D0392588

Thief of
HAPPY
ENDINGS

Thief of HAPPY ENDINGS

KRISTEN CHANDLER

VIKING

VIKING
An imprint of Penguin Random House LLC
375 Hudson Street
New York, New York 10014

First published in the United States of America by Viking,
an imprint of Penguin Random House LLC, 2018

LIBRARY OF CONGRESS CATALOGING-IN-PUBLICATION DATA IS AVAILABLE.
ISBN 9780425290477

Printed in the USA   Jacket and interior book design by Jim Hoover

10   9   8   7   6   5   4   3   2   1

For Dylan, who got back on

&

For Quinn, who finds horses

"If you want a happy ending, that depends, of course, on where you stop the story."   —ORSON WELLES

Before

I WAS TOO stupid to be scared back then.

It just felt like the ground had a heartbeat. My grandfather was next to me, snoring like a bagpipe. We were in his big, smelly tent out on the edge of his place. My heartbeat sped up to the pounding I felt coming up from the earth until I jumped up out of my sleeping bag. Everything was going too fast to lie down. I don't know why I didn't wake up my grandfather. Maybe because my grandfather, indulgent as he was, was not the sort of man I wanted to startle out of a dead sleep.

I ran out into the cold morning with my tender city-girl feet. All I saw was dirt and sage and the sun sending its first blond streaks across the pale Wyoming sky. But damn I felt them. Pound pound pound. And even in the wind, I heard the trilling and snorting of something big.

I raced over rocks and thorns to the cliff edge my grandpa threatened me to stay clear of. I ran right to the very precipice and *felt the sway of the valley beneath me reaching at my stomach when I got too close. I held my arms out for balance and reeled back. And there they were.*

Hundreds of mustangs, all running, all together. Through the swirl of dust they raised I could see their heads and tails and legs flying all in unison, one big graceful creature, moving over the ground like the god of freedom, so hard and fast and fearless I wondered how they didn't trample one another to bloody pieces. But they didn't. They ran like the wicked wind itself, going who knows where and what for.

And then I felt my grandfather's bony hand clamp on my shoulder. He didn't say anything, but when I looked up his face was soft, like it never was, soft like he was happy and sad all at the same time, and he let go and we stood there looking at all those horses running together for about one more second before they evaporated over a hill and left nothing but a cloud of dust and a permanent stamp on my little pink brain.

It would have been easy for those horses to come a different way, come up on the hill and run me down like August thistle. But that never occurred to me. I thought that stampede was the best thing I'd ever seen. Because I was young and happy and not afraid.

I thought just because something was wild, it was free. And because I loved something, it wouldn't hurt me.

Chapter One

IT'S A LONG drive to Wyoming.

I stare out the window at dirt, sagebrush, and an endless blue sky. It's as dry and empty as a clay bowl, but the sky is so bright it's nearly blinding. I put my head in my arm and lean against the car door. Then I check the lock. It's fine. I put my head down again.

I've been trying to sleep since we left Denver so I won't have to talk or think, but I can't. Mom doesn't want to talk either. That leaves plenty of time to consider the reasons I shouldn't be going to Wyoming. First, I'm afraid of horses. I didn't used to be. But then, I didn't used to be afraid of a lot of things. Second, I haven't exactly been lighting the world on fire lately. As in, I sort of stopped getting out of bed for the last three weeks of school. Third, even as a five-foot-one slug, I've been the stabilizing influence for my sibs during this "difficult time," which is the super crappy way Mom and

Dad refer to taking their perfectly storybook marriage and putting it in the garbage disposal.

I look at the pink mountains in the distance. Our family wagon drives fearlessly on. I'm glad that something in my life is fearless.

I say, "The mountains don't seem to be getting any closer."

"Oh, they're coming," Mom says.

Mom's dark waves of hair are pulled up tight onto her head. She doesn't look much like the girl in the framed photograph I found stuffed in the living room drawer a week ago. In it, my parents are standing arm in arm with the ocean twinkling behind them. Dad's thick hair hangs to his shoulders. Mom's smile is easy and wide. The way she holds herself is billowy and graceful as fabric. Across the bottom of the picture, in Dad's messy handwriting, are the words *I always knew you were the one.*

It's probably the sappiest thing Dad has ever written. And my favorite.

Before we left this morning, Dad showed up to pick up the sibs. The twins and Wyatt wandered out to the driveway in their pajamas. Jessie Jane and Oakley stood there shoving their matted mops out of their faces. Oakley started crying, which is typical, and Jessie Jane punched her in the arm to get her to stop, even more typical. Then Wyatt grabbed me like I was going off to war. "Why is everyone leaving?"

I rubbed his fuzzy summer crew cut. "Hey, I'll bring you back some magic rocks."

He's seven, so he played it cool. "Rocks aren't magic."

When Dad hugged me, he said, "Do you really want to do this, Cassidy? You can change your mind." His voice was terse. His dark Irish eyes bored a gut-size hole in what was left of my resolve. "That's a woman's prerogative, you know."

Mom said, "I've paid her deposit, Peter. Get in the car, Cassidy."

I hate it when they do this. I'm not choosing between them. But they make it that way. Like about anything. Like about everything.

"I'll be home in a few weeks."

He sighed and rubbed his professorly stubble. "I'll have my book done when you get back. You can be my first reader."

"I can't wait."

He smiled in that tight way that feels like he's frowning. "Dammit, Cass, just look at you. All this black shiny hair and a face like a china doll. You stay away from all those cowboys. They're nothing but trouble." He hugs my head to his chest and then lets me go.

Because every cowboy in Wyoming is looking for a pale, short girl who's afraid to get on a horse. But Dad doesn't need to worry. I'm on a drama-free diet this summer, thank you very much. It's not just cowboys that are trouble.

I look out the window again. For reals, the mountains are not any closer. We pass a scenic oil rig sticking its fangs in the ground. And then another. A tumbleweed blows across the road and gets stuck under the wagon. Mom doesn't seem to notice. She looks as stressed out as I am.

"I brought some apples if you get hungry," she says.

"I'm not," I say.

A big red semi passes us going the other direction. The draft shakes the wagon. The fumes make me carsick. I sit forward and keep my eyes on the road.

It's weird to take this drive after not seeing it in so long. We used to go this way to get to my grandparents' place outside of Cody. That drive is even longer. The road just goes on and on, winding up through the dust for-friggin'-ever until you finally hit trees, and then like one bathroom stop later you're into mountains so fierce you can't even see the tops of them from inside your car. The landscape in Wyoming doesn't mess around.

When I was little I could barely hold still I was so into going to see my grandparents. My head would be all tingly when we started early, early in the morning, and Dad would buy a big box of doughnuts that he put in the backseat with me and the twins. I thought of the ranch like my own private amusement park. And I was the star of the show. Until I got bucked off into the fence and sort of brought the house down.

I didn't die, obviously. Just got a concussion and a scar on the back of my head where my hair didn't grow back. But Dad was pissed about the whole thing, Mom had Wyatt a few months later, and then my grandparents died before any of that got sorted out.

"You feeling okay this morning?" asks Mom.

I shrug my shoulders and smile. But truthfully, I don't know how I feel. Scared, I guess. I let Mom con me into this trip by showing me old pictures of myself at Grandpa's ranch. Happy. Stupid. Riding bareback. Riding double with Mom. Standing up on the backs of horses. I looked so all-out audacious. So much cooler than I am now. Somehow I fell for my own advertisement.

Mom tries to pretend she isn't checking her cell phone every five seconds to see if Dad is taking care of the kids. The twins will be okay, but Wyatt is so hyper he wears out our dog, Kidd. I can't think about Wyatt or I'll jump out of the car and go after him.

"What did Mr. Coulter do for Grandpa again?"

Mom doesn't talk much about Grandpa and Grandma. Neither of my parents talk about their parents. Dad doesn't get along with his folks. But I think the opposite is true for Mom. She misses her parents too much. I miss them, too. Once in a while, she'll tell a story about growing up on a ranch with no television and one bathroom. Or about how tough Grandpa was or how sweet Grandma was. But she almost always ends up with her voice cracking. And Mom hates to cry like a cat hates to swim. She made an exception to talk me into doing this.

Mom says, "Coulter worked for Daddy as a foreman. But I think he stuck around because he liked your grandmother's cooking. It was awfully nice of him to squeeze you in and let you do the work scholarship."

"I just have to do extra cleaning every day?"

"Exactly. So pretty much like home. And it will save me a bundle."

She rotates her head to look at me. "Did you notice I put your grandpa's hat in the back there? It's probably still too big, but it'll keep the sun off."

The hat in my closet. I didn't notice. I look in the back-seat and see the black felt thing perched on the seat. It has a small pheasant feather in a black band. I always thought it looked like a bad guy's hat. I told Mom I didn't want it in my room because it smelled like cigarettes, but truthfully it just made me feel funny. That's why I shoved it in the closet. "You want me to wear that?"

She sighs and passes an ancient farm truck. "Think of it as a talisman."

"Aren't talismans supposed to do stuff? Like make you invisible?"

Mom's smart about Englishy things, like talismans. She was an English major until she met Dad and switched to accounting. "A talisman is supposed to bring you good luck, is all."

"Why did he leave it to me in the first place? It's way too big."

"Who knows?" says Mom. "Maybe just to remember him by."

"Or to haunt me. He was mad about me giving up horses, wasn't he?"

"I don't think he was mad at you a day in his life. Your grandfather loved you very much. He'd be proud of you for doing this."

I turn and look at the hat again, sitting alone on the seat. "I'm just saying, maybe it's not exactly good luck."

"It's gotten you this far," she says.

We drive for a long way without talking. Everything turns flat and barren. Like nothing grows out here but the dirt and rocks I promised to bring Wyatt. And nothing looks very magical. I turn on the radio to slow down the churning in my stomach but only get static and a Christian station. I wonder if I packed enough clothes.

Then, in the middle of all the silence, Mom asks, "You don't remember the accident at all?"

"Just what you've told me. That the horse bolted, I split my head open on the fence and got twenty stitches."

"Thirty. But don't let it worry you. The past is the past, right?" She smiles and pushes my shoulder with her fingertips.

I look back at the hat following me in the backseat. "Right," I say.

We watch the dirt turn to grass, then the grass to hills, then the hills to mountains. Just like I remember it, both sides of the road become vertical angles, and then we turn and we're winding on a gravel road. I feel hard pressure on the car. I check the lock on the door again.

"It's the wind," says Mom. "That's what they make the most of in Wyoming."

When I think I can't sit still one more minute, the mountains part and we come to a four-way stop with a thin green sign that says POINT OF NO RETURN YOUTH RANCH, with a small white arrow pointing left. I've seen parking stalls with bigger signs.

When Mom showed me the website for this place, I thought she was kidding. "What kind of name is that for a summer camp? Is it like a correctional facility?"

She said, "It's a leadership camp. Where you train mustangs and learn leader-y things."

"Leadership—with horses." I made a gagging sound. "Isn't that code for 'Messed-up rich kids, apply now'? Last time I checked I was only one of those."

"Like I told you. The man that owns the place, Tim Coulter, is an old family friend. He said we could work out the tuition. He also said that they get all kinds at this place, including kids with reasons for being away from home for the summer. There's nothing wrong with that."

"So I'll be doing manual labor with banished, potentially deranged rich kids at a ranch with wild horses. I feel better already."

She pouted at me and pointed at the screen full of smiling teenagers chopping wood and sitting on perfectly behaved equine specimens. Okay, the kids in the pictures did look like they were having fun, I'm sure because they were told they wouldn't get rations otherwise. And the mountains looked sort of breathtaking. But it was one line on the website schmoozefest that got me: "Whatever your personal mountains are, they'll look smaller after you've lived in ours." I thought that was good manipulative writing. I can appreciate that.

I mean, I guess I get the "what doesn't kill you makes you stronger" bit. But I still don't see how horses, which can *actually* kill you, can really make racing thoughts and stomach cramps go away.

Mom turns left and keeps her eyes on the road. "You need to get away from the mess to get better, Cass. I know it's going to be hard, but I want you to try to tough it out until the end of summer. Sometimes you just have to ride things out."

I count ten telephone poles before I say what I'm thinking. "Are you and Dad trying to ride things out?"

Mom tightens her grip on the steering wheel. "Don't worry about that right now, Cassidy. This summer your job is to ride horses and worry about yourself. I'd love to do something like this. It's a once-in-a-lifetime thing."

In front of us the canyon splits open to a primeval-looking mountain range jutting up into a crayon-blue sky. Even though it's June there's still snow on the peaks. On the other side of the road, the wind bends wild grass to the ground. Out of nowhere, a hawk dive-bombs the car.

"Redtail," Mom says, pointing.

The hawk circles in front of the car once and then flies off. I roll down the window. Wind floods into the car. The air outside the car is so clean I can actually smell the wildflowers jabbing up on the roadside. I turn to Mom. "Have I ever been here before?"

"No." She smiles. "Does it seem like it?"

After a few minutes we see a cloud of dust blow up over a ridge. The cloud is in a canyon opening surrounded by scrubby trees. It looks like a tornado coming from the ground. "Is that a dust devil?"

Mom pulls the car over and reaches for her binoculars in the glove box. Of course she has binoculars in the glove box. "Will you look at that," she says. "You have a welcome committee."

"What?"

"Mustangs. I read that there were a few wild bands left in the area."

"That cloud is horses? Just running loose?"

She hands me the binoculars. I put the heavy black lenses to my face. I move the glass back and forth. But all I see is dust, swirling in the gnarled branches like ghosts. But that tingly feeling I had when I was a kid fills my head. Now it comes with butterflies in my stomach. I look around me at all the open space. I can't believe this is where I'm spending my summer.

At last we drive under a wooden archway with a sign that says POINT OF NO RETURN and a big dead pine wreath swinging under it in the wind.

We drive up over a quick hill into a valley surrounded by pine- and aspen-dotted hills. Late afternoon clouds float overhead. Down in the valley there's an old two-story ranch house with great big windows and a deep wraparound porch. Bright yellow flowers spurt out all over around the outside of the house. "How pretty," says Mom.

"Yeah," I say.

Next to the main house is a large fenced pasture, one big arena and a small one, a long gray horse barn, and something that looks like a red dollhouse—maybe a chicken coop. The pasture is full of shaggy horses. Just the sight of all these horses makes my stomach flip-flop. And then flip-flop again. Dang. I don't want to be this scared. Maybe I can just take care of the chickens. I would fit in there.

Down the road are barrack-style tents that I'm going to guess is where they stash the campers in question. Behind the tents are some small one-room cabins, and in front are four wooden outhouses.

Mom says, "That's . . . rustic."

"I don't have to clean those, right? Can you even clean an outhouse?"

"No. I'm sure those are just back-up facilities."

A man wearing a denim shirt and an actual red kerchief tied around his neck walks up to the truck as we start to unload. He tips his chocolate-colored hat to us just long enough for me to see his short black hair with a white skunk stripe in the front. "Welcome! I'm Darius Pike, head babysitter and bottle washer here at Point of No Return. Are you the Carrigans?"

"Yes. It's nice to meet you, Mr. Pike." Mom puts out her hand graciously.

"Oh, just call me Darius. We're pretty informal up here in the sticks. It's a pleasure to meet the descendants of Guthrie Parker."

Mom brightens. "Did you know my dad, Darius?" she asks.

"No, but I've heard the stories. Quite a guy." His face seems snagged on one side, like he's got a permanent smirk.

"Yes, he was," she says.

Over by the outhouses I hear kids' voices.

Darius taps the dirt with his boot. "Well, thanks for coming and dropping her off, Mrs. Carrigan. You have yourself a great summer."

"Oh." Mom's face drops. I think for a minute she's going to break down. "I'd love to see Mr. Coulter, if I could. Shouldn't I help Cassidy set up her room?"

"Coulter's not around right now. Don't worry about your daughter. She looks like she can roll out her own sleeping bag." He taps his hand on my back, which I don't like. "We'll take good care of her. Have a safe trip home."

"My mom's been driving since early this morning," I say. I turn to her. She's making the worry face. "Maybe you should rest or walk around before you go."

"Oh no, I'm fine." Mom tries to open her car door, but the handle sticks. She pumps the latch. I think I should do it for her, but I don't want to embarrass her. She leans through the car window and jumps back out again holding my grandfather's hat. "Do you want this, then?"

I nod. Words aren't my best thing at the moment.

She puts the hat on my head. It drops over one eye. "Still

a little big, huh? Should I put it back in the car?" Her voice is shaking.

"No, it's fine. Just fine." I try to sound enthusiastic, but what I want to do is get in the car and drive straight back to my room and climb under the covers. But what if something happens to me up here? I can't let her see me panicking. "Will you be okay driving home?"

She puts her hands on my shoulders and looks me right in the eyes. "I'll be fine. Cass, honey, I want you to stop trying to rescue everyone else and just rescue yourself for a few weeks." She smiles. "Do what Mr. Coulter says. And don't worry about me or anyone else at home. Is that clear?"

Oh, I'm worrying about myself right now. In addition to my messed-up family. But as terrified as I am of staying here, if I go home, I'll just keep being a mess, and I will have to face every person who thought I couldn't do this. I will be the chicken they think I am. I will be the chicken I think I am. I'm practically growing feathers just standing here.

Mom looks at Darius and then looks at me, reading my mind in that psychic way she has. "You don't have to do this, Cass."

I say, "No. I'm good. Totally good. See you in August, okay?" I smile and act like I'm checking my bag so I don't have to look her in the eyes. She's put a deposit down. I'm doing this. I can't believe I'm doing this.

Mom lets out a gasp of air, which may be a tad dramatic. "You sure?"

I nod. One hundred percent not sure.

Then she gives me one really good, long hug, and one quick one after that, and before you can say *hyperventilate* she's gone, leaving nothing more than red dust behind her. And then *wham*. I'm standing next to a guy in a bandana, a hundred years from anywhere.

Chapter Two

"YOU BEEN AWAY from home before?" Darius says.

"Yes," I say. Because fifth grade school camp totally counts.

"You get used to it."

I grab my duffel. It feels like Wyatt stuck a few of his pet rocks in my bag.

"You need some help with that?" says Darius.

"I got it." I'm short, but I'm not helpless.

We walk to an area with a dozen or so army-style canvas tents. In the center is a fire pit surrounded by tree stumps and a wooden flagpole. The United States flag flies above a flag with a bison in the middle.

Darius points his hairy finger. "Ladies in these tents here on this side of the road. The tents over there are for guys." He points to the one-room cabins situated above the tents. "That little bungalow up there is mine. And that one with dried flowers hanging on the door is for the counselor who isn't a guy. The far one in the corner there is for the junior staff. We got one of those right now, which is about one and a half too many."

We walk into the first tent. "This will be your place," says Darius, picking his teeth with some straw. "Home sweet home."

The canvas drapes over wood beams and doesn't even go all the way to the ground. For what they charge for this place I was thinking that there would at least be walls where we slept at night. Beneath me I see a live mouse run past my feet. I step backward. Darius laughs.

"Don't scare him now," he says.

There are four cots, with two sleeping bags already laid out. There are hooks on the beams by each cot with dangling name plaques made from barnwood and baling wire. They're painted green with pink swirling letters. It's a sweet touch for such a depressing place.

There is also one giant trunk with an open padlock.

"What's that for?" I say.

"Anything that smells. Including toothpaste. It's bear protection."

I'm digesting the news about bears when I hear a rustling noise. I jump a full six inches before I can stop myself. A petite Asian-looking girl walks through the canvas.

"Don't worry, Baby Parker," says Darius, chuckling it up. "It's just your roommate."

The girl has oil-black hair and creamy olive skin, and

she isn't much taller than I am, but much more delicate. She's wearing a padded lime-green coat that reminds me of a caterpillar.

"Hi." My voice suddenly sounds loud.

"Hi." She comes over and politely shakes my hand. "It's nice to meet you. I'm Alice."

"I'm Cassidy."

"I noticed," she says, letting her eyes go to a plaque behind me. She has a shy smile, like she thinks a lot.

Alice drifts over to the bed, unzips her coat. I turn away because I don't want to be nosy and because I'm danger-to-myself nervous. I stand still and look at Darius.

He stares right back at me. "Well, alrighty then. Banner ought to be along in a minute. You three can set up your Barbies until we have bugle call."

"Bugle call?" I snort. Not loud. A little loud.

"Yes. *Bugle call*." His face narrows, like he's thinking something not all that pleasant. "And one more thing. I'm going to need your cell phone."

"I don't have one," I say. It's not something I like to admit around people my own age.

"Sure you do. You all have cell phones. Even little Alice here."

Alice doesn't turn around.

"I really don't have one, Mr. Pike."

"I said call me Darius." Darius moves closer to me. "This is going to be a long summer if you can't follow the rules."

I don't know about the rules, but I really don't have a

cell phone. Dad moving into an apartment has jacked the family budget. A phone is an optional expense according to Mom. I unzip my suitcase and dump it on the bed. Have I come to the right camp? I thought this was a rah-rah, get-your-crap-together, be-the-hope-of-tomorrow camp, not reform school.

Darius walks over to my cot, suddenly furious. Which I don't get, since I'm the one who doesn't have a cell phone. I look over at Alice, who is taking a very long time to unzip her suitcase.

"You are a little Parker, aren't you?" says Darius. "All spit and piss."

"My grandparents' last name was Parker. My last name is actually Carrigan." I try to say it nicely.

A honey-skinned woman with long black hair down one side of her neck peeks into the tent. She has dark eyes and a wide, brilliant smile. Whoever this person is, she looks like she belongs on a parade float or a stage somewhere. "Hi, Cassidy," she says, her smile getting even bigger. "I'm Kaya." She pats Alice on the shoulder, so I guess they've met. "I'm the other camp counselor."

Darius laughs, condescendingly as all crap. "Cassidy was just telling me she doesn't have a cell phone."

Kaya looks at the mess on my bed and then at me and then at Darius. "Do you have a cell phone, Cassidy?"

"Am I supposed to? I mean, I'm sorry . . . I don't own one. I thought the packing list said we weren't even allowed to have them." This isn't at all humiliating, promise.

Kaya looks me over. "Good for you, sweetie. Darius, could I speak with you outside?"

Just as Darius pushes through the canvas flap to go have a chat with Kaya, a tall, flame-haired girl walks in. All this coming and going through that tent flap is making my head spin.

"Hello, Banner," says Kaya.

The girl lifts her chin. "Hey."

Kaya turns back to me as she leaves. "Cassidy, don't worry about the phone thing. It was just a misunderstanding, okay?"

"Okay." I nod. So Kaya's cool.

"But, hey, since you're one of our work scholarship recipients, I'll be getting you up a little earlier than the other girls tomorrow. So get some sleep."

Work scholarship. I guess it's better than calling me the poor kid, or the charity case, but not much.

"Scholarship, huh?" says the new girl, to me this time. "You must be good at school."

I feel my face flush. I am not talking about this. She can think what she wants. I mean, I used to be good at school. Not that you'd know that by looking at the hatchet job I did to my grades last year.

She gives me the once-over. "Everybody has to be good at something." Her accent is faintly southern, but not hillbilly. She's wearing a tight sky-blue tank top that makes her freckles and other parts of her stand out. And she has a lot of freckles. Her face is muddy with them. She looks a lot older than Alice and me, and not just because her fingernails are painted black.

"You must be Banner," I say, hoping to change the subject. "I'm Cassidy."

"Hey, Cassidy." She half smiles. "Darius kife your phone, too?"

I shake my head. "What's up with him?"

"A stalker for sure," says Banner. "That guy has got to be registered."

Alice says, "He makes the hair on my arms stand up." She holds up her tiny arm, covered by a heavy T-shirt, then looks away like she's sorry she said anything.

Banner spreads out on her sleeping bag. She also has a cherry-red blanket that could stop traffic. I guess she likes red. A lot.

"Where you from?" I ask Alice.

"San Francisco," she says. She sits down on her bag and gets three inches taller from the padding. Her extra-strength arctic winter bag matches the coat.

"Denver," I say. "Well, actually, a little suburb outside."

"I'm sorry," says Banner.

I laugh, but I don't think she's kidding.

"I like your accent," says Alice to Banner. "Are you from the South?"

Banner shrugs. "Charleston."

I say, "I've seen pictures of Charleston. It looks like heaven."

"Oh yeah, it's heaven. Just ask my dad. He's tight with Jesus. You two bring any cigarettes?"

I stir the mess on my bed, just to be polite. "I don't smoke."

Banner says, "Me neither." She pulls a cigarette out of her bag and sticks it in her mouth but doesn't light it. "It's against the rules. A girl could get sent home for that."

This is more attitude than I have the stomach for right now. I look around the room for something that isn't cigarettes, bears, or bra sizes to talk about. "Is there a fourth girl coming?"

Banner swirls her long legs under her until she looks like a cat. "She bailed. Freaked out before she even got here. That's what Darius said anyway. Couldn't handle the whole mice and dirt thing, I guess. What'd you two get sent here for?"

I don't answer. It's not like I'm going to either.

Alice looks tweaked by Banner's question, too. But then she digs in her pack and holds a small box out to her. "I don't have any cigarettes, but I have matches. My parents thought a horse camp would be relaxing. I enjoy riding."

Banner looks behind her at the opening to the tent, then stuffs the small box in her pocket. "Thanks, Alice." She picks at her black nails. "I think the diagnosis for me is a pain in the ass. But I ride jumpers. What's your story, Carrigan? Do you ride cow ponies and bake cookies at home?"

"I don't really ride much," I say, understating things a tad.

Banner recoils her legs and giggles. "You do bake cookies though, don't you?"

A knot of embarrassment settles in my chest. I actually do love to bake cookies. And every other thing you can frost or put sprinkles on. I take it back. Banner's less like a cat and more like a redheaded puma.

"So what did you get shipped here for? Depression, drugs, sex . . . teacher's-pet-ness?"

What is her problem? I feel like I'm back in freakin' school.

A dying animal sound comes from outside the tent.

"Bugle call," says Alice, popping up sharply and zipping on her caterpillar coat.

"That's the bugle?" I say. "I'm pretty sure it's giving birth."

No one laughs.

Alice puts her thin eyebrows together and walks out, making a swish-swish sound with her coat, followed by Scarlet O'Scary. *It's fine*, I tell myself. *I can do this.* Having a mountain lion for a roommate is just another hard, slightly aggravating thing. That's how all stories start, right? You have to have a little pushback to know you're headed in the right direction. *Besides*, I tell myself, *heroines are always misunderstood.* That's how you know, deep down, you're the heroine.

I look at the empty bed next to mine. I wonder who that girl is and how she's doing, wherever she is. I hope she's okay. I may be scared and suck out loud at riding horses, but I'm here. And that's something.

Chapter Three

I JOIN ABOUT twenty kids standing around an empty fire pit. Everyone has the same dazed look, and there's no way to avoid looking at the person standing next to them. I scan the crowd. What I notice real quick is that everyone is dressed better than I am. Which isn't hard because I'm in beat-up jeans and a pair of cowboy boots my mom got on the discount rack at the Boot Barn. Most kids are dressed in outdoor gear, not Western stuff, but the kind of outdoor stuff you buy at stores that sell Sport Beans and yoga mats. Although there is one guy wearing the dorkiest cowboy bolo tie I've ever seen.

"Good afternoon, campers! Good afternoon!"

I turn to see the man from the website stride up the path to the head of our gathering. He has an impressive beer gut, legs about six feet long, and a snowy owl beard. He's decked out in jeans, a leather coat with fringe hanging off the arms, and a cowboy hat that has a sweat stain around the hatband. "Good afternoon."

His voice is rich, deep, and seriously loud. He puts his arms out like a circus ringmaster. "Welcome to Point of No Return Youth Ranch. You may all call me Mr. Coulter. I may call you whatever I want. How does that sound?"

Three guys with hipster haircuts standing over on the other side snicker to one another.

Mr. Coulter reaches into his fringed coat and pulls out a coiled whip. He loosens the whip and cracks it right up in the egg-blue air, and the *GQ* brothers stop laughing. I glance over at my other fellow campers to see if they are as freaked out as I am. What I see is even more startling than Mr. Coulter. Alice's head is missing. More accurately, the top of her head is poking out of her collar like a human turtle. I don't know what to do. Is she cold? Is she scared? Did her neck collapse?

I step toward her. "Alice?" I whisper. "Are you okay?"

Kaya's hand comes from behind and perches on my arm. She shakes her chin at me, and I step away. I look back over at Alice. My headless roommate puts her hands in her pockets. So at least she's breathing. I look around. Banner seems preoccupied with the main event.

Mr. Coulter's words boom across the campsite. "You are about to embark on a great journey. I want this time we have together to leave you so utterly altered that you can't help but take hold of your destiny with new hands. And believe me, children, those hands will have calluses."

Alice's hands come out her pockets, squeeze together, and then disappear again.

"Because you are going to work. Harder than you have ever worked in your soft, entitled lives. You want to be leaders? Well, here's the dirty little secret. Leaders work." He turns in a slow circle while he speaks, clicking the heels of his cowboy boots on the rocky ground.

I'm not sure, but I think Alice might be trembling inside her coat.

"Your parents have deposited you here, thinking that after a lifetime of their screwing you up, I will feed you pork and beans, put you on a horse, and the fresh air will magically develop confidence and character. It will not. But I am going to teach you what it takes to run a horse ranch and get a herd of mustangs to auction. And when you're done, that work will make you men and women. What kind of men and women will be up to you."

He looks across our heads, then lowers his voice. "There are rules while you're a camper."

A boy who looks about twelve rubs his shirtsleeve up under his nose. A thin girl with too many blonde highlights and mascara-plated eyelashes makes a scowl that could crack paint. I just stand there. I'm nervous about the oxygen in Alice's coat.

"No drinking, smoking, drugs, or shenanigans. I don't give a shit who your parents are. I'll send your butt home. You will go home knowing you backed away from one more thing."

We all look down. Except Alice. I don't know what she's looking at.

"But rules are not why we're here, ladies and gentlemen! Our goal this summer is to ride and sell horses and have a fine time doing it. I have twenty mustangs that need homes. We lost one camper this morning, so her horse goes on to the Rock Spring holding facility. Horses sent there have a much poorer chance of ever being adopted because they are not trained. In a little over two months there will be an auction at the county fairgrounds. This truly Western event is known as the Wild Card Mustang Festival. Anything your horse brings in above my cost is yours to keep."

"And how much would that be, Mr. Coulter?" says this tall, sturdy kid in the back.

Everybody stares at the kid for a second. Not only is he the only African American on the premises, he has an amazingly chill grin. I can't tell if he looks more out of place because he's black or because he seems so likable.

"I'm sorry, Ethan, were you addressing me?"

"Yes, Mr. Coulter. I'm just wondering, how much money are you talking about?"

He has a slow Texan drawl. So basically, epic charisma. What is a kid like that doing here?

Coulter nods. "Thank you, Ethan. That depends. Some of these horses may not sell at all. But if you clean 'em up and gentle 'em enough to walk around a show ring, there's a good chance you'll make a few hundred dollars."

"You say on the website that one rider can earn back their tuition," says Ethan.

"You have read the fine print, young man. I like that in a person." Coulter strokes his white beard. "Indeed. There is a second part to the mustang event. The riding competition. We pick our best rider and put him or her on our one adult mustang. We only take on one adult because they're harder to deal with and harder to sell. But last year a camper made enough money to pay his tuition and had a thousand to spare." Coulter cracks his whip again. "How does that sound?"

There's barely a murmur in the crowd. Most of these kids probably spent that much money on their cell phone bill last month. But it sounds fan-freaking-tastic to me. I mean, for people that can do that sort of thing. Ride, I mean. For a minute my mind goes back to the pictures of me in the scrapbook.

"I asked you a question." For some reason Mr. Coulter seems to be looking at me when he says this.

I say, "I'm sorry, Mr. Coulter. Do you mean me?"

"Am I looking at anyone else?"

"I'm sorry," I say again. "What's the question?"

"Come out here," he says. "This, campers, is Cassidy Carrigan. Granddaughter to the greatest horse thief I ever knew." With his daddy longlegs he steps close to me and sticks out his fringed arm, drawing me into the center of the fire pit area where everyone can see me. "Guthrie James

Parker, my former associate and a ruthless scoundrel." I look up expecting to see Coulter wink or do something to let everyone in on the joke. He says, "Guthrie was as crooked as the day is long, but he never met a horse he couldn't ride. And I've heard this one doesn't fall too far from the tree."

I would be insulted if I wasn't so confused. First, why is Grandpa's friend calling him a horse thief? And second, what the crap has he heard about me?

"So, Cassidy, let's get back to the question. What do you know about mustangs?"

I look out into the gawking crowd. I see that Kaya is taking Alice back to the tent. I worry that Alice will trip if her head is too far into her coat. I worry that the guy running this camp has me confused with someone else.

I try to pull myself together. What do I know about mustangs? "They're wild horses?"

"What else?" Coulter's eyes narrow.

"I'm not really a horse person. I mean, I like them, I'm just not that comfortable around them."

"Oh, I see. Cassidy is not much of a *horse person*. Which is why she's here. What do you think, campers? Should we help her out? Who thinks we should help her out?"

Banner says, "I'd love to help her out." She smiles at me. She actually has beautiful teeth. Shiny and sharp.

Coulter leaves the fire pit and walks quickly away from the camping area, down toward open ground, talking and waving for us to follow him. "Fifty or so years ago, the US government made themselves a law to stop folks from butchering mustangs for dog food. The problem is there aren't any predators left to kill 'em, and mustangs reproduce like jack-rabbits. So the Bureau of Land Management, or BLM, started rounding up mustangs, putting 'em in holding pens. Now they've got thousands of horses to feed. They're sponsoring programs like the one we will be participating in to get people to adopt 'em. Which is about like trying to put out a forest fire by pissing on it, if you ask me."

We walk to the edge of a large meadow with knee high grass and wildflowers in the center of the valley. The new grass tips in the late afternoon breeze. Behind us, more in the direction of the ranch house, is a pasture area surrounded by a log fence. On the other side of the meadow is a steep rise thick with aspen all the way up to another bluff overlooking the camp. Off to the left of the trees is a trail that disappears into a large draw but seems to circle up, back to the top of the hill.

The kid in the bolo tie stands next to me, shifting his weight, which is ample. Except for dressing like my grand-father, he looks about as much like a cowboy as an accent pillow. He shoos a mosquito off his sleeve without killing it, then looks at me and grins. "Good afternoon," he says, and puts out his hand.

"Hi," I say, putting out mine.

Coulter latches on to my shoulder and drags me up next to him. "Right here, Cassidy. I want you to have a front-row view. We keep our mustangs up on higher ground at night for better grass up on the hill, then bring 'em down in the morning to work with 'em. Which means every day we have a little show." He bellows, "Ladies and gentleman, I give you the orphans of the American West."

First, Coulter waves everybody to stand behind us, like we're about to see a parade. Then he sticks his pinky fingers in his mouth and whistles hard. Above us on the bluff trail we hear a murmur and then a low-grade rumble, accompanied by angry whinnying. In seconds the rumble turns to pounding. I can feel it coming from the ground, up to the part in my hair. The trail fills with dust. Then, at the base of the trail, out of a cloud of flying dirt flow heads, tails, and hooves.

The sight of those horses lifting the ground up with their hooves sends my heart into my throat. They're rip-your-guts-out beautiful. But I don't like the direction they're headed. Not at all.

Behind the horses there is a single rider. He is whip thin and wears a hat the color of the dirt. He comes whistling and galloping behind the herd. Calling. Once he's in the meadow, his dirty-yellow horse darts around the edge of the herd, smooth and agile. His body seems built into his horse. He bends and leans with the herd, like he's part of that, too, but driving it at the same time. I've never seen anything like it.

I turn to Coulter. It's too loud in my brain to say anything, so I shake my head, trying to tell him I'm not okay with this. I can't stand here. My chest's so tight I think I'm going to pass out. Coulter glares down at me over the crest of his white beard. "Don't move now. You'll have to wait to ride until later. These are the wild ones."

I face the charging herd. I can do this. There must be twenty or more. They just keep running, grabbing the ground with each stride as they enter the open meadow. I mean, it's a big meadow, but there are people in it. Me. What's happening? Why are we standing here? A huge gray horse leads them in a crushing gallop. I cross my arms over my chest and try to steady my feet. The horses are still running. I feel sweat on my forehead. I need to yell. No one is moving but the horses and the rider.

I can't help it.

I bolt. My feet won't hold still. I have to get away. But almost in the instant that I lean to run I feel a hand pull me from behind. Coulter grabs me by the belt. "Whoa there," he yells. "Whoa."

I don't like being grabbed. I fling around. It's like I black out or see red or turn green or something, because without any other thought at all I swing at Coulter so hard I nearly break my hand. Coulter lets out a yell and reels backward. I go sprawling forward into dirt. When I look up with my belly on the ground, all I see are hooves and that godforsaken rider.

The rider darts to the side and swings out in front. The horses in the herd bend to his lead, as if he's guiding them with his hand. Instead of trampling me, or anyone else, the mustangs flow away from us like channeled water. They bend and run and bend again. Before I know what's happened, the horses are flooding into the pasture and circling inside the fence, safe as rain puddles and far from me.

"Holy hell, you little runt!" yells Coulter, still holding my busted belt in one hand and his chin in the other. "You're dumb as rocks, but you sure swing like your grandfather." He laughs from his swollen gut.

Because this is hysterical.

The rider gallops to our side where all the other campers are gawking at me. Under the hat I see a kid with square, bony shoulders. But that's not what I'm looking at. I'm staring at the most messed-up nose I've ever laid eyes on. It's like somebody relocated the middle of his face with a combat boot. It hurts to look at. Or maybe that's my hand. "What the hell was that?" he shouts at me.

I'm shaking. His shouting, especially from the top of one of those beasts, makes me furious. "You were coming right at us."

He yells, "You could have injured all those horses."

"Who cares about your stupid horses? Are you crazy?"

"Hush, Cassidy," says Coulter.

"I'm crazy?" His voice is low and dagger sharp.

Coulter's big voice booms. "Not another word, Justin. Get off your horse."

The rider swings down. "I never even came near you. Until you ran out like a stupid . . ."

"Justin, I'd like you to meet your newest pupil."

"Like hell," he says.

I rub the red dirt off my face. Every part of me hurts. I hate this place. I hate this kid. He could've crushed me to death. I swear if I cry, I'm going to kill someone. "I'm out of here."

"Oh, both of you, shut up," says Coulter.

I stomp to the back of the group. Everyone moves away from me, which I couldn't care less about.

"All right, campers. Enough entertainment. I want everyone to meet Justin Sweet. He's our junior wrangler. Justin's a mere seventeen, but he knows plenty about horses. What he says goes around here, just like with Darius, Kaya, or myself. We don't want anybody getting hurt or any horses getting hurt."

I fix my best skunk eye on the rider. Justin *Sweet*? Someone has a sense of humor. Under that terrible nose, he's built like a yield sign. Wide shoulders with poles for legs. He shoves up the sleeves of his ridiculous ripped-up cowboy shirt, showing off his dirt-brown arms.

Coulter says, "We'll be starting with the domesticated horses first thing in the morning. I'll assign you a counselor, according to your skill level." He glances at me, letting me and everyone else know that I will be in the level without skills. That knot of embarrassment I had in my throat earlier has now transformed into a body-length net of humiliation.

I dig my hands into my pockets. It's only for an entire

summer of my life. *Keep on breathing*, I tell myself. I wanted to get out of my bedroom. I wanted an adventure. I guess I got one. But now all I want is to sleep and wake up at home.

When I finally get to bed that night, I lie in my sleeping bag listening to a mouse scuttle across the floor. I think I would rather hear approaching zombies than those creepy little feet sprinting across the dirt floor. What if it climbs onto my face in my sleep or jumps into my sleeping bag? My roommates drop off to sleep like they've been drugged, which I'm pretty sure they both have. Or maybe they were just exhausted by all the entertainment I provided today. I lie frozen, wrapped in homesickness, worry, and a sleeping bag that smells like a gym sock.

I wish more than anything I could sleep. Instead, all I do is remember.

MY SIBS RAN across the wood floor with our mutt, Kidd, sliding after us like a black-and-white missile. Dad was sautéing something with butter and onions. Mom pulled bread from the oven. The whole house smelled like you could eat it. We all sang along to "Brown Eyed Girl" because even Wyatt knew the chorus. Well, some of the chorus. Well, "gwirl."

Halfway through the second verse, Dad took the pan off the burner, put it down, and grabbed Mom's hand. She brushed him away at first because she was turning off the oven. He lifted her other hand and swirled her around the kitchen island. She was light across the floor. He took her out into the open space by the table and spun her again until he dipped her backward and a laugh popped out of her mouth. We pretended not to watch, but we did. At least I did.

I danced with Wyatt, and the twins danced with each other. Kidd barked for a partner, so Wyatt and I circled around him until he jumped straight up.

That's how they were. Until they weren't.

Dad says everyone loves a love story. I loved ours.

Chapter Four

KAYA'S FLASHLIGHT finds me before the sun comes up. "Look at you, you're already awake. I love that."

Actually, I've barely slept. Some horse kept whinnying, reminding me that today I'm supposed to ride one of those things. And, pathetically, I miss my family.

"Good morning," says Alice. Her voice is so small I think it's just her sleeping bag rustling until I see her head pop up.

Banner growls from her bag. "This is NOT morning." She sounds a lot more southern first thing in the morning. "GAWWD. Am I still here? No one talk or I'll cut your tongue out."

Kaya motions for me to hurry and then takes her flashlight outside. I try to get ready quietly in the dark, but I can't make my nervous stomach shut up.

"Did you eat a garbage disposal or something?" says Banner.

Alice laughs like teacups clinking together.

My stomach growls again.

Kaya's cowboy hat peeks in. "You comin', Cassidy?"

I hustle out of the tent. I'm not sure what I'm wearing, but my boots are on.

Outside the tent the sky is lightening, and I can see Kaya. Unlike me, she looks amazing. Her beige hat has a woven turquoise braid that matches her turquoise earrings. Her black braid falls all the way to her tiny waist.

She holds out a granola bar. At least I think that's what it is since my eyes haven't focused all the way. "This will hold you over until breakfast."

I could eat an entire box of granola bars. "Thanks," I say.

It's hard to keep up with Kaya in the half-light. She hustles up the trail with way more pep than should be allowed at this time of the day. After a few steps I notice the birds are up, too, and the air smells like wet grass. It's cold, but in a good way that wakes me up. "What are we doing?" I say.

"Outhouses," she says. "You'll have to start with them every day. I'll help you this morning, but you'll be on your own after that."

"For the whole summer?"

"For the whole summer."

Once I get past the smell it's not that horrible. Which is kind of like saying once you get past the wetness of it, swimming isn't so bad. But I don't have to do much more than restock the toilet paper, wipe everything down, and make sure that there's no gross-out mess. I get to wear gloves and a nice denim apron Kaya gives me, so it makes me feel like a high-class maid to my fellow campers.

"Is anyone else 'on scholarship'?" I ask, making air quotes with my fingers.

"Ethan's stacking wood for the breakfast fire."

Ethan is the tall kid from Texas. It makes me feel a lot better to know I'm not the only one working the early shift. Although I'm pretty sure I got the short end of the job stick.

"You're excellent at this," Kaya says. "You must be a big help to your mother."

Guilt floods my head for a minute. I am a big help to my mom, and she sent me here. I hate to think what the bathrooms at my house are going to look like by the end of the summer. I have a little brother who can't aim and two clutter cyclones for sisters. I hate thinking of Mom doing all the work alone.

When we're finished, Kaya gives me a lilac tree air freshener to hang in the corner of the outhouse, which actually works. She nods at me and smiles. "It's the little things that change the big things."

I like Kaya.

We meet Ethan down by the campfire. He's finished stacking and started a roaring fire in the pit for breakfast. He's covered in sawdust, but somehow he still looks tidy. He gives me his chill smile. "Hey, how's the morning treating you, Colorado?" Ethan's like a foot taller than I am. He has hair

40   KRISTEN CHANDLER

on his chin. I look like I'm in fifth grade. If he wasn't so nice I'd think he was making fun of me. "I knew being a boy scout was going to useful one day," he says.

He was a boy scout? I didn't know people still did that. "How did you know I was from Colorado?"

Ethan looks at me, suddenly very serious. "Didn't you know I read minds?"

Kaya shakes her head and smiles. "Or he read your sweatshirt."

I look down at my clothes for the first time today. I'm wearing one of my dad's old University of Denver sweatshirts.

"What's your job, Colorado?"

"Cleaning outhouses," I say.

"Outhouses, huh?" He pinches his nose. "You must really want to ride horses bad."

"You'd think," I say, mostly to myself.

Kaya looks at Ethan's stacks of wood. "You are an excellent worker, Ethan. You and Cassidy have that in common. That will make your summer and mine much better."

"Go, team morning shift," says Ethan, like it's cool to be the poor kids. Actually, with Ethan doing it, maybe it is cool. At least cooler.

Ethan puts a little more wood on and then leaves Kaya to watch his fire and start the coffee. He jogs up the trail to his tent whistling as loud as he possibly can. I wonder what it would be like to feel so confident and cheerful every morning. I'm seriously proud of myself for just being out of bed.

Then I remember what we're supposed to be doing in a few hours.

"Are you going to be around when we ride today?" I ask Kaya as we walk back to my tent.

She nods. "Are you going to punch Coulter again? Because I wouldn't want to miss that."

I snort, which makes everything that much more embarrassing. "Horses make me panicky. When I was little I got bucked off . . . into a fence."

"I bet that was scary for you," she says. "But you know the first rule of horses."

I do. And I hate it.

"When you fall off a horse, you have to get back on." She puts her arm on my shoulder. "You're not going to get hurt today. You need to trust that."

I wish I could. I really wish I could. But nobody can promise that.

Darius blows his sick horn. It's even louder than Ethan's whistling. The man can make some noise. I figure that ought to wake up everything in Wyoming. But the worst part is that it means the day is officially starting.

Coulter stands on his stump with the smoke of the campfire rising behind him. He holds his hands up. "Today, campers, we begin our study of the horse. The first thing you must know is that a horse is a large animal that can accidently hurt or even kill you if you are reckless. Is that clear?"

So that's not at all terrrifying. I see a few other kids nodding, including the dude with the bolo weirdness.

"The second thing you should remember is that a horse has the power to transform you."

I keep nodding. It seems a little out there, but I'm willing to go with it for now.

"You won't be riding your yearling mustangs. We like to give 'em time to grow a bit and stop being so stupid. You'll gentle the mustangs and ride our saddle horses. Most of these saddle horses know more than you do, so please be respectful of that."

"Let's ride already," whispers a painfully thin blonde girl standing next to me. She's wearing riding leggings, tall English-style boots, and a shirt that looks like a pink tablecloth. She has a tiny black mole by her mouth I'm pretty sure she had surgically implanted there.

"Respect, Miss Devri, is the hallmark of a true horsewoman. And a requirement for riding privileges."

Devri rolls up her lip. It makes her mole almost disappear. "Whatever."

Three girls behind her giggle. I can't really see the girls laughing, but I don't need to. I can just close my eyes and remember high school. Honestly, we have been here for less than two days. How do girls like Devri recruit minions so quickly? I guess there is never a shortage of people who are looking for someone to mindlessly giggle behind.

"I am so sure," says Devri.

Coulter puts his hands at his side and looks up, as if he

expects rain to fall out of the sky. Then he drops his eyes to Devri. "Unfortunately, Miss Devri, you will be returning to your tent now. At noon you can try again. We'll see how fast a learner you are."

Devri shrinks a little but doesn't move. You can almost hear the look of surprise on her face. Coulter looms on his stump, waiting, staring at Devri. She turns around and faces her squad behind her, but the other girls look down. Devri walks back to her tent.

Coulter continues. "This is how the morning is going to go. We eat, do chores, and then ride. How does that sound?"

I walk to breakfast with Alice. Her head is still in the right place, but she looks close to doing that turtle thing again. I ask her how she slept, but she doesn't answer. She didn't sound scared of getting on a horse in the tent yesterday, so I wonder what she's afraid of.

Mr. and Mrs. Sanchez are the ranch cooks, and for me it's basically love at first sight. Mrs. Sanchez wears her thin gray hair tied in a knot. She hunches a little and wears a bright orange parka you could see from space. Mr. Sanchez is short with small, swollen fingers. He walks like his hips need grease and his shoes are too big, but he smiles incessantly.

We all line up at the griddle where Mrs. Sanchez is already flipping pancakes and scrambling eggs. It's maybe the best thing I've ever smelled.

Mrs. Sanchez says to her husband, "Old man, where are the bottles of syrup?"

"Syrup takes sugar." His mouth turns up at her, and he starts to back toward the kitchen.

She holds her spatula up by her face and waves it at him. "Don't sugar me, Mr. Sanchez."

"Can I help it, Mrs. Sanchez?" he says. He moves about as fast as the syrup he should be hunting.

I step next to him. "I can get it," I say.

Mr. Sanchez looks confused. I wonder if I'm being stupid or insulting. I'm probably being stupid and insulting.

"No, *pequeña*, you get in line." He smiles. "But you can help with dishes."

We all kind of hunker down together and shove the food in our mouths as fast as we can. Kids are already dividing up into little groups. For some reason Banner comes and sits with Alice and me instead of the Devri drones. She tucks her red hair behind her ears and sits between us.

She turns to me. "What did you do this morning, scholarship girl?"

Here we go. "I cleaned the outhouses."

"Are you serious?" she asks.

I nod and keep eating. It's not like I can hide it all summer.

She surveys the other kids, as if she's looking for somewhere else to sit. "That's so depressing."

I swallow my food. "Kind of crappy," I say.

Alice chokes a little from laughing and swallowing at the same time.

"Well, I'm glad you have a sense of humor," says Banner. "That must make being you a lot easier."

Alice doesn't laugh at this. She just looks at Banner like she doesn't agree. I think Alice is about the nicest person I've ever met.

Banner says, "I just mean that, on top of last night and all, that's so sad."

"You aren't going to take that on your belly, are you, Colorado?"

I look up, and Ethan is standing behind us. A big group of kids are standing behind him watching.

He says, "Big Red, what you so mean for? How about some of that southern hospitality."

A few boys next to Ethan laugh.

Banner glares. "And who are you exactly?"

"Ethan Fredrick Philips the First. You want my phone number?" He laughs happily at himself.

"I want you to stay out of my business," Banner says.

The crowd makes an *Ooooo* sound that I really don't like. Alice's head is completely gone.

I say, "I'm going to go help clean up."

Ethan says, "Easy, Cassidy, don't let Red here pick on you. Just not right."

"No one is picking on me," I say.

The chubby kid with the bolo tie walks up to us in the

middle of all this. Today he's sporting a camo shirt, extra starch. "Hello, ladies. Charles Remington. But people call me Charlie, except my mother, who calls me Charles," he says, putting out his hand to Banner.

Banner looks at his hand like he used it to clean the outhouses and then walks the other direction. Alice brings up her head and walks back toward the tent.

"Is it something I said?" asks Charlie.

Ethan puts his big arm around Charlie like they're best friends, except Charlie looks like he's going to a Halloween party dressed as a middle-aged man, and Ethan looks like he runs this place. Ethan says, "Charlie here is smarter than he looks."

Charlie seems completely unbothered by this commentary. "Actually, I am smarter than I look." Charlie drags something out of his pocket that looks like a piece of rock. "I think it's an arrowhead."

Ethan shakes his head. "I said he was smart. I didn't say he knows anything."

Justin Sweet walks past and says nothing at all. I get that he's an employee and we aren't, but seriously.

"Now, that dude is tightly wound," says Ethan.

"But what he did with those mustangs yesterday was impressive," says Charlie. "If I could ride like that I'd clean up at that contest Coulter was talking about."

"If it was a toxic waste contest, you'd win," says Ethan. "I thought I was going to asphyxiate last night. You are the smelliest dude I have ever met."

Charlie doesn't even look embarrassed. "I know, right? I'm almost as bad as you are."

While Ethan and Charlie bond over flatulence, I watch Justin walk down to the pasture where the mustangs are milling around. I can't help but notice his strut. Or whatever it is. That cockiness that comes off him like a smell. When he gets to the horses he hesitates for a minute with his hand on the fence. He surveys the horses, then throws an apple over the top.

All the horses look at the apple lying in the dirt, but when a black mare steps forward, the big gray horse jumps forward and takes a bite out of her neck. The mare shrieks, kicks up her back legs, and runs. The gray horse jumps, flicking out his front hoof at the mare half-heartedly.

Justin doesn't even flinch. It doesn't seem to bother him a bit that he probably just caused that black mare to get bit.

The other horses all go flying to the other side of the arena. Even after they've all moved back away from the apple the gray horse keeps kicking, running the band into a smaller and smaller corner of the arena. He's so big compared to the other horses he makes them look like ponies.

"Is that the horse that someone gets to ride? He looks vicious," says Charlie.

Ethan says, "He's just a frontin' bully, like Justin. Not a fan of bullies." Ethan smiles when he says that, but I'm surprised at the edge on his words. "On the other hand, maybe he just needs a little schooling. Somebody to show him how to behave."

Justin stands at the fence, and then he opens the gate and walks in. The horses are still moving around. But Justin looks as calm as if he were walking into a living room. I don't think I'm ever that calm, even in my own living room. He stands inside the arena, horses flying around, and waits. After a few seconds everyone except the gray drops their head and looks at Justin. The gray stands off by himself with his backside, ready to kick, turned to Justin.

I get a funny feeling in my stomach.

"I don't know," I say. "I don't think that horse is very interested in school."

Chapter Five

"CAMPERS. WE WILL now begin the main event," says Coulter. He stands near us at the opening of the log pole corral that is in between the ranch house and the big meadow. He surveys the herd of saddle horses behind him and then turns to face us. He smiles through his beard. His voice is softer, like he's talking to each of us personally. "Before we ride our horse we have to catch it."

"You mean like chase it?" asks a little kid with gold curly hair and a hardcore Bostonian accent standing right next to Coulter. He seems agitated, because he keeps wiping his nose on his sleeve and then looking side to side. It's like watching a metronome with congestion.

Coulter looks down. "No, not like chasing it. Danny, who let you in here?"

"You did, Mr. Coulter."

"Well, don't make me regret it. We catch a horse by communicating. We approach a horse with confidence and consistency. You will only hear me use those words about four thousand more times this summer." He stretches his arm out and shows us a harness-looking thing, which I remember is a halter. "Always approach from the left so they can see you. No sneaking up on a horse. They're like fat deer and will assume you're trying to kill them." He opens the gate to the corral. Almost all the horses instantly turn their noses to look at him.

"Horses feel what we feel. So I walk up to the horse with the idea that I like him. I watch what he does. If he turns to me, I keep coming. If he ignores me or turns his butt to me, then I stop and make noise to get his attention. Like waving hello before you get to your friend down the hall. I want him to invite me. Once he does that, I keep going. Until I'm all the way to his head."

A square brown gelding turns his head as Coulter walks to him. The horse drops his nose right in Coulter's hand when Coulter reaches him. Coulter stands parallel to the horse and looks forward. "I don't look him in the eye. I stand parallel. This lets the horse know I want to be part of his herd, but also that I respect his space." Coulter takes the halter and drops it over the square brown gelding's head. The horse barely moves except to put his nose in. Coulter brings the horse to Alice. "You want to saddle this old boy for me, Alice?"

Weirdly, Alice keeps her head up and even smiles. She walks with the gelding over to a hitching post where she quickly ties some knot I've never seen, then grabs a grooming brush and goes to work.

I think Alice has had more than a few lessons.

"Who wants to go next?" says Coulter.

Banner grabs a halter from Darius and walks into the corral full of horses without a ripple, just like Coulter. The horses turn to watch her, but they don't move away. Which kind of disproves the thing about how horses can smell a predator.

Everyone else gets a halter and wanders out to find a four-legged friend, with Coulter and Darius making recommendations. I stand there. I don't want to be pushy.

Kaya is right next to me. "Do you know which horse you want to catch?"

"Do you have a Labrador retriever?"

Kaya points to a brown-gray-blackish horse hunched over in the corner of the pasture by himself. He reminds me of old paint that's splattered on the outside of the can. "How about we start with Smokey? He's twenty-five and has arthritis. You two will be perfect for each other."

She seems nice, but I think Kaya has an edge to her.

She shows me how to catch poor old Smokey and lead him to the post. He's basically a bag of bones in a gray hair suit. Not that he's skinny, but he's just so ancient that everything is poking out in all the wrong places. I like him.

When I finish brushing him, Kaya shows me how to put on a western saddle. It's heavy and awkward. There are a lot of knots and straps. Smokey paws at the ground and nearly smashes my foot.

Kaya smiles. "Horses are mirrors of our emotions. If you're relaxed, then he's relaxed."

"What if I'm not relaxed?"

Kaya smiles. "Relax."

"What if I can't?" I ask, feeling myself become much less relaxed every second.

"Think about something calming," she says.

"How about not being here?"

I look up to see that most of the kids are saddled up and riding. Banner is trotting in tight circles out in the middle of the arena for Coulter and Justin. Dang Banner. Alice rides by with Darius walking beside her. Even Danny is mounted. Darius asks, "What's the matter, Cassidy? You having trouble getting on?"

Kaya brings over some plastic steps for me. "This mounting block will help."

When I was little I could climb into the saddle, no problem. Well, there was a problem. But I try not to think about that. Unfortunately, that makes me think about that.

"Come on, Cassidy," says Kaya. "You can do it."

Smokey is moving around again, so I wait. I don't want to scare him. I do not want to scare me.

"Are you okay?" says Kaya.

For some reason the worried look now on Kaya's face reminds me of my mother. And then all I want is to be home.

Who rides horses anymore anyway? It's like driving a stick shift. It's a completely useless skill. "I'm not going to ride," I say. "I don't want to."

"Cassidy. You came all the way to Wyoming to do this."

"It was a mistake. I thought I did. But I . . . I need to lie down."

And then it's all I can do to keep my feet from buckling right out from underneath me.

Kaya asks, "Do you need me to walk you back to your tent?"

I know where my mice-infested tent is. I start walking. Behind me I hear the voices of the other kids talking and laughing. I ignore them. I've heard those voices before. They're just voices. I have lots of voices louder than those in my head.

"CASSIDY!"

I turn around. It's not really a choice. Coulter isn't walking toward me. He's just yelling.

"Cassidy, get the hell over here with that horse. You don't have to get on him. But you sure as hell have to take charge of your own animal."

For the second day in a row everyone is staring at me. I go get my horse.

Kaya stands patiently waiting for me. She beams at me as she hands me the lead rope, like I've just done something wonderful. "Just go get acquainted. This isn't a race to get on. Just make friends with him, like you did with Alice. That was wonderful."

"He's a horse, not my roommate."

I take the rope and walk. The horse follows me. He doesn't immediately step on me. He actually sticks his nose in my armpit. Then he sneezes and blows horse snot all over my side. "Oh!" I yell.

"Keep walking, kid," yells Coulter. "All the way to the arena."

Smokey nudges me. I can feel the warmth of his dirty nose through my shirt. All right, I'm going already. When I get inside the arena I walk to Coulter with Smokey still basically in my armpit. I feel like I'm being escorted to the first day of kindergarten. Except by a horse.

"That animal bothering you, Miss Cassidy?"

"No," I say. If I cry, this is all going to crap. I'm not going to cry.

"Okay, then. I got a phone call before you got here. Your mother says you showed some unusual talent as a little thing."

I say, "I'm not seven anymore, Mr. Coulter."

"You sure as hell aren't. So I want you to work that horse of yours from the ground today. I want you to walk him up to the big house and back. And then down to the pond. Then go show him your tent. Make sure he gets a good look at it. Don't let him step on you or eat the weeds. And when you're done with that I want you to take off his saddle and brush him until he shines like a new spoon. Can you do that?"

"I can try," I say.

"I have no interest in your trying. Can you do it?"

"Yes," I say.

"That's what I thought. Now get going."

I walk through all the kids looking down on me from their horses. I hope they can't see my hands shaking. The surfer kid with the white-blond hair, I think his name is Scotty, says, "You have to get on the horse to ride it."

Doesn't matter. Smokey and I are getting out of Dodge.

Smokey wants to eat, so I have to keep tugging on him to keep him out of the weeds, but other than that he's decent. He follows me. I wouldn't follow me. If he's a mind reader like they keep telling me, he's getting an earful right now. Anyway, at least he stays out of my way and I stay out of his. When we find some shade at the big house I stop and scratch the blaze on his face. Dust flies in the air. Dust flies when I touch anything on him. He's like an overfull bag in the vacuum cleaner.

When we get to the pond I let him drink the water, and he slurps and slurps and my heart beats at its normal speed. Then I show him my cool digs and tell him about the mice. He cocks his ears to me like he's listening. So I tell him about Banner, too. Just to give him the heads-up.

It's weird the way a horse can take the mad out of you. By the time we get back to the barn to take off his saddle, I feel almost cheerful. "What do you do around here all day, Smokey?"

He licks his lips and nods his noggin at me.

"That means he likes you," says Kaya.

I startle. "Oh, hi. Yeah?"

"When a horse licks and chews he's basically saying he trusts you. Smokey's old and set in his ways. He doesn't usually warm up to people this fast."

"Well, good," I say. I'd lick and chew back if Kaya wasn't standing right here next to us.

Kaya shows me how to tie him with that cool cowboy knot and take off all the tack. I'm still embarrassed that I'm not riding with everyone else. But I like it, too. This way I can concentrate on the horse. I brush Smokey until he starts stamping and scratching with his hooves again. When I take him back to be with his buddies I barely lead him. He walks right next to me.

The rest of the day is chores and eating and chores and eating. There are a lot of chores on a ranch: feeding, watering, shoveling, sweeping, cleaning tack, feeding chickens, weeding the garden, stacking the firewood. As soon as you do one job, another job grows in its place. But I know how to work, so I don't mind. It's easier than doing something that scares me.

When I get back to my sleeping bag that night I want to kiss it. Home sweet pillow. I survived the first day.

Alice says, "I could ride horses all day. Wasn't it great?"

"Yeah," I say, mostly because that is the word I can say with the least amount of effort and the least need to say more words after. Even my eyelashes are tired. And it was a great day, just not in the way Alice's was.

"You and Smokey have a good time?" asks Banner, her voice flipping in just the perfect way to imply everything insufficient about me.

I can't stand Banner, but I like Smokey. He likes me. "Yeah. We had fun together."

"That's darling," says Banner.

Not long after the lights go out, I fall asleep. Unfortunately, I don't stay that way for long. I wake up to more whinnying. It's a shrill, angry whinny tonight, like something is wrong. I lie in the dark of the tent, listening to the horse calling or crying or whatever it is until I can't stand it anymore. I throw on my coat and boots and step outside the tent.

I smell cigarettes.

"What's got you up, Cassidy?" asks Banner.

I look into the dark up on the hill and see Banner sitting on a camp chair stuck in the trees. The light at the end of her cigarette looks like a tiny red coal. I guess we're both crappy sleepers. She doesn't seem too worried about getting sent home. Maybe that's the idea.

I say, "That horse. It sounds miserable."

"Probably one of those mustangs. They don't like being trapped any more than we do. You want a smoke? Calms me right down."

"I'm okay."

"Whatever."

I feel like I'm being unfriendly not to smoke with Banner, but I don't care enough to actually smoke. Maybe that's my problem with friends. I wish I had them, but not enough to do what it would take to make them like me. The horse keeps whinnying. Coulter must hear it. "Somebody should do something."

"Yeah. Somebody should do something."

"Good night, Banner."

I go back into the tent. Alice is silent. After a few minutes Banner comes back in. She makes the tent smell like cigarettes. I wonder if the telltale smell will be here in the morning. At first she rolls back and forth on her sleeping bag like a boat in bad water, but eventually she stops moving, and I can hear her breathing evenly. I let myself think about home for a while, but it just makes the lonesome hole in my stomach get bigger. Who gets homesick when they're sixteen?

Me, I guess.

The horse keeps whinnying. I wonder if I should do something. Maybe Banner's right, maybe the horse does feel trapped, or lonely. Or maybe that's just me. Maybe it had a decent life before it got cornered and rounded up and everything started to suddenly suck like a giant gale-force wind tunnel. And now the horse is wondering when that feeling of not being okay is ever going to stop.

It's dark in the tent. I close my eyes. But I keep seeing things.

SOPHIE LOOKED AWAY down the hallway. "It's just that Haley's locker is closer to most of my classes." Sophie and I had four out of eight classes in the same room at the same time. Sophie's idea, not mine. Because we'd been best friends since sixth grade when she moved into my neighborhood. Even when the whole world made fun of her for smelling like an ashtray. Even in seventh when she got fat eating peanut butter. Even in eighth when she got braces and looked like a Transformer.

She's skinny now and has bleached teeth and hair extensions. She also has new friends and a creep for a boyfriend.

"You don't mind, do you?" She says it like a question, but it's not a question.

I tried to hold it together. Dad and Mom were fighting nonstop. I had slept zero hours. I felt like I'd swallowed razor blades. I wasn't above being needy. "Kind of," I said.

"I mean, this way you'll have more room in your locker. So, okay then?"

The hot mess of tears started backloading in my face. I had to make it quick. "If this is because of Gavin? I swear I never . . ."

"God no. Gavin and I are great. It's just you aren't . . . you and I are going in different directions now."

"What does that mean?"

"Nothing. Just. I like to go to parties. I have lots of friends, Cassidy. You sit at home and make food for your little brother."

That cued the waterworks. And the panic. Sophie wasn't just my best friend, she was my only friend. I was too stressed to do the social thing. Who would I talk to now? Who would I sit with? What if I never have another friend because I'd become unfriendable? "You know why I have to make food for my brother."

"Yeah. I mean, of course. But you might try a little harder."

"Excuse me?"

"Just because your parents are getting divorced doesn't mean that you can't be presentable."

I was wearing the shirt I didn't sleep in the night before, with tights and flip-flops. I had no idea what I was wearing until she mentioned it.

"Everyone has problems, Cassidy. You just have to stay positive like I do. Maybe you could get your own boyfriend if you'd be a little more cheerful."

What I thought: If I had Gavin as my boyfriend, I would go to the health department and ask for the douche bag vaccine. He could varsity letter in cheating on you. And I did not ask him if he wanted to make it a threesome even though he told his jerk off buddies that I did. I would never do that to you. We are best friends. Best friends don't dump you when you're down. They don't say the things you fear most about yourself in the hallway so that you feel naked in front of the entire school.

What I said: "I gotta go."

What I did: Stopped going to school.

Chapter Six

I WAKE UP before my alarm. It must be the birds gossiping outside the tent. And the smell of the air warming up. I get dressed quietly and hustle out into the dark, wondering what wildlife besides the birds are up this early. And then I walk really fast, in case it's something that wants to eat me.

When I get to the outhouse I creak open the door and check around for critters. Not even a mouse is stirring. The outhouses still stink, but being alone is okay. I clean fast, and it's kind of therapeutic after the last couple of days. It's a lot easier to sweep out a floor than my head, but doing one seems to do the other.

On my way back to my tent Ethan erupts from behind a pine tree. I totally jump and make a *yee* sound. He nearly chokes laughing.

"Did you think I was a horse?"

My heart is still pounding. I'm not in the mood.

"Now, don't be mad, Colorado. You're scary when you're mad." He raises his fists like he wants to box with me.

I don't get Ethan. He seems more like one of those kids with an Internet start-up that pays his parents' mortgage. Everyone likes him and does what he says already. I don't see what he gets out of a "leadership camp." I also can't figure out why he talks to me.

"So are you going to ride today?" he asks. "Or let that Banner girl make fun of you again."

I shrug. "Probably the last one."

"Why'd you come here, if you're so scared of horses?"

A little nosy. "Who says I'm scared? I'm an advanced horse walker. Why'd you come here?"

"Governor of Texas has to ride a horse."

I stop walking. "You want to be the governor of Texas? What? Really?"

He shakes his head and laughs. "No. Not really."

"So why are you here?"

"Can you keep a secret?" He looks at me when he says this, so it's possible he's serious, although I have yet to see him be serious, so I'm not sure what to look for.

"Yes. I can keep secrets." I try not to let the irony of this statement sound like sarcasm.

"My parents are both schoolteachers."

In spite of how crappy I feel, I laugh. "That's your secret?"

"It turns out schoolteachers don't make enough money to send their kids to expensive camps, and they sure don't make enough money to buy them a horse that costs more than a car. I need to learn how to ride. Really ride. Like in the mountains and across rivers and shit."

The image this conjures up in my mind is entertaining but doesn't make any sense. "That's your secret? You want to be the Lone Ranger?"

For the first time since I've met Ethan he looks surprised. But maybe it's ironic surprise. "A *Texas* Ranger. The Lone Ranger was a fictional racist. Texas Rangers are legal officers of Texas government. That can never be done away with, by order of the Texas constitution. And it turns out if you want to be a Texas Ranger, you have to be good on a horse."

"They still have Texas Rangers? I mean, I thought that was just in books and stuff. Didn't they save some president from being killed or something, and then they helped get Bonnie and Clyde?"

"Yes, ma'am," he says, smiling. "They solve murders and investigate people and the whole thing. It's harder than being an astronaut. Okay, not harder than that, but about that hard."

"And you professionally rescue people? On a horse?" I ask.

He nods happily at himself. "They also have helicopters and cars. But yeah, they chase people on horseback when they need to."

I get why Ethan would want to do that, actually. You ride horses and save people. I mean, that's not a bad job. I look at Ethan again. "Are you kidding?"

He shakes his head and looks deliberately innocent.

Honestly, I'd like to believe anything Ethan says. But I'm not sure. You can't tell with Ethan. He could totally be jacking with me just for fun. The Texas Rangers. Ethan starts whistling. We walk along like that. He's a good whistler. He gets the highs and the lows. Maybe he's telling the truth. It'd be pretty cool if he is.

Banner is standing in the tent talking to Kaya when I get there. They're both standing too straight. I recognize the posture. My parents have done a lot of standing up too straight. Alice is sitting on her bed with her eyes glued to the floor. There's enough estrogen in the tent to start a cage fight.

Banner's red hair is pulled back into a ponytail so her high cheekbones jut out. "Darius told me it came yesterday."

Kaya leans back in her boots and nods. "That's what I'm saying. I have to drive down to get it. But really, nothing comes this early in the camp. Sometimes we go for weeks without mail to campers."

Banner winces. "I have mail coming."

"Are you expecting something?" asks Kaya.

Banner digs at her fingernails. "That's my business, isn't it?"

"Of course," says Kaya. "There's no reason to get upset." She steps toward Banner.

"I'm not upset. I'm incarcerated," says Banner.

Kaya folds her arms across her chest. "Speak with respect, please."

"Respect? Is that what I'm learning, Pocahontas?"

Kaya straightens up like a rope being pulled at both ends. Banner kicks her way back out of the tent, hits the flap of the entrance, and leaves it swinging behind her.

I say, "Wow. Just wow. Sorry, Kaya."

"Never apologize for something you didn't do," says Kaya. She frowns at the swinging tent flap. "And don't worry about me. I've dealt with girls like Banner before."

Coulter strokes his Santa beard. "We're going to do some character-building today. How does that sound?"

Nobody looks thrilled as Kaya hands out pieces of paper with the lists of jobs written next to everybody's name. Four guys compare lists and grumble. A girl with aviator sunglasses says, "I'm allergic." I think it's the girl who got in trouble before, Devri.

"To what?" says Coulter.

"Dust mites," says the girl.

Coulter stops what he's doing and looks at the sunglasses. "I've also got a shit-covered chicken coop that desperately needs a makeover. That sound good?"

"Not really," the girl says. I think her glasses are fogging up.

"All right then." Coulter smiles. "I suggest you get to work."

My first job is cooking breakfast with Alice and Banner.

I wish somebody would shuffle the deck a little better for the work groups.

Darius shows our group how to construct a fire in the shape of a tepee. "You've got to get the fire going, then wait a second while everything burns down to coals. Part of the trick of cooking this way is not stepping in the fire while you're working. So watch the coals. You girls think you can handle that?"

Alice has her fire blazing two feet in the air while he's still talking. He steps back. "Hey there!"

"You little pyro," says Banner.

Alice says, "My family owns a fireworks company."

Two of the younger boys bringing firewood up from the cutter come close, amazed by the height. They look at Alice and then back at the fire, then go back to work in a hurry.

I need to spend more time with Alice.

Banner gets her tepee up fast, too. I have less fire-building skill.

Banner asks, "What does your family do, Cassidy? Clean outhouses?"

Once my fire is up, Mrs. Sanchez hands us all a pan, which is just fine with me. She hands us some eggs, and we get our coals all shipshape and go to work. First I get my pan going with bacon grease, and then I crack my eggs with one hand.

"That's good, Cassidy," says Mrs. Sanchez.

Alice heads off to slice potatoes. I grab my pan with

the two hot pads and shimmy it backward. I can feel eyes watching me crack the eggs and toss them back into the egg keeper in one swoop. I check my feet to be sure I'm not too close to the coals and shimmy the eggs again. My favorite part is the sizzle they make when they hit the pan.

Mrs. Sanchez hands me more eggs. A lot more eggs.

I stop showing off and start cracking and scrambling as fast as I can. The air fills with snapping sounds of breakfast happening. When I finish the eggs, I stand up. Banner is still frying bacon. She looks up at me. "Impressive."

"Thanks," I say.

She keeps looking at me. "Like you're on fire."

"Thanks," I say.

I don't even notice Mrs. Sanchez until she's almost on top of me. "*Fuego! Fuego!*"

I simultaneously see her towel and the end of my jeans smoldering. Mrs. Sanchez throws her rag on my leg, pushes me on the ground, and kicks dirt on me. I get dirt in my mouth. The eggs are in the dirt.

When I sit up Mrs. Sanchez is hovering. "*Alma mia.* You have to be more careful!"

I look across the fire, trying to figure out what just happened. Banner is frying bacon. "Wow. That was a close one, Cassidy. Are you all right?"

I get on my feet. "I'm fine."

Because I ruined a flock of eggs, breakfast is late, chores are late, and everything else, like me, is a mess. My pants have a sexy new scorch on them. The knot is back in my throat. And the worst part is that I'm not sure the accident was totally my fault. Maybe it was. Maybe somebody helped the coals while I was cooking. But I swear I stood back to keep out of the fire.

After the chore-fest is done, Coulter gathers us all in the first small arena. Everyone kind of hangs on the fence like they'd like to go back to bed or at least stand in the shade over by the ranch house. It's not even halfway through the morning and it's already so hot the back of my neck is sweating, or maybe that's just the steam coming out of my ears from being secretly ambushed.

"Today Darius and Justin are going to teach you how to be a good partner to your horse, aren't you, gentlemen?"

Justin looks out at us and tips his hat farther down on his face. Darius takes off his baseball cap and shows his two-tone 'do. He bows slightly, and we all clap. He's funny at least. Justin is about as much fun as a tick.

Coulter says, "Yesterday we haltered our horses in a corral where they were all close together with nothing to do. Today we are going to go out into a pasture with grass and plenty of room to run. The horses like being with their buddies, eating and kicking and running. The idea is get your horse to come to you so you can get a halter on them. Any ideas?"

We all just stand there swatting at flies, shifting weight from one boot to the other.

Coulter waves open his arms. "Here's a hint. Horses are social. They depend on the herd to survive."

Everyone stays quiet, but the wheels inside my head are cranking almost on their own. Why do horses let people halter them?

Devri says, "Easy. You take a grain bucket out and bribe them."

Somebody should give Devri some grain. She looks like she lives on lip gloss.

"Thank you for your comment, Devri. Let me see if I got this right. We have to go get twenty grain buckets to get our horses for the rest of the summer?"

Devri frowns. "Well, yeah."

Banner's steps forward from the back. "You show the horse who's boss."

Coulter walks through the other campers with a halter and hands it to Banner. "Excellent. You can pick any horse you'd like, Miss Banner. All you have to do is get that horse to lie down by showing him who's boss."

"You want me to get the horse to lie down?" Banner holds the halter for a moment, looks out in the pasture, and hands it back to him. "I'd need more than a halter for that, Mr. Coulter. I'd need a whip."

"You wouldn't do that, would you, Mr. Coulter?" asks Alice.

"I've seen that at rodeos," says a kid wearing a beanie cap. "It's totally cool."

A girl in a red tank top asks, "Why do you want the horse to lie down?"

Coulter takes the halter from Banner and returns to the front of the crowd where Justin and Darius are waiting.

"Justin," Coulter says, "our campers are wondering why we would ask a horse to lie down. Can you show them?"

"Right now, sir?" He doesn't look all that happy about it. But I have yet to see him do anything but scowl.

"Right now," says Coulter.

Justin walks his buckskin next to a patch of cheatgrass. He takes off the saddle and blanket, then props them up sideways in the low-growing weeds. He takes off the bridle and hangs it over the saddle. If the horse wanted to bolt, there would be no stopping her, but the buckskin barely twitches at flies.

Justin turns his back to us and leans into the side of his horse. There is something measured and graceful about the erectness of his shoulders. Nothing he does is fast or slow, just fluid. He rests his hands on her back and under her belly, almost hugging her. His back rises and then recedes, rises and recedes, as if they're breathing together. Then he steps away, keeping a hand on the buckskin's middle. "Down, sis," he says.

The horse drags her head around and looks at Justin, who nods back with his whole head. "Down."

Nothing happens.

Justin leans on the horse again. Nothing. This is a strange trick.

Finally, Justin leans in and says something I can't hear and then backs away.

After a second or two the horse's legs seem to tremble. She sticks her butt backward, almost like she's squatting. Then the horse drops completely onto her side in the dirt and rolls over on her back, hooves waving in the air. Which sounds cool, but with a horse it feels like something serious. Anybody can see horses' legs and bellies aren't supposed to be upside down, exposed to the world with no way to run.

Everybody oohs and ahhs. Coulter's eyes go all twinkles and moonbeams. I don't get it. To be honest, the whole thing bothers the crud out of me.

Justin nods to Coulter and then looks at us like *here you go, idiots.* He turns back around to his horse and makes a clucking sound, and the horse flips right up on her feet and shivers off the dirt. He pats her gently and hugs her around the neck. There's a sweetness about the two of them that makes me feel funny again, like they have this hidden thing that only they get.

Coulter says, "That, campers, is being partners."

Banner raises her hand again. "We couldn't have done what Justin did. He already knows that horse. They practically live together."

Coulter smiles. "Exactly right."

"But why do you do it?" I ask. That's not being a partner. "Why do you want the horse to do that?"

"Excellent question. But I'm not going to answer it. You are. The first one who answers it right gets this." He pulls a gigantic candy bar out of his jacket. I'm not sure how he hid it in there. I don't want to think about it too hard.

At least ten kids raise their hands. The kid with the running nose moans out loud, "Sweet mother of candy."

Devri says, "I thought you said you don't offer bribes."

"There is difference between a bribe and compensation. I should note that if you guess wrong, you get to clean the outhouses with Cassidy."

Everyone puts their hands down.

Coulter bellows, "No takers?" Nobody moves. "All right then. Let's make it interesting. How about the chocolate and a one-hour riding lesson? But if you lose, you have to work an extra two hours."

I look at Justin. Then I look at his buckskin, just inches from him, standing quietly without her halter. That mare would follow that broken nose off a cliff, and he'd probably do the same. So why roll in the dirt? That's the worst way to get away from a cougar there is. I raise my hand. "Okay."

Coulter looks at me triumphantly. "Are you sure, Cassidy? That's two *extra* hours of work."

I want to clean two extra hours tomorrow like I want to have my eyes poked out, but heaven knows I need more help than anyone here. Plus I think I know the answer. "You ask the horse to lie down because you want her to trust you." I stop to see if Coulter's face changes. It doesn't. "There's no way she'd do it otherwise. It goes against her instincts. And if she does, then you know you can trust the horse."

Coulter's eyes narrow. I think I see a flash of something serious, and maybe even anger, but then he smiles and hands me the candy. "You'd think I'd learn not to bet against a Parker by now."

When we get back to the tent, Banner is not a happy camper. "What was that?"

"What?" I say.

"Coulter really is your sugar daddy."

I lay the candy trophy on my bed. I'm not a huge chocolate fan, but I can't believe how big this thing is. And I won it. For answering a question no one else knew the answer to. About horses. Are there taxidermists for chocolate bars?

The tent feels stuffy. Alice lies on top of her sleeping bag like a deflated balloon. Banner pulls off her boots and pours dirt out of them. "Why's Coulter obsessed with your grandfather? Was he some kind of bank robber or criminal or something?"

"He died when I was little. But he was just a rancher." Then I add, "At least, that's all my mom ever talks about."

Banner takes off her shirt and sits on her bed in her bra and jeans. "Bless your heart. That's what families are best at. Keeping secrets."

Alice nods. "All my parents talk about is money. And me becoming an accountant."

I think about this for a second. "My mom's an accountant. But she doesn't talk about money, not much anyway. She talks about accountability. Which is not the same thing." My mind leaves the state for a minute. My parents do keep secrets. I look at my trophy. This is going to be a long, hot summer. I need friends a lot more than I need chocolate.

I offer the first half to Banner. "I hope your letter comes soon."

"Shut up and give me the chocolate," she says.

I give the second half to Alice, whose smile barely fits on her face. She breaks her chocolate in half and hands the biggest piece back to me.

I smile back at Alice.

"That's so sweet," says Banner.

It actually is.

Chapter Seven

BANNER AND ALICE go right to sleep. No such luck for me.

After a while the horse starts to whinny, and no one seems to care. It's not loud, but it doesn't stop. I wonder if I should do something. But what would I do? My mind wanders. I look at the outline of my grandfather's hat in the darkness.

Maybe Banner is right about my grandfather, too. Maybe he did do stuff he shouldn't have. I know how Grandpa was with me at least. He was strict and foulmouthed, but he never cheated me out of anything except more years as his granddaughter. Anyway, I have enough family problems to worry about.

The horse isn't quiet for a long time.

When I finally fall asleep I see Grandpa's long, skinny arm arching over the green bar of the gate to the horse pasture, opening it to me like a kingdom.

Chapter Eight

BY THE TIME I get a shower on Sunday morning I feel like I have lived at Point of No Return for seven weeks, not seven days. To be honest, if I'd known I was only going to get to shower once a week, I might have bailed. A good shower is hard to compete with.

Like everyone else, I get only five minutes at the back of the big house. By the time it's my turn the hot water is long gone, but I use every butt-freezing second. The dirt runs out of my hair in a brown stream into the rusty drain. I see a spider the size of silver dollar clinging to one corner of the ceiling. I have to say that standing there naked and freezing in front of a spider, I feel tougher than I did a week ago.

The highlight of the day, besides washing off eight pounds of dirt, is something that Coulter has billed as "Sunday Suppositions." He tells us we'll be "sharing a moment" in the cathedral of the great outdoors. Not optional. When

Banner asks about her freedom of worship, Coulter says, "Don't worry, Banner, nobody gets saved in Wyoming."

I sit on a beat-up old blanket next to Ethan, Charlie, and Alice. We're like a thing now. Which I'm pretty happy about, really. Ethan hangs out with everybody, but I think he's taken us weirdos on as a service project. Ranger work.

"Your family religious?" asks Ethan.

"No. My dad's an English professor." It occurs to me only after I open my mouth that people can be religious and work at a university.

He nods. "My family are Methodists."

"Do you like being a Methodist?" I say.

He smiles in kind of a serious way. "It's not bad. We forgive people. We help people who need it. The people are nice. I first got started riding at a Methodist Bible camp with horses."

Charlie says, "My parents are religious, too. My mother is religious about exercise, and my father is religious about golf. I am an exercise atheist. I have no proof it doesn't work because I haven't tried it." He stares into the fire. "They sent me here to trim down a bit."

Two blankets up, Banner says, "How's that working for you, slim?"

We all turn around to glare at Banner but instead get an eyeful of Izzy from San Diego and Andrew from Arizona making out under a tree. They seem to have fallen in love in one week and are inseparable. Behind them Justin is sitting on a rock carving a branch with a knife. He's flicking his shavings in their general direction.

Kaya walks up to the couple. "Excuse me," she says. "You two!"

Andrew and Izzy sit up quickly.

"Do you want a window or an aisle seat on the next plane home?"

Banner says, "Y'all better look out. That happiness, it's sin, isn't it?"

Coulter doesn't exactly make a grand entrance. In fact, he looks haggard as he ambles across the meadow to where we are all waiting in the shade. He has a guy with him dressed in some kind of forest ranger suit. I wonder if we're going to get a Ranger Rick lecture.

Kaya sits down next to me as the two men approach.

Coulter waves us all to silence. "I'd like to welcome you all to our first Sunday get-together. This isn't church. But it is a day of rest for the horses."

"Hallelujah," says Banner.

"Put a cork in it, kid. We have a guest. He has an announcement."

The late-twentyish-looking guy in the forest ranger uniform steps out from behind Coulter. He has sandy brown hair and a big jaw. His wide shoulders tip forward, like he's ready to tackle something.

"Good afternoon. I'm Officer Miles Hanks. I work for the BLM, or the Bureau of Land Management. I have the honor of caring for this beautiful land"—he lifts his hands stiffly—"on behalf of the United States government." I wonder if he's been an agent very long.

Coulter's face doesn't look right when Officer Hanks is talking.

"You kids are going to get a great opportunity to work with mustangs this summer. I get to work with them, too. Unfortunately, there are too many mustangs on the range here, and it's my job to see that the horses that are selected by the government to be gathered and put up for adoption are gathered safely and efficiently. We've had some problems with horses being released after they've been captured. This is a danger to the horses, who have to be captured again, and it's costly. So we're asking you kids to keep a lookout for the people doing this. We also want to let you know that there is a three-thousand-dollar fine for harassing mustangs or vandalizing federal property. Anyone caught doing this could even be looking at jail time."

He stops talking. His eyes seem to drop by accident and land on Kaya's face. He quickly looks up and starts talking again. "So I need to let you know that if anyone from this group were to be found harboring information about this behavior, we would have to cancel our contract with Mr. Coulter and not allow kids like yourself to train horses anymore. That would be sad, wouldn't it?"

Nobody even cracks a joke about how stupid this question is.

"Okay, well, I much appreciate Mr. Coulter making time for me."

"Don't mention it," says Coulter.

The man stares out into the group as if he's looking at all of us, but I see where his eyes pause, and then he tips his shoulders toward where he came and disappears.

After he's off the hill somebody finally talks. Ethan. "Was that dude for real?"

Coulter rubs his beard. "Our tax dollars at work."

Darius pipes up from the back. "He's a pain in the ass is what he is."

Coulter shoots Darius a look of warning and then readjusts his hat so we can see his wrinkled face. Then he uses his booming voice. "Nobody here is to chase, harass, or have anything to do with loose mustangs. Is that clear? I'll take you out to see them, but if you so much as try to sneak up on them, I'll take it out on your hide personally. How does that sound?"

"Does he think we're doing that?" I ask.

Coulter settles back down. "Officer Hanks is doing his job, which is notifying everyone in the county that there are rules around here and consequences for breaking them. He's been making the rounds since he got here. Not making many friends on either side of the fence, I'm afraid. Which is what brings me to my Sunday Supposition."

Runny-nose Danny asks, "What's a *supposition*?"

"A supposition, my small, allergic friend, is a wonder. Something you suppose, or have a hunch about. And we are all full of them."

"Like, I have a hunch you don't like Officer Hanks," says Danny.

Everyone laughs, and Danny looks pleased with himself.

"I like Officer Hanks just fine. But that is part of the reason we suppose things, because we don't know the whole story."

Coulter folds his arms across his chest and looks out into our band. Then instead of booming it out like he usually does, he drops his voice so we all have to listen. "In one of God's books he says, 'I have seen servants upon horses, and princes walking as servants upon the earth.'"

"Kill me now," sighs Banner loudly.

Coulter doesn't look at Banner.

"What does that ancient supposition mean?" Coulter asks. "I believe it means that whatever you did today, and yesterday, you can't tell what greatness you have inside you. And you don't know what other people have inside them either." He pauses here. I look around. For a microsecond everybody is listening, even Banner. "So in essence, every relationship is a supposition."

He continues. "All you know is what horse a person is riding today. What's important is that this supposition goes for us, too. Sometimes we're sitting on a horse we don't much care for, but we get the idea that's all we can do. That's who we are. But we choose the horse we ride every day."

Banner sighs again. Devri and the drones start whispering.

"Hey, don't," I say.

"Looks like somebody got saved after all," says Banner.

Coulter says, "That's all I got, kiddos. You have the rest of the afternoon to lollygag. Don't kill each other when you're throwing the axes, and don't get more than a mile from the ranch without a counselor. You should be able to hear the dinner bell if I ring it, and you come a-runnin'. Other than that, it's like every day: no drugs, no drinking, and no shenanigans." He looks directly at Izzy and Andrew when he says this.

Everybody gets up and goes off to play horseshoes or go fishing or whatever they want to do. I lie on my blanket and close my eyes. The wind starts to blow, because Wyoming, and it feels good just to let it blow right over the top of me. I don't want to *do* anything. I need a minute to remember why I came here in the first place, besides that my mom basically forced me to. I think about whipping around on the horses at my grandfather's ranch. Happy. Fearless. The wind flying through my hair. And today I feel one step closer. At least I have the wind in my hair part.

When everyone is gone, I look up into the wide-open blue sky. I wonder what horse I'm on, like Coulter said, or if I'll ever even get on a horse. Or if I'll stay stranded on the ground, too scared to do anything different but too stubborn and ashamed to go home. Pathetic. That's the horse I'm on today.

But somehow the sadness I normally have doesn't stay. I don't know why. Maybe because there's no ceiling to hold it. Instead I wonder, *If I could get on the right horse, where would it take me?*

Chapter Nine

THERE'S A SURPRISE for me when I go to do my first job for the morning. In the middle of the night, someone has dumped horse manure on the floor of one of the outhouses. At first I just stand there looking at it. I try to imagine how a horse could accidently walk in a door that was left open and unload all over the floor. Then I realize how deliriously tired I am. This is a message, or a joke, meant for me. Either way, I wish I could return to sender.

I walk down to the barn and get a pitchfork and a wheelbarrow. Darius walks by.

"What you doing?" he asks.

"Someone left a horse pile in the outhouse."

Darius looks at me. Then he laughs. Then he stops laughing. "Someone doesn't like you all that much, Cassidy."

Trust Darius to make something unpleasant even more so. I guess it's like Banner says: everybody has to be good at something.

When I go back to the tent I don't say anything. My hands are washed. Nobody died. It's just horse manure. But I'm not happy either. I know how this goes. When you let jerkwads dump their garbage on you they just keep doing it.

I change my clothes without talking to Banner. Alice is already up and gone. Banner seems cheerful as a fed squirrel. All my happy chocolate love is gone. I look at my pants with the burn mark on them. Coulter said we can choose our horse. I think I'll choose a horse that kicks back today.

I mean, I don't know for sure it was Banner. But then, her gloating grin isn't exactly subtle. Why she hates me I don't know. I mean, I know my stomach growls, I don't smoke, and I buy my clothes at stores where you can also buy groceries. But hate, that usually requires something sexier than just thinking another kid is a teacher's pet.

When I'm done I reach up and take my grandfather's hat off the hook over my bed. Its black rim feels enormous around my head, but my Irish skin is already screaming from sunburn, so it will have to do. I slide it onto my head and teeter it back and forth with my hands. I'm buried to my eyebrows in smoky felt. Since I have no mirror I have no idea how it looks.

Banner watches me tucking my hair in. She spurts out a laugh. "Nice hat, Cassidy."

"Thanks," I say. "Nice hair."

She puts her hairbrush down and looks at me. "Somebody poop in your oatmeal this morning, half-pint?"

"Not in my oatmeal," I say.

I don't see Alice at breakfast. And thanks to Darius's big mouth, everyone has to make poop puns while I'm trying to eat. I go looking for Alice with no luck. In fact, I don't find her until I start my second job for the day. A group of us are supposed to help bring the mustangs in from the pasture. Alice is waiting by the fence post.

"Hey," I say. "What's up?" I don't want to let on how much I'm dreading this. Banner's in our group as well.

"Hey," Alice says. She looks at my hat but doesn't say anything. She's wearing a pink San Francisco Giants baseball cap tipped to one side of her head. "I'm sorry about the outhouse."

"Nah. What have you been doing this morning?"

Her baseball cap droops forward.

"What's wrong?" I say.

She leans on the post. Her hand shakes.

I say, "You should go back to the tent."

"Coulter told me to stay out here."

"Did you tell him you're sick?" I say.

Alice stares without focusing. "He talks too loud."

Just for a second, the way Alice looks off into space reminds me of my sister Oakley. She faints if she cries too hard. For real. Like one of those goats you see on YouTube. I hope Alice doesn't faint. The turtle thing is enough of a health hazard up here.

I say, "Don't laugh, but I'm worried I'm going to freak when I see those mustangs."

Alice's face cracks into a smile.

"I told you not to laugh."

"What do you want me to do?" she says.

"I could follow you." I say. This works with Oakley every time. She knows I'm doing it and it still works. But then, Oakley isn't Alice, and I don't really know how bad things are for Alice. "But no pressure." Alice looks out from underneath her pink brim. She seems to be adding and dividing something.

Banner marches up with her ponytail swinging. She ignores me and stands next to Alice. "What's up with you, turtle?"

Alice's hat dips down.

"Don't call her that," I say.

Banner stops swinging her ponytail. "Who made you cruise director, poop maid?"

Justin rides up on his buckskin. Walking behind him are two guys I recognize from Ethan and Charlie's tent, Granger and Andrew. Andrew, a husky kid with a baby face, seems lost without Izzy glued to his side. Granger is pale and skinny, with a near-beard that looks more like mold than facial hair.

Justin barks down at us. "The old man wants you to see how the herd works. We're going to walk up and watch them, and then you'll get up on the sides of the trail and we'll run down."

"With the horses?" I say.

"I said you walk up on the *sides* of the trail. You stand up there on the turns and make pressure that keeps them all together, then you fall in behind them and drive them down. I can do it myself, but if you all do your job it makes my job a little easier. Can you all do that?"

Banner narrows her puma eyes. "We're not retarded. Well, most of us aren't."

It's astounding just how much I don't like Banner at this moment.

Justin turns to the boys. "You two help me with the gate when we get up there. Let's move."

The guys stand there with their hands in their armpits while Justin circles back behind us. Granger leans over to me and Alice. "Don't worry, ladies, we got you covered." He raises his narrow eyebrows at me and Alice.

Alice and I just look at each other and try to hold on to our laugh-to-death reflex.

Alice leans over to me. "Let's go."

Alice may not be strong, but she's fast. We book it up the trail. The boys and Banner tag behind, with Justin at the back on the buckskin. I like hiking with Alice, especially when it gets me away from Banner. Every once in a while, Alice will turn and smile at me to make sure I'm keeping up. She doesn't look nervous at all now. The girl's got purpose.

When we get farther ahead of everyone else, Alice and

I walk closer together. I don't know what's going on with Alice, but I wish I knew how to be a better friend. To distract us both, I tell Alice about Oakley fainting. "It's like her brain just turns off."

"Maybe she needs it to turn off," says Alice.

I take off my grandpa's hat and fan my face. It's getting warm. "Sometimes I wish I could turn things off."

"No you don't," says Alice.

When we get to the meadow and I see all those manes and tails and hooves swirling around, my back starts to sweat. I'm not even close to them. You'd think they were dragons or something. But my head can't talk my body into making sense. In fact, the more I worry about worrying, the more cumulative worry happens.

"This way," says Alice.

"Right behind you," I say.

When Banner gets up the hill she walks up to Alice. "You walk pretty fast for a turtle."

Alice looks off in the other direction.

"Her name is Alice." I can feel the heat in my face.

Justin rides past us. We're just one more herd to him. "Let's make this quick." He jumps down from his horse and walks to the fence. The horses back away. They're definitely still wild. They want nothing to do with people, even Justin. He pulls a handful of something out of his pocket and shakes it in his hand, then throws it to the ground. "Horses get two things. Fear and connection. Fear comes naturally. Our job is to make the connection."

"What are those tattoos on their necks?" asks Alice, touching her own.

Each horse has a set of white angular symbols stamped just below their manes.

Justin says, "Freezemarks. If you know how to read them, they tell the year and place the horse was born and a registration number."

"Does it hurt them?" I ask.

Justin spits on the ground. "The BLM says it doesn't. But that doesn't make it true."

The stout gray horse lifts his massive head and steps to the front of the herd. His ears and tail point up. He swings his imprinted neck side to side. And then he whinnies. Low to high, just like the one I hear at night. But how? We must be over a mile from my tent here.

Justin says, "Every band has a leader. In this band, everybody stays out of the gray's way. We don't have a boss mare like a real herd would, because we only have one horse that isn't a yearling." The black mare I saw the other day stands blowing air out of her nose but doesn't come closer to the food littered on the ground. No one crosses in front of the gray. "In an actual herd, mares are boss. Stallions are muscle. But that's enough horse psychology for one day."

"So the gray's a stallion?" I ask.

"No." Justin sticks a blade of wheat grass in his teeth and

looks at the angry horse. "He just thinks he is. Sometimes that happens with geldings when they cut them too late. They call it proud cut. It just means he doesn't know the fix is in."

"What does that mean? *The fix is in*?"

Granger and Andrew laugh.

Alice says, "It means he's been castrated, but he still tries to mate mares."

Justin walks to the generator that powers the electric fence. He nods to Andrew. "When I give you the signal, open the gate. You others get clear on the edges of the trail. Stay high. I don't want anyone going mental on me today."

"Got that, Cassidy?" says Banner.

I'm still thinking about the gray. No wonder he's mad all the time. I mean, he's scary, but in an epic way.

Alice taps my arm. "This way."

"Does he have a name?" I ask.

Justin scowls. "They aren't pets. Would it be possible for us to start now?"

"If he were my horse, I'd call him Goliath."

"He's not your horse," Justin says. "Get going."

He hits the switch and gives the sign. Andrew reaches for the wire gate. The horses back away, raising dust. As soon as the gate drops they pour onto the plateau. Horses' hooves beat the ground. My stomach flip-flops. I stand back as far as I can and try to stay calm.

And just for an instant, when I stop being scared, they're beautiful. Their heads rise and their long, tangled manes fly along their necks. They move in and out of one another, lifting their legs and heads but not touching each other. There's a liquid energy in their dancing that's terrifying but, dang, it's sort of beautiful, too.

"Cassidy." The blare of my name startles me. I see Justin waving his hat. His face is twisted in frustration. "Cassidy. Get moving."

I jog to catch Alice. She's running parallel to the trail above the horses. The other kids are far ahead. Alice moves full tilt along the sandy incline, shadowing the animals five or six feet closer in than I am. The pounding of the horses' feet fills the draw as we start to descend the hill. Dust swirls everywhere. Alice turns to me, still running full speed.

It's when she's looking back for me that she trips. One minute she's light and fast. The next she seems to catch on something and torque sideways, so instead of just sprawling to the ground, she launches like a slingshot toward the oncoming stream of horses. Her pink hat sails off her head onto the trail.

Justin's behind us, on the other side of the horses, and everyone else is below us, already farther down the draw.

I shout at Alice. "Hey. Hey! You have to get up."

The horses are roaring.

I take off at full speed. "Get up! Get up!"

Alice is moving around in the dust but not fast. The horses are mostly running inside the main trail, but if they veer off to the perimeter, Alice is in trouble. I pull off my grandfather's hat. I wave it as big as I can. I yell, "Hee-yaw, hee-yaw," like I've heard Coulter do. I put it way above my head and go straight at them, yelling. I don't even look at Alice because after a few strides she's behind me.

I'm too small. They don't see me. There's too much dust. I wave my hat bigger. I yell, "Look at me!" I just keep waving and jumping and running so they can't miss me until I think I've made a terrible mistake. "Look," I scream. "Look!"

Then it's like some lever gets pulled on the giant switchboard of the universe. The gray and a palomino give my hat a wide white eyeball. They startle and instantly move away, taking the rest of the herd with them. And in a few pants-peeing seconds, the herd is past us.

I guess there's more than one way to talk to a horse. And one of them is loud.

I look down at the trail. Alice's hat is out in the middle, trampled. Mine's in my sweaty hand. I walk out and pick up the cap and shake it. Behind me Alice stands with her hands out to her sides. Her face is powdered in dirt, even her mouth. I jog back to her.

"Are you okay?"

She doesn't answer.

I put her crushed hat back on and give her a quick hug. She's stiff as a post.

Then I sit down in the dirt. I just have to sit.

Justin rides up, stopping just long enough to shout at me, "That's it. You're done with horses."

Chapter Ten

"WHAT THE JACK Daniels were you thinking?" bellows Coulter over his desk. His office is dusty and barren. Alice sits next to me, fidgeting in her chair.

"I was thinking the mustangs might run over Alice."

"And why were you thinking that? Besides the fact that they are mustangs and, therefore, deadly in your strange little mind."

I take a deep breath. I realize I don't have a stellar track record with acting calm around horses. But that doesn't make me wrong. "Mr. Coulter, Alice tripped so hard she wasn't getting up, and I thought if they turned the wrong way they'd squash her. I also want to add that having us run next to stampeding horses is reckless endangerment."

"Reckless endangerment?" He snorts over his beard. "That's a two-dollar word."

It's two words, I think. *And man I wish I would shut up.*

Justin sniffs behind Coulter. His hat is off, so I can see his ears are red. Like they're burning. "The horses weren't stampeding, they were safely driving down the trail like they have every morning since they got here. And she's the reckless endangerment."

Coulter turns to Alice. "Were the horses going to trample you, Alice?"

Alice is shrunken up like a pill bug. Her face is still dirty. She looks at Coulter, and then she looks at the floor. Her hand is shaking, so she folds her arms across her chest to steady herself.

"It was pretty scary," I say.

Coulter says, "I am aware, Cassidy." He looks at her, waiting. "But I would like Alice to talk for herself."

Alice blinks back at him and then pulls her hat out of her back pocket. She puts it on his desk. It's impressively trampled.

Coulter shakes his head. "Well, I'm glad your head wasn't in that. Do you feel good enough to find Mrs. Sanchez?"

Alice nods and beats it out of there. Coulter doesn't even wait until the door is all the way closed behind Alice before he starts in. "What's wrong with that one?"

I'm not sure if this is a real question, but I answer anyway. "She doesn't like loud noises."

"Like horses?"

"Like your voice, sir."

Coulters pauses and then lowers his boom box. "You say

what you think, don't you?" He spins around on his chair. "Nevertheless, I can't have you causing trouble like this. You're like a bomb waiting to go off every couple of days. What is your problem?"

It's easier to explain about Alice.

"She's scared a' horses. She shouldn't be here," says Justin with thick disgust.

Coulter grabs his suspender straps. "Is that really all that's going on here?"

It's a simple question. I just don't have a simple answer. Yes, I am afraid of horses. But if I was only scared of horses, I wouldn't be here. I'd just avoid horses, which is easy to do in a suburb. I'm scared of something a lot bigger and harder to explain, even to myself. The weird thing is that when I was charging at those horses that really could have hurt me, I was hardly scared at all. I just wanted to keep Alice safe. And I can't explain that either.

"She didn't used to be afraid of them." Coulter spins around in his chair again, then stops with his boots facing Justin like a roulette lever. He looks up at Justin but seems to be still talking to himself. "She just needs a little desensitization."

Justin bursts out. "Hell no, Coulter. Hell. No."

"Sir?" I say.

Coulter ignores me. "Justin is an expert at helping our mustangs get over their fear of people. You could say he has a gift. He's less gifted with people. So in a way, I'll be killing two birds with one stone."

"How are you going to kill birds, sir?" My brain is still rattled from the whole Alice adventure.

"By having Justin give you riding lessons. You won a free lesson, remember? But we'll give you a few extra as a bonus. We need to get you up off the ground and in the saddle where it's safe."

I glare at Justin. "Nothing about that sounds safe."

"Because I couldn't teach you?" says Justin. His nose looks even more bent out of shape than usual.

"You couldn't teach a polar bear to swim," I say.

"And you're about as teachable as brick."

Coulter laughs. "Oh, you two are adorable. Does this come in a box set? Now go make good choices together. You'll have to start with some groundwork, but I want Cassidy on a horse by the end of the week. Do you both understand me?"

"No," says Justin, swinging his head back and forth. "I won't do it."

I don't say anything because all I can think is that I won't do it either.

Coulter turns on Justin, "If you want a shot at being a real horse trainer, you are going to have to learn to train more than horses. Do I make myself clear?"

Justin doesn't answer.

"Do I make myself clear?"

Justin kicks the floor.

"All right. I'll make it clear. You get this girl on a horse, or I give that hellion of a gray gelding to Darius to train."

Justin's face twists up like he's going to blow fumes out his eyeballs.

Coulter stands and towers over me. "Cassidy. You have to promise me you'll stop running in front of my horses. Can you do that?"

"I wasn't trying to . . ."

"I don't care if the Virgin Mary appears to you in a dream. Can you stop running in front of my horses?"

"Yes, sir."

"Fair enough. You start tomorrow." Coulter sighs heavily. "And Justin, you work on getting a sense of humor."

"I work for you, don't I?"

"I don't have a sense of humor, boy. So you watch your mouth."

I think Coulter has a sense of humor. It's just not a very nice one.

Chapter Eleven

TONIGHT RAIN PELTS the canvas and rattles the flaps. After an hour or so it slows down, but it never really stops. None of us feels like talking, especially Alice, who disappears into her bag without eating dinner. I bring her a plate of lasagna, but she isn't interested.

Banner asks, "Haven't you wrecked her enough for one day?"

It hadn't even occurred to me that I was the cause of Alice getting hurt. But I guess that is one very sucky way of looking at it.

I try to write a letter home, but I have a hard time thinking of things that are okay to say. Banner smokes just outside the tent under a tree, then comes back in and sprawls on her cot without talking. She tosses back and forth and then is finally quiet. Alice kicks at her giant green cocoon long after she falls asleep. I lie still, thinking about how I'd love a warm shower. If I had a shower, maybe I could sleep.

The rain keeps falling. The horse doesn't whinny to-night, which is good. I couldn't bear that sound right now. I turn off my flashlight and promise myself to finish my letters home tomorrow. After what seems like forever, Wyo-ming style, my mind drifts. Unfortunately, it drifts all the way back home, to a shower I would rather forget.

SHE DIDN'T ANSWER, *but I could hear the water spraying. She'd been in there a long time.*

"Mom?" I waited. "Mom?" No answer. I left for a few minutes and then came back. "Mom, are you okay?"

Our dog, Kidd, came in the room, and Wyatt followed him. "Where's Mom?"

"She's in the shower." I said.

"I'm hungry."

I went downstairs and microwaved oatmeal for Wyatt. Kidd circled my feet. Kidd always knows when something's up.

I went back upstairs with a knife to jimmy the door. My plan was just to peek in. If she was in the shower, she'd never know. When I got it open Mom was standing in the middle of the floor in a bath towel. Her eyes were swollen.

"What's wrong?" we both asked at the same time.

Then we both said, "Nothing."

I asked, "How come you didn't answer?"

She tightened her towel. "Go downstairs. I'll be down in a while."

I called Dad on his cell phone. He didn't answer. Dad is never without his cell phone. I called two more times. The first thing he said was, "Is everything okay?"

I was standing in the pantry looking at canned vegetables. My chest was tight. I was trying to think of a reason why Mom would be staying in her room so much and crying in the shower. Good reasons. "Mom's sick. When are you coming home?"

When he finally spoke his voice was flinty. "I might not be home tonight, honey."

I asked, "What's going on?"

"I'll see you soon."

"Where are you, Dad?" I had assumed he was at a conference, but I hadn't asked. I was careless that way. Dad went to a lot of conferences.

"At work."

"So why don't you come home?"

"I'm far, far away at work." He sounded like he was telling me a fairy tale. Like I was Wyatt. "Are you doing all right?"

I didn't feel all right. I felt worried. Where was far, far away? "Does Mom have cancer?"

"Of course not. Why would you say that?"

"She's been in her bedroom all day. There's nothing to eat." Which was totally selfish, and I was sorry right after I said it.

He didn't talk for a few seconds, but it sounded like he was crying. "She doesn't have cancer."

I started crying, too, even though I didn't know why.

"I'd better go," he said. "Love you, Cass."

"Love you, Dad."

And then he hung up.

He showed up four days later and stood on the porch. He and Mom sent us inside and stayed three feet apart while we watched through the blinds. The twins went to the basement to play a video game. Wyatt kept trying to go out, and they would scoot him back inside to me. I finally turned on a movie and made popcorn.

Dad didn't say good-bye. He just left. And just like that, he didn't live here anymore.

It happens. I get that. But my parents loved each other. And then they didn't. And Dad went from being "Daddy" to "your father." Mom went from "my darlin'" to nothing at all, because Dad wasn't there to talk to anymore. Then everything seemed to break all at the same time, including "the children."

Chapter Twelve

KAYA SILENTLY HANDS Banner a letter over her hoagie sandwich. Banner drops her plate on a rock and bolts.

Alice kneels next to me. "I hope that's good news, don't you?" She doesn't seem mad at me for nearly getting her killed yesterday. But that's probably just Alice.

Charlie asks, "Do you think she wants the rest of her cookie?" The Sanchezes outdid themselves with dessert today. Charlie doesn't wait for me to answer before he inhales the chocolaty thing.

When Banner finally comes back from our tent her mascara is smudged, but she's smiling.

I ask, "Good news?"

"Shut up," Banner says.

Alice moves off to the other side of the fire and then drops in some firewood.

Charlie, who is wearing an orange-and-green poncho,

says, "That's an interesting expression. *Shut up.* It originally meant that a person was quarantined."

Banner looks at her empty plate. "Did you eat my cookie, fat boy?"

"I did," I say. "I thought you left it."

She moves from Charlie to me. "You and all your girlfriends need to all stay out of my way today. I don't want anyone ruining my good mood."

"I'd hate to see you in a bad mood," I say.

"Yeah, you would," she says. "You really would."

My first lesson with Justin goes like this: I get the word through Danny to meet Justin at the mustang corral. The other kids are all meeting at the big corral to saddle and ride the regular horses. Justin watches me walk up, while he hangs on the fence. He's wearing a T-shirt with a cow skull on it. Of his own free will, I think. Now I have to look at the top half of his arms, which are, like, bizarrely sinuous. That is not the kind of thing I need to be noticing right now.

"I'm not going to be working with Smokey today?" I ask.

"No," says Justin. Then he just stands there, toeing the ground with his crusty boot.

I look around. Behind him is the corral full of mustangs. I ask, "Do you want me to put a halter on one of the horses?"

Justin wipes the back of his hand across his face. It leaves a streak of red dust on his cheek. Which makes me notice, completely against my will, that his eyes are muddy brown. Luckily, he opens his mouth. "You don't just walk out and halter a wild horse."

"Okay," I say. I'm bothered now in a different way. "Do you whisper to them first?"

He takes his dirty hat off and spits. "It's a load of crap, you know. You don't whisper in a horse's ear or anyplace else."

I remind myself that I promised I would not freak out, even if Justin is a jerk, which he is. "Can't you pretend I'm a horse and be nice?"

Justin looks off at the mountains. He shifts his shoulders. Then he shifts them back again. If he were to look at me, he'd know I'm about ten short seconds from packing it in. I can't handle so many emotions fistfighting in my head. He doesn't look at me. Finally he says, "I've never met a horse that irritates me as much as you. But I could try that."

"What do you want me to do?"

"Nothing," he says. "You stand outside the corral. Don't stand near the fence either."

Using a stick with a flag on it, Justin runs a scrawny brown mare with white speckles on her back through a corridor that connects to the round pen and corral. That way he doesn't even have to halter her. Which is good, because she's a full-throttle mess. Her mane's half torn off, and she's got a wound on her rear that looks like one of the other mustangs bit her this morning. Once she's in, there's no place to go but up or in circles. She tries both. Every time she strikes the air with her hooves Justin holds his hands out to his side and says, "Easy, girl." The horse gets back up against the fence and starts running again.

Soon the horse is foaming with sweat. Her eyes are bugging out. Justin stands in the center, one leg cocked forward, watching her.

He raises his hand. The horse flies up and goes the other direction. Justin puts his hand down. "Whoa," he says. The mare keeps running. He drops his body down like he's sitting. *"Whoa."* The horse slows to a jog and then stops.

He steps toward her. She keeps her head down. He takes another step. She moves her head side to side, but she doesn't run. When he reaches her, he puts his hand under her mouth. There's a gentleness in the way that he touches the horses that completely throws me off. Even from a distance I can see the horse settle in his hand. "Aren't you a beauty?" His voice is warm and easy. Even I like him when he uses that voice.

"Should I come in now?" I ask.

The friendliness drains from his face. "No."

I have got to remember that Justin is one person around horses and another person around humans. And he may save his extra-irritating self just for me. "Are you going to let me do anything today? I could at least feed one of them. I could feed Goliath."

"His name's not Goliath."

He spends five whole minutes rubbing his hand up and down the mare's back. Every time she shivers he holds his hand still, and when he starts again he says, "Easy, girl." Then he puts a lead line slowly around her neck and guides her back into the corral with the other mustangs. When he comes out he looks at me from underneath his hat. "That's it."

I say, "You didn't teach me anything. You just parked me in the dirt and did what you would have done with the horse anyway."

"That doesn't mean I didn't teach you something."

He keeps walking. I follow after him. "Coulter told me to get on a horse. I have one week, and all I did today was stand here."

He sniffs with his smashed-up nose. "You either get it or you don't."

I'm kinda over being dumped on around here. "Get what?"

"It's not about you."

That's fine. It isn't about me. It's about me getting on a horse. The horse I choose. And Justin isn't the only person in the world who can teach me how to do it.

Chapter Thirteen

AT DINNER I slide next to Kaya. She blinds me with her smile. "How was your lesson with Justin today, sweetheart?"

I look over my shoulder. Justin's talking to Coulter and Darius about something life changing, like how to spit farther. "About like I thought it would be." But I have other things to do tonight than talk about that jerk. "You ever had anyone besides me scared of getting on a horse?"

"Sure." She keeps eating. It's barbecue tonight, and everybody's ravenous.

"How'd they get over it?"

She munches her coleslaw thoughtfully. "They got on. I mean, I stood next to them, but it comes down to that really. I've even kept the horse in a halter and led them, but they had to get on."

I try to imagine myself climbing on. I drop my spoon in my food. "I can't do it."

"Why not?" says Charlie. He sits down right next to Kaya. He's having seconds on beans. I'm glad I'm not in his tent tonight. But I love the denim jacket he's wearing. Red kerchief pockets. I mean, it looks a little out of place compared to the T-shirts the rest of us are wearing, but the kid has style.

"I just can't," I say. "It doesn't make sense."

"Everything makes sense if you understand it all the way through," says Charlie.

Surprisingly, that makes sense, even if Charlie said it. Behind me I hear Banner laughing. I didn't mean to start this conversation in such a public place. "There ought to be a better reason why I'm afraid. On the other hand, it also seems logical to me that if doing something hurts, you don't do it. Maybe the illogical part is that I'm here at all."

Alice sits next to me. She must have had a great ride today because she's eating enough for two Alices. She has barbecue sauce on her cheek.

"Maybe you're making this too hard," she says. "The best part about horses is that when you get on them you don't have to think about anything else."

"Great," I say. "But how do I get to that part?"

Ethan shoves in. I'm having an intervention. "Alice is right. You just have to do it. You can't overthink it."

"Spoken by the person who has been afraid of nothing ever," I say.

Ethan laughs. His plate is so full it's bending at the

edges. "I'm afraid of things. I'm afraid of sleeping in the same tent as Charlie tonight."

"Me too," says Charlie.

The mustang is having as bad a night as I am. First he blows, and then he bellows. How can no one else hear him? I look at Banner's cot. Her breathing is steady. Alice is silent but I think she's out, too. I go for the bear box as quietly as I can. I take out the two beautiful red apples I stashed from dinner tonight and put them in my jacket next to my flashlight.

The mustang corral is a walk. But it's blissfully chilly after a day of heat and flies. And the moon is full. I walk close to the trees. Crickets and wind cover the crunch of my footsteps until I hit the soft dirt trail. I almost turn back when I get to the draw. In the dark, the trail feels twice as skinny and three times as long. But after a night of people telling me how to stop being such a baby, I can't go back.

The mustang's whinnies get louder once I get on top of the plateau and am near the fencing, so it's not hard to locate where he is. The electric fence is hot, so I just look through the wires at him. In the moonlight, he glows white. He looks so huge and miserable. He runs back and forth. The other horses give him ample room. I think about what Justin said about the fix being in. He whinnies again.

I hold the apples out. "Hey, Goliath," I whisper. "What's up?"

He stops whinnying.

I stand stock-still and hold the shiny fruit out. He blows through his nose, but quietly, like he's thinking. Maybe he thinks too much, too. I feel prickles on my skin as he walks closer. He sniffs the air. "Goliath. You like that name? He was a bully, too. But he kicked some butt for a while."

I chuck one apple just over the fence so he'll come right next to me. He lifts his head up and down, shaking his long mane, but doesn't move farther forward. I chuck the other apple. He waves his head at the apples irritably but stands his ground.

"Come on, you do it for Justin. And he's a complete ass."

It feels nice to talk to Goliath. I think he gets it. Also I bet he agrees. Even if Justin does mesmerize him with horse sorcery. That nose. That attitude. Those stupid arms.

The gelding looks off, shunning my petty bribe. He can't be had so easily. Go, proud cut. But I hear him chomping the fruit as soon as I turn my back to return to the tent. And I don't hear him whinny afterward. Not once as I fall asleep.

I don't know what I've accomplished. But something.

Chapter Fourteen

THE NEXT MORNING Justin is standing by the outhouse waiting for me.

"What brings you here?" I ask.

He doesn't laugh. "We need to start over."

I probably should almost-apologize, too. "Okay," I say.

"Let's do our lesson right now. Before everyone gets up."

I haven't even brushed my hair. I'm wearing a hoodie with tree sap on the shoulder. "Can I go do my jobs first?"

"No," he says. "I'll explain to Kaya. Let's go." Then he starts walking across the field. His long, skinny legs take one step for my two. Luckily, there's enough pink-and-yellow light coming up over the mountains that I can see the holes in the ground. Plus I just did this walk a few hours ago in the dark.

We walk up the hill to the mustangs in silence. Well, I can hear the rooster waking up. I breathe too loudly. Being alone with Justin is hard on my nervous system.

He asks, "How did you get hurt from a horse? When you were little, right? Tell me the whole thing." He doesn't even turn around to ask me. Like we're doing a tour and I'm supposed to show him the room with my crazy in it. Plus I love that Kaya or Coulter blabbed this to him.

"I got bucked off. Thirty stitches."

"Yeah, what else?"

"That's it."

"No. I don't believe that."

What? "Why would I lie?"

"I don't know. Why does anybody lie? But if we're going to get you on a horse in three days, then the first thing we've got to do is figure out what you're scared of. Fear's an animal. I want to know what we're hunting."

"Do you always talk like that?"

We walk a little ways more. Logically, I know he's trying to help. But it doesn't feel like his business. I don't need a therapist. I need a riding instructor. So I don't say anything, and he doesn't ask again.

When we get to the pasture the horses aren't there. I try not to act surprised, since I wasn't exactly supposed to be here socializing in the middle of the night. "Where are they?"

"I moved them to the second pasture to give this grass a rest."

"This morning? How long have you been up?"

He says, "I'm not much of sleeper."

"Me either," I say.

He tips his head. "I noticed."

We walk across the top of the bluff until we reach a dense patch of trees and stream, then we cross the stream on rocks. There's still a layer of mist on the ground that makes everything smell like sage and cheatgrass. As pretty as it all is, I'd like to know where we're going. My feet are getting blisters. And we are a long way from anyone else. "Are we walking to town?"

He frowns. "Are you tired?"

"No," I say.

A breeze pushes through the pines. The stream bubbles. I guess walking's not the worst thing I could be doing this morning.

"There," he says.

The mustangs are grazing in lush undergrowth on the other side of the trees. They're enclosed by two strands of electric fencing. "How'd you get them over here?"

"I haltered the gelding, and they followed me."

"They followed the gelding? I'd think the other horses would want to stay as far away from him as possible."

"Horses follow strength." He nods. He's using that calm voice he used on the speckled mare. But the way he treated me yesterday is still fresh in my mind. He puts out his hand. "You can find a stump and sit on it if you don't like standing."

"What are we doing?"

"Watching."

"For what?"

"Just tell me what you see."

The gray gelding is in the corner by himself, and the other yearlings are milling around each other, grazing off the buffet table of grasses. They all have their heads down and their ears flopped over forward. Most of the horses are two or three years old. Big, but not full-grown. They flip each other with their tails. Two geldings chase each other around the perimeter of the fencing. I wonder if the gray gelding remembers me. He doesn't seem to.

"I guess I see horses hanging out. They seem to like each other."

"Yeah. So what do you think this has to do with riding?"

"I don't know."

"Why does a twelve-hundred-pound animal let a one-hundred-pound animal get on his back?"

I think about it for a minute before I answer. "I guess it's because they're either afraid or they trust the person."

"Right, in a way." Justin's voice warms up even more. "You can force an animal to do what you want if you know which levers to push. But if you are forcing something on a horse, you have to keep the lever there all the time or you have no control, and after a while the horse will get used to the lever and you'll have to get a bigger lever. So you have no room to back up and let the horse figure anything out for themself. If I let the horse get to know me, if the horse feels a certain amount of friendship or trust in me, then he likes to be with me. Like you like to be with your friends."

"I never thought of that," I say. Riding a horse is a kind of friendship. "That's totally cool. My grandfather said something like that. He said you make the horse think it's his idea."

"Your grandfather said that?"

"Yeah." It's weird what I'm remembering about him now.

"Coulter says that, too. He probably learned it from your grandfather. What else did he teach you?"

"I don't know. I don't remember most of it. I feel like I don't know anything."

"That's fine. Most of the problems that happen on a horse are because someone thinks they know what they really don't."

"Well, I should be a great student then."

Justin almost smiles. "Tell me more about your grandfather."

Before I know what I'm doing I'm blabbing my guts out about how my grandfather let me sleep in the hayloft with the cats and taught me to swim in the creek behind his house by chucking me in.

Justin smiles. "I'd love to have a grandfather like that."

"What's your family like?" I ask.

"Not like that," he says. "I've been chucked around plenty of times, but never to teach me to swim."

While we're talking I notice the gray gelding moving around in the field. He's all muscle. Set against the trees his coat shows off all the dark rings of his dappled coloring, like raindrops. His mane flips over his eyes. "Hey, Goliath," I say without thinking.

"That's not his name," says Justin.

The gelding takes a step forward. I hold my hand out. "Are you sure? Come here, Goliath."

The gelding comes toward me. No doubt he thinks I have another apple.

Justin stands there with his hands in his pockets.

I put my hand all the way out over the fence, careful not to touch it. The gelding walks past two mares and steps within a foot of my fingers. He shakes his head and stops, then he sniffs and lifts his head to me. And right about the moment I'm feeling smug, Goliath leans over and nearly takes my thumb off with his mouth. I pull my hand out of the way just in time. "Hey!" I yell.

Goliath doesn't back away. He stands at the fence watching us.

Justin's voice is sharp. "How did you do that?"

I look at my hand. All five fingers. "Yeah, I'm okay." I look at the horse again. I know he's a horse, but if he weren't I would think he was laughing.

"He never does that," says Justin.

"Eat people's fingers?"

"He likes you."

"He does? Wow, I hope he never loves me."

All the way back to the ranch Justin asks me questions about my grandfather. Which is not exactly what I expected from a riding lesson, but it's also cool because I start remembering even more. The accident wasn't all that special, but my time before it happened was. My grandparents spoiled me with things like homemade ice cream and shopping trips to town. My grandmother watched old movies with me and my grandfather did magic tricks with peanuts. I mean, I was messed up by the injury and the shock of it. But I should have been okay. I should have gotten back on, and I didn't. My parents should have put me back on, but they didn't. My grandparents didn't come see us in Colorado. There were just lots of didn'ts.

"The horse just threw you in the air and split your head open. What scared him enough to buck?"

Of course Justin asks about the horse. "I don't remember, and my parents don't like to talk about it. My mother says I could have had brain damage."

"So you got thirty stiches and then you never rode a horse again. After riding like a wild thing before?"

"Yes," I say, my face heating up.

He looks me up and down. "You lack resilience, girl."

It's hard to believe how much it hurts me to hear Justin say this. Maybe because I lack resilience. But his words pound in my ears like a drum. I march to the beat of a faint-hearted drummer. We walk across the bluff and down the trail in silence, at least on the outside. I'm listening to failure drums that could drown out a football stadium at half-time.

Then, right before we're out of the canyon, Justin grabs my arm. Hard. I pull back from him, but he won't let go. His face is expressionless. Not mad. But blank. I think he's gone crazy. I'm walking alone with a cowboy psychopath. I reach out with my other hand and swing, like out of nowhere, hard. Lightning quick, he ducks and lets go of my arm. And then he laughs.

I jump away from him and yell. "What is wrong with you?"

"Sorry," he says, still laughing. "I just had to know. You've got resilience. You just gotta get mad first. Then you're fine."

"Look at my arm." I pull up my sleeve, and there's a puffy red fingerprint. I don't know what gets into me, but when I look up and see him smirking I reach over and hit him in the shoulder. Hard. At least for me. He doesn't stop laughing.

"Yep," he says, with a wide smile. "I can work with that."

I turn my fainthearted face toward camp and walk as fast as I can without running. But it does no good. The memory of that day I got hurt follows me. It's like the wind around here. Once it gets going I can't stop it or outrun it, so I let it roll right over the top of me.

WHEN GRANDPA ASKED me if I wanted to ride Hurricane I wasn't worried. I mean, I had no reason to be. Riding a more advanced horse was just another thing I could brag about after I was done.

Of course, I noticed this horse was different when we were saddling him. He tried to bite my arm when I brushed him. He flipped his head when I put on the bridle. When I picked out his hooves I had to have Grandpa help me because he wouldn't lift his legs. By the time I finally got on him I was in as bad a mood as he was. Well, almost.

He seemed okay through the warm-up, just pulling on the reins here and there. Then the wind came along and ruffled the trees by the arena fence. He broke away into a trot. Grandpa yelled at me to get my horse under control. So I did what any self-respecting seven-year-old would do. I yanked back hard on the reins and yelled, "Whoa."

Instead of stopping, everything just happened in slow motion.

When that bridle's bit smacked his mouth, Hurricane came up off the ground like there was a bomb underneath him. When he came back down, he seesawed back and forth bronco style. I grabbed the horn with both hands to save myself, but that just meant I dropped one of my reins. Within a second the rein was under his feet, snapping in half, scaring him back up on his hind legs. With the one rein I had left, I pulled his head. He spun sideways and pitched me backward into the air, slamming my shoulders and the base of my head into the fence.

I always say I don't remember. And I don't remember hitting the fence, not the impact anyway. But I remember in sharp, clear color the details of what came before. And what I remember the most is the feeling of knowing that I was about to be hurt and there wasn't a damn thing I could do about it.

Chapter Fifteen

WHEN I GO to bed that night I hear Goliath calling. I'm tired. I'm so far past discouraged I don't remember what it looked like when I crossed the state line. I'm hundreds of miles from home but not one inch closer to riding a horse than I was when I got here.

I can only listen to my roommates sleep peacefully for so long. I find the apples I've hidden in my sleeping bag. I put my dang boots on and walk up the long hill one more time. When I get to the pasture Goliath is whinnying at the fence. I throw out the apple instead of holding it in my hand. I want to keep my fingers this time. At least, I'm getting a little braver standing next to horses. I just don't dare sit on one yet.

When I get back to the cabin Alice is actually snoring, although it sounds more like a cat purring. I walk over to the bed of the girl who didn't come and stare at it. I reach out my hand and run my fingers over the empty cot.

"What the freak are you doing?" asks Banner.

I jump. "Sleepwalking," I say.

"Gawd, you're crazier than Alice."

"Yep," I say. I climb into my sleeping bag and fall asleep in my clothes.

I snooze completely through my time for cleaning and nearly miss breakfast. Alice has to shake me awake. I throw my clothes on, and she pulls me down to the campfire. She says, "You need to go to bed earlier."

Most of the food's gone so I grab an apple.

Mr. Sanchez asks, "You got some kind of dietary restriction?" With his accent it sounds kind of exotic to have a dietary restriction. "Apples are good. But you need food for *coraje*," he says.

I'm guessing from my two stellar years of Spanish that he means courage. I wasn't aware that came in a breakfast food.

He goes into the cooking area and comes back with a small bowl full of salad that looks suspiciously like the weeds from my front lawn at home. "Are those dandelion leaves?"

"When everything else dies, it makes a flower." He raises his gray eyebrows at me. "Plus it's high in vitamins, minerals, fiber, and protein."

"You want me to eat dandelions?"

He hands me the ranch dressing and a plastic fork. I could probably eat horse manure with enough ranch dressing this morning. Although that would take more dressing. I dump some on my bowl of weeds and eat up. It's a little bitter, but I eat the whole thing.

I don't see Justin or Kaya at breakfast. Darius is in prime form though. Banner and Devri are cackling at his jokes all through cleanup. He should have his own comedy club. The two lovebirds Izzy and Andrew gaze into each other's eyes over granola bars. Coulter's around but only sits in his camp chair over by the mess tent drinking coffee. I give him a wide berth while I wash my dishes.

Finally, he calls me over to him. "Justin has to make a house call this morning. You'll have to tag along with everyone else."

"Sure," I say. I wonder why anyone would need a house call from Justin.

"You gonna cause problems?"

"Probably."

He pauses over his coffee cup. "That's my girl."

I take the halter out to Smokey without any fuss. He seems happy enough. I saddle him without help. Not that I'm going to be using the saddle, but at least I can put it on.

"Today," says Coulter, "we are going to discuss the basics of pressure and release. Anyone know what pressure is?"

"My mother," says Charlie.

Scotty says, "Allison Cameron at homecoming."

Granger laughs. He laughs at everything Scotty says.

Coulter nods. "Yes, that all sounds very life-threatening. But my point is that when you feel pressure you have a choice. Most of us choose to move away from pressure. A horse is no different. So we use that."

He walks up to Ethan's bay gelding, Whiskey, and leans against the horse's neck. "This old boy is a stubborn one. That's why I put him with Ethan, because Ethan is strong." Ethan nods his head and gets a few whistles from the crowd when he shows his bicep.

"Ethan, I want you to get this horse to bend its head back to you by slowly pulling on one rein."

Ethan grabs the rein on the big bay and pulls backward. The horse looks more irritated than interested and keeps his head forward. Ethan pulls harder, and the horse flips sideways. Ethan tries again, and the horse sidesteps again. Coulter takes the horse.

Ethan's easy smile is long gone. "You aren't going to let him get away with that, are you?" he says.

Coulter nods at Ethan to step back. "Ethan has a highly developed sense of fairness. Horses do, too. But if you only use force on a horse, you will have to keep using more and more force. If I want him to soften up, get him to give me his head willingly, I pull only as long as he resists. The moment, and this is important, *the moment* he gives, I release the pressure. That's fairness. It's also known as compromise."

Ethan taps his big boot impatiently in the dirt. "Sir, I disagree. Fairness isn't compromise. It's what's right."

Coulter nods at Ethan like he's putting up with him, but just barely. He picks up Whiskey's rein and gently pulls it back. At first the horse kind of lifts his lip and flicks his ears, but he sure doesn't give. Coulter calmly stays on him. Then the horse gives, and Coulter drops the rein and pets him. One more time, and the bay bends his neck all the way back to Coulter. Coulter loves all over him. "It's what works. Everybody give it a try."

We all go to try it. Except that Smokey bends for me on the first pull.

"Look at that, children. Cassidy has a boyfriend," says Coulter.

I look around. Banner and Devri sputter laugh to each other. I realize he's talking about the horse, and I relax a little. I rub his nose.

"Okay, children. What does this have to do with riding? Banner?"

She stops laughing. "If you're always forcing your horse to do what you want, she starts to resent you?"

Coulter lets that hang in the wind between them for a second. "That's about the size of it. And if the horse figures things out, she gets what she wants, which is less pressure."

Banner says, "She still has to give her head."

"Are we talking about horses still?" asks Ethan. "Because that sounds like something else."

"Get on your animals, campers," says Coulter. "Let's apply the principle. One of you knuckleheads needs to get smart enough to ride that gray mustang for the auction. Just remember, whatever you ask for, the second your horse gives to you, you take away the pressure. Make it a conversation, not an order."

Everyone starts to get on. Some horses move around a little when their riders try to mount, or prance around once the rider is on. I take Smokey over by a pine tree to get him out of the chaos. Then I stand there looking at him and the stirrup, listening to everyone else get mounted.

I wish Kaya was here. I'm glad Justin isn't. I wish I was alone. I wish I wasn't afraid. I look at Smokey. He wouldn't hurt a charging lion. And we dig each other. I just have to do it. But everyone will be watching if I fail.

"You gonna actually get on now?" asks Banner. "Praise the Lord."

I turn to my horse. "Listen, Smokes. I know you won't hurt me," I whisper. "And I sure don't want you to miss another riding day. You might croak tomorrow." Smokey is looking forward, but his ears are backward. He hears me. I close my eyes. I remember swinging up on Grandpa's paint. I put my hand up on the horn. Smokey steps back, but I manage to keep my foot in the stirrup anyway.

Coulter booms, "What are you doing back so soon, Justin?"

I hear Kaya. "Coulter, look at Cassidy."

I keep my boot in the stirrup and focus on my picture of me at seven. I hear my grandfather yelling, "Saddle up, Cassygirl." I see my little-girl legs lifting me up and over, my pink boots flying. I can do this. I swing my right leg. My left leg shakes but stays in the stirrup. I pull myself over. I look around. Re-freaking-silient. I'm in the saddle.

Chapter Sixteen

I EXPECT THE world to stop. But the only thing that holds still is me.

A bunch of kids, led by Ethan, cheer like I've scored at the World Cup, which scares all the other horses. Except Smokey, who is virtually napping he's so chill.

Coulter yells, "What the hell happened?"

Alice rides over to me and beams. "You did it."

Horses and riders circle around. I'm worried that they might smack into Smokey. And then somewhere, in all the horse havoc, I see Justin standing beside Kaya with his eyes closed. He looks like he's in pain. Not irritated pain, but real pain.

Then Kaya is at Smokey's side. "You did it, Cassidy. Now walk him forward. Don't stop."

I'm already stopped. Smokey's eyes are closed. And I'm good with that. Coulter never said I had to actually move around, did he? Then Justin is next to Kaya, pushing her out of the way. His face still looks drained, but he's smiling. He says, "Okay, Cassidy, ride this old horse. Come on. I'll let you hit me after."

"Are you okay?" I ask.

His head jerks up. He smiles again. "I'm fine. Go ride."

I tap with my legs, and Smokey moves. And then it's the bicycle thing. My head doesn't remember as much as my legs do. And my legs are longer and stronger than when I was seven, so it works better. Before I know it, I am walking past Coulter. "There you go, Cassidy. Keep moving. The fun hasn't started yet."

We ride toward the arena. My heart is up in my throat because I'm afraid to have this go bad. Everything is rushing inside, so I slow everything down on the outside. I look at the fence and try to remember it's just wood, not something I'm going to crash into. I follow the other kids. Then I use my reins and legs to move Smokey away from the other horses. I'm hazardous enough without other horses helping me. I focus on moving slow and staying out of trouble.

"That's it," yells Coulter. "Look at Cassidy, everyone."

Which is exactly what I would like them not to do.

Banner rides past and yells. "Skip-de-do, Cassidy, you got your big-girl pants on."

I look the other direction. I'm too busy for Banner right now.

Everyone rides faster than we do. Ethan, Charlie, and Alice all ride together, but I can't keep up with them. I move as far as I can to the outside and try to stay out of the way. And we keep going. When I start to feel nauseous I look at Smokey's tattered old mane and think about how he needs a haircut. I could braid it and put flowers in it. Daisies. I just keep telling myself this crap.

But the truth is that when I ask Smokester to go, he goes. When I pull back and say "whoa," he stops. He is calm and easy to sit on. In fact, he seems pretty bored by the whole thing.

"Reverse your horses," yells Coulter.

Everyone's horse circles around, so I pull my inside rein and tap my outside foot, and Smokey rotates his nose around. It's as if I'm turning on my own two feet. I don't think about it as much as I just do it. I look up and see Justin watching me. He has one hand in his pocket and one on the fence. His head is tipped back and he's chewing one of those delicious pieces of wheat.

"Get your heels down," he says when I ride past.

Coulter says, "Very good, everyone. Now spread out and get yourself a little room. I'm gonna ask you all to trot."

Trotting is just another word for bouncing. I don't want to trot.

We walk past Kaya, and I can see she doesn't want me to trot either. She's looking at Coulter and looking at me. She says loud enough for everyone near me to hear, "You don't have to do that, Cassidy. You just keep walking."

"Leave 'er alone, Kaya," says Justin.

I ride away. It's just me, Smokey, and all the butterflies

that just invaded my stomach. All I have to do is stay on. What's the worst that could happen?

Coulter yells, "Trot your horses, campers. No crowding or cutting in."

Horses jump and lunge, and then they move past us. Danny's horse is totally a mess. He's switchbacking all over the place. I go around him. Everything speeds up. Alice trots past. "Just move to the outside, Cass," she says. "Keep walking, you're doing great." Her smooth black hair flips behind her, and she's gone, as graceful as a bird.

"Yeah, you just keep walking," says Banner, gliding past.

I can feel Smokey getting ready. All the other horses are trotting.

I grab the horn of my saddle like a little kid. "Hey, Smokes," I say softly. That's it. I don't even tap him with my foot. I just let go of the brakes in my head, and he slips into a trot.

My body jiggles and smacks all over the saddle. It's like someone greased my butt. The only reason I don't fall off is I'm holding so tight to the horn that my hand turns white. Then I shove my heels down to get some traction, and it helps. I straighten up. I lose sight of anything but Smokey. I don't know if people are talking. All I see and feel is this body under mine that I'm trying to match and sync up with. I shut off everything. There isn't even sound. And then I'm trotting past Alice and trotting past Charlie and trotting past Ethan. I let go of the horn. And I'm riding and the sun is on my face and I feel like I'm not bouncing, falling, or failing. I'm dancing.

The next thing I know Banner is riding in front of me. She holds her hand up for me to stop. "Stop. Don't you hear me?" she says.

"Did you say something?"

"Gawd, you're a freak. We're done. It's time to put your horse away."

Chapter Seventeen

THE BUZZ INSIDE of me doesn't go away all day. I shovel manure. Still happy. I chop and stack firewood. Still happy. I weed the garden. It's hot and dirty and I get blisters on my hands. Still. Happy. Even when I'm not thinking about the ride I just feel lighter.

Ethan stands by me as I dump out the wheelbarrow. "You've been sandbagging that shit for a big entrance or what?"

"I'm not sure what you just asked me," I say.

"First you act all scared to get on the horse, then you're like, 'Imma ride like this horse so pretty'?"

"When I was little I rode. So I guess I remembered stuff once I got going. But I *am* afraid to get on a horse. I mean, what if next time is a disaster?"

"What next time? What if next time a volcano erupts in Yellowstone and blows us all to bits?"

Charlie says, "The probability is one in seven hundred thousand. Over the next few thousands of years."

"You make shit up," says Ethan.

"I actually don't."

They start smacking their shovels into each other like hockey sticks. Three other guys join in. Kaya walks up to us from the campfire. "You boys stop that. I just brought in the mail. And you *all* got something." She smiles and hands me a letter.

I'm almost afraid to take it, but I do. Maybe today is just my lucky day.

My letter is from Oakley. Just the sight of her handwriting makes me so homesick I have to walk up the trail and find someplace to be alone.

> Dear Sis,
>
> How are you? Are you riding horses now?
> I am so jealous! I wish I was riding horses.
> We go with Mom to work every day and play
> around with the other kids but it gets boring.
> One of the boys there smells like brussel
> sprouts. Jessie Jane says it's because his mom
> is a health freak and that's all she will feed
> him. At least our mom lets us eat popcorn.
>
> Mom and Dad are still mad at each other,
> so I don't like that. AT ALL. Since you aren't

here they argue more. When are you coming home? AWWWW!

> Love, your
> favorite and best
> sister,
> Oakley

P.S. Your less cute sister Jessie Jane says hi.

I lie on top of the rock I'm sitting on and stretch out my legs and arms. I close my eyes and get busy having a full-scale guilt attack. What kind of sister leaves her sibs holding the bag of crazy at home just so she can get away? But if I go home, what will I do? Nothing will change. Mom and Dad will still fight. Or is that just what I tell myself to feel better? Because I don't feel better.

That night I wait in my sleeping bag, dying for everyone to go to sleep. Banner and Alice write letters. Alice reads some book she hides in her bag. Banner waits till we turn off the lights and smokes outside. She got a letter today, too. When she finally comes to bed I ask, "You okay?"

"Do I seem like I'm okay?"

"Not really," I say.

"You gonna tell me a bedtime story about your perfect little life?"

I say, "My life isn't perfect. Believe me."

"I don't," she says.

Chapter Eighteen

GOLIATH SEES ME coming and nickers. I'm late.

Even with a bright moon I can see a zillion stars tonight. The sky is bursting with them and they're so sparkling and bright. I never see this many stars at home. I know it's not true, but the sky feels bigger here. Everything feels bigger here, even me.

"What are you doing?"

Justin steps out of the dark. In the moonlight I can make out the outline of his baseball hat and his pointy shoulders.

"What are *you* doing?" I ask.

"Nothing much." He uses his soft voice. "That was a pretty good ride you had today."

"Yeah, it was." I look down and realize I only have on the super thin T-shirt I sleep in. Not that it matters on me. Sort of it does. I fold my arms.

We stand there in the dark. I'm not sure what we're waiting for. He tilts his hat back and leans against the fence, looking up at the stars. "Did you know that in India the stars don't look the same?"

"Stars don't change," I say. I wonder how well he can see me in this light.

"Yeah, but what we see does."

I stop thinking about my T-shirt for a minute. Justin never stops confusing me. "Have you been to India?"

He laughs. "I've never been anywhere. I stole a book from Coulter's library."

"Coulter has a library? Wait, really?"

"Pretty good one, actually. In the big house."

It gets quiet between us. I rub my arms, more because I'm nervous than because I'm cold. But it's not awful nervous, just quiet nervous. Finally, I ask, "So why are you up?"

He tips his hat back a little more. "I'll show you if you give me that apple you brought for big gray over there."

It's nice to be out here in the dark, talking like this. "You aren't mad I've been feeding him?"

"Nope." He shifts a few times onto either foot.

I toss Justin the apple.

"Now hit that switch for me," he says, pointing to the circuit box.

As quick as I pull it he's in the pasture holding out my apple to Goliath. The horse doesn't pull back or turn away, just muzzles the apple and gathers it in his mouth. A chunk falls out on the ground. Justin reaches down slowly to get it for him and then strokes the giant gelding. The horse drops his head and smacks his lips together as he chews. It's like Goliath is a normal horse or something. And then dang if Justin doesn't slide a hand on that huge mustang's mane and swing onto his back.

"Justin!" I yell.

But it's too late. Goliath goes up in the air, and Justin goes with him, a gray blur under the moon. Then it's three hard hops and one full-out buck that lands Justin flat on his back with Goliath running around the pasture scaring the other horses.

I can't believe what I'm seeing. My brain floods. I slide through the wires and run in.

Justin isn't moving on the ground.

Goliath and the other horses are still swirling around, kicking at each other in the dark. I dodge them and run over to Justin. "Are you okay?"

He pops up on his elbow. "Help me up."

I wrap my arm underneath his and reach around his back. His shirt is damp. I'm so short I'm like a crutch. I feel him up against me, pushing, shaking. "Dammit, Justin."

We hobble out of the pasture, and Justin leans up against a big rock. He straightens, like he's getting his wind back. I leave him and get the fence turned back on. Goliath stops snorting, and the other horses settle down.

I stand in front of Justin. I'm ready to be mad now. "How stupid can you get?"

"That wasn't my best idea. Guess I was showing off."

"I guess you were. What if he'd stomped you right in front of me? For what? I have to go."

Justin waits until I've gone a few steps and then calls to me. "You want to start feeding him? Goliath, I mean."

I turn. "Yes," I say. "I'd love to."

Chapter Nineteen

"WHERE DID YOU go last night?" says Alice.

I tip my boots over to check for mice and then slide them on quickly. Banner is outside brushing her teeth. Light rain is pitter-patting on the canvas of the tent. The sky looks gray and drizzly outside. "I couldn't sleep so I took a walk."

"You should wake me up then," says Alice. "What if something gets you?"

"I'm fine." I hear a mouse scurrying in the corner of the tent. "All the wildlife is in here."

Alice frowns. "Where'd you go?"

I can't tell her about Justin. It sounds wrong. Like I meant to meet up with him. "No place really. I was looking at stars."

"Take me with you next time, okay?"

"Okay," I say. I feel a weird heaviness between us. "Are you doing all right?"

Alice turns away from me and doesn't answer.

At first I think she doesn't hear me. "Are you okay?"

She shakes her head but keeps her back to me.

I stand behind her, not sure what to do. Her hands are curled up in fists. "Alice?" I put my hand on her shoulder.

She turns her head, and her eyes are rimmed with tears.

I look around. It's just a regular morning. There are no loud noises. A few birds are singing. "Did something happen again?"

I get her to sit down with me on her cot. I slide close so we're smashed up against each other. I know this could be making it worse by invading her space, but I do it anyway. I'm a hundred percent on instinct here because I don't even know why she's sad. I rub her back a little. She doesn't seem like she's bugged by it.

Finally she says, "I got a letter from my parents."

"Oh?" I've been so jealous of everyone else's letters from home it never occurred to me that she might be getting anything but good news.

Banner walks in. "Y'all comin' or what?"

I say, "We're going to be late."

"You should go," says Alice.

"Banner, can you tell Kaya we'll be there in a minute?"

Banner grimaces, "Because the rules don't apply to you, right?"

I look up at Banner, trying to let her see in my face that this isn't the greatest time to discover the rule book, but she just glares back at me. "Don't worry about it then."

Banner shoves the flap of tent out of her way for her exit. The smell of rain rushes into the tent.

Once Banner is good and gone, Alice breathes in hard and lets her words wash out all at once. "I have been accepted into the Whitmore Academy. I've been working to get in since fifth grade."

I'm guessing by her clenched fists this is not a good thing.

She makes a weird chirping noise and then gets ahold of her voice. "I'm not actually that smart. But my parents think I'm a genius. I already study eight hours a day for public school. This place will kill me."

It takes me a second to add up what she's telling me because I go to public school and all. "That's like a fourteen hour day with school. When do you sleep?"

"My mom supported her family when she was my age. She cleaned houses starting when she was twelve. She hardly slept at all for fifteen years. She always makes a joke that this is why she is so short. But now she is very successful."

As Alice tells me this I notice that she hasn't brushed her hair recently, and there is a dirt smudge on the end of her nose that looks like stage makeup it's so perfectly round and brown. She looks like an orphan in a musical.

Outside I hear someone coming up the path to the tent. We're going to catch it.

I say, "Here's the thing, Alice. You aren't your mom."

Alice's face tightens, and I think she's going to start crying again.

I say, "It's okay. We'll figure something out. I promise. We'll figure it out."

Alice nods and rubs her fingers under her eyes.

A black hoodie pokes into the tent. It's Kaya. "You two have missed roll call. And, Cassidy, you haven't done your morning job. Do you want me to report you?" Kaya's voice is sharper than I've ever heard it. She steps into the tent all the way and takes off her hood. Her hair is unbraided and messy. Her eyes have dark circles under them, and her mouth is set in a line.

"I'll go do it now," I say.

"You can do it after breakfast. We won't be riding for a while with this weather. Justin and Coulter have gone into town."

I jog down to the fire with Alice and find Mr. and Mrs. Sanchez arguing in the kitchen. It makes my stomach roil. I ask them if they need more firewood, and Mr. Sanchez tells me the work has been done. Ethan comes in and asks for ketchup, and Mrs. Sanchez tells him that the eggs shouldn't be wasted with ketchup.

I stand under the kitchen tarp for a second, and I feel the old tightness in my chest. I felt this way at home all the time. *Con-ten-tion*. Why are humans like this? It was way worse at home, of course. Way. But even the reminder of it makes me cold all over. Why can't people just act like I want them to—stop fighting and play nice. I mean, how am I supposed to figure my crap out if I'm always dealing with everybody else's?

And it hits me how stupid I am. And how annoyingly right Justin is.

Maybe the only way I'm going to start feeling better is to stop trying to get people to do what I want—they never do anyway—and help them get what they need. Which is to cheer the smack up.

I sit down on a food crate in the tent, which is leaking rain, by the way. I look around at the other campers, getting wetter and more ornery. I don't just *feel* cold. I *am* cold. It's so muddy most of our chores are pointless. At home on days like today I would make everybody grilled cheese sandwiches and tomato soup, then we'd bail and go to the library.

I find Kaya in the first aid tent with Danny, who has developed a scab under his nose. I think he's allergic to the whole state.

I say, "I heard there is a library in the big house. Can campers go in and check books out?"

Kaya says, "You can borrow them, if that's what you mean." She squeezes the ointment on Danny's finger and demonstrates how to put it on "What kind of book are you looking for?"

"I want to learn more about mustangs."

Kaya stops working on Danny. "Why do you want to do that?"

I smile casually. "Just seems like I should know something about all the stuff that BLM guy was talking about. Like the politics and stuff."

"The politics and stuff?" Kaya frowns at Danny's finger, which is mostly going up his nose. "Yeah, I can find you some books. But I can't promise they're going to explain anything. And it's not very cheerful reading. It's a sad situation."

"Is that why somebody is letting the mustangs go? Because the BLM isn't treating them right?"

Kaya gives me her full attention. "Some people hate the mustangs and think they're a nuisance. Some people think the BLM is needlessly incarcerating animals they can't humanely care for."

"What do you think? I mean, is that BLM guy hurting the horses?" I put my hands out like pistols. "Is he a good guy or bad guy?"

She raises her perfect eyebrows. "I think you ask a lot of questions."

Danny gets off the table before she goes after his face again. She takes the rubber gloves off her hands and looks up at me. "Not sure what to make of you, Cassidy. But I like your try, and your curiosity. Don't make me regret that, okay?"

Devri and her two buddies walk into the tent. "We're bored and it's freezing. And we totally hate it here. Can we go into town?" Devri's blonde hair is flattened with the rain, and she's wearing her sweatshirt backward. I've seen cranes with more body fat.

"Absolutely not," says Kaya.

I say, "I was actually wondering if we could all go hang out in the big house together and read there. Like a read-a-thon."

"A read-a-thon?" says Devri. "What are you, like, seven?"

Ethan walks into the tent, like we've called a meeting or something. He's soaked from trying to get plastic over the firewood. He has little drizzles of water coming out of his hair and onto his face. "Did I just hear someone say we're getting out of this mudhole and sitting around a fire with a pretty little book? I am all over that. Like literally, all over frickin' that."

Devri looks at Ethan and nods. "Yeah, that sounds okay."

Of course, if Ethan suggests it. I ignore Devri and give Kaya the puppy eyes.

"I'll get the Sanchezes to give me the stuff to make grilled-cheese sandwiches," I say.

Danny says, "Grilled cheese. We get grilled cheese?"

Kaya shakes her head at me. "Remember what I said about regretting? Coulter's going to kill me."

Almost everyone comes inside just to get warm. Charlie reads a trashed copy of *Romeo and Juliet*. Ethan reads *Les Miserables* (the real book) and doesn't make a peep all afternoon. Alice reads something called *Common Parasites and Their Treatments*, which sounds like one hundred percent disgusting. Banner writes in her journal. The way she's scribbling, I'm surprised the pages don't catch on fire. But we all sit together. The fireplaces crackles. It's warm and dry and kind of wonderful. Except what I'm reading.

The first mustang book I dive into is like an encyclopedia of bad news. It isn't like the Internet fluff I read before I came here. It talks about how the mustangs were brought over by Spanish conquistadors. Over hundreds of years wild horses changed the way Native Americans did everything from war to courting. And wild horses supplied cowboys with a way to settle the West. The mustang became the symbol of the Wild West, but when people started driving cars instead of riding horses, wild horses stopped being useful. People started to think of them as feral, especially ranchers who wanted to run cattle where the horses lived. So the horses were hunted, killed, and used for dog food.

When they passed a law to protect them, the horses stopped being butchered, but they started being locked up. The last chapter of the book says that nobody knows what to do. The authors don't even try to give a solution. I close the book with a loud slap.

Banner says, "Don't tell me you read that whole book just now."

"It has a lot of pictures," I say.

"You must make your parents so proud."

Alice lifts her eyes over the top of her book.

"I drive them nuts," I say.

"What a shocker," says Banner.

After I make the sandwiches with the Sanchezes, I read all day. The rain stops, and most of the kids leave and go do other things, but I keep on reading. The picture gets darker in my mind as the clouds roll away. I keep reading, thinking I will find something that could fix everything. But I just get more depressed. The whole idea behind the Wild and Free-Roaming Horses and Burros Act was to protect them. But now half the wild horses are in holding pens, and the other half are being chased, harassed, and sometimes even killed. And the money and effort being expended to keep things this way could feed and house a small country.

When I come to bed Alice has gone back to being silent and sad. Banner looks at old letters.

Turns out, just because you want to help doesn't mean you can.

At night I don't hear Goliath. Maybe Justin has decided to feed him for me. I don't know because I haven't seen Justin all day. When the sun goes down I read with my flashlight until my head and my eyes can't take any more.

I should write Oakley a letter. But I don't know what to say.

It rains for two days. I read every book that Coulter has on the mustangs. Banner goes over to Devri's tent, and they watch videos on the movie player Devri smuggled into camp. Alice, Charlie, and I sit around and lose at cards to Ethan. And then we divvy up the romance novels, because a person can only take so much reality.

I watch for Justin. He seems busy with other things.

Chapter Twenty

THE RAIN FINALLY stops and the mud dries up. Coulter jumps right back into lessons.

"Fear. You can only beat fear with knowledge. You have to beat fear to feel right with your horse." Coulter marches in front of us. We're all paired off with a saddled horse in the middle of a field not far from the ranch. There's sharp, nasty thistle all over, and the horseflies are already awake. I don't like the sound of this lesson. Smokey and I hang in the back. Alice motions for me to come stand with her and the boys in the front. Nope.

Coulter grabs Scotty from the group of mouthy kids messing around next to Alice. "Scotty, how would you like to be our volunteer today?"

Scotty flips his white bangs. "Yeah, whatever. Sure."

His buddies all laugh and bump elbows.

Ethan says Scotty's okay. He just has a little too much

attitude and has inhaled a few too many things. I wouldn't mind him if he wasn't always making fun of people, like me for instance.

Coulter says, "Scotty is a surfer."

Scotty waves hang-loose fingers for applause.

"He's not afraid of anything. Is that correct, Scotty?"

"Damn straight," says Scotty, smiling.

"Excellent. Get on this horse then, please."

I glance over at Darius, who's smiling. Kaya has her arms folded across her chest. Scotty shakes his white bangs to the side of his face. His buddies cheer as he gets on. I can barely stand to watch.

Coulter says, "Walk Tequila across that stream over there." Coulter motions to a shallow bed of water that runs around the meadow.

Scotty walks Tequila through the tall grass swinging his arms, trash-talking, and laughing. The horse gets along fine until he gets up to the water, then he sniffs and backs up. Scotty spurs him, and Tequila turns in a circle. Scotty leans in and spurs him again. I can tell Scotty's scared now because he's clinging to the horse, digging into him. Then out of nowhere he kicks Tequila in the gut, like that will help. Tequila crow hops about a foot and then rears. Scotty yells and then tumbles backward and lands in the grass. The horse hops away and stops.

"Scotty, are you okay?" asks Coulter, jogging up to him. Kaya and Darius exchange a knowing nod. Justin grabs Tequila.

Scotty stands up, swearing his living guts out. But he's fine. I breathe out. He's fine.

Coulter says, "Scotty. Will you get back on your horse now, please, and stop screwing around?"

Scotty spits out a premium selection of expletives.

Coulter gives him a warning look. "Who do you think you're talking to, your mother?"

"I'm not getting back on," says Scotty.

Coulter puts his hand on his shoulder. "That's the first rule of riding."

Scotty shakes Coulter's arm off. "I don't care. I'm not getting on that piece of shit."

Coulter says, "Okay, children. Let's review. Scotty's afraid, the horse is afraid. And if we don't get this figured out, we've taught the horse and Scotty that the way to avoid fear is to quit. The pressure goes away when you come off. Then if you're Scotty, you go home, cry to your nanny, and die a little inside. You hate horses, and you stop riding them. If you're the horse, you've just learned how to win an argument by hurting someone."

Scotty's wipes the dust off his pants. He's going to cry in front of everyone.

"Are you scared, Scotty?" asks Coulter.

"You son of a bitch. You knew he'd do that."

"You're the lesson today." Coulter turns to us. "The first thing you have to do is admit that you're scared. At least to yourself."

Scotty says, "I could've had my head kicked in, you mean

old bastard." I don't like Scotty, but he has a point. A good one. "I'm out of here."

Coulter laughs. "Your nanny's going to be disappointed in you, Scotty."

Kaya says, "That's enough, Coulter."

Coulter looks bored. "No one has a suggestion for Scotty here? How can he get the horse across and conquer his fears?"

I look at Justin. He knows how to get the horse across. He only looks at the ground. Banner glares at me. "You got something to say, Cassidy?"

Justin looks up and shakes his head at me.

Scotty is already walking away. His guys are all elbowing each other. Scotty's best friend, Dalton, says, "He's crying."

This is ridiculous. Tequila is about as mean as a wombat. If Scotty goes home, that's one more horse that goes to the holding facility in Rock Springs with a crap chance of getting adopted.

"Hey." I feel like a Labrador, but I chase him.

Scotty pushes me out of the way. "Get away from me, freak."

"Get Tequila across the water on the ground. Then ride him back."

Scotty stops walking. "What do you know, freak? You're afraid to even sit on a horse."

I shrug my shoulders and back away. "That's how I know."

Scotty takes three more uneven steps and then storms back and grabs the horse from Justin. Tequila doesn't want to go near the water at first. But after Scotty slows down, Tequila does, too, and then he bends his muzzle and steps a hoof into the stream. Scotty's boots get wrecked. His whole body is soaked by the time the horse is across. Then Scotty sloshes up onto Tequila and walks him back across the creek.

"You couldn't be any more adorable, could you?" says Banner.

"Who's next?" asks Coulter. "Everyone's going to cross today."

Dalton raises his hand. I don't care much for Dalton either. Maybe it's his sculpted eyebrows, but it's probably because I heard him call Alice a dumpling on the second day. "I'll go," he says.

Coulter hesitates. "Okay, Dalton. But I need you to listen to me now."

Dalton nods his head.

"We just had a little scare. It's important that you don't rush into this. Brandy is a good little mare, but you have to go slow. You got that?"

"Got it," says Dalton, already walking to Brandy.

"I'm not playing about this. You give that mare a second or she'll buck you. You just give her time, and she'll get you across."

A few boys fist-bump Dalton, who's acting like he's all about it. Scotty gives Dalton a big grin, but I wonder if he's worried that Dalton's about to make him look bad.

Dalton mounts his bay mare, Brandy, gracefully. She's one of my favorites. She's like a little race car the way she zips around the arena. "Let's go," he says, leaning forward and tapping her with both legs. Not hard, but harder than he should.

Brandy zips up to the water's edge neatly and starts to go in. Dalton sits her like a general. I'd kill to be that confident on a horse. A few people cheer. Dalton raises his left hand like he's a bronco rider. He's totally rubbing this in Scotty's face. Brandy gets a few feet farther into the shallow water, then stops. Dalton looks startled. Coulter moves toward the water. "Easy, son."

Dalton kicks Brandy again, this time hard. She doesn't move. He unloads on her with both legs. "Go! Go!" he yells.

Coulter yells, "Stop, Dalton!"

Just as Coulter yells, Brandy explodes up into the air. All four legs eject upward, and her back arches. She comes down in a deeper pocket of the stream and goes up again. Dalton's hand flies high into the air, and his body flops and jerks in the saddle. Brandy stumbles on the rocks when she comes down and barrels forward, dropping her front left leg, nearly going down in the stream, and then rights herself, terrified. She jumps toward the other side of the water and falls forward on the muddy shore, throwing Dalton underneath her, then she bounds up and runs into the trees, reins flying.

Dalton lies on the ground and screams. Everyone's horse freaks out, except Smokey, who stands almost completely still. Kids shout at their horses and at one another. I just stand there holding on to Smokey, trying not to keel over.

Coulter bounds across the stream like he's been shot out

of a gun. Darius is right behind him. Kaya calls to the rest of us. "Stay calm. Get your horses under control. Now." Her voice is hard and loud. "Now!" Justin rides across the stream on his buckskin, past Dalton, and goes after Brandy, who is long gone in the trees.

Coulter gets over to Dalton, who is flailing in pain. Dalton grabs at his leg but can't seem to control his body. He keeps screaming and sobbing and grabbing at his knee. Coulter scoops Dalton up in his arms and carries him across the water. Darius runs back across the stream, faster than I can believe he's capable of, toward the big house.

For some reason my brain empties. The thing I was afraid of has happened. Someone is seriously hurt. Dalton's leg is almost certainly broken.

It's like there's an echo it's so empty in my head. I go over to Danny, who is completely losing it. His horse is backing away from him, and he's crying. "Hey, it's okay," I say. I don't know what else to do but take the reins from Danny and stand there. Danny's horse doesn't like me either, but at least I can help Danny start to pull it together so he doesn't get hurt, too.

I look over at Alice. She's standing close to her horse. Her face is pale, but her head is in the right place. She has a muddy streak on her sleeve and a little clod of something in her shiny black hair. Alice is tough in her own way.

Ethan walks around making sure everyone is okay, while Kaya gentles down the horses that are causing the most trouble. Charlie's horse is still snorting and stamping, but

Charlie's totally handing him. Ethan comes over to Danny and puts his arm around him right in front of everyone.

Ethan says, "Listen, everybody. I've seen this before. He'll be okay. Everybody just calm down."

Scotty nods and wipes his face with his sleeve.

Ethan and Kaya get everyone down to the barn and get the horses put away. Coulter and Darius splint Dalton's leg and get him in Coulter's truck before anyone says good-bye. They'll have to drive two hours to the hospital in Jackson Hole in case they have to operate. I wouldn't want to be in that car ride.

We get the word over dinner that Dalton's okay. His mom is flying in. But his leg is fractured, and he's going home. I rehear all the crummy things Coulter said about going home and feeling like a bigger failure than when we started. Dalton was stupid, but it's not like I've never been stupid on a horse.

"He shouldn't have kicked her," says Danny, who's basically been sitting next to me at the picnic table since Dalton got hurt. "Coulter told him not to."

Scotty says, "Coulter's an ass. If I didn't have to do rehab, I'd go home right now myself."

Mrs. Sanchez dishes up another plate of fried chicken that everyone just stares at. "*Cómanlo.*"

I poke at the food on my paper plate. "Will his mustang get sent to Rock Springs now?"

Justin is sitting at the end corner of the table by himself. "Yep. That's how it works around here."

Everyone looks at Justin, surprised that he is joining the conversation, I think. Of course, that's all he says. We all go back to staring at our food, but no one seems hungry. Except Banner, whose appetite seems positively normal. When Mr. Sanchez brings out the final, generous attempt at distraction, little pieces of chocolate cake, Banner leans over to Charlie and points. "Are you going to eat that?"

Charlie looks at Banner and rolls his eyes behind his glasses. "It's all yours."

I stay awake almost the whole night, seeing Dalton's accident over and over. Probably everyone else does, too. One minute everything was fine, and the next minute Dalton's screaming. First I worry about Dalton, like that helps anyone. Then I worry about Dalton's mustang. He'll have to go to the holding facility. Then I worry about myself, and it feels like I'm starting all over again.

I don't go out to feed Goliath. He whinnies, but I don't go. Sometime I'm brave. Sometimes I'm not.

Chapter Twenty-One

THE BLM TRUCK is out in front of the big house with a trailer. With Dalton's mustang in it, I guess. Coulter is back from Jackson. I see him and Officer Hanks standing inside the window of the dining room when I go to clean the outhouses. They both have their hands up in the air. Kaya and Darius are sitting out on the porch drinking coffee, which they never do at this time of the day. Almost like they are guarding the door or something.

Ethan comes up behind me. "Man, if Coulter didn't have it bad enough already, you see that BLM guy is here?"

"Yeah," I say. "Any idea why? I mean, he doesn't care if kids get hurt up here, right?"

"I don't know what's going on, but I don't think it's good, Colorado." Ethan scratches his hairy chin. "You might need to go into the big house to get toilet paper though, right? 'Cause, we could be out."

It occurs to me that one of the reasons that everyone likes Ethan is that he pays attention more than the rest of us do. He collects information about people like other kids collect World of Warcraft scores or moves on the basketball court, which I find both impressive and mercenary at the same time. And something I wouldn't mind being a part of.

I have to go all the way around to get into the back door without Darius and Kaya seeing me. I open the door carefully, but it still squeaks a little. Luckily, the two men inside are shouting now. "You think I want to be out here at this hour?"

"Look, Miles, I have a lot on my plate this morning. What you do with your free time is your business."

"Free time? Half the county's looking over my shoulder, telling me these horses are destroying their land, and the other half's stealing my horses as fast as I round them up."

"You want to talk to me about people looking over your shoulder? I just spent the night with a trial attorney from New Jersey whose son has a broken leg."

"I'm sorry for your trouble, Tim, but this has to be looked into. I have ranchers who want to cull the whole herd. They're even pushing the feds to thin the herds at Rock Springs. Things are getting ugly. So when I catch them and somebody lets them go . . . Can you imagine how that makes me look?"

"You're in Wyoming now, Miles. No one gives a shit how you look. They care what you do. I am not letting your horses go. Why would I do that? Why would anyone do that?"

"I was hoping you could tell me."

Coulter grimaces. "I would not presume to tell you anything. It sounds like you have it all figured out."

"Perfect. Even the people who work for the government won't tell me anything. All right. You have it your way. But if you see that boss mare, I want you to notify me. Henry Helford thinks she's the ringleader that's been messing up his water hole."

"It's not the horses that mess up that water hole, it's those overgrazing cattle. They're so chemically engineered they can't piss straight. And I'd be surprised if Henry could find his butt with both hands."

I don't hear exactly what Officer Hanks says in return. I have the toiler paper, and I think it's time to get out of there before I laugh out loud.

Chapter Twenty-Two

WE HAVE LESSONS with the saddle horses right on schedule that afternoon. All Coulter says about Dalton is, "He's going to be fine. That's my first broken leg in twenty years at this ranch. But when I tell you to do something, you damn well better do it." The next thing he says is, "Cassidy, get up on this horse."

The sorrel gelding standing behind Coulter is sixteen hands, which is the way they measure horses for no good reason at all. In other words, he's big. The other thing that should be noted is that his name is Highball.

I feel the muscle in my stomach constrict. "Sir? You want me to go first? Maybe someone else would be better."

"You were pretty good with telling Scotty what to do yesterday. Let's see if you can ride."

It occurs to me as I walk over to Highball that the bad thing about doing something right is that it raises expectations. I look at the stirrup and wonder if my leg goes that high. I look at Coulter. He's all smiles and moonbeams. The man is evil. "You have a problem, Cassidy?"

"No, sir," I say.

"Cassidy, we always tell the truth at this ranch. Are you scared?"

"Spitless, sir."

"Okay. Why don't you tell us what you're worried about?"

"I don't want to get bucked off, mainly."

"All right. Let's take care of that right now. Hop on."

I have to try three times to get on, I'm so nervous.

"Now. Take your feet out of the stirrups and spin all the way around on the saddle."

I look at him. "I'll have to let go of the saddle horn if I do that."

"You will be okay, Cassidy. Do what I tell you to. I'll stand right here and hold your horse."

Highball sits quietly. I tell myself that this will be fine. That Coulter has the reins. But mainly I just force myself to move and not think. I pull my feet out, and using my butt to center me I lift my boots in the air and rotate all the way around. Highball is slow and easy to sit. When I get back to Coulter he says, "Good. You're doing great. Now jump off."

"What?"

"Trust me. You'll be fine."

I look down. It looks like a long way.

"Push up with your hand on the middle of the saddle and jump. Do it!" His voice is so stinking loud I feel like I have to, but also that I want to. I hate being a chicken. I liked how I felt when I rode Smokey. I tell myself I am not Dalton, and I come flying off the horse with both legs. I land on my feet. Dust flies. I stand up.

"Great work, Cassidy! Now get back on. I'll keep holding the reins, and you reach up in the air."

I get back on in one try. I'm feeling scared but better. I put my hands over my head while he leads the horse. I sit up like there's a thread up my spine. I stay on.

"Now close your eyes."

"Do what?"

Coulter turns to his attentive audience. "Yesterday is yesterday. Half of what we're afraid of in this life isn't half as bad as we think it'll be."

"What about the other half?" I say.

"It's worse." He turns back to me and uses that low, gravel voice. "You'll have to trust me on this one. Trust me, and you will be fine."

I close my eyes.

"Now we're going to walk. You hold your hands out to the side like you're balancing."

Having my eyes closed actually helps. I can concentrate on what I'm supposed to be doing, and since Coulter has the horse I know I'm not going anywhere.

"Now put your hands over your head."

Underneath me I feel the tip and pull of the horse's body, the beats of the horse's legs hitting the ground. I feel my body stretch up through my arms. I move along smoothly. My chest tickles.

"Great work, Cassidy. So good. Keep it up."

We walk faster. I can hear the birds and crickets as I pass. I feel us going around the arena.

"Now put your heels down and really shove them down hard. No peeking. Put your hands all the way out, balance like before. Shoulders back. We're going to trot. I'm right here with you, okay? You trust me?"

Trot? The tickle in my chest keeps expanding. I'm going off for sure. But the horse is being good, and Coulter will stop him if I fall. "Yeah, okay."

"Go Colorado!" I hear Ethan call.

"Hush," says Coulter. "No distractions. Hands out now."

I put my hands out, and Coulter clucks to Highball. His powerful body lifts up, but he has a super gentle, quiet trot. The beat of his legs changes. I'm bouncing, so I shove harder in my heels and straighten up taller. I take the bounce out through my hands and feet. All I hear is quiet. All I feel is the horse and nothing else.

"Cassidy!"

I open my eyes. I'm in the far end of the arena. Trotting. Coulter's like ten feet away. The reins are tied to my horn. I'm trotting with no reins and no Coulter. My body goes stiff. I'm still moving.

"Cassidy! Say 'whoa.'"

Highball drops to a stop as I grab the horn, like he's controlled by Coulter's voice. My guts come up in my throat.

Coulter is at my side. Now, anyway. I could have ended up just like Dalton. I trusted Coulter. He is a mean old bastard.

"You did it! Cassidy. There aren't one in a hundred kids that'll do that. Look at you!" His face is beaming.

I jump off the horse.

"What's wrong, Cassidy?"

I look up at Highball. At least I don't hate him. "I'll tell you what's wrong. Actually, no, I won't tell you what's wrong. You figure it out."

I take off my hat and go back to my friggin' tent.

I know what I've figured out.

The minute a person tells you to trust them, you might as well stab yourself in the back and get it over with. You'd think I'd know this by now. You really frickin' would.

THE WEEDS SMELLED like licorice on the trail by our house. It was blazing hot. When Kidd ran through the tall July grass, the grasshoppers erupted like popcorn.

Dad said, "I'm sorry you didn't make the tennis team. But it's just junior high stuff, right? Keep at it, you'll make it by high school."

"It's okay. The girls are all jerks anyway."

"I thought you liked tennis."

"No," I said. "I'm not coordinated."

Dad kicked at the tall grass. The grasshoppers jumped every which way. Kidd went crazy trying to nip at all of them, flipping back and forth, thrashing up more as he went.

I jump back from the trail. "Gross, Dad." I used to let grasshoppers cover my legs and spit on me.

Dad nodded and kept doing it. "I've read they find their way by jumping into the wind. Whatever direction the wind blows, they turn to face it and then jump. It helps them find food during the dry season."

"Really?" The wind wasn't blowing much that day. The grasshoppers catapulted all over the place. But I liked the idea of it. Finding your way from opposition and all that inspirational stuff. "That's cool."

"Okay. Well, if you don't do tennis, you'll find something else."

"Like what?"

"I don't know. Maybe the circus is having tryouts."

Obligatory eye roll. "Has this ever happened to you? Totally losing at something?" I wasn't the oldest thirteen-year-old.

"If it didn't, what would I write? 'Life is always what I expected it to be. The end.'"

We walked a little way. "It still sucks to lose."

Dad took a slightly irritated breath. "Come on, Cass. What have you lost? You're still smart and healthy and full of talent." He gave me the fake dad scowl. "Like burping. You are excellent at burping."

"No, I'm not," I said, punching him in the arm. "That's you."

"Oh yeah. You're right. Well, you have me. I'm not going anywhere. Trust me, Cassy girl, you'll always have me." He pulled me close to him, even though it was too warm for that. "So what have you lost, really?"

Trust isn't motivation. It's a promise.

And the answer is you, Dad. I lost you.

Chapter Twenty-Three

JUSTIN IS WAITING for me by Goliath's fence, and Goliath is standing next to him. Even in the moonlight I can see Justin doesn't have his hat on. When I get up close I see he's shaved and he's wearing a nice shirt. It even has sleeves. He has an apple in his hand. "You blew Coulter away today. You blew everyone away today. It's hard to sit a trot like that, even on Highball."

"So don't want to talk about it."

Goliath whinnies. It's a friendly noise. I know he just wants to be fed, but it feels like he likes me.

Justin hands me his apple. He holds it over my hand for a second too long. On almost any other night that pause would interest me, but I'm all stretched out in the wrong places so that no thought fits and everything seems to be falling apart. I take it from him and toss it over the fence for Goliath.

"You're making some pretty good headway. You gonna try out for the mustang challenge?"

"I haven't thought about it."

Goliath practically swallows the apple whole, then puts his head over the fence for another. Justin rubs the horse's muzzle affectionately. "Whoever rides this old boy is going to make some bank."

I look at Goliath and try imagining what people would pay for him. He is a gorgeous animal. His size and muscle alone probably make him a hot horse commodity. "It feels kind of rotten to work all that time with the horse just so you can sell him."

"It's better than cleaning toilets," he says.

Justin walks around me and stops at my shoulder so we're both facing forward. He's awkward. He puts his arm around my back and gives this uncomfortable side hug. He pulls tight on my shoulder and then lets go. His hand is startlingly strong. I brace myself not to fall into him, which is all variations of embarrassing.

As awkward as it is, the feel of him next to me shuts my brain off. He even smells good.

"What's that's for?"

"For calling Coulter on his bullshit. He shouldn't have tricked you."

"Yeah. He shouldn't have," I say.

I let myself lean against him. Not a big deal. I mean, we're friends. Sort of. "It was like that thing you did with the horse, where you got it to roll over? He was using me like that horse." I feel the blood rising in my skin just thinking about how he was saying "trust me" across the arena. What a jackass.

Justin doesn't move away from me. "That's about the size of it, I guess."

I look up at Justin. Without his hat on, I can see that broken nose of his clearly in the moonlight. His deep, sunken eyes are staring right at me. He smells like . . . Nope. I step backward. Then I step backward again. I am not making the same mistake twice in one day, thanks.

I say, "I have to go."

"Sure," says Justin. "Yeah. Me too."

Chapter Twenty-Four

I FEEL SOMEONE shoving my shoulder. They aren't being gentle. I stick my head out of my bag to see whom I owe the honor of yelling at. Coulter is standing over my bed.

"We have a problem," he whispers.

Alice doesn't move. Banner rolls over in her sleep. "Shut the hell up, Cassidy." Banner had a restless night. Not that that matters.

"What's wrong?" I whisper back. I'm not too happy about seeing Coulter anywhere right now, but especially in my tent after not sleeping all night.

"Chickens are out."

I'm sorry to hear this, but this is not my problem. And I'm still mad at Coulter. In fact, I'm planning on staying that way. Then I remember I gathered the eggs last night, so I could have left the coop fence open. I get dressed. Outside the tent Coulter is already walking. "A coyote dug a hole under the back fence. The ones he couldn't eat ran off. We lost at least three hens."

"Three? Where's the coyote?"

"Darius is after him. That son of a bitch can smell coyotes."

Takes one to know one, I think.

I find a few of the hens and baby chicks in the bushes, and most of the other feather balls find their own way home. The chicks are so absurdly adorable that I almost forget I've only had two hours of sleep. Their little yellow bodies teeter back and forth across the ground while their heads bob up and down. A gust of wind could knock them over. I'm surprised any of them survived a coyote raid. I'd think running away would kill them.

I walk around inside the henhouse fluffing up their nests and readjusting everything to make it look like it did before. The hens peck in circles, checking the hay and making chirping noises.

Coulter runs in chasing the rooster.

"You got all those hens and chicks back in by yourself?"

"I used that bucket over there."

"You are a real mother hen, aren't you?"

He doesn't say it like a compliment.

"I just lie to them and tell them they'll be safe in here."

"Also a bit of a grudge holder, aren't you?" Coulter sighs. "You'd a never done that on Highball if you'd known I wasn't there."

"Maybe not." I check the nest for eggs and start arranging the hay.

He says, "Sometimes you need to improvise to get things done."

Adults are hilarious. "I'd rather not get things done."

"Life isn't that simple." Coulter fluffs a little hay and walks around the house. He finds an egg and sticks it in his pocket. "But I won't lie to you anymore. You have my word. You can ask me anything at all. Take your shot."

"Unless you're lying right now." I'm so mad I feel like I might say anything. I feel like I could say all the things to Coulter that I haven't said to everyone else. And he would deserve every word. But only one question fills my head. "Why didn't you like my grandfather?"

Coulter looks at me in surprise, then he chuckles. "I did like your grandfather. Most the time."

"Why do you call him a thief then?"

"He took things that were precious to me."

"Like what, for instance?"

"Your grandmother."

"Oh." I think about this while I fluff up the coop and then sweep. My grandmother was old when I knew her. She was bad at Scrabble and had a big mole on her neck. It's hard to imagine her as a heartbreaker. She made great strawberry-rhubarb pies, though.

Coulter pushes the rooster with his foot. The rooster crows at him but runs away. "Your grandfather was something else. He made people feel like anything was possible, even if it wasn't."

"That doesn't sound criminal to me."

"It wouldn't." For a second Coulter doesn't look as tough as usual. His sunspotted cheeks flatten out, and his mouth makes a little hollow circle like he's concentrating.

I herd an escaping chick back into its nest with a stick I pick up off the chicken coop floor. The crazed furball heads off to Coulter, who cups his hands and shoos it back into its place. He's not always a mean old bastard.

"So that's why you call him a thief?" I ask.

"That wasn't the only thing he stole," says Coulter, looking away. "Now I need coffee. All this truth crap is making me cranky."

I stamp my foot like one of the chickens. "You can't do that. Finish the story."

"I said I'd tell you the truth. I didn't say I'd tell you everything."

I'm not going anywhere. I pat the last nest into place. One of the hens pecks her head in the straw nearby as I finish up. She hops to her spot and dusts it with her tail feathers. She clucks her four chicks to her, and all but one climb under her left wing. The loose chick chirps noisily. I cup my hand and guide the chick to the other side until it disappears under the hen's feathers.

Coulter shakes his beard. He seems sad. "I will tell you

this much. Some apples just don't fall too far from the tree."

"What's that supposed to mean?" I look at him seriously. I don't want a punch line or a dodge. I need to know. "You promised to tell me the truth."

Coulter sighs heavily and opens the coop door. "The truth is you should never trust what people say, Cassidy, not by itself. Trust what they do. Anyone who promises to always tell the truth has probably already lied to you."

This I can believe.

Chapter Twenty-Five

AT THE END of the third week we get some good news. "We're going to the rodeo," says Coulter. "Take a shower and brush your teeth. When we go into town we like to class up the joint. And as an added bonus we get to watch our own Kaya Tree run a clover around three barrels as fast as she and her horse, Prairie Dog, can go." After twenty-one days of being away from civilization, this sounds like a trip to Disneyland.

We drive into town in an ancient white school bus that Coulter keeps behind the hay barn. I'm shocked it runs. I thought Coulter was keeping it around as a sort of cultural artifact, since it looks like it was built before they invented roads. It may be the only thing at the ranch older than he is.

When we all pile onto the bus I check the seats for mice. I don't find any. But the vinyl is so brittle I'm afraid to sit on it. A bunch of kids are throwing one another's hats around.

The girls are all wearing makeup and earrings. The boys look polished up, too, or at least clean. Alice braided my hair, and I lent her a cowboy shirt with snaps that looks way better on her.

Mr. Sanchez drives, and Mrs. Sanchez tells him how to drive. Alice and I sit toward the front so she won't get carsick. I know she doesn't want to go, but she's trying to power through. She puts in the earplugs Charlie brought as soon as we get on the bus. But for me the dusty, teeth-rattling ride into town just adds to the feeling that we are going back in time to a boot-stomping, butt-kicking Wild West show.

The town nearest the ranch is called The Big Empty. According to the sign at the entrance to town, 274 people live here. There's also a hardware store, a post office, a convenience store, two bars, and a good-size mobile trailer park. Coulter says the town is named after the nearby Red Desert, which often gets called that nickname. When I ask him why people call it that he shrugs. "It's only empty if you're a damn fool. But there are plenty of those to go around."

The vacant lot near the rodeo grounds is overflowing. I've never seen so many trucks in one place. It's a big facility for such a puny town: two big stock pens and the covered pavilion with picnic tables. The rodeo arena including the seats must be twice as big as any building in town, including the hardware store. Coulter says they don't even have a school here. The ranch kids all ride a bus into Big Piney. The whole county must be here tonight.

I haven't been to many rodeos. A couple. But only indoor,

citified ones, where the whole deal is more about the rodeo queens and the clowns than the bull riders. My mother complained so much about how phony these events were that we just stopped going. I'm not really sure what to expect, but it's nice to have a change of pace. I'm excited to see Kaya ride at least.

We pile into the bleacher seats. It's so crowded we have to fill in where we can, and there are a bunch of us. Alice and I are jammed between Ethan and Charlie. As luck would have it, I get to sit behind Justin instead of in front of him. So I get to look at his wide shoulders and the back of his sunburned-red neck. It's funny, until this moment I never realized why people from the country get called that.

I bump him on the shoulder. "Is this a good rodeo?"

"If you like this sort of thing, yeah."

"Don't you?" I ask.

"No. I don't," he says.

"Why not?"

"My old man used to do it. Not my thing."

"Your dad was a rodeo cowboy? Where is he now?"

"Not really sure. He shows up now and then."

"I'm sorry." The rodeo isn't the place to be talking about this.

He shrugs. "Shit happens. You get over it or you get under it."

I turn and see Alice disappearing into her jean jacket collar.

"Are you okay?" I ask her.

She doesn't look at me until I put my arm around her. They must be really good earplugs.

While we wait in the heat for the rodeo to start, I check out the crowd. The men wear mostly ball caps and cowboy hats, and the women have cowboy hats, too, but not as many. The girls my age mostly wear skintight jeans or teeny tiny Daisy Dukes with big old clunky boots. I see half a dozen boys with chewing tobacco stuck under their lips. Maybe it's the heat outside, but people seem to be throwing back their red plastic cups pretty hard, and I don't think it's soda. The faces at this rodeo look more worn than the faces at home, but tougher, too, which is really starting to grow on me.

The rodeo starts with the whole flag-ceremony-anthem-singing thing and girls speeding back and forth on their horses with giant flags whipping at their sides.

"Man, let's start this thing already," says Scotty. He's sitting, trying to get the candy out of his giant box of licorice.

An older man in a plaid shirt says, "Stand up, kid. We have respect for the flag in this town."

Scotty stands up. I think this is a wise move, considering the dirty looks we are attracting. I'm sure this isn't the first time that Coulter's brought a bunch of spoiled out-of-towners to sample the local entertainment. But I really wish that Coulter and Darius would come in and sit with us instead of getting reacquainted with half the town.

A man in a BLM shirt, not Officer Hanks but some other dude with a pie-shaped picture of trees on his arm, walks up and sits on the front row of the bleachers directly in front of us. The two men on either side of him say, "Hello, Riker," and make plenty of room.

He nods to them. "Henry, Tom." This BLM officer looks twice as old as Hanks, with gray in his beard and salt-and-pepper hair. But he's got a lean, grizzled look and pale blue eyes sunk back in his face that say no freaking nonsense. Once he gets seated he turns around and gives all of the campers the once-over. He looks up at Justin. "New greenies?"

Justin looks at the man. "Yes, sir."

The man turns back around with no response.

The announcer booms out a speech about how this is one of the most authentic rodeos in the world—no gimmicks or fakers, just the real deal. Everybody cheers. Then three girls with tiaras on their hat brims and very shiny shirts blaze through the main gates on their long-maned horses, whipping everybody up by riding around the arena a hundred miles an hour while waving like crazy. I look over at my friends. Everybody has their mouth open except Alice, who is standing quietly with her hands folded. The announcer blares, "Let's rodeo!"

The first event is steer wrestling, which is where two burly cowboys come flying out of the chute on their horses, chasing after a steer. Then one of them up and jumps off the horse going full speed and tries to flip the steer over on his back. I feel sorry for the steer, which has done nothing to deserve this harassment, but I can't imagine how these guys do it. I mean, it's like football with horns and hooves. One guy misses, overshoots the horns, gets trampled by the steer, and stands right up like it's nothing. Cowboys are crazy.

The next event is barrel racing. Kaya's event. Only women run the barrels, but it's not exactly a trip to the spa. Riders come through the gate like someone has shot their horses out of a cannon, and then instead of flying into the air they find some way to bend their horse around three barrels and then fly to the finish line, legs flapping and hands up high. Of the seven riders before Kaya, three knock down barrels. One rider nearly comes out of her saddle. I can barely stand it I'm so excited.

The announcer says, "Miss Kaya Tree. A local beauty who's been racing horses around barrels since she was old enough to hold the reins. Let 'er rip, Kaya."

Kaya's sorrel mare explodes into the arena. Her horse's lower legs are wrapped in bright turquoise tape, so you can see just how much ground those legs cover. Kaya's dressed in a white dress shirt and jeans. And she's all business. Her mouth is puckered tight in concentration, her chin and shoulders reach way over the front of the saddle, while the bottom half of her rocks like crazy to take the full-on gallop. When she flies past with her silk black hair streaming, Alice and I cheer our heads off.

When she crosses the finish her time is 0.23 seconds faster than the next closest rider. "Yes, ma'am!" I yell, jumping up. "Go, Kaya!" Charlie and Ethan and a few of the other campers are on their feet, too, jumping up and down.

The crowd gives her a good round of applause. After a few

seconds we all start to sit down. The noise settles suddenly, so it is not hard to hear the BLM officer say to the man next to him, "...squaw meat." The man on the other side of Riker, or whatever his name is, jerks his head around to the officer and then turns quickly to his wife and daughter sitting next to him. The older man, the one the BLM officer was talking to, kicks his head back and laughs. "Yeah, but I wouldn't mind some of *that* squaw meat."

"What did he just say?" says Ethan.

"He just called Kaya squaw meat," says Charlie.

Ethan raises his deep voice. "You mean that cracker jack just said something about the rider who just kicked butt all over everyone else?"

The old man sitting next to the officer turns around in his seat. "You better shut your mouth, boy, if you want to stay in one piece."

I'm suddenly very aware that there are mainly white people in the bleachers. Like, all white people. But still, I mean, so what? So freakin' what?

"Did you just call me *boy*, old man?" says Ethan. His voice just keeps getting louder and carries farther in the crowd.

The BLM man turns to us. "You little shits put a cork in it. That includes you, boy. You want to cheer for that red bitch, you can go elsewhere."

"You can't talk about people like that," I say, standing up.

The man with a wife and daughter says, "Let's everybody just watch the rodeo."

His wife stands and picks her daughter up in her arms.

"No way, Tom. I'm not going to sit here and let my daughter listen to that kind of language. Riker, Henry, I don't care how much you've had to drink, you ought to be ashamed of yourselves."

"Why don't you control your wife, Tom?" says the older BLM man.

"Why don't you shut your mouth, Riker," says the big man, standing up.

Then everyone is standing up. Scotty and Devri and Banner and the whole crowd of kids are on their feet, and everyone in between. I'm sure people don't even know what they're standing up for. I grab Ethan's arm like a break switch. Ethan's big, but those old men look like the worst kind of trouble. Ethan shakes my hand off. He's ready to hit somebody. I look down. Alice has gone into her coat completely. I drop down to put my arm around her again, and I see that Justin is sitting calmly in his seat, like he's waiting for the next event, which he wouldn't be able to see through all the people about to punch one another.

I hear some talking and scuffling and see a white beard. I hear people start to sit, and a few start to yell, and then Coulter laughs and everyone starts to sit down. Except Ethan. And Charlie. So I stand up next to them. I don't know what else to do.

Coulter waves his hands to the direction of the exit. "All right, campers. Time to go. Rodeo's over."

Once we're on the road back to camp Coulter makes every-one shut up so he can talk. "I am going to give you future leaders a story problem. So I want you to listen, even the ones who normally don't. How does that sound?"

We're all dead quiet.

"Let's say you live in a neighborhood with a bad dog. Maybe a couple of bad dogs. Those dogs live in a house that you pass on your way to school. What do you do? Do you walk past the dogs and take your chances? Do you shoot the dogs in the street? Do you stop going to school? Or do you walk on the other side of the street?"

"I don't have to take that shit off anyone," says Ethan. "This isn't the 1950s, in case you haven't gotten the word up here."

"Thank you, Ethan. You've had a shocking experience. Adults acted badly, no question. Now, what is your answer?"

"Mr. Coulter," says Charlie. "If you are using rabid dogs as a philosophical metaphor, I would say dogs shouldn't be allowed to attack people. That's what laws are for. To protect people."

"What if the dog catcher in town owns the dogs?"

"If a dog tried to bite me, I'd shoot that hound in the street," says Banner. "Catcher or no catcher."

"The Big Empty is not the kind of town where you can shoot every ill-mannered dog. Dogs have to be tough, and sometimes that brings out the worst in them. What would you do, Ethan? What gets you the result you want?"

Ethan looks out the window instead of answering. "We

got bad dogs in my neighborhood, too, Mr. Coulter. And nobody calls me boy there either."

"No, they don't. Because you and your family have been smart enough to pick your battles and win, right?"

Ethan doesn't answer.

"Sometimes being a smart leader is losing the battle so you can win the war."

"We didn't win anything tonight," I say.

Coulter says. "Kaya did. And you did. Because you all stuck together. Don't forget that. And also please try to remember all the good people you met tonight. Like the Anderson family, who were trying to help. There are more good people than bad in The Big Empty, and more good people than most towns have period."

I think I will remember everything about this night. The good and the bad. When I finally get to bed I close my eyes and think of Kaya flashing around those barrels while those men talked trash about her in the bleachers. I think about Ethan and Charlie standing up to those men. And Alice going to the rodeo even though it was so hard for her. My friends make me want to be brave other places besides the saddle.

Chapter Twenty-Six

"TODAY IS EVERYBODY'S birthday," says Coulter. "Or pretty close to it. In just a few minutes you get your yearling. And just like when you were born, you can't pick your legs, but you can pick what you do with them."

Match day. When we get the yearling we will work with for the auction. I'm sweating I'm so excited and nervous. Plus it's hotter than Hades in this field we're standing in, and ghastly botflies are everywhere. I love that Wyoming even has flies that eat your flesh.

Coulter continues. "Your mustang has a freezemark on the left side of his or her neck that we've translated for you and written the individual four-digit code on the horse's halter. All your mustangs have a halter on them already. We had that picnic this morning.

"Now, I know you all think you're going to walk out into the pasture and find your soul mate. But the reality is that horses, like people, are not perfect. Soul mates are earned, not found. And as you've hopefully noticed, these horses are young, so you won't ride them. The reason we work with yearlings is that buyers want to train their own horse, but they want someone else to do the hard work of getting them used to people."

Coulter looks funny. His eyes are watery and his arms are extra floppy. "So the way this works is that you stick your hand in this bucket and get a number. We don't name them so you don't get attached. Of course you will, but we try to keep that to a minimum."

Darius walks though the crowd, letting all of us pick a number out of a feed bucket. My number is 4748. That sounds lucky enough. Everyone bumps over to the fence to get a peek at their equestrian match. I'm so short all I see are heads. But I hear people sounding happy. That's promising.

When I finally get to the front I see a red roan marked 4748 wandering near the gate. I've noticed her before. She looks like she's about two years old, and she's already pudgy. Or maybe that's baby fat, but I'm not sure how you get fat as a baby mustang. It's like getting fat on lettuce as a toddler. Anyway, she has straight legs and a pretty head. And gorgeous strawberry coloring. I'll call her Roanie. I turn to Alice. "Who'd you get?"

She points to a tall black yearling with a white blaze down his face. He's bumping around with the other yearlings in the corner. "Wow. Your horse is beautiful," I say.

"All horses are beautiful," says Alice. "Who did you get?"

I point to the red roan.

"Is she pregnant?" asks Alice, smiling.

"Weird, huh?"

"She's pretty. She just needs some exercise," says Alice.

Coulter makes us all stand and watch our horses inter-act with one another. Goliath has been separated out already to the small round pen so no one gets kicked while we go out to get our yearlings. Coulter says, "Starting now you will all get a chance to feed them, and we will supervise you getting them out and walking them around on a halter. All of these horses have been worked in a round pen with us already, and nobody has been an idiot but that one."

Coulter points to Goliath. All the boys laugh. I guess they recognize a bully when they see one. "He's Justin's problem. If Justin gets a saddle on him, one of you can ride him at the auction. If not, we'll have to ship him off to Rock Springs."

"What really happens in Rock Springs?" I ask.

"Nothing," says Coulter. "They put the mustang's picture up on the Internet. Then they keep 'em there until someone takes them. Which is never for most of them."

"Never?" I say.

"Never," says Coulter. "And that goes for any of these horses who don't get adopted. This is their shot at something more than standing in an overcrowded pasture with noth-ing to do but get older for the rest of their lives."

All the kids get quiet.

"That's like jail," says Banner.

"Call it what you want to, honey, that's the way it is."

We all watch as everyone catches their horses. Ethan's bay follows him almost instantly. Alice's horse rears when she tries to lead him out of the pasture, so Darius comes to help her, but Alice doesn't shy away. When the horse comes back down she stands opposite and pets him until he settles down.

Banner stands next to me with Devri behind her. "Nervous?"

"No," I say.

"You aren't going to have a seizure or something?"

"Tomorrow. I thought the first day we'd go for ice cream."

"Darlin', it looks like your horse has done that a few too many times already. You might want to get her some diet hay."

Devri thinks this is hilarious. If she were a horse, Devri would eat diet hay.

Coulter calls Banner to come get her horse. "Hey. Look at that. My guy's gorgeous. What do you know?"

And he is. He's a paint with dark brown patches on pure white. Banner strides out to get him, and he stands quietly for Coulter, but as soon as she gets ahold of him he's all over the place. Coulter steps in and takes the horse. "You might want to wait on this one. I'll work with him this afternoon."

Banner says, "He's mine, isn't he?"

Coulter has Justin move Goliath from the round pen while he gets Banner's mustang under control. Banner and Coulter walk into the round pen together, and then Coulter turns the horse loose. He stands behind Banner's big red hair. "Have at it."

Banner stands up square to the horse. And when I say square, I'm not counting the curves that come out of that skintight T-shirt she's painted into. I can see her belly button indentation. Then she flips out the lead line like a whip. The horse takes off running and works himself into a lather. He looks like he wants to quit, but she keeps running him. Finally, when the horse is breathing smoke, Coulter nudges Banner, and she puts her hands down. The horse stops and gasps for air.

"What did you just teach that colt?" says Coulter.

Banner walks out to the horse, swinging her hips. The horse looks nervous, but he's too tired to run. She strokes his neck. She scratches his head. She talks to him, but I can't hear what she's saying. I look around me. Every male with eyeballs has his tongue hanging out. Some of them look like they might fall over if I pushed them with two fingers. She hooks the lead line back into his halter. "He'll be right as rain after a week."

Coulter nods. "You've done this before then?"

"I break all my daddy's horses."

"We don't break horses here, Banner, we gentle them."

Banner walks out of the round pen with the horse trailing behind her. "He looks gentle to me, Mr. Coulter," she says sweetly. "In fact, I think I'll call him Sugar."

Coulter drops his head. Every guy is making the same

stupid face. It's revolting. And I'm not at all hypersensitive.

"You're next, Cassidy," says Coulter.

"Someone else can go next if they want to," I say.

"Get your horse," says Coulter.

I look out into the corral. Darius is approaching the roan. She spins back from him. Great.

"I'll come get her," I say, rushing in. She spins even wilder when I move too fast.

"Hold up, you two," says Coulter. "She's a spooky one."

I stop walking. "Darius, can I catch her myself?"

Darius gives me the king of dirty looks and then comes out, dropping the lead line in my hand. "She's all yours, genius."

I feel my face go pink. He's right, of course. This horse is way more than I can handle. But he wasn't doing her any favors. I just stand there. I mean for a long time. Then I take a step forward. When she looks, I step. When she doesn't, I wait. After several minutes, I make it to her side. She dances off to the right. I turn and see Kaya standing right behind me.

"I'm here just in case," she says.

I know I'll probably be sorry, but I think that having two of us in here is just making it more dangerous for everyone.

"Can I try it alone for three more minutes?"

"Cassidy, you barely started riding."

I think of Dalton and step back. Kaya gets the horse for me and hands me the lead rope. Then I walk with the roan out to where Justin is standing against the fence, leaning up against it with his boot stuck in the gate.

"Don't let Kaya do your work for you. That roan isn't spooky unless you think she is."

Why does Justin come at me like that? I know how the horse feels. Then it hits me. *I know how the horse feels.* Not exactly, but something like it. I stop there in the middle of the walkway. The roan sidesteps, watching my every move. I look at Coulter, waiting for him to compare me to Banner. I start humming and walk away in the opposite direction.

"Where do you think you're going?" says Coulter.

"For a walk," I say.

When I pull, she gives, and I let go. When she stops, I stop, too, but I keep pulling. In about nothing flat she gets it, and I take her all around the outside of the arena area. She's smart. If I was that smart, I'd have figured out how to ride the first day I was here.

When I get back to where Coulter is standing he's smiling. "Well done."

"Thanks," I say.

I look up and see Justin's hat facing down. I know underneath it he's smiling, too.

That night I go back to feed Goliath. But when I get to the upper corral he isn't there. I panic for a second and then remember how Coulter kept him separate earlier today. But in the morning when I go to get Roanie I find him back with the yearlings. I wonder how I could have missed him.

Chapter Twenty-Seven

EVERY DAY IT'S something else at Point of No Return. Today the adventure is a trail ride. Coulter meets me outside the outhouses when I finish cleaning. I swear it's like my dad's office hours. People know they can always find me here. Coulter points at a mountain that juts into the sky off to the south. "Can you handle that today? There will be some tight spots."

Every time I do something I think is impossible, Coulter raises the bar higher. "I don't know."

"You're welcome to stay here and help Darius clean out the clog in the shower drains."

I hustle to finish my chores and get saddled. I decide not to think about all the ways I could get hurt on the trail ride. This horse stuff seems to be coming back to me, at least some of it. But it's like finding a hundred-dollar bill in my pocket. I'm not quite sure what to do with it, or if it's really mine. Anyway, riding in the mountains sounds a hundred times more fun that riding in circles in the arena. I just hope Smokey and I are up to it.

The morning goes like a dream. Smokey's in a great mood. I saddle him quickly. The sun makes pink layers on the morning clouds. Everyone is quiet and busy getting their gear set. There's a lot to do before you can set off for an all-day ride, like packing clothes and food and going to the bathroom about seventeen times. By the time we're ready the sun has burned off the morning mist. I look across the valley up at the mountain. It seems impossibly far to go, but then again, just being here seemed impossible a few weeks ago.

Right as we're getting into our saddles, a cloud of dust shows up on the horizon, and Officer Hanks's truck speeds into the yard. The truck makes a hard stop, throwing up dust. A bunch of the kids nearly lose control of their horses trying to get out of the way. "Aww hell," say Coulter.

"Morning," says Hanks, swinging open his door.

Coulter says, "Hello, Miles. I'm afraid we were just leaving."

"I can appreciate that. I don't want to interrupt. But we've had a little mishap at one of our holding pens. Wondered if you'd seen these horses?" He holds up his cell phone to show Coulter, like Coulter's gonna look at his phone.

"I keep pretty busy watching the mustangs I have," says Coulter.

Kaya steps out of the crowd of kids. "Hey, Officer Hanks. Sorry, we really have to get going. The horses get anxious." She turns. "We're all ready, Mr. Coulter."

Officer Hanks steps right next to her. "You haven't seen them then, Kaya?"

Kaya glances at his phone and then folds her arms across her chest. "I thought the BLM was done rounding horses up for now. You have your quota."

"Just a few ranchers complaining about some trouble-makers. We had to pick up a few extras," Officer Hanks says. "But they weren't there this morning. I don't want this to get out of hand."

"Good idea. All right, kids, let's go," says Coulter.

Officer Hanks says, "So I take that as a no. You haven't seen them?"

Coulter climbs on his big dun horse and looks down at Officer Hanks. "If I see anything on our ride, I'll be sure to let you know." Coulter puts his reins in his teeth and tightens up the knot on the lariat hanging off his saddle.

Kaya waves good-bye and walks back into the crowd.

We all get in line. Banner swings in front of me. Justin stands right behind me. Banner turns and asks, "Is Justin teaching you to stay in the saddle?"

I feel the heat in my face. "He's just watching me to make sure I don't fall off."

"That's not all he's watching," says Banner.

"Hey, Banner," says Justin. "You're holding up the line."

Coulter leads us on a narrow path that cuts behind the ranch. The ground is still wet, but it's so sunny the grass twinkles. Soon we hit a steep hill, and I keep right on pace with the other riders. I'm getting the hang of this. Once we are on the plateau we cross a sea of sagebrush. I can't get used to how much open sky there is. Giant clouds sleep in the upper valley. We let the horses drop their heads so they can pick their way through the brush. I had no idea anything could be so much fun.

Justin trots up close. "You look better. I mean, on Smokey."

Banner turns around and raises her eyebrows. "Isn't she a peach?"

"I think we all look amazing today," says Charlie, coming up right next to Banner. Charlie's wearing a sombrero with a red sash. I don't get how his wardrobe fits in his tent, but he does look grand.

Banner bursts out laughing and walks ahead.

"Can I talk to you?" Charlie asks me, popping into Banner's spot.

"What's up?"

"What's your opinion on summer romances? I mean, are they inherently doomed?" He's asking all this over his shoulder.

The heat is back in my face. Have I been that obvious? I feel like I'm riding my horse naked. I cough into my hand. "They never work out. That's what I think. You both just go back to your real life when you're done."

Charlie turns. "Yeah. I mean, maybe. But it doesn't have to be like that, does it? I mean, if you're really into each other."

I can't believe Charlie is outing me right here in the horse line. It's time for defensive action. "Why are you asking? Do you have a crush on someone, Charlie?"

He turns and nods. He looks surprisingly serious for a guy in a red sash. "Devri."

"Devri? Like, really?"

Luckily, Coulter yells for the trot, so we all stop talking. "We're going to extend out here. Get up in your stirrups and balance."

The other riders charge ahead, including doomed Charlie. Smokey's trot is just not as speedy as the other horses. Justin jogs his buckskin slowly behind me. Because that's inconspicuous. I nudge Smokey a little harder.

When we get to the base of the next big incline we cross a good-size stream. Two horses, including Scotty's, buck as they cross, but nobody goes off. I'm not going to lie. When I see those horses buck it scares me, but not like it used to. And after we're across I notice the air is warm and breezy. Aspen and pine dot the low hills. We trot past a field of giant limestone boulders covered with bright green and orange lichen. The sun flickers on my face as we ride under a small grove of aspens.

I look from hill to hill.

I turn to Justin. "Is it true mustangs used to fill this area?"

"That's what I hear," says Justin.

"And people killed them for dog food until they made that law to stop it. And now people are saying they want to go back to killing them."

Justin jogs his buckskin up to me. "Why are you asking me?"

"Because I need somebody to explain what's really going on around here. I mean, we put people in jail for cockfights and neglecting their pets. So how is slaughtering horses for dog food okay? Or sticking them in horse jail for that matter. How is that right?"

"It isn't. That doesn't mean it doesn't happen," says Justin. He looks like he wants to say more but doesn't. Or maybe he just thinks I'm a sheltered city kid who talks too much.

He says, "We're getting farther behind the other horses. Let's see you lope."

I look at Smokey. "You want me to lope right now? I've never done that outside the arena. What if he takes off on me?"

"Stop worrying, Cass. You're a good rider now. Or haven't you noticed?"

What I notice is he just called me Cass, all nice and slow. And that we're way behind the other riders. I cluck to Smokey and I feel him shift, looking at the horses ahead. I tap on him with my foot, and he bounds forward. He wants to get to his herd. In two steps, we're galloping, but it's not scary at all because it's faster but easier to sit than the trot. I tilt forward and watch the world go by. Justin's buckskin canters close behind. When we finally catch up to the other kids I have to keep my mouth shut to keep all the happiness from whooping out.

"Ride 'em, cowgirl," says Banner as I pull in line behind her.

We ride past giant-size boulders that have come out of the mountain, then meander up a rocky draw that finally opens up on wide plateau. Below, the world is a gray granite tub filled with aspen treetops. Everything else is sky.

Far ahead Coulter stands up in his stirrups. He points at the trail that crosses the ridge. "Short canter to that big rock. Nice and easy. Everyone ready?"

Darius and Kaya jog to the edges of the plateau. I guess it'd be pretty bad if one of their riders cantered off the edge of the mountain instead of going to the rock. I make a mental note not to be that stupid. Justin leans over to me. "Nice and easy."

Banner turns her head and whistles at Justin. "I'll baby-sit her, Justin. Let's canter up to that rock together, Cassidy."

I back away from Banner. Smokey is still prancing around he's so wired up. Other kids are cantering their horses. With the waving grass it looks like the earth is moving instead of the horses. Banner moves up between me and Justin and whacks Smokey right on the butt with her hand.

My brain cracks loose. What is her problem? She didn't have to hit Smokey.

Smokey must be mad, too, because when I barely touch his side with my boot his bony old body lunges forward. The only reason in the world I stay on is because I'm so ticked I'm already clamped on to him like a fist.

And then we cover ground. We leave Banner's mare like she's glued to the dirt. We pass the horses that are already galloping. My hat flies off and whips behind on my chin-strap. Smokey's feet grab the ground and throw it behind us.

Behind me I hear Coulter's voice. "Whoa! Whoa! Stop that horse!"

But I don't whoa. This is amazing. But then we're almost at the rock and we're past the rock and I'm running out of mountain. I ask Smokey with everything I've got in my legs and hands to whoa the heck whoa. I vise-grip the horn with both hands to keep from flying off into the rocks.

And when Coulter and Justin and Banner and everyone else catch up and start to yell at me, I barely hear them. Because that was the best thing ever.

Coulter asks, "How the hell did you stay on?"

I don't answer. Because I don't know. I just did.

After the wild ride everyone looks at me funny. Maybe because I can't stop smiling. There isn't much talking. Alice asks me if I'm okay. Coulter spits a lot. Banner doesn't say a word. We divide up into groups so we can be more carefully supervised. Coulter doesn't put me in a group with Banner.

Justin doesn't look at me when he rides past, but I still hear him. "Ride 'em, cowgirl."

Chapter Twenty-Eight

THERE ARE GOOD mornings and there are great mornings. A morning when I get to make buttermilk muffins with Mrs. Sanchez is a spanking-great morning. Plus, I may be a little hopped up on horses and Justin. We are well into our fourth dozen when Justin comes riding right up to the kitchen on his buckskin.

"I need some help with the mustangs." He's back to being sour-faced.

Mrs. Sanchez says, "She's busy."

"It will only take a minute, Mrs. Sanchez. *Por favor. Es importante.*" His accent is worse than mine.

"Biscuits are important," says Mrs. Sanchez.

Justin employs the face of sadness.

"What's up?" I ask.

He holds his arm down to me. "Do you think you could ride double if we just walk? We're only going up the hill."

His buckskin seems safe, but you never know. "Where do I sit?"

"On the back." He holds his arm down farther and kicks his foot out of the stirrup so I can put mine in. "I don't have all day."

Mrs. Sanchez rolls her eyes. "*Ten cuidado.* I like this one."

I have to put my arms around Justin to stay on. I know Justin can keep the horse calm. I just don't know if I can stay on. I feel like a five-year-old. His shirt smells like hay. "What's wrong?"

"What's wrong is you. You don't learn about mustangs in a book," he says, all the ornery gone from his voice. "I'll show you something way better than a book."

"I like books." My words bounce out of my mouth and fall behind me. "Are we going far away? I really was helping Mrs. Sanchez."

"Trust me. Mrs. Sanchez doesn't need any help. And you'll like this better."

Having him say that, about trusting him, makes me feel immediately worried. I realize that if I'm sitting on this horse with him, I must trust him in some way. At least when it comes to horses. I'm just not sure how it happened or if it's a good idea. We ride up the hill like we're going to bring the mustangs in from pasture, but then we keep going. He asks, "You okay?"

I am still holding on tight. My skin itches. "Is this going to get me in trouble?"

"Not if you don't tell anybody."

Justin clucks his buckskin to a trot.

"Seriously?" I say, bouncing. He keeps trotting. I squeeze tighter.

"I need to breathe once in a while," he says.

I say, "And I need to stay on."

About a mile from the mustang pasture I see them. Popped out, on top of the hill. And they don't evaporate into dust when we get closer, either. A sorrel horse stands off from three smaller horses, snorting and stamping. The sorrel's head is cocked and jutting forward. The other three pace around a white, round-bellied horse. They watch us approach. These are mustangs that are still wild. Justin is right. This is way better than a book.

I whisper, "Why aren't they running away?"

Justin points three fingers to a nearby ledge. We get off behind a big rock and climb up the side of the steep ridge. Rocks sputter under our feet, and I have to bear-crawl with my hands to keep my balance. He nods to me like a question. A smile creeps onto his face. I nod and keep moving.

When we reach the outcropping of rock we stop and peer over at the small herd. The stallion is running fast in a circle around the other horses, raising dust. Three other horses braid into one another around a white mare.

They look like the mustangs at the ranch, but they move more quickly with lighter steps. Standing on the ridge with the sky behind them they look chiseled out of the ground in all its different colors, except the white mare who looks like she is made of porcelain. She's so beautiful, I almost miss the tiny brown ears poking up through the patchy grass. The mare is standing in front of a foal, no bigger than a lamb.

"A baby," I say, louder than I mean to.

The foal lifts its head up one more time and then drops down. Its small legs are tucked under its belly. It can't be much more than a few hours old.

Justin spits and says pretty much every cuss word I've ever heard times two. I turn just as he digs his boot into the ground. I have no idea what's going on. "Let's go," he hisses. "This isn't what I brought you out here for."

"What's going on?"

"The BLM is what's going on. They have no business chasing mares like that. They run 'em up and down with trucks and ATV's and even helicopters if they can get 'em. They run 'em until they drop their foals. It's murder."

"You mean she had the foal early because Officer Hanks was chasing her?" It's one thing to read about this kind of thing, but it's something very different to be standing here. I turn back to the horses. I hold still. The foal stays down. "It's okay. It's resting."

Justin grimaces. "It's not resting."

After a few minutes the sorrel stallion circles the herd, snorts, and then charges down the hill behind him. Two horses follow. Eventually the third peels off and leaves the mare standing alone. She cocks her head to the wind. I don't think she has taken a step since we got here. The foal still doesn't move.

Justin's shoulders bend toward me. "Let's go."

"No," I say. "I want to stay. I want to see what happens."

The sorrel rushes back up the hill with his ragged mane flaring along his neck. He rushes the mare, nipping at her, pitching, and whinnying. The white mare turns her head and teeth to the stallion, but she doesn't move her legs. "What's he doing? Does the stallion want to hurt the foal?"

"He's trying to get her to come with him."

"But she can't leave . . . Its head was just up."

The stallion bites at the mare. She swings her head into his. Their skulls clap together. She rears up but quickly comes back to position. He kicks his hind legs at her flanks, just missing.

"We have to stop him."

"He's trying to protect her. We have to go."

"We have to do something."

"The colt's dead, Cass."

"You don't know that."

"I'm sorry. But we have to go now." Justin takes hold of my hand. I shake it off. He reaches for my hand again, and I push it away. "You're acting like a baby."

"You're acting like a bully."

"I'm trying to take care of you," he says.

"Well, don't," I say. I didn't ask to come out here. I'm not listening to him. I turn to the white mare and start walking.

He puts his hand on my shoulder. "They'd stomp you to pieces if you went down there."

The stallion kicks at the mare again, and this time he connects. The mare stumbles and nearly falls on the colt. When she turns I can see open skin on her hip. A red line runs down her leg. The stallion spins and runs into the brush. In seconds he returns and kicks at the mare with his front hoof. She steps back and misses the full force of his leg but drops to the ground.

"Stop it!" I yell.

Both horses look to me and then each other. The mare staggers. The stallion waves his head, snorting. The mare drops her nose down into the brown lump in the grass. At last the stallion runs to the bush, drops off the hill, and doesn't come back.

I wipe my face. "She's bleeding. Let's take them back with us. Maybe . . ."

Justin is right behind me. He shakes his head and talks to himself. "There's nothing we can do now. They might as well shoot 'em. I hate those government bastards."

I say, "You're the one, aren't you? The one Officer Hanks is looking for. Letting the horses go."

Justin looks at me sharply. "No, I'm not. Get on the horse."

"You are." It's like a punch in the stomach. "It's against the law, Justin. You could go to jail."

"It wouldn't be the first time. I've done six months before. But it's not me. We have to go now."

Neither horse is moving. "What will happen to them?"

"At least it didn't die in some warehouse. Or worse yet, live in one."

"But what about her?"

He stands by the buckskin, waiting for me to get on first.

I look behind me as we ride away, holding on to Justin, but not really. I see the mare standing over her silent colt, a square white object getting smaller and smaller the farther we go toward home, until we turn into the trees and she's gone.

Chapter Twenty-Nine

I DON'T GO out to feed Goliath for a few nights. Instead I visit him before it gets dark with my portion of fruit from dinner. He still whinnies in the middle of the night, but I stay in my bag. One night I sleep under my pillow. The next night I stay up late talking to Alice until Banner tells us to shut up and go to sleep.

And this is the question I ask myself: Which is worse? To hide that you know someone is doing something wrong, or to hide from that person because you don't know if what they're doing is right or wrong? Here is my answer: I don't have an answer.

During the day there's plenty of work to be done to get the yearlings ready for auction and take my mind off of Justin's extracurricular activity. We have to walk the yearlings and groom them and teach them how to stand and move. I thought horses knew how to stand and move, but apparently in a horse show they're supposed to walk and move like people want them to. And then there's all the regular work of running the ranch.

I don't talk to Justin. I'm sick about the way the mustangs are being treated, but I'm also worried that if Justin gets caught, Coulter will lose the ranch. Justin could get sent to jail. And that colt could have died for lots of reasons. But mostly I don't want to think about it because I can't stop feeling sick about it.

In the afternoons I ride with the group. My tutoring is over. It's good to be with Ethan and Charlie and Alice. They tell dumb stories that make me feel normal. At night I keep reading the books from the big house. I puzzle over the pictures, tables, and charts. So much information but no solutions. Millions of dollars are getting poured into this problem. My mom says when I have a problem I have to start from the bottom line and work up. But the bottom line on mustangs is fifty thousand horses in holding facilities all over the country. Just waiting to be adopted. Who is going to adopt fifty thousand mustangs? How do you work up from that?

Saturday I burn through my chores so fast I finish them by midafternoon. It's so hot, everybody is walking in slow motion, but I can't stop moving. Even the clouds are stuck in the sky. I ask Mrs. Sanchez if she needs help making dinner, but she says she is already finished. Darius is sitting on the porch drinking iced tea. His shirt is covered in sweat and hay.

"Is there anything you need me to do this afternoon?" I ask. That's how desperate I am.

He hitches up half his lip. "Yeah, why don't you go finish stacking those hay bales."

He's being sarcastic, but I'm fine with it. "Okay," I say.

He snorts. "Right. Those bales weigh about as much as you do."

"I'll figure something out," I say. "Enjoy your iced tea."

I love being polite to Darius. It really pisses him off.

The bales are heavy. But not so heavy that I can't move them. We got a hay shipment in two days ago, and the delivery people did a terrible job, so Coulter wants the whole thing redone. It's a lot of packing up and stacking. Darius must be getting old. I mean, the barn is like a stuffed sauna, so I don't do it fast, but I can do it. Just one beastly bale at a time.

After I've been alone in the barn for ten minutes, Justin comes in with his work gloves on. "Are you going to keep hiding from me the rest of the summer?" he asks.

I straighten my already-sore back. "I'm not hiding. I'm working."

"That thing with the colt was more than you were ready for the other day. I didn't mean to upset you."

When he almost apologizes I almost want to like him for it. But I am upset. Now I have to carry around this knot in my stomach about the colt, but also about Justin. Who knows who's on the right side of that mess? I lift another bale. "I'm just going to finish this job."

"Some jobs go faster if you have two people." He picks up a bale.

"I didn't ask for your help," I say.

He says, "I'm not asking for yours."

I look up and our eyes connect uncomfortably. He doesn't look away. I know exactly what he means, but I wish I didn't. I keep stacking. Finally I say, "They'll catch you."

Justin tosses the bail in front of me. "Who'll catch me? You? You've never seen me buck hay before."

Justin can lift twice as much as I can twice as fast. I stack faster to keep up. He speeds up, too. Then I get momentum and start catching up. Until one of the bails I grab has a stowaway. A mouse spurts out and scampers right across my thigh. I drop my bale and let out a whoop. The bale poofs in the air, and little pieces fly up in my face and mouth so I blow like a geyser. "Swit," I puff.

Justin drops his bale, too, he's laughing so hard.

"I hate those things." I say, inhaling hay and spitting it back out again. My hands and arms are too dirty to clean my face.

Justin pulls his hand out of his glove and reaches out across the foot between us. He takes my arm with one hand and wipes the hay off my lips by dragging his thumb across them. "You're going to choke yourself, Cass. It's just a mouse."

I stop spitting and inhaling. I shake off his arm and step

back. I swallow the hay dust in my mouth. "Thanks," I say. "I'll go get a glass of water."

That night I lie in my bed, unable to sleep. I think about Justin lifting me off the ground onto his horse. I think about what he's doing with the mustangs and how dangerous it is for everyone, but especially for him. I think about the men I saw at the rodeo and how they seemed rotted out by prejudice. Those men wouldn't think twice about shooting a kid sneaking around letting horses go. I think about the colt and the white mare. Why do people hate what's free? Why is freedom so dangerous?

Outside I hear Goliath's frustrated whinny. I'm sure not a horse, but what I hear is his impatience for freedom. I feel that, too.

I think about how good it felt to race along the top of that mountain, flying on Smokey's back. I think about Justin's rough thumb on my lips. How my insides light up like a chandelier when we're together. A mouse's tiny feet skitter across the tent floor. I pull out my flashlight and wave it side to side. I don't see any beady red eyes, and the skittering stops. Then I realize, with a shock, it doesn't matter that much to me what the mouse does. He's probably not going to bother me. I'm fine.

I settle into my sleeping bag and go to sleep.

Chapter Thirty

"HANDS QUIET AND shoulders back," yells Coulter.

The cool thing, he isn't yelling at me. I post past Devri. Her face is tight and miserable. Highball is dropping his head to resist the bridle and giving her fits today.

"Nice, Cassidy. That's what I like to see." Coulter's given me Shooter to ride today to get him collected back up. Danny rode him yesterday, and he bolted. He's doing fine for me so far. He's not even ornery. I pick up his head and gently ask for the canter.

My riding skills are still rough. It takes years to develop the timing of an experienced equestrian. But I've improved fast. Coulter is letting me ride all of his horses. And my mustang, Roanie, is letting me put a noisy piece of plastic on her back, to simulate loading her with rain gear. That's crazy advanced for a yearling, because horses usually hate that kind of stuff. Kaya has me help her with some of the younger campers, getting their horses groomed each day and making sure the horses are getting the gentling that they need. Kaya says I'm not a horse whisperer; I'm a horse listener. Which is fine by me.

Banner rides by on Thunderbird. "You're on the wrong lead," she says as she passes me.

I look down at Shooter's shoulders. No, I'm not. I don't know, maybe I am. I do a half-halt bounce and switch my timing.

Coulter yells, "What's a matter, Cassidy? You just switched to the wrong lead. Can't you tell which lead you're on yet? Just look at the horse's legs."

I look at Shooter's shoulders and switch back. Banner is galloping on the other side of the arena by now. Justin is hanging on the fence. Of course he's seen the whole thing. He just shakes his head.

The closer we get to the tryout day for the mustang challenge, the more Banner fills my life with her charming sense of humor. Yesterday she told me that Mrs. Sanchez wanted me to start dinner without her, and when Mrs. Sanchez got there she about tore my head off for poking around in her kitchen without permission.

In a way I guess it's a compliment. Banner sees me as competition instead of pathetic. But I can think of other compliments I'd rather have.

When I come to get dinner going I make sure not to do anything until Mrs. Sanchez tells me to. She's in a mood, and I don't want to do anything to make it worse. We're making stew and cobbler today. Coulter's favorite. It's not that hard, really, but there is a lot of chopping and peeling to feed a group our size. Mrs. Sanchez leaves me alone with the peaches. "A peach is little gift from God. Don't waste them by being sloppy."

I peel each gift from God slowly and try to get it right. The rich, cheerful smell makes me feel hungry and satisfied at the same time. Maybe Mrs. Sanchez is right.

"Whatcha cookin' up there?" asks Banner, coming to visit me in the kitchen.

I turn around quickly. "Dessert."

Banner picks up a plastic spoon and licks it. Like, seriously. "Because you're so sweet?"

I go over to the fire. I'm warming up shortening in the pan near the coals. I have to keep my eye on it so it doesn't burn.

"Have you decided if you're trying out for the riding spot?" she asks.

"Not really," I say.

"Yeah. Me neither."

We are both lying. She's been planning on winning since the camp started. And why wouldn't she? She can do flying lead changes and jump fences without messing up her hair. Justin can train horses to do things, but even he can't ride like Banner. Something weird happens when she sits on a horse. Instead of being mean old Banner with a perfect bod, she turns into graceful Banner with perfect timing. Of course, the whole perfect-bod thing doesn't hurt.

Just the same—I've been thinking about how I don't want her to ride Goliath.

I walk back over to get my juice and one of the bowls of peaches. Banner reaches for the second bowl of peaches I've just peeled, sticks her fingers under the plastic wrap, and helps herself.

"That's disgusting, Banner," I say as calmly as I can.

"That's a little harsh, isn't it?"

"Your hands are dirty."

She licks her fingers. "I'm not the only one with dirty hands, am I? I've seen you sneaking out in your pajamas. I'd hate for that to get back to Coulter. He might have to fire smash nose."

I squeeze the spoon I'm holding. "What is your problem with me exactly?"

"*I* don't have a problem." Banner gets up and sticks her hand in the bowl again before walking off. "But you might."

I squeeze the wooden spoon so hard I'm afraid it's going to snap. I don't hurl it at her.

Mrs. Sanchez has me chop vegetables for the stew. I imagine the carrots are Banner.

"You are chopping with gusto today," says Mr. Sanchez. He puts some more wood in the fire.

Mrs. Sanchez points at Mr. Sanchez. "Go bother those boys who do nothing. Cassidy is my little chef."

I stop thinking about Banner for about two seconds so

I can appreciate how nice it is for Mrs. Sanchez to call me her "little chef." She blusters past me and sets out the Dutch oven. "If you don't pay attention, you make mistakes," she says. "Don't get distracted."

That rings a bell in my head. I think about how much I'd like to sneak up and steal the spot from Banner for the mustang competition. How good it would feel to win because I care about my horse instead of how I look on top of him. How it would feel to win at something, and maybe even make money doing it. But I'd have to do what Mrs. Sanchez says. Not get distracted.

And then there's Ethan. He wants the spot, too. But I can't think about that.

Mrs. Sanchez shows me how to layer the ingredients for the cobbler. The layering changes the way the heat gets around in the pan. Then she explains what she wants done with the stew. "I can do things in this pot you can't buy in a restaurant," she says.

I think Mrs. Sanchez could make a neutron bomb in a Dutch oven if she felt like it.

"The redhead gives you trouble?"

"Yeah," I say.

"No one is more prized than a good cook."

I like Mrs. Sanchez. She doesn't get distracted.

Right about the time everything is in its rightful Dutch oven, doing its beautiful thing, Justin hijacks me at the water spigot. "I'm going out to check on the white mare tonight."

So much for not asking me to get involved in this. But then I still ask, "Is she back with her band?"

"Yeah. But I've only seen them from a distance."

"Banner threatened to tell Coulter about us meeting at night."

"She's yanking your chain like she always does."

"What if she's not? What if Coulter lost this whole place because of you?"

"Why do you care? You're never coming back here."

"Why *don't* you care? You live here. Coulter's your friend." Not to mention the fact that there is a three-thousand-dollar fine if we get caught, and Justin could get his butt slammed back into juvenile detention. "It's not safe."

"What's your deal with safe? When has that ever gotten you anything?"

"I'm behind schedule getting dinner ready."

"You know what your problem is?"

"I'm sure you do."

"You let everyone tell you what lead you're on." He kicks his boot in the ground and walks off.

I drink water in the tent with Alice. It's so hot even the flies are taking naps. Alice sits on her bed reading a book from Coulter's library.

"What are you reading?" I ask.

"Meditations."

"What kind of meditations?"

"It's kind of like horse yoga. Like things you can say to yourself when you ride. You know, to be more enlightened," says Alice.

"You should tell me some."

Alice closes her book and looks at me. "You have that restless look again. You're going to take me if you go anywhere tonight, right?"

I need to get a better poker face. "I'm not going anywhere."

"Okay," says Alice. "But you'll take me if you go, right?"

I stand up and look for my canteen. I feel like I've been thirsty since I woke up.

Alice holds another package from home. She gets them so often that sometimes she waits to open them for a day or two.

"What did they send you this time?" I ask.

"Hand warmers," she says.

We bust up laughing.

An hour or so before dinner I'm supposed to pull all the ovens out and check on everything and salt and pepper the stew to taste. It's hellish hot, but if I focus I can get it done. Everything smells amazing. At least there is one thing I'm doing right around here. I cover them up and go wash my hands for dinner.

The Sanchezes make a big fuss about how I helped with cooking dinner. We all gather around the picnic tables. Everyone is laughing, smelling the food. Coulter's eyes squint in a smile as he drinks out of his canteen. Justin sits on the edge of the adult table and doesn't look at me.

I bring Coulter a corn bread muffin and a heaping bowl of stew, and he belly laughs. "Cassidy, sometimes you're downright useful."

Coulter sits back in his chair and crosses his legs. He puts a big spoonful of the stew in his mouth. His smile withers to a pucker and then twists into a tight oval. In front of everybody he spits the stew out on the ground. "What is that?"

Mrs. Sanchez looks as if she's been mortally wounded. She grabs a spoon and sticks it in the pot. Her face says it all. "What did you do to it, Cassidy?'

"I seasoned it, like you told me to."

Coulter stands, kicking dirt over his mess. "It tastes like you dumped a cup of salt in there, hon."

I can barely talk. "I did it just like you told me to."

Alice walks up behind me with her bowl in front of her. "What happened?"

All the kids are spitting the stew out. Except Banner, who is sitting innocently on a rock looking at the ground. She doesn't even have a bowl.

Mrs. Sanchez is already diving into each of the three Dutch ovens. Her face gets angrier each time. I feel myself sinking in humiliation.

Not this time, I tell myself. *This time it's not even my fault.*

"Banner," I say. I don't care if she rats me out. She's probably going to do that anyway. "You did this, didn't you?"

"Did what?" asks Banner, snorting with laughter. "Wreck dinner? I'm pretty sure that was all you, Cassidy."

"Why would I wreck dinner?"

"I don't know. Why do you do anything?"

"You can't stand the thought of me doing anything right, can you?"

"Cassidy," says Alice. "It's okay. You don't know that for sure."

"Yes, I do," I say, stepping in front of Banner and her big obnoxious red hair.

Coulter steps up to me. "Campers need to take responsibility for their own mistakes."

"This isn't my mistake."

Mrs. Sanchez marches off holding one of the pots with hot pads. Everyone else starts moaning. And they stare at me, the killer of dinner.

I don't step back from Coulter. "She did it. To spite me."

"Cassidy, get ahold of yourself."

I look through the crowd and see Justin with his head down. Thanks for that.

Banner looks so innocent it's revolting. I've had enough of everyone. I turn to go.

"Where do you think you're going?" asks Coulter. "You need to apologize, Cassidy. Now."

I look at Banner. "I'm not going to apologize for something I didn't do."

"You won't?"

"No."

"Well, there's another way you're related to your grandfather. Fine. You're welcome to return to your tent for the night. You lose all your riding privileges until you can own up to your mistakes."

"I didn't do it," I say.

"Have it your way," says Coulter. "Guess we'll break out the beef jerky and hot chocolate, compliments of Cassidy."

Everyone groans again.

Then I remember.

I grab the tongs and get down to sweep the briquettes off my last oven. I lift it up out of the fire pit with the tongs so I can put it on the serving rock and dazzle everyone. It's ten times heavier than when I put it in there. I hear a noise as I move, but I can't see anything because I'm holding a giant swinging hot thing. Suddenly, Charlie bumps me from behind. Or I bump him. The cobbler flies like fiery peach pellets into the air. Burning hot juice scalds my hand.

"Whoa," yells Coulter. "Whoa, Cassidy."

I frantically wipe my hands on my pants to get the burning juice off. It still burns. I stand up and face straight ahead. Everyone glares. Let them.

I walk past Alice, Ethan, and Charlie on my way to the tent. Even they don't look up at me.

Chapter Thirty-One

I HEAR THE scratch at about eleven. I'm wide awake. I rolled into my sleeping bag before everyone came back so I wouldn't have to talk to my roomies. The only good thing about faking sleep is that I'll hear it if Banner tries to get out of bed to do something else to ruin my life.

The second I hear that scratch I know what it is. It's not a mouse. I put on my jeans and boots and slip outside. I know that Banner could be fake sleeping, too, but it's not a crime to walk outside the tent.

Justin is in a dark sweatshirt and beanie. The whitest thing on him is his smile. I know he's not going trick-or-treating in that costume, but doing what I'm supposed to hasn't really kept me out of trouble. I follow him.

When we get outside camp I whisper, "Where are we going?"

"I told you. To check on some horses."

"Where?" I say a little louder.

He looks away, like he's figuring something. "I'm sorry about what happened tonight at dinner. Banner's a wench."

I don't want to talk about Banner. I want to talk about what we're doing. I want to talk about the questions I have piling up in my head. "Do you really think that the BLM's intentionally hurting the horses? Don't they have to gather them up or the horses will eat all the grazing grass to nothing?"

Justin says, "You'd have to see how they chase them. If a horse dies in a gather, it's one less horse to feed." He walks faster.

I jog to keep up. "So you're the thief. Are you doing all this alone?"

"I am not a thief. Thieves steal things. I let them go," says Justin. He turns to me. "And I'm not doing it alone anymore."

"Have I been recruited?"

"Do you want to go back?"

We head up the hill to the mustang pasture. The crickets are loud tonight. But not as loud as Goliath. He whinnies and snorts as we approach him in the dark. All the horses are restless and moving.

"Wait here. Just for a minute," he says.

"What for?"

I watch in the moonlight as Justin gets inside the fence with the horses, hands over an apple to Goliath, waits for him to chew it, and then bridles him. Goliath barely nickers.

I ask, "How did you do that?"

"We've been practicing," says Justin. "We've had some good progress."

Justin takes Goliath out of the pasture and over to a big rock. He ties a strap underneath Goliath's chest. "You'll hold on to this with one hand and the reins with the other. Come on. You're going to need a step up."

"You want me to ride Goliath?" I ask. "Without a saddle? Are you kidding?"

Goliath leans his head down to me, looking for more apples. He seems as gentle as Smokey. If I didn't know him better, I might believe it.

Justin laughs. "It's just in that arena he's hot now. On the trail he's solid."

"You've had him on the trail?" Justin never stops surprising me. It's both endearing and super disturbing. Mostly disturbing.

"It's not like I can ride the stable horses down below. Darius and Kaya will bust me for sure if I get into the pasture right where they can see me. And Goliath is a gladiator on the mountain. He loves it."

I look at Goliath. His huge gray body is lit up like the moon itself. It will be a glorious death.

I step onto the big rock, and Goliath doesn't move away. I reach a leg over and climb on. He whinnies but stays put. I hold my breath, waiting for the worst. But he stays quiet. He feels double the size of Smokey. And without the saddle to separate us, it's like we're fitted together. I am sitting on

Goliath in the moonlight. I breathe out. I feel like someone should make a statue of me right now. "Who are you going to ride?"

Justin reaches back in his bag and pulls another apple out of his pocket and gives it to Goliath. Then he steps on the stump and swings up behind me. He puts his arm on mine. I flinch. "Don't worry," he says. "We're both harmless."

Goliath is moving around but not bucking. "It's impossible. What did you do to him? He tried to throw you over the fence last time you rode him bareback."

"I'm persuasive. It helps that he likes you, too."

He covers my hand and puts it on the strap he has wrapped around Goliath's chest. "Don't put your hand under that rope. If something bad happens, it's better to fall off than lose your hand."

"Is he going to be okay with two of us?"

"I guess there's only one way to find out."

We start off walking. Goliath is well padded. I hold the rope and mane, and Justin holds the reins. It's not bad. Justin wedges me still with his back and his arms, which makes me feel safe and vulnerable at the same time. We start moving. Goliath is amazingly smooth. For a few seconds I'm thinking about Goliath and not Justin. Up until Justin reaches across my shoulder with his chin. "You have a very secure seat."

"Excuse me?" I say.

"I mean, you don't move around a lot on the horse. It makes this easier."

"Yeah. Okay."

We don't talk for a while after that. I can feel Justin breathing on my shirt. I concentrate on staying in the center of the horse and not fainting like a goat. I worry that we're too heavy for Goliath. I worry that we'll get caught. I worry that I really like having Justin wrapped around me.

After we get off the plateau we walk up switchbacks, and then we get up onto a wide ridge that takes us up over the mountain. The full moon gives off a soft gray light. When we come to the edge of the ridge a big dark valley sweeps below on the other side.

We're high, but not Empire State Building high. And in that valley, straight below us, are a sad little mobile home and some makeshift corrals. There's a single lit window inside the mobile home and a light up on a pole above it. I can see a truck. A BLM truck. I can faintly hear horses whinnying. Maybe it's just the wind. Or the sound of my heart pounding a hole in my shirt. I had no idea they were so close to us. No wonder Officer Hanks thinks it's our fault his horses are being released. And then there's the fact that it is our fault.

"They trapped them yesterday. They have so many in Rock Springs, sometimes it takes a week to get permission to bring a new group in."

"Justin, I thought we were going to check on them."

"We are checking on them. Then we're fixing a few things."

"I'm not ready for this."

"Okay," he says. "Do you want to go back? I'll take you back. I'm serious."

I look down at the corral and see the faint outline of the horses moving inside. "No."

"I'm going to go down there and let some horses go home. And I could sure use someone to hold on to Goliath and be my lookout. You can see everything from here. All you have to do is whistle if you see anything. Sound carries like it's in a microphone in this valley. But if I get caught, you go home without me. You haven't done anything but whistle."

He's off the horse and in the dark before I have time to explain I don't know how to whistle, not loud anyway. I sit there in the dark with hulking Goliath wondering what to do and about all the things that could go wrong. Goliath could just decide he's had it and take off. And it makes me so nervous I have to go to the bathroom.

The worst part about that is I have to get off the horse to go. And believe me, if this was anything less than a five-star emergency, I would not get off. "Goliath, can you help me out here? Just don't freak out. I will also try not to freak out."

The second bad part is I have to keep a lookout. Right there on the ledge I find a spot that I can hold on to Goliath with one hand while I hang on to weeds and lean backward with the other. Whatever I'm holding on to makes my hand sting.

When I'm done, I stand by some big rocks to get out of the wind. Goliath hangs his head toward mine, looking me over. "What?" I ask. "You do this in front of me all the time."

I decide to practice my whistle. Nothing. I mean, nothing. I try to whistle in earnest. Air, but no sound.

Just as I realize how pointless I am, Justin's shadow appears in the moonlight moving toward the corral. The horses whinny. He has zero ground cover. He walks right up to the gate of the BLM corral. Officer Hanks could come out of the mobile home and catch him any second. And I can't whistle. This is bad.

I turn to Goliath. "We have to go down there."

I stand on a big boulder, then scramble onto Goliath. It's a miracle, but I get on. We start down the steep hill. I slide all over. Even at a walk, I nearly come off. I grab the reins, the mane, and the strap to keep on. I listen for sirens or gunshots but hear nothing except the sound of Goliath's enormous steady feet.

We come off the hill. We're within a block of the house. More whinnying from the pens. I carefully slide off and walk toward the back of the pens. Justin is nowhere in sight.

I walk past a sturdy tree and hear a hissing sound that I really hope isn't a snake. A hand grabs me from the side. It's a good thing I went to the bathroom already.

"What are you doing here?"

I stare into Justin's angry face. I whisper, "I can't whistle."

"You shouldn't be down here."

"Neither should you."

I walk with Goliath for camouflage toward the pens. The horses nicker. We get all the way to a gate. It has a big, fat padlock.

The horses in the pens come toward us. The white mare is in front. She walks unevenly, dropping forward more carefully on the left side. She has dark markings on her legs, hip, and face. Her left front leg is soaked. Even in the dark I know what that is.

I draw in a loud breath.

Justin grabs my mouth.

I get it. I shut up.

The white mare whinnies shrilly at Goliath. Goliath whinnies back in a baritone. Then other horses join in. Too much whinnying.

A light goes on in the mobile unit. A small one in the back. The bathroom. I hear something crash to the ground. A man curses. We're dead.

Justin throws his hand into his backpack and yanks out clippers. He cuts through the padlock in two tries, but the horses go nuts. We yank the gate open together, and the horses flood out behind the white mare. They run for the canyon. Dust fills my nose and throat.

There's a loud banging and shouting in the mobile unit. Justin grabs on to Goliath and swings himself up. He reaches for me, and I nearly pull him off. Goliath is prancing all over. Justin hangs off to one side and yanks me off the ground. I nearly fly right over the top of Goliath, but I stop myself and swing around. I glue myself to Justin's back. Two strides and we're cantering. Goliath follows the other horses' dust into the canyon.

As we head into the trees we hear three angry gunshots explode in the air.

We head up. Way up. I keep my mouth shut. If I open it, I might scream.

We reach the top of the ridge. Justin turns his head to me. "Hold on."

I squeeze my arms even tighter around his rib cage, afraid I'm going to cave in his internal organs. He takes one of my hands and puts it on the strap I was holding before. He leans forward and boots Goliath. We're on a flat spot on the ridge, so I don't immediately go off. But oh my freaking gosh there must be rockets inside this mustang.

Everything moves past and under me. It's terrifying. Everything I've been learning and doing seems to come together because it has to. I mean, it has to. Right now. I'm with Justin on Goliath riding across a mountain after rescuing the mare and her band. The idea flashes across my mind that even if I go to jail, or to the hospital, maybe tonight, this moment, is worth it.

We reach the end of the flat trail quickly. Goliath stops hard, and I nearly go off. Justin grabs me as I lean to one side. He points way out on the road to the headlights speeding toward the ranch. "He'll be there by the time we get there. And he'll tear the place to pieces looking for us."

"Officer Hanks?"

Justin says. "That's not Officer Hanks."

"It's the other guy?"

"It's the other guy."

"Oh." I feel like I'm still flying across the ridge. "Come on. We're almost to the pasture, right?"

"We don't have enough time. I'm sorry I got you into this." He lays his head on Goliath's neck. "Sorry, boy."

"There has to be something we can do. You can't just quit right here," I say, looking around.

"No. You've been, like, I can't even believe how tough . . . it's not that. I have a way that's faster. But it's not safe."

"What's your deal with safe?"

Justin points to a break in the trees. "Do you want to see it?"

In a few steps we're at the edge of a drop-off. It's pretty much a ski jump down the mountain from here, but if we survive, this way drops us right into the mustang pasture. It's not a bad drop for long. But where it's bad, it's ridiculous. I don't know if Goliath can handle anything that steep, but he knows. He won't go if he can't do it. That's what I tell myself.

I grit my teeth and grab the strap Justin put on Goliath's neck and wedge down my arms onto Justin's thighs. Justin literally jumps backward when my hands go shooting forward, which is perfect. Now we're wedged in. It's a hundred-percent awkward.

"Wait," says Justin.

But I kick Goliath before I can think too much.

"Stop," yells Justin, pulling back on the reins.

I ignore him. So does Goliath. The hillside drops away beneath us.

Justin yells and lets up on the reins. I lean almost all the way back, vise-gripping Justin with my arms. He leans back on me, too. My arms feel like they're popping out of their sockets. My hands burn. Everything goes blurry. At one point I see my boots flap like wings when we go over a log. Goliath keeps moving, and so do we, dropping down and down the side of the hill. It's like sliding down a twelve-hundred-pound banister that's moving side to side, up and down, and forward, with hooves.

It's probably only a few seconds. We stay on until the end. And then there's another log and my hands and arms pop free and we both go sideways off the front and drop like a sack. I hit my head on the log. Why do I always have to hit my head?

Justin lands next to me. He has managed to hold on to Goliath by one of the reins. The other has snapped off. Goliath is going nuts, stamping and hopping. He may kick us to death as punishment. I taste blood in my mouth from biting my tongue. Justin jumps to his feet and yells, "I said wait!"

I get to my feet and shake myself off. My head is still ringing, but we take off running to the pasture. Goliath lets Justin drag him with the rein. I have a stick bobbing in my hair and rocks in my boots. I breathe in dirt. I throw the switch and rip open the gate. Justin has Goliath loose in a heartbeat, yanking off the bridle and strap and throwing them under a rock. Goliath spins and kicks up his heels as he runs from us.

We run on the deer trail. It's narrow, steep, and full of

things to trip over. Even in the shadow of the pines I feel like I can see everything. The edges of rocks. Water on leaves. Changes in the slope of the ground. My eyes are burning. I feel locked in, synced to everything around me.

As we come out of the trees I see headlights again. Under the ranch sign. Justin points, and I nod. I know. I know. I have to go faster. Ahead of us the tents are dark and silent. I hurdle rocks and weeds, puffing like a freight train. I focus on my tent. But I know it's no good. There isn't time.

I suddenly realize I'm going to either wake up my evil roommate when I go in or be caught outside. Once again I've worked myself to death only to screw it up in the end. I stop hurdling.

Justin slows and gently jogs for his private cabin. No one will see him change his shirt and put on baggy sweats and tube socks.

Think, Cassidy. Think.

I run past Justin and head straight to the outhouse. I step inside, shut the door as quietly as I can, and collapse onto the toilet.

In the privacy of this heavenly hideout I pull the twigs out of my hair and wipe the dirt off my face. I swallow the blood in my mouth. I inhale the lovely lilac chemicals of the room freshener. It's a beautiful thing. I'm sitting on my alibi.

Chapter Thirty-Two

THE KNOCK DOESN'T come to the outhouse for a long time. Long enough that I have time to consider what a big mess I'm in.

"Hey, Cassidy. You in there?" It's Kaya.

"Yeah," I say in my sick voice. I'm not faking it.

"Okay, just checking. You all right?"

"I'm sick to my stomach." I can't talk to Kaya. I know I'm going to give myself away for sure.

Silence.

"Do you have a fever?"

"Maybe," I say. "I'm sweating."

"Have you been up long?"

"Hours."

"Gotcha," says Kaya. "We'll fix you up a little room in the big house. It might take a minute. The men from the BLM are here asking a few questions. You okay to stay in there a minute?"

Nothing could make me happier.

By the time I come out of the outhouse, there is no BLM truck and the breakfast fire is burning. Kaya keeps a foot or two away from me. "You poor thing."

I feel bad keeping the truth from Kaya and Mrs. Sanchez. But I let them fuss over me and put me in a room with a cot and a shower down the hall. I can't say no to that.

When I wake up the sun is on the other side of the sky. I'm surrounded by walls and a door and a clean blanket. I'm a terrible person. A dirty rotten liar and a thief. But a deliriously tired one. I fall back to sleep. When I wake up the second time there are voices in the room down the hall. I open my door a crack.

"If that beer-breathing jackass comes on my place waving his badge in the middle of the night, I'm going to give him a Wyoming welcome with my Colt." Coulter's voice is hard and sharp. "And that goes for his ten-year-old boss, too."

"I'd like to do some target practice on both of them," says Darius.

"You two both put your pistols in your pants," says Kaya.

"We can't let this escalate. You have to talk to Miles and reassure him you had nothing to do with this."

"Miles," says Coulter. "Since when did you start calling Officer Hanks Miles?"

Darius says, "Since he bought her drinks at the Grizzly Bar after the rodeo."

Kaya snaps back. "How is that your business, Darius?"

"You had drinks with Officer Hanks?" asks Coulter.

"My personal life is not the issue," says Kaya. "We have a real problem here. Riker is a bomb waiting to go off, and if he does, you know who's going to get hurt."

"Oh, Riker's a harmless drunk who talks tough," says Darius. "He can barely hold a pen to sign an IOU at the bar. It's that little prick from Washington we need to get fired ASAP."

"I think you underestimate the damage a mean drunk can do, Darius. My life has not afforded me that privilege." She looks at Coulter. "Officer Hanks has made mistakes. He's making one right now. But Riker is hardly harmless."

"They never proved that," says Darius.

Kaya says, "People prove what they already believe. I don't want Riker walking around this camp looking for trouble. Dealing with Officer Hanks is the best option we have for keeping the peace."

"Is that what you call that now?" asks Darius.

"Darius," says Coulter coldly, "Instead of asking you to take your dirty boot out of your mouth, I'd like you to go out and make sure all the gates are locked. Head up to the mustang pasture, too, and check on things. We'd hate for horses to get loose after we gave Riker such a hard time about not checking his."

"The gates are fine," Darius says.

"Check them anyway."

The screen door slams shut.

After a pause Coulter says, "I might want to refresh your memory about what happens to plenty of those horses."

I can see Kaya walking in a half circle around Coulter with her arms folded. "We both know whose fault that is. Riker ought to be put in jail. Whose side do you think I'm on?"

There's another long pause. I lean forward so I can see better through the crack in the door. Kaya is staring out the window, and Coulter's staring at her. Finally he says, "We all work hard to keep this place alive. God knows it's harder than it ought to be. But there's a certain amount of trust I have to have in people who work for me. I'd like to know you're on the right side of this thing."

"There's no right side to this. There hasn't been one of those since this country became property. You don't own this mountain or those horses, Coulter. Nobody owns those horses. And you sure as hell don't own me either." Kaya spins and moves out of my view. The door slams again.

I go back to my bed. I lie still and close my eyes. There is a barn full of stuff I don't know where to stack inside my head. Why is Riker so dangerous? Why would Kaya stick up for Officer Hanks? I saw that mare. The way the BLM treats the mustangs is terrible. It's wrong. But Coulter can't run this place without Kaya, and he knows it. I don't know who is on what side around here or anywhere. I think maybe the adults don't know either.

Chapter Thirty-Three

TWO DAYS LATER I am covered in flaming-red poison ivy blisters. On my face and hands and everywhere. I have it in places you don't want to show people. I have welts the size of quarters. Everything on my body itches, including the insides of my eyelids. I have to wear gloves to keep from scratching in my sleep.

Maybe it's a punishment for lying or letting the horses go. Or maybe it's the bush I grabbed in the dark when I was out with Justin. Or both.

I sit on the cot in my undershirt while Mrs. Sanchez coats my arms. "You have been working in the heat. This is why it's spread. But you must tell me, where did you get into it?"

"I don't know." I rub my arm.

"Don't scratch." Her eyebrows knit crossly at the top of her face, but she continues to slather on the cream. "You sure? We should kill it if it's in the camp. Is it by the garden?"

I shake my head. "I don't know." That much is true, in a dishonest sort of way.

"Wear the cream and don't get too hot. Or you'll spread it more. You have to be more careful." She narrows her eyes at me. "Things that don't get taken care of get worse before they get better. Do you understand, *mija*?"

"Okay," I say. "I'll be careful."

It's terrible thing to lie to someone who calls me *mija*.

Chapter Thirty-Four

JUSTIN AND I hardly speak for a week. He rides constantly, I'm grounded from horses for not apologizing, and I'm still decorated with welts. At dinner he never even looks up to say hello. I have no idea why, beyond that I'm hideous. Which is to say, him not talking to me is not all bad. I prefer to be hideous without feeling hideous in front of him.

Since I look like scab art, I clean. I polish all twenty-five saddles and bridles in the tack room. I sweep every hard cement and wood surface at the ranch. I wear long-sleeve shirts and a hat. Alice hangs out with me at lunch. Everyone else treats me like I'm contagious.

"Is it starting to itch less?" she asks.

"I'll live."

"Charlie, Ethan, and I are going to the pond after dinner. Do you want to come?"

"I'm invited?"

"Not really."

"Okay."

"Banner says you got poison ivy on purpose, to make people feel sorry for you. I told her that's a stupid idea. People already feel sorry for you." We laugh for a second, and then we sit and frown at the dirt together, which really is nice. I've never had a friend like Alice.

After dinner Ethan says, "No offense. But that rash looks nasty."

"It feels great, too," I say.

Charlie smiles. "My mother claims a trip to the spa can cure anything for ninety minutes. Could I interest you in a small surprise?"

We walk up a path that forks off to the trail I went on with Justin. I hate that I can't tell my friends what really happened. But if I do, then I'll just drag them into trouble. And I will have to admit to Alice that I am a horse thief, a liar, and a bad friend for not taking her with me.

"Are you still going to try out for the riding spot like that?" asks Ethan.

"I'm still grounded for yelling at Banner, remember?"

"You're grounded because you won't apologize," says Alice.

"You're grounded because you're being an idiot," says Ethan.

Charlie says, "Enough. I'm sick of horses and work and being hot."

"You can't stop being hot, Charlie," I say. "You'll just have to live with it."

"I know," he says. "I know."

We walk into a patch of trees, and suddenly I can smell the muddy weeds. I step past the pale yellow willows, and I'm standing in a holding pond. It's not the cleanest water I've ever seen, but out in the middle it looks fine.

Alice raises her eyebrows. "Mud is good for itches."

Before I know it, both boys have grabbed my pant legs and shirtsleeves. I don't fight that hard because, well, I don't want to kick them when they're talking to me again.

"One and a two and a three," they all chant.

My body lifts up sideways into the air. I feel weightless, and my stomach spins and twists. Then I am in ice cold pond water, and I don't think about itching or poison ivy at all. All I think about is getting even. I grab Charlie first. His pant leg is closest. He goes in pretty easily once I trip him from running away.

"You're mean for an invalid," he says.

Alice giggles at the edge of the pond to keep away from the splashing. I grab her by the wrist and pull her in, up to her knees.

She yells, "Swamp thing!" Then she tears her wrist away and disappears into the muddy water with a minnow jump.

Ethan jumps in full cannonball. He about overflows the pond. He pops up with his eyes wide and his mouth puckered. "That's co-o-old."

We all laugh. I'll take the cold over the itch any day of the year.

Things seem to be looking up until the next afternoon, when I get a letter from home. Actually, Kaya brings me two letters right after I finish morning chores. I sit down with the other kids under the trees by the big house. I have a letter from each parent. I know before I open them that this will be either very bad or very good. I open the one from Mom first because she gets down to business.

> Dear Cassidy,
>
> It's taken me a few days to write. There's been a lot going on here. Your dad has decided to file for divorce. He's moved on. I'm sorry to tell you like this. I'm afraid I'm not good at talking about it yet. I'm glad you're away. There is no reason for you to be here and go through this with us. It's inevitable now, and at least one of us should be happy. I'm glad you're free and doing something fun.
>
> I'll be fine. So will your siblings. So will you.
>
> I'm sorry this had to happen. I did everything I could. Your father refused to wait until you got home, and I thought you should know.

Stay strong, sweetie. Ride one of those horses for me.

> I love you,
> Mom

Dear Cassidy,

    I'm sorry to write this to you. I wish I had some softer, more humane way to be with you right now. I'm heartbroken to tell you that your mother and I have not been able to work out our differences. I wish there was a way. I wish I knew how to change her heart. But the heart is a complex and, at times, bitter thing. I hope you will be all right. You call me if you need to. If you need to come home, I think I could arrange that with your mother.

> I love you,
> Dad

I stand up under the trees and look around me, disoriented. I'm surprised to see people around me I feel so totally separated from everything but the pounding in my head. My legs feel uneven. My tongue feels too big. I go down to the creek with a rag and get it wet and then put the rag on my face. It doesn't help. I knew they wouldn't wait. What difference does it make if I'm home? I mean, I'm just their daughter. And my life will only be changed in every way by their decision. My favorite part is how they both signed their letters.

I don't hear him until he's standing on top of my boot tips. That's how far gone I am.

I sit up and shove Justin off my feet.

"What are you doing?" he asks. He sits down in the dirt with his arms behind him, like we're about to have some great chat after he's ignored me for days. "You look terrible."

I can't even be mad. All my emotions are in overdrive, like, all of them. I just need him to leave. I need everything to go away. I am capable of doing and saying anything. I'm not safe for conversation. "Can we talk later?"

His shoulders hunch over. "I'm sorry, Cass. It's my fault."

My brain isn't able to hold anything. All the space is taken with those two letters. "What are you talking about?"

"You got into this mess all over your skin when you were out with me. That makes it my fault."

Somewhere in the back of my head I know he's trying to be nice, and on a different day I'd probably be over the moon about him caring at all. But there's a full-blown cyclone spinning around in my head right now. "It doesn't matter," I say.

He looks up at me from that handsome, wrecked face of his. "You were my responsibility."

This feels like about the worst possible thing he could say to me. "People aren't responsible for each other. Nobody is." I scratch myself hard on my arms and neck.

Justin has the pained look I saw him make when I rode Smokey for the first time. "You're just going to stay mad then?"

I lift up my shirt and scratch my stomach. I don't want to explain. There is no explanation. I want to scratch my skin off. "My parents are getting divorced."

He tips his baseball hat back. His eyes look funny. "I thought they already were."

"Separated. Implying the possibility of being together again. But that's past tense. Adios." I pull on my shirt and scratch the crap out of that spot on my neck.

"I'm sorry," he says. He looks around, like he's suddenly as itchy as I am.

"They could work it out. But they won't. Because neither one of them can admit they might be wrong." My voice is sailing now, flying out of control.

He puts his hand down to me. "You want to go for walk?"

"No. I don't want to go for a walk."

"I have this place. I mean, it's not really a place."

We walk along the stream until we come to a muddy spot where our boots start to sink. Trees and weeds poke out of the mud. Bees and flies buzz. All of a sudden Justin reaches over, picks me up like I'm nothing, and throws me over his shoulder. Then he carries me across the mud. It's not romantic. It's like he works for the Coast Guard and he's rescuing me from a rooftop. I don't feel like being picked up, but I let him. I don't feel like being tough or mature or anything but sad right now.

Then he puts me down and shows me this place behind the trees that isn't muddy. It's like a spot where animals sleep with pines needles and flattened weeds. It's quiet. There are white flowers growing under the trees. I just stand there.

"You want to sit?" he says softly.

"I'm okay."

Justin steps uncomfortably close to me. "You are a lot of things, Cassidy. But okay isn't one of them." Then without any more warning than that, Justin reaches over and pulls me next to him. I look up. He's not working for the Coast Guard now.

"What are you doing?" I ask, pulling away.

He turns his head. His arms come up behind me and wrap around my back. Those ranch-kid arms I've been trying not to stare at all summer. His hands are too heavy. The air between us is too thick to breathe. It's everything I wanted but wrong. His mouth presses against mine. I feel like I'm being smothered.

I jerk away with my whole itchy body. "What the hell are you doing?"

His face is covered in surprise. "I'm cheering you up. I swear it works like a charm on girls."

Nope. *That* is the worst thing he could say to me. I take about eight steps back until I'm right up against the tree.

"My parents are getting divorced. I'm not one of your girls. And I don't want you to cheer me up."

He stands with his hands on his hips, staring at me. "Are you sure?"

"Pos-i-tive!" My face explodes in weak, horrid tears. And I'm not even sad. I'm so mad I want to flatten something.

"Wait, I'm sorry," he says.

I sit down on the mud and take off my boots. I'll never get this out of my clothes, but I'll be damned if Justin Sweet is going to make me ruin my only pair of cowboy boots. I stand up with the boots in my hands and shake them at him. He actually looks afraid of me. "Don't you ever . . . kiss me because you're sorry for me. Ever." I cross the thick, muddy mess with my boots in my hands and get out of there fast.

Chapter Thirty-Five

I GO TO my tent to clean up, but I can't cool off. The tent is empty, so I don't have to explain why I look like a hurricane victim. I huff and puff and clean my damn jeans. I walk myself to the big house and find Kaya inside. "I need to call home."

Kaya is working on the computer, and I'm pretty sure she doesn't even hear me she's so startled by my appearance. "You look . . ."

"I'm ugly and dirty. I know," I say, almost yelling.

"I was actually going to say your sores look like they're scabbing over. You may be on the mend. But I'm sure it's still uncomfortable. Is that why you need to talk to your mom or dad? Did you say which one?"

"It's personal. I'll start with my dad." I want to ask Dad about Mom's "moving on" comment first.

"I see," says Kaya. "Boy problems?"

"My dad is honestly the last person on the planet I would talk to about a boy."

"You can't just call because you want to. I need a reason."

I would stamp my feet and throw my fists in the air if it would help me get my way. I'm about three weeks past thinking straight. "He has cancer."

"That's not funny, Cassidy. People's dads really get cancer."

I don't care what anybody says. Adults want you to lie to them. And this is none of her business. "A boy problem, a really big one."

"You poor thing, Cassidy. I get it."

She doesn't. She really doesn't.

The phone rings five times before it goes to voice mail. I hear Dad's recorded greeting, and it sends me all to pieces. I don't leave a message.

Kaya is in the other room. I dial Mom. She answers on the second ring. "Are you okay?"

"Yes." The sound of her voice distracts me. *Don't get distracted*, I tell myself. *She's half of this.*

"Are you sure?" she says.

"What does 'moving on' mean?"

Mom breathes heavily into the phone. "This isn't the time or the place to discuss that, Cassidy. I was angry. We need to talk about this when you get home."

The thing about having parents who speak in code is

that I have learned to speak it myself. I hang up without saying good-bye.

Just like I used to do, I get in my bed and stay there. That night I am visited by Coulter, Kaya, and Mrs. Sanchez. When I have nothing to say to them they eventually send me off to take a shower. My roommates give me a wide berth. Alice brings me a flower, and I thank her. But once the lights go out and Banner starts snoring, I can't lie in my bed for another second. I walk to the river, away from the horses. Away from everyone. I hear thunder someplace far away.

"Did you read my mind or something?" Justin asks, jumping out of the dark. He's had a shower. I can smell the soap on him.

"Leave me alone," I say. "I mean it."

"Okay," he says. He stands there like I didn't just ask him to go. "Did you see the storm coming in?"

A skiff of wind dusts up some pine needles onto my pant leg. He might be right, about the weather at least. "I told you to leave me alone."

He walks away for a few steps and stops. "All I want to do is apologize."

"You don't want to 'cheer me up' again? Because that would be something."

He keeps his distance. "Can I come closer so I don't have to talk so loud?"

As mad as I am, I don't want an audience right now. I

motion to him with my hand, and then when he gets close enough I put up my hand to tell him to stop.

"I was trying to cheer you up. I did it wrong. I'm sorry about that." There isn't a shred of defense in this voice. Just a flat-out apology. He rubs the front of his jeans like his hands are dirty and stares down on the ground. "I've got two gears with girls. Park and high. I don't know how to be around a person I actually care about."

He's doing this now? Now, so I can't even be mad at him. Fine. Let him be honest. But my insides are still shredded about my parents. I mean, I should have figured. But I didn't want to. I hoped for the best. I guess that never goes unpunished.

He shifts his weight uncomfortably. "You have every reason not to, but will you walk with me?"

"Are you serious?"

"I'll leave you alone. I just want to show you something. You don't even have to talk to me."

I don't move. "What kind of stuff? I'm not up for surprises right now."

"You'll like this. At least, I think you will. It's just pretty."

"Huh," I say.

"I swear," he says.

We walk out into the moonlight a few feet apart and stop. The thunder is letting loose on the other side of the valley. "We're going to get wet if we go very far," I say.

"Yeah, let's cut up here," he says. He points to a small hill that juts out from the mountain.

Above, the stars are being swallowed by an enormous gray cloud that is lit from the back by the moon. We walk up to a big boulder with a flat spot and sit down. We're above the horse corrals, so the sound of the horses' bells clink up to us in the dark. The river rushes over rocks in the distance. I watch Justin's silhouette. He tips his head like he's about to talk, then doesn't. It makes the air feel charged. Finally he says, "I'm sorry about your parents. You must love them a whole lot to want them to be together so bad."

I ask, "Don't most people want their parents together?"

He leans back. "Bet they're real smart, like you."

"Way smarter. About some things."

"Like what?"

I sigh. "My dad's a poet and a professor. My mom does the mom stuff, and she's an accountant."

He says, "That's cool. My dear old dad's a drunk. My mom died when I was two."

I want to crawl into a hole. "I'm so sorry," I say.

Justin says, "No. It's okay. I mean, it isn't. But . . . anyway, I've seen pictures of her. We look a lot alike, except she has darker hair and a normal nose."

"What happened . . . to your nose? Is that okay to ask?"

He flinches. Not okay to ask. *Nice one, Cassidy.*

He touches his face. "A horse kicked me."

"I'm sorry," I say. "You've had some terrible things happen to you."

"It's not that bad. Look at me tonight. I'm sitting here with you." He laughs. "Look at that."

A giant rosy cloud is moving into the valley. In less than a minute it fills the horizon.

"I've never seen a cloud that big in my life. How come it's pink like that?"

"It's a cumulonimbus cloud," says Justin. "It's bringing the storm."

Right as he says this, the enormous cloud lights up. Explosive bright yellow flashes inside, silhouetting portions of the cloud too dark to light with a flash and a puff of smoke. "You can't hear it because it's too far way," he says. "There's enough electricity in that cloud to light up half of Wyoming, but there's no way to catch it."

"How come you know so much about clouds and stars?"

"No reason, really. I see them all the time, so I thought I'd find out how they worked."

The light changes color. First orange, then white, then back to yellow. It makes pockets of shapes like rooms. Suddenly, a lightning bolt escapes and shatters the sky. The thunder rattles the air so hard my teeth shake and my hair tingles.

I move closer to Justin. Not close enough to touch him, but close enough to feel him next to me.

The lighting inside the cloud strikes again and again. Each time, different parts of the cloud light up in brilliant color. It's like fireworks in a see-through house. My mind scrambles for a word. "Incandescent."

"What's that?" Justin asks.

"It's a word my dad taught me. It's a kind of light you get

when you heat things up. The heat makes the light."

Justin looks up. "That's a good word."

We sit still on the rock while the lightning and thunder continue. Justin turns to me but doesn't touch me, like he promised. I put my hand under his hand and feel the hot charge go through me. He slides his fingers into mine. Our skin is rough and calloused. I pull his hand tight to mine.

This time, Justin doesn't smother me. He keeps his hand in mine and takes the other so that we face each other. His wide palms and long fingers radiate up through my whole body. Something winces hard inside and stops in my chest. I'm scared. I feel all the things that can go wrong. I feel all the heaviness and hurt and waste of what's happened to my mom and dad. I know this isn't going to work. It can't. And maybe when it doesn't, it will burn the last bit of life out of me. But when I look into Justin's face, all I see is Justin, lit in the bright broken flashes of a cumulonimbus cloud as big as the Wyoming sky. He leans closer. I lean closer, too.

When his mouth finds mine, I feel the hardness shatter. And I'm weightless. Brilliant.

Incandescent.

Chapter Thirty-Six

THE BEAM FROM the flashlight is blinding. "How's Justin?" Banner asks.

I sit down on my cot and get in the sleeping bag with my clothes on. I'm too kissed to care. "Can you put that light down, please?"

Alice is sitting up in her bag. She doesn't say anything.

Banner sighs. "What have y'all been doing out there in the rain, Cassidy Carrigan?"

"Watching the lightning."

"You know what Coulter says about shenanigans. He might have to send you home. And fire scar face."

"There weren't any shenanigans," I say.

Alice says, "It's not safe to be out in the lightning."

"It was far away. I'm sorry, Alice, I didn't mean to worry you."

"What do you think, Alice? Should we help our roommate by telling Coulter about her unsafe behavior? It only seems fair."

Alice drops down on her sleeping bag and turns her back to both of us.

I say, "If things were fair, I wouldn't have lost my riding privileges."

I turn my back to her and close my eyes. With my lids closed I see the sky in dangerous little pieces. Everything spins. How can I have opened those letters, hated Justin, and kissed him all in the same day? How can I have so many edges loose in my skin?

Banner puts the flashlight at the back of my head. "If things were fair, I'd be home sleeping with my boyfriend instead of weirdoes."

It's funny, when Banner says this I realize something that should have been obvious to me. Things aren't fair. Of all the lies I've believed without realizing it, this is maybe the worst one.

I taste the cold rain on my mouth. I shiver under my blanket, but I'm not sure if it's from the cold or Justin.

Banner says, "He's just going to break your heart. You know that, don't you?"

"Good night, Banner."

"Don't say I didn't warn you."

"Okay."

She's probably right, but tonight I choose not to believe it.

Chapter Thirty-Seven

THE NEXT MORNING Coulter and Justin aren't at breakfast. I pretend to eat something before nonchalantly asking Kaya where they are. "They went to town for groceries," she says. "Your mother called three times. I can't keep telling her no. She would like you to call her tonight. Your dad said he'd like you to call anytime."

I nod noncommittally. I have no intention of calling my parents in this decade.

"They sound like very nice people."

"They're nice," I say. "Just not to each other."

Kaya looks at me with all the pity her enormous brown eyes can generate. "I'm doing the Sunday Supposition. So you'd better come."

I don't want to seem as hostile as I feel. "Yeah. I'm tired," I say.

"Sleep after. I need you there."

Kaya gathers us in the meadow above the tents and coaxes us into a few hokey songs. And after every song we sing I feel more miserable. My body itches and aches, and my head is throbbing from trying to not think. I love Kaya, but what I really want is a ten-hour nap and another shower.

"I'd like you all to take a mental journey with me," she says enthusiastically. She walks around us, trying to get our attention. "Come on, guys. Help me out. Everyone partici-pate. I'd like you all to imagine yourself going on a long, dif-ficult hike. What do you pack, Ethan?"

"Food," he says. "Lots of food."

"Medicine," says Devri.

"Clothing that wicks," says Charlie.

"A sleeping bag," says Alice.

"A map," says Danny.

"A gun," says Scotty.

"Porn," says Granger. Everyone laughs.

Kaya asks, "What would you pack, Banner?"

Banner is propped up on one elbow on her blanket. She doesn't answer. There's an awkward pause while Kaya waits and then speaks. "Anyone else?"

"How about a plane ticket?" asks Banner. "Can I have one of those?"

"Not exactly," says Kaya smiling. "But let's talk about that. At times we all want to escape. Danny, could you come up here?" Danny hustles up to the front, and Kaya puts a backpack on him and opens the flap. "What if I offered you heavy rocks?" Then Kaya picks up a big rock off the ground and puts it in his pack. Then she does that a few more times until Danny sags a little. "What if every time somebody lets Danny down or does something deliberately to hurt him he gets a rock? And the bigger the problem it makes for him, the bigger the rock."

Danny looks stressed now.

"If somebody's jacking me up, they aren't going to be messing with my backpack," says Ethan. "Because that is going to stop."

"Exactly," says Kaya. "But if you're angry at someone, that's what you do. You let them put this heavy thing in your pack, and then you carry it around for them. And if you did something wrong that you can't get over, you carry that around, too. Pretty soon there's no room for anything else."

At this point I come out of my daze to realize that Danny is not the subject of this supposition. And I am genuinely not in the mood. Sometimes people do stuff. And it's their fault. And you know it is.

"Yeah," Banner says. "What if you like the rocks?"

"Can you explain that?" says Kaya.

"Maybe the thing that you hate is the thing that makes you strong."

"That's wise, Banner. But how can carrying around anger and frustration hurt you, too? Or slow you down?"

"You know what? Forgiveness is bullshit," says Banner. "It's for suckers and saints. And have you seen what happens to saints? Nobody wants to be them."

A handful of kids laugh, but mostly it just feels awkward.

What's really awkward for me is that I agree with Banner. Which is why I'm not going to apologize to her. I raise my hand. "May I be excused, please?"

Kaya doesn't say anything for a few seconds.

Finally she flutters her hands in the air, like she's waving insects away. "Okay . . . good discussion. Let's get some rest before the week starts up again."

Alice and I go out to the mustang corral with some pilfered snacks. Goliath comes right up to me. I think he smells the potato chips on my hands. I'm not giving him potato chips. But I'll scratch him all day long if he lets me.

Alice says, "That's amazing. How do you do it?"

"Bribes."

Alice shakes her head. "That's not true. I've seen you with him. I've seen you with all the horses."

"No, I totally bribe him with food."

"It's only a week before the tryout. Are you really not going to compete because you're too stubborn to apologize to Banner?"

I stop scratching Goliath. "I'm the worst rider here. And I'm not apologizing for something I didn't do."

Alice sighs. "I would love to be able to ride like you. So free. And what about Goliath? Do you want Banner to ride him? And what if there was some other reason that the soup got spoiled? I mean, you aren't sure, are you?"

"Did you see her smug face?"

"So you're going to let this chance to ride get away from you. Just like Kaya said."

"Not like Kaya said. Kaya acts like people can get over all the crap that's happened to them by tipping it out of their backpack. Sometimes you can't do that. Sometimes it's part of the backpack."

Alice kicks a rock. She won't look at me. If I can make Alice mad, I am a truly horrible person. "What about a friend who won't take me with her? Should I stay mad at her?"

"I'm so sorry, Alice. I couldn't . . . I had to go alone."

"That's a terrible apology. I want you to ride Goliath in the horse show. Ethan can't beat Banner on Goliath, but you can."

My mind is a few circuits past blown. I can't believe that Alice has this much faith in me. I can't believe she's even talking to me after what a jerk I've been.

I start scratching Goliath again. Finally I say, "You're a really nice person, Alice. Not just nice. You're generous. You see the good in people."

"Thanks," says Alice.

Goliath's gray muzzle drops in front of me. I think about the ride, the jump we made together. The feeling of flying, of being totally caught up in riding, trusting him to carry me over the edge of the cliff. It still doesn't seem real. If we can do that, it shouldn't be that hard to ride in circles around an arena. But I'll never know as long as I keep being "right."

I hate it just the same.

I find Banner. She's sitting on a rock painting her fingernails. Only Banner would go to the trouble of painting black on her nails when we're all up to our necks in actual dirt. Behind her, Devri and her backup singers are all giving themselves skin cancer on some flat rocks.

Banner looks up at me as I approach, and I have an overwhelming urge to turn and run. I picture Goliath. "I'm sorry I blamed you without proof," I say.

"No, you're not." She smirks. She's an excellent smirker. "You're just saying that so you can compete against me."

"I don't like the way you treat me or anyone else who gets in your way. But I shouldn't have blown up like that."

She looks at her nails. "I'll tell Coulter you apologized."

"Thanks," I say. Then I wait. Where's the rude dig or the sarcastic swipe?

Banner blows on her nails. I'm think I'm dismissed.

Chapter Thirty-Eight

I WATCH THE BLM truck coming down the drive to the ranch all the way from the entry sign. It's a bigger truck than the one Officer Hanks drives, with a much older paint job.

Coulter has already had Darius bugle us into formation. We're doing something today called the "spook alley," which is supposed to help us get our horses ready for the auction. I have Roanie haltered behind me. She starts swishing around all over the place the minute that truck comes over the hill. She's a sweet horse, but sometimes I hate how sensitive she is. It makes me feel like I have a five-foot display screen on my insides.

Ethan steps beside me with his bay. "You see what I see?"

I say, "I see a truck. What do you see?"

"That's not Hanks's truck," says Ethan.

Justin joins the party a little late. He walks up to Roanie

and runs his hand on her to let her know he's there. For once she doesn't broadcast my emotions or even flinch. Unlike me, who goes stiff as an ironing board. He stops right behind me.

Ethan looks over at Justin and me. My face burns, but I keep looking straight ahead. I don't need to be Ethan-ized this morning.

"Have I missed anything?" Justin asks.

Ethan says, "Looks like I have."

Roanie paws the ground. So much for not broadcasting. I say, "The BLM's coming to visit."

"I saw 'em," says Justin.

I try to ignore Ethan looking at me and Justin. Coulter is talking, and I'd like to know what he's saying.

"The next two weeks will make or break you and your horse. Maybe you'll go home and tell your nanny that you trained a horse or you won't, but your horse will get adopted or he will go to Rock Spring and face a fence until he dies. And if that pressure bothers you, I'm glad. Everyone is going to have to do a whole lot better than I've seen so far if we're going to get these horses ready."

The BLM truck stops a ways from the arena. The truck doors slam. It's the jerk from the rodeo. The one who followed us from the holding pen. Coulter keeps on talking.

"There is a pattern to things. But often we have to be out of the pattern to know how much we're in it. So we have to break our pattern by letting go of what makes us feel safe."

The BLM officer comes to the edge of the arena but

doesn't interrupt. He's a bulky man with broad shoulders and a paunch. He hasn't shaved, and his gray hair could use a comb. But it's his mouth that gets me. His lips don't close all the way, like he's about to take a bite out of something. Everyone steps away from him.

Coulter readjusts his hat and then softens his voice. "Alice, would you be able to help us out today?"

"Yes, sir," says Alice.

"You play the violin, and I hear you are a very good student. You're a successful young woman."

"Thank you, Mr. Coulter."

"How do you do it?"

Alice holds her neck still, but you can tell she's forcing herself to because she stops blinking. "I practice and study a lot."

"Wonderful. What else do you do?"

She's quiet for a few seconds. "I imagine how good it will feel if I don't make any mistakes."

"Alice, come out here. I'm going to ask you to play a game with me. Is that all right? It will kind of be like Simon Says. Do you know that game?"

Alice looks at Coulter and then nods. It's obvious that she's sorry she agreed to be part of the lesson today. But she walks slowly out to the middle of the arena. I can feel how much she hates being the center of attention. Coulter holds his hands under his chin, pressed together like he's praying. "Now hop on one leg."

Alice looks at him in surprise and then hops.

"Now stick your arm out."

She sticks out her opposite arm. It's hard to keep going in the dirt. Her foot teeter-totters on the uneven ground.

"Great. Now sing," he says with urgency.

Alice looks at him again, her eyes enlarged. She puts both her feet down. "I can't sing."

"Alice, I asked you to sing. And I'm sure you know plenty of tunes, but you are deeply, and I mean deeply, afraid of failing. And today I am going to ask all of you to fail." He looks out at all of us. "I want you all to find something you and your horse are terrible at and fail the hell out of it. That's your job. At least for now."

The BLM man skirts around the campers and edges toward us. I feel Justin stepping away from me. He sidesteps into the cluster of the guys. Scotty and Granger look behind them. No one talks, but they make room for Justin.

Coulter blares on. "All our patterns have their uses. But the old stuff isn't going to get you through today. Alice, you are going to go first through our spook alley. And all you other campers are going to follow her. Listen to your horse. If he hates something, you stop there. Go slow. Figure it out. You let it feel like it's his idea to fix this fear. You don't put any limitation on how long it will take. Until you fix it as a team, you fail as a team. How does that sound?"

"Like a load of horseshit," says the BLM officer. His voice is deep and carries into the arena.

"Good morning, Riker. How convenient of you to drop in during a period of instruction."

The man casts his eyes around and locates Justin. He doesn't look at anyone else. Justin looks only at the ground. "I need to talk to your employee."

My legs get soft under me. I knew they would find out it was us. I knew they would.

"If you mean Justin, he was about to assist me," says Coulter.

"He can assist you later," says the man.

"Of course. Where are my manners?" says Coulter coldly. "Justin, let's you and I step into the big house with our guest. Kaya and Darius will start the obstacle course. Remember, campers, I said fail. This does not mean get kicked. Two horse lengths between horses."

I try to make eye contact with Justin, but he's buried under his hat. Coulter swats me on the back as he walks past. "You fill in for Justin, will you? This obstacle course can get a little much."

I bust over to Kaya. She's going over a clipboard, checking off people as they go into the arena. "What's going on?"

"Nothing to worry about," she says, not looking at me. "This isn't your concern."

"Why does that guy want to see Justin?" At least I can try to find out if Kaya knows.

Kaya hits her pen on her clipboard, obviously irritated that I am still talking to her. "Justin will be fine. Coulter is looking out for him."

"How does somebody like that keep his job? I mean, he's horrible."

"He's local," says Kaya. She looks like she's swallowing something that doesn't agree with her. "He used to be okay. Started drinking too much when his wife died, and it got the better of him. People overlook things if they consider you one of their own."

Darius yells, "Cassidy, get out there and start walking around with Alice."

I look into the arena. I can make out blue plastic tarp, a ramp, barrels on their side, and some old tires in a circle. There's more, but all I can think about is what is happening in the house. What if they know? What will happen to Justin and Coulter? To everyone? Roanie starts prancing all over the place. The poor thing doesn't need a spook alley. I am scaring her to death all by myself.

Ethan walks next to me. He lets out a long breath. "I didn't even punch the racist. All this country living is making me soft."

"Will you hold Roanie while I go help Alice?"

"Sure. Fail the hell out of it," says Ethan.

"Absolutely," I say.

Alice's horse is jumping across a barrel away from her. Then his back legs go up and strike at the air. Alice yanks on the lead and gets him on the ground, but he's dancing all over. I get next to her as fast as I can.

"How are you two doing?" I ask.

"He's scared," says Alice. Her voice is trembling.

"Let's figure out why."

She backs him off the barrel, and her black gelding stops moving, but his ears are straight up and his eyes are wide. Poor guy. I look at the barrel. Then I look at Alice. "Did you have him sniff it?"

Her arms are shaking. "He's too scared," she says.

"How about I hold him while you show him? Go sit on it. Show him it doesn't hurt you. Make it fun."

"Fun? Will that work?" She hands her horse to me. He bounces a few steps and then freezes, his eyes popping out of his raised head.

"We're failing, right? It doesn't have to work."

She goes to the barrel and straddles it like a horse. Everyone is so surprised they break out laughing. Alice isn't usually the queen of comedy. She looks at the kids cracking up and then leans all the way backward. Then she lies on the barrel like she's sleeping. When she stands up everyone claps. I hand her back her horse, who has started to settle down.

"Now what are you going to do?"

"Fail until we figure it out."

I turn to the campers, stroke my chin like Coulter, and talk in my deepest voice. "How does that sound, everyone?"

Everyone whoops.

Darius walks in with Danny, and they go down to the far end of the arena where the blue plastic tarp is spread on the ground to simulate water. Horses are terrified of it at first. Darius talks to Danny the whole way and isn't a jerk for a change.

As they pass me I say, "Do terrible, Danny!"

Danny smiles. "You too."

I go out and get Roanie. Ethan comes in with Scotty, who is still trying to look cool, but his paint yearling is bobbing like a balloon in the wind.

"Come on, Scotty!" I yell. "You get to fail, too."

Scotty flips me off, but he walks a little faster into the arena. Ethan nods in approval.

A door slams. I look toward the big house. The BLM officer is walking fast, but he doesn't have Justin with him. He's headed for his ugly old truck, hallelujah. Then the door slams again. This time it's Justin. He's also walking fast and alone. He storms off to his cabin. Last but not least, Coulter comes out and slams the door one more time. That door is going to pop off its hinges.

Coulter walks to us. He looks like he's ready to rip somebody in half. Roanie instantly starts channeling how worried I am by jumping around. I tell myself to knock it off. I was supposed to screw this up. It's okay if everyone is a disaster out here. Coulter stomps out to the center next to me. "Ladies and gentlemen. Please shut up."

The arena is instantly silent. Even the horses are quiet.

He yells loudly, "Alice, what have you learned?"

Alice freezes. I see her start to pull her head down and then stop.

"Alice!" he yells.

Her head bobs, and then she extends her posture until

she grows three inches. "I don't know if I have learned any-thing, sir."

"What were you supposed to learn?"

"To fail."

"Did you do that?"

"Not really."

"What happened?"

"I took my horse to the barrels."

"Did you go over any barrels?"

"No."

"So you failed."

"No, Mr. Coulter. You asked me to fail as a team. And we were successful in that."

"What happened?"

"Well, at first he nearly kicked me. But I worked with him and Cassidy helped me and I started laughing and I re-laxed and then the horse did, too. I think if I keep doing this, practicing, but not really getting upset when it doesn't go right, he'll do it."

"Alice. You've failed me."

She tilts her head back and sticks out her chin. "No, I haven't."

"Is that right?"

"Yes, sir. I can't fail."

"Why not, Alice?"

"I don't know. I just can't. Not if I'm trying."

"Trying to do what, Alice?"

"Trying . . . until we figure it out."

"Thank you, Alice," says Coulter. "Now, which of you brave hearts are still going to try out for the riding position? This will mean more work on top of me working your guts out anyway. Justin has been doing his best with this mustang gelding, but if you decide to do this, you'll be riding a horse that can hurt you. This isn't for beginners or crybabies."

Ethan steps forward. "Me."

Banner steps forward. "Me."

I cover my eyes with my hand. "Me."

"All right then," says Coulter. "Tryout in one week. Auction in two. We have ourselves a horse race. Now, one last thing. There has been some activity with the mustangs that the BLM are collecting. My contract to train mustangs is dependent on a good relationship with them. So I cannot have anyone involved in that kind of activity. Is that clear?"

A few people nod.

"No. I mean, I need you to promise me to stay away from the wild mustangs. Even seeming to be the problem is a problem. Things are tense. Some ranchers are looking for target practice."

He goes around the circle, and every one of us promises to leave the wild mustangs alone, including me. Unfortunately, the person who should be making this promise isn't even here.

Chapter Thirty-Nine

JUST BECAUSE YOU throw down doesn't mean you automatically acquire discipline. In fact, I'm so scared that working hard is the last thing I want to do, because then I have to face what I'm trying to do. And Justin's big brown eyes aren't helping. It's like someone has unscrewed my head and poured heart-shaped marshmallows inside. To say that I'm distracted doesn't quite capture it.

The first day I ride in an arena, Goliath lets me know what I'm in for. All three riders get a turn to ride him. I get picked to go first, which I think will be grand because he's not grumpy yet.

But the minute I take him in the arena I know that what I'm asking from him here is not what he wants to offer. We're not on the trail, I didn't bring him an apple, and he's not feeling it. He lets me get on, but he crow hops, drops his head, and kicks the fence post. All of which is better than what he cooks up for the other two. He rears up halfway on Banner, and with Ethan he intentionally trips, trying to throw him off. So I guess I should be grateful. Justin is mortified. He's been telling everyone what a great horse Goliath is turning into.

Darius, Coulter, and Kaya give each other knowing nods of disappointment.

"Well, there goes this year's trophy," says Darius. "They'll laugh us out of the fairgrounds if he acts like that at the auction."

"Maybe we can get him calmed down enough to get him sold," says Coulter. "These kids will ride him two more weeks."

Kaya taps her pen on her clipboard. "I don't think you should have kids on this horse, Coulter. The last thing we need right now is another injury."

I stand next to Coulter and Justin. "He's not like this with Justin," I say. "Tomorrow, let's just have one person ride him, and we'll rotate. I think three riders a day is confusing."

"They'll only get one more ride before the tryout," says Kaya.

"That's not enough," says Banner.

"No, Cassidy's right," says Coulter. "This horse's a different kind of customer. Let's make it one rider a day, and we'll have the tryout Saturday. Justin, you hop on him today and let him know that he can't act that way."

Justin gets on, and Goliath drops his head and trots the fence. I could swear he picks his legs up when he comes around to us to let us know how much he would rather have Justin ride him. Both Ethan and Banner scowl at me, as if it's my fault Goliath is a butt. But I don't care. Three different riders a day will just make him confused and angry. You can't bully a horse like that.

And, by the way, Justin looks incredible on Goliath. I wish he could show him, but I guess since Justin works for Coulter he loses his amateur status.

Ethan leans over to me. "Just because you're hanging out with him now doesn't make you an authority on that horse he rides."

Banner stands with her arms folded, watching every move Justin makes. I can see that she thinks that Justin looks incredible, too. "I'm really going to enjoy this competition."

The schedule for the week is that we do the spook alley obstacles in the morning with the yearlings and start the chores in the afternoon so we don't wear the horses out in the heat. We groom, feed, water, shovel, polish tack, mend fences and equipment, chop firewood, chase chickens, and work in the kitchen and garden. We do everything at a new level of intensity. Well, we're supposed to. I love the work, but I'm intensely aware of Justin.

On the afternoon before the tryout it gets so hot that Coulter makes us stop so we don't all get heatstroke. He tells us to go jump in some water and team build, which I think is leadership talk for "have fun." There are two places to swim at the ranch. The closest one is the pond. It's muddy, and you can see it from the big house. The best spot is a hike from the ranch. Kaya and Darius say they don't want to walk that far so Justin can supervise us. Right. We all throw on our cutoffs and get going.

We follow the creek that flows through camp upstream about a mile where it gets deep in a stand of willows. The guys all cannonball in the second we get there, because that's a rule written in guy DNA somewhere. Devri and her friends try to lay out and immediately get thrown in. Then there is a frenzy of pushing and daring and jumping until we're all in dunking one another and officially having a good time.

The water is dark and cold, which is heaven after a summer of dust and heat. And for the first time I think since we got here, we're all having fun together without being supervised. I'm not sure what I love more, the cold water or the freedom.

It's deep enough that we can get in up to our armpits in some spots, or float on our backs. A few kids start having chicken fights, which is where small people sit on bigger people's shoulders in the water and try to push another team's small person off into the water. It usually takes about ten seconds for it to become more like Mortal Kombat.

Granger yells at me. His shagster beard still hasn't filled in after growing it all summer. It's just long in patches, which makes him look feral. "Hey, Cassidy, be my partner. We'll take on Banner and Scotty."

Banner stands on the side of the stream looking like

the calendar girl shot for July in her microscopic shorts and soaking-wet T-shirt. Scotty looks at her hopefully. She doesn't immediately say no.

I say, "I'm okay. Thanks, though."

"Oh, come on," Scotty says. "Are you scared?"

Scotty just wants Banner to climb on him.

"I'm like a foot shorter than Banner," I say.

Granger laughs. "You totally shanked Coulter. You can take her."

"I didn't shank anyone," I say.

"Don't bug her, now" says Banner. "Nice girls don't play chicken, do they, Cassidy?"

After a summer of saying it, she still manages to make my name sound like an insult.

"I wouldn't know. But I don't want to."

The boys moan. I look over at Justin, who is still sitting on a log dangling his feet and supervising. He's the only guy wearing a shirt, so it makes him look like he's the lifeguard. Even Charlie is going topless. But that's Justin. Man apart.

Charlie is flirting with Devri by splashing her with water. Scotty keeps doing backflips right next to Banner, and she's fluttering her lashes like tractor beams. Alice and Ethan are looking for frogs together. Izzy and Andrew are making out, as usual. There's something in the air. I look up at Justin. He's looking at me. I put my head under the water.

This team building could get out of hand if we stay here too long.

I slide off under the water and flip over onto my back. I

let my feet bob up. The stream carries me, and soon I'm slipping downstream, floating like a stick in the sun. Over me is a painted blue sky and large Wyoming clouds. The water level drops, and my feet skim the mossy rocks. My hair floats behind me.

"Excuse me, ma'am. Where you going?" Justin asks, floating up next to me.

I look at our toes bobbing side by side. "No place."

"I'm afraid I'll have to supervise that." He takes my hand, and we let our bodies float together, laughing as we try to keep the perfect balance while holding hands. Inside I am so light I think I could float without water. I lean my head back all the way so I can see the whole sky. Justin's hand is wrapped around mine. I want to stay floating right here forever, but the current keeps moving us, taking us farther downstream.

After a few minutes we come to an eddy shaded by willows. On the riverbank the grass squawks with grasshoppers. The willows hang over, heavy in the heat. Justin drops his feet and takes my shoulders so I float in front of him, anchored by his arms. The cold and the heat and the way Justin is looking at me make my head spin. I close my eyes, letting the water pull at my sides. Justin drops down behind me, his chest pressed against my back. Just for a second his hands relax. I open my eyes, thinking he's letting go. "I got you," he says.

I swivel around in the water until I'm facing him. My legs loosely wrap around his. "Maybe I have you."

He raises his eyebrows and then pushes at my legs, but

my legs are a lot stronger than they used to be. Justin says, "Now you stop that, before I lose my mind. Except it's about two months too late for that."

"What does that mean?" I say.

He looks away.

My face heats up. I drop my legs and try to stand up in the current. When we were floating, the current felt easy. When I try to stand, it feels like it's shooting past. I don't mind. I really don't. I put my hand behind Justin's neck. His muddy brown eyes are on mine. He leans down and kisses me. His lips are cold like the stream.

"You know they are going to come find us down here, right?" I say.

He looks upstream. "They're busy."

We step farther toward the bank to get out of the current. The willows make black shadows on the water. I feel a chill run through me from the shade and from standing halfway out of the river. He pulls me next to him, and his wet T-shirt is cold on my skin.

"How come you wear your shirt in the water?" I say.

"How come you do?"

I laugh. "Should I take it off?" I'm kidding, but after I say it I don't know if I'm kidding. I have a suit on underneath my shirt. Well, sort of a suit. A sports bra. A smallish sports bra.

"You first," he says.

"No, you," I say, and I whirl around his back. I tug at the back of his shirt, and just to be stupid I lift it up. He jerks away. "Don't."

Justin's back is covered with ugly red slats of skin. The scars aren't new, but they look deep.

"What happened?" I say, floating back from him.

He pulls his shirt down. "I did some bronco busting before I knew better."

"You got those from getting bucked off a horse?"

"I got dragged."

His face is wrong. I don't know what my face is doing, but I have to grab a handful of willows because I'm floating away. "What happened?"

"I got dragged," he says. "That's all."

I'm not a doctor, but I don't see how being dragged could make those scars. I feel so messed up I don't know what I think.

"God. Don't be stupid. Have you never seen a cowboy with his shirt off before?"

I don't answer. But I see his nose differently now.

"We'd better get back," he says. "Scotty's probably broken both arms trying to show off for Banner."

We get out of the water without touching each other.

I walk back to camp with Alice. She talks about looking for frogs with Ethan. It's like she's obsessed with frogs. Maybe she and Ethan were looking at more than frogs. All I can think about is Justin's back. Who does that to a person? What happens to a kid who is treated like that? Could that be from riding a horse? I mean, could it?

Chapter Forty

IT'S HOT, REALLY hot, the day of the tryout. It's hot enough that I expect Coulter will call it off. We've all had a full day of work already. It's not like we couldn't do it in the morning. I'd be fine with that.

Instead, every last camper comes to the big arena to see who is the fool who will get to ride Goliath at the auction. Coulter holds out three pieces of straw to his three contestants and lets us draw. Ethan will go first, then Banner, and then me. Which means Goliath will be tired and out of patience by the time he gets to me.

The tryout is pretty simple. Coulter wants each of us to come in, saddle, and mount Goliath. Then ride him around at all three gaits. And then, if we would like, demonstrate a small trick. Since we haven't really practiced on him, we just show what we can do with him cold, and then Coulter picks the rider he'll train with.

Justin stands next to me hovering. "You ready?"

"I'm pretty nervous," I say.

Justin frowns at me. "Stay off the reins. Keep him focused. Make it about him."

Banner is wearing a long-sleeve black shirt with silver snaps. In the heat. She has her hair tied back and make-up on. She looks professional. Ethan and I look like ranch hands. "Good luck, y'all," she says smoothly.

I help Ethan get his rope and everything ready to go. Charlie is slapping him on the back making him more nervous. Ethan leans over to me. "Banner looks good, huh."

"Don't worry," I say. "You'll be great."

"That's one big horse," Charlie says, walking away.

Goliath is antsy the second Ethan takes his lead line. Ethan's size alone makes him look more like a cowboy than any of the other campers, but Goliath doesn't buy it. Ethan gets Goliath out into the arena okay, but Goliath strikes out his front hoof when Ethan pulls on the cinch. Ethan freezes.

Coulter says, "You got it, son, just keep easing him into it."

Ethan keeps going slow, and he manages to get on. But he rides Goliath like he's waiting for an explosion. Everybody else is, too. On the trot Goliath starts dancing sideways. Ethan takes hold of him hard. I don't like how hard, and neither does Goliath. He flips out his back legs and bucks Ethan to the ground.

Ethan gets up okay and shakes it off. He didn't get stepped on or hit or anything. But his ride is over. We give Goliath some water, unsaddle him, and get ready for round two.

Banner takes ahold of Goliath's lead rope like she's having her hand kissed. He backs up on her, and she startles. *Good boy, Goliath*, I think. *Nice instincts.* Then instead of cracking him like I've seen her do with every horse she's ridden since she got here, she slows way down. "Come on, sweet boy," she says.

Sweet boy? I want to hurl.

And he totally goes with her.

She walks out into the center of the arena where the saddle is sitting on a rack. Goliath is calm and attentive. Then she saddles up Goliath flawlessly and swings up. The whole time she's sweet-talking Goliath and rubbing her painted fingers all over him. Once she's in the saddle, she walks him an extra long time to warm up. She keeps talking to him and rubbing him. Her legs and posture are perfect. She looks happy and poised. The way I want to look.

Then she executes her pattern. Like, totally executes it. She moves from walk to trot to canter like a machine. I keep waiting for Goliath to buck in the corner or fight the bit or do something. But he doesn't. He's fine. When she's done, she stops Goliath with one gentle jerk of the bridle, and he stops.

"Well done," says Coulter. "What do you have for the grand finale?"

Banner pats Goliath's neck and whispers something to him and then jumps off his back by pushing her hands in front of her and throwing herself backward. It happens so fast Goliath doesn't even kick. She lands on the ground like a gymnast and walks around to grab her reins.

The bleachers erupt in applause. Like Banner is so great. Okay. She is. That was gutsy and brilliant.

"You're up," says Justin. He tries to smile. We both know that Banner just won.

Goliath and I have history. We've shared produce and midnight rides together. Unfortunately, that history means he starts off by walking right up behind me, looking for his apple. I'm so nervous I'm going to screw up, I don't realize what he's doing until he knocks my hat off and nearly charges over the top of me. Coulter tips his own hat down. "Are you walking that horse, or is he walking you?"

While I'm picking my hat off the ground, my eyes catch Banner watching me through the gate. Coincidently, as I see her smirk I remember what an inexperienced rider I am. Then I remember that Goliath doesn't like arena riding. And I don't like it much either. I breathe as slowly as I can, which isn't slow. I get the big guy to the tie-up and get him saddled. I talk to him, but I don't say much.

Finally, I lift my short legs into the stirrup and shotput myself onto his back. He holds still for me, which is generous on his part. We walk without a problem. We trot. I'm not pretty or smooth like Banner, but I stay upright. I'm feeling like this is going a lot better than it could have. Then I brace myself and ask for the canter. I feel every bit of my breakfast in my throat, but I try to stay calm.

I finish and stop. As I do, I see Banner staring at me through the fence, still grinning. I have to do something spectacular to finish, or it's all for nothing. I haven't ridden well enough to beat her on horsemanship. But doing things gracefully has never been my style anyway.

Justin carries a wood box from the spook alley out into the center. As he walks past he says, "Give him time to get up there."

Of course I will. We can do this. We're going to do this. I can feel it.

I scoot Goliath up with a tap-tap of my boots. He tugs backward, and I tap again. He moves away from the wood box. This is not the start I had in mind. He's supposed to be going the other way.

"You getting up on that thing or not?" asks Coulter.

I circle the podium, kicking and prodding impatiently. Then I do it two more times. It's no use. I'm not a good enough rider to fake my way through this. He just doesn't want to do it. But I need him to do it. He has to. This is the tryout. I give him one more kick. He bursts away from my feet onto the podium and goes right over the top, bucking but not throwing me off. Finally I get him under control and bring him back to the gate.

I can't look at Coulter or Justin.

I get off Goliath. The best cowgirl won. And Goliath's her horse to ride now.

My mom and dad call that night. I tell Kaya that I'll call them back tomorrow. I know Coulter says failure teaches you something. But right now it just feels like it teaches me to fail.

Chapter Forty-One

THERE ARE A lot of things I expect the day after I blow the tryout. Like Banner victory dancing until the summer ends. Or Justin not talking to me. Or Coulter and my friends being disappointed in me. Or just a nauseous sadness overtaking me. What I'm not expecting is Banner lying on her sleeping bag silently crying in the middle of the afternoon.

To be honest, at first I think she's making fun of me.

She's staring up at the tent roof like I'm not there. They look like real tears. But how can you know?

"Banner?" She doesn't answer.

I don't know what to do, but it seems like I ought to do something. "Banner?"

When she finally talks, her voice is sharp and weirdly high. "If you try to make me feel better in any way, I will tell Coulter that you are sleeping with Justin."

"I'm not sleeping with Justin," I say.

She turns her head. "That's your problem."

I start to walk out of the tent out of sheer uncomfortableness, but then I can't. "Is it your boyfriend?" It hits me that I've been watching Banner read her mail from this guy all summer and I've never even asked what his name is. "I guess I don't know his name."

She pauses. She reaches for her journal, and I think she's going to throw it at me. But instead she opens it and pulls out a letter. "Spider. Spider Garcia. And he says he has to think about the consequences of us being together." She looks up. "Can you believe that? I fall for a guy who has more ink on his body than this stupid journal, who races motorcycles, and now he wants to be responsible. You just can't trust people."

I sit down a few feet away. "So what do you like about him? Other than the ink."

Banner sits up all the way and pulls her legs underneath her. "Are you trying to cheer me up?"

"No," I say. "Would you rather not talk about him?"

"I could talk about that idiot all day. That's the sad part. He's out of control, like, completely no fear," she says, a smile stealing across her face. "He has a perfect butt. And he gets me. At least, I thought he did."

"I'm sorry, Banner. Really."

"It's fine. Guys are nothing. Lose one, find another one, right?" She drops back down on her bed and puts her back to me. I pat her on the shoulder as I head back outside.

I'm not sure what just happened there. But Banner and I were almost friends for five minutes.

Justin and I haven't talked much since I yanked his shirt up in the stream. I was busy blowing the tryout and all. I know I need to apologize. Not halfway. All the way. I don't even know what that was on his back. And I had no right to assume or act differently around him because of it. I stole that information.

I find him picking ingredients for Mrs. Sanchez in the garden.

"How's the cilantro?" I ask.

"You might want to go help with your roan. They're trying to trim up her muzzle, and she won't hold still for nothin'."

I look at Justin's arms and shoulders, the way he stands with his feet out. The way he's leaning forward toward me. I say, "I'm sorry I got into your business in the stream." And then I do something I feel bad about. I pretend to believe something that I don't because it's easier. "I've just never seen someone get scratched like that by a horse."

He stands up and grimaces. He shakes out the delicate green leaves. "You want to come to my cabin tonight?"

"Your cabin?" The words just don't want to come out of my mouth.

"Is that okay? I want to talk to you."

I could point out that we will probably get busted by

Darius or Kaya before I even walk in the door. Or that he could talk to me right now, here, in the daylight. Or that it seems like a really, really bad idea for us to be hanging out in his room, considering who my roommate is. Or that I don't know what he's really asking me. Instead I say, "I'll come when I can."

I wait so long for my roommates to fall asleep that I'm sure Justin will be in REM sleep by the time I tap on his rickety cabin door. He opens the door before I even get my first tap. I stand there with my fist in the air as he pulls the door away. He's in a pair of basketball shorts with a tank top on. He invites me in without talking. I feel guilty instantly. This is a bad idea.

But I do want to talk to him. And maybe you can't say some things about your life in the middle of a cilantro patch or in the doorway.

I walk in and look around because I'm nervous. There isn't much to see but Justin. A bed, which I do not want to look at. A beat-up chair. Clothes lying around, shelves and a desk made out of boards and bricks. Justin is pretty much the only amenity. So I look at him. Even in the yellow shadows of this poorly lit place I can see red stripes showing from under his tank top. If he got those scars from a horse, he was dragged a long way.

"Banner give you trouble when you left?"

"No," I say. "But she's going to be tough to work with tomorrow. Her boyfriend dumped her."

"Oh great," says Justin, scratching his hair and making it stand up on his head. "Why am I always working with emotional women?"

I cross my arms over my chest. "Is that what I am?" I'm kidding. Of course I'm emotional. The first time I met Justin I yelled at him.

He steps forward and uncrosses my arms one at a time. We stand that way for a moment, with our hands together like we're dancing. Then he puts one of his arms around my waist. "I like your emotions." His fingers touch a hollow spot in my back I didn't know I had. It sends a shiver all the way up my spine. "Like that one." He pulls me even closer and moves his fingers up my back. "And that one."

I say, "I don't like the sound of this list."

He relaxes and leans back. He tilts his chin to the side like he's making the list right now, a painfully specific list, like not just the thing, but the kind of thing he notices about me, which means he may notice me a fraction of the same obsessive amount as I notice him—and this makes me feel more naked than if he was making the list out loud.

We stand loosely against each other, waiting. Then he kisses me, just as I am thinking I'd like that. And that alone, that feeling of him knowing what I want, right as I wish for it, is so electric that even without a cumulonimbus cloud, there are small sparkling explosions in my head. He kisses my chin and then works his way around to under my ear. His hands are slow and warm. More fireworks. I hold his neck with my hands. And then we're kissing like we're starving. And it's the Fourth of July, flashing and exploding until I think the sky is going to catch on fire.

He picks me up with those arms I've been gawking at all summer. Why am I so short? He can tell I'm not comfortable so he puts me down and sits on his squeaky bed. And then I'm really uncomfortable. It smells musty but not awful. Like Justin. He sits next to me. Everything about this is a bad idea, but if I'm kissing him I won't have to think about it.

"Are you okay?" he asks.

"Do I look not okay?"

He half smiles. "Maybe it's me who's not okay." He looks up at his ceiling like he's going to break some bad news to me. "When you look at me with those green eyes of yours, I sometimes stop breathing."

"Don't stop breathing," I say. "Definitely don't stop breathing."

And then we both stop breathing because our mouths are doing something better. He pulls me down on the bed next to him. And I'm suddenly the perfect size. It's like I was made to fit here next to him on his squeaky, musty bed. His hand moves up my arm and stops on my face. He sighs, and I think maybe he forgets to breathe again.

And then, just as I feel myself surrounded by my own happiness, twisted perfectly under his arm, I remember this is me. I know what happens when I feel this happy. Maybe

I've never been this happy. I'm not supposed to get my hopes up. Justin is flammable. You don't get to keep that kind of pure imploding energy if you're me. Or anyone maybe.

He leans across me and starts kissing me again. A lot. And then everything is too much. The bed and the fireworks and the way he's wrapped around me. The crazy-happy-cloud feeling turns to suffocation. Too much Justin, too much being in his room, too much making out, too much of the crazy feeling inside me, kicking to get out.

I pull away from him and make a space between us. "You said you wanted to talk."

"What?" He laughs softly.

I think about this for a second. I sit up and straighten my shirt on my shoulders. "What did you want to talk about?"

"Do you want to talk right now?"

I stand up and back into something behind me. "Sure."

He sits up on the edge of his bed. "Did I do something wrong?" His voice is gravelly.

"No. I mean, you said you wanted to tell me something."

He gets up and walks past me and finds his flannel shirt. I watch him button it up with tight, precise fingers. He does have something to tell me. Something that he was going to tell me, after whatever he thought was going to happen had already happened.

He turns around and faces me. "That rancher, Henry Helford. He talked the BLM into helicopters. They'll fly those god-awful machines around, scaring the horses so bad some of them will get their legs broken. They'll push as many into holding pens as they can Thursday night and then haul them out of here Friday while we're gone."

"So you want to go out after the gather." Here it is. Like I knew it would be.

"It's not a gather, Cass. It's a mob." Justin voice becomes urgent. "They have no right to do it. They've already met the quota. This is personal. Pure mean-spirited vendetta, and Hanks is not just going along. He's paying a damn helicopter to do it."

"I promised Coulter. We all did."

Justin rubs his face with his hand and walks in a tight circle around the room. "Coulter made you. That's not a real promise."

"If I make a promise, it is one."

"That's fine." Justin looks away. "I didn't say you had to come with me."

"Don't act like I'm a coward. I still have the battle scars from the last time."

"So you blame me."

"I don't blame anyone but myself. But we promised. And the BLM is out for blood. What if they catch you and then they close this place down and no one can train the twenty horses that get homes every year? For all you know, they are setting you up. This whole thing could be to bust you."

"Maybe," he says bitterly.

"So don't go."

He slaps his hands against his sides. "You don't get it. These horses don't belong to us. We act like it's our job to catch them and train them, but our job is to leave them alone. They already know how to be horses. Live or die, no one has broken them or beaten them or whipped the living shit out of them yet. No one has tried to make them something they aren't and cut their hearts out for free." His voice shifts and cracks. His eyes are watery. What's happening? "Don't you get that?" he asks, covering his face.

And then I do.

I finally do. I finally get the part about Justin and the mustangs that I have been blind to—because whatever hard thing has happened in my life, nobody, absolutely nobody, has ever beaten the shit out of me. No one has ever broken my nose and blamed it on a horse or carved a map of hate on my skin and called it an accident. The scar I have on the back of my head really was an accident. So I don't get what Justin has been through. But at least now I get what we're talking about. He's every chased, beaten, whipped, trapped, broken horse he's ever touched.

Our eyes collide. We're both scared. Really scared. I reach my hand out to his shoulder. "Justin. Who did that to you? Are they . . . where is your dad?"

He slaps my hand away. "Are you coming with me or not?"

I take a deep breath in. He's upset. I need to stay calm. "They're baiting you. This is totally a setup."

"You're just afraid." He knocks the books off the table with the back of his hand. The pages flutter open like escaping birds and drop lifelessly to the floor. I should get out of here. But I don't care. I care about what we are finally talking about. Him and the mustangs.

I get in front of him, staring up at his angry face. "I want to keep the mustangs safe just like you do. I want to run out and throw open every gate from one end of this stupid country to the other. I want to jump over the edge and not look. That's what I want. But that isn't real. It's just some romantic idea. Sometimes you can't get what you want, and you have to make something else work. God, Justin. Don't go."

There's a knock at the door. My heart stops. Or it feels like it. We both stand frozen.

The knock comes again. It's quiet. Justin walks to the door and pushes it open. A woman's low, unhappy voice says, "You know better than this, Justin."

"I do," he says. "She was just leaving."

I can't get out of there fast enough.

Kaya's face is tight and pale. Her coat is zipped up to her chin. "Do you want to get sent home, Cassidy?"

I don't answer. I don't apologize.

"Tomorrow you call your parents. First thing in the morning. And if you don't, you will be on the next bus out of here. Is that understood?"

I nod. I understand.

"I thought I could trust you, Cassidy."

I thought she could trust me, too. But no one trusts me now. And they shouldn't. What do I know? The more I try to help, the worse things get. I'm so mixed up and mad and sorry and embarrassed and guilty and scared I just go back to my tent, past Banner curled up smugly in her red blanket, and climb into my rotten, no good, villainous sleeping bag. That's how I know I'm the villain of my own story. Not even I like me anymore.

Chapter Forty-Two

I TAP MY teeth with my fingers before I pick up the phone. I cross my legs and then uncross them. I look at the dirt in my fingernails. Kaya is waiting out in the hall to make sure I call my parents. I look around Coulter's office. Without Coulter staring me down in his chair I can actually look at something besides him. The room is full of trophies of all shapes and sizes. There are pictures of old clients and kids from twenty years ago. I get up and walk down Coulter's memory lane, wondering what has happened to all these people. Did coming here turn them into teachers and ranchers and activists and leaders, or was it just another thing they did? A way they spent their summers before they ended up like everyone else.

I call my mother first. "Hello," she says politely. My mother has impeccable phone manners.

"Hi, Mom," I say. "How are you?"

"Well . . . I'm glad you called. Finally."

"I'm sorry. I was upset."

"Are you still upset?"

"I thought you were going to at least try to work things out."

"Cassidy." There is long pause on the other end of the phone. This is how it is talking to both of my parents now. Everything is this calculation where they think about how to say things that are going to be awful no matter what words they use. "I've been miserable for a long time. Making it official is hard, but it feels more honest. Parents don't need to share their misery with their kids. But you're old enough to accept someone else's disappointment besides your own."

"Okay," I say. There isn't much more to talk about, I guess. And if I keep talking, I'm just going to get mad. We're all disappointed. We all don't get what we want. Everyone loses. It seems so pointless. "Why?" I ask. I'm not even talking to her.

"Why what?"

"Why now? Why not in a month or a year?"

Mom doesn't answer for a long time. I wonder if I've lost the connection. I wonder if she's going to tell me what's really been going on with Dad this last year.

Finally, she says, "You just can't love some people. They won't let you." It's like a slap in the face. I tell myself she's just upset. She doesn't mean to be that cruel about Dad. She makes a breathy sound and then clears her throat. "I shouldn't have said that. It's just . . . I need a new dream, honey."

Mom lets me be quiet now. I hear the twins come yelling into the room where she is, probably the kitchen, and then Kidd barks, and I realize that even though I'm homesick, I'm also glad I'm here in Coulter's office, where I have something else besides that tiny kitchen with all its broken pieces of what could have been. I don't know what it's like to be my parents. It must be soul crushing. Nothing makes up for what we all lose now, but at least sitting here I can imagine a time when it won't always be about what went wrong.

My mind surfs over the summer. Unpacking that first day with Alice and Banner, and feeling like I'd made the biggest mistake of my life, and then looking up from the dirt at Justin an hour later and being absolutely sure. Doing chores with Ethan, cooking with Mrs. Sanchez, getting on Smokey for the first time and losing the chance to ride Goliath in the auction. Fighting with Justin and then making out with Justin and then fighting again. Lying, running, cantering, laughing, spinning, spying, and being shot at in the dark. The world is much more complicated than when Mom dropped me off two months ago, but it's bigger, too, and the mistakes I make, all four thousand and nineteen of them, are mine.

"I'm sorry, Mom. I'm really sorry."

"We all are," she says. "But maybe things can get better now."

I should call Dad. He'll be pissed if I don't, now that I've called Mom. But talking to Mom, hearing her beaten-up voice, doesn't make me feel like "things can get better now." It makes me furious. At him. Mom has her problems. No question. But he left us. For weeks I've been feeling calmer and calmer about the whole thing. Now everything has gone back to being a giant suck storm. I shouldn't call him when I feel like this. It's a bad idea.

"Dad?" All I need him to do is tell me there has been a terrible, terrible mistake.

"Cassidy?" His voice isn't just far away, it's at the bottom of the ocean. That is not what I need right now. He clears his throat. Twice. "How are you?"

"Guess how I am."

"I'm so sorry, Cassidy. This isn't what I wanted."

"So why is it happening?

Pause. Longer pause. "It's complicated."

"Make it simple for me."

"Cassidy . . . this isn't going to help anything."

"Did you cheat on Mom? Yes or no."

"Yes."

"Why?"

When he speaks again his words are drier. You could make croutons with each arid syllable. "That's not any of your business."

I can't stop myself. Somebody has to say what's really happening. "Why not? We're a family. You're wrecking our family."

In the geological age of silence that follows I get some of my sanity back. I feel a little bit sorry.

"Sometimes people change, Cass. Your mother and I don't fit anymore. We're not getting a divorce because I cheated. I cheated because I wasn't happy."

The smallest, tiniest part of me remembers who this is. But it's too small to slow down the rest of me. "Are you happy now?"

"I'm heartbroken. But it doesn't mean I'd be happy with your mother. It means that we need to find another way to be happy. All of us. Your mom and I love you very much."

Nope. I'm furious again. "Until I don't fit?"

"You're angry. I get it."

"You don't, Dad. You really don't."

After a few minutes Kaya knocks on the door. "Are you all right, Cassidy?"

That would be cool. If I was all right. But I my hands are shaking. And my blood is pumping so hard I think I'm going to blow up my eyeballs. I open the door.

"You want to talk about it?" says Kaya.

I look at Kaya's face. Something about the creases around her eyes tells me that she has yelled at people in her family, too. More than once.

"Not really," I say. "But thanks."

Chapter Forty-Three

I'M DREADING SEEING Justin the next day, and when I do we act like strangers. He eats his eggs by himself, and I surround myself with Ethan, Alice, and Charlie. The space between us should make it easier, but it doesn't. Just the sight of him turns me inside out. I give Charlie my breakfast and head off to do chores.

It's good to sit alone on the tack room floor scrubbing silver on the show halters. It gives me time to cool down, but it also gives me time to realize how little time is left here. We have one week to get ready for the auction. And a few days after that we go home. Even with everything going on here I don't want to go home. In fact, it shocks me to realize I'm dreading going home more than I was dreading coming here.

After chores Coulter leads us all to the arena, where the mustangs are corralled. He holds out his hands to us as if he has to shut us up, but we're patiently listening for instructions. "You are all doing wonderful things with your yearlings. Now you must prepare them and yourselves for separation. Your job, like any good trainer, is to teach your student to become independent. Your yearlings should be able to work with all of you, switch back and forth, stand next to other horses, walk over obstacles, and adapt to change."

Adapt to change. Yeah. Not my specialty.

I play some games with my mustang gal pal, Roanie, like dragging the lead line over her legs and running my hand all over her ears. She's a good sport. But when I take her for a walk, we pass by Justin's cabin and she jumps all over. Has a total meltdown. Roanie and I are a little too connected.

After I work with Roanie I decide to apply the "change lesson" to myself and go out to the small arena where Banner is riding Goliath. Justin is leaning against the fence on the inside, watching them both intently. He doesn't look up when I approach. It seems appropriate that I'm talking to him through a fence. Kind of a warm-up for when I visit him in jail.

I put my arm on the rails and watch silently for a minute. I'm not sorry to say all three of them look way stressed. For some reason Banner is wearing spurs. Goliath needs someone to kick him with sharp metal like a fire needs a bucket of gasoline. And on top of it she's bumping his nose with the bridle. Poor guy.

"Why's she doing that to his head? He hates it." I say this loud enough for Justin to hear me through the fence. Banner can hear me, too, as she rides by, which I am fine with.

A gust of wind blows up the dust in the arena. Justin drops his hat down to cover his face. It also makes it so he doesn't have to look at me when he talks. "She's trying to get him to collect up, tuck in his head. Show horses are worth more."

"Nobody's going to buy that mess," I say. "Goliath doesn't need spurs. He needs her to calm down. Why can't she ride him like she did in the tryout?"

Banner rides past again. "You lost, remember?"

Justin smiles at that. Because it's hilarious.

"That doesn't mean I'm wrong," I say. "He's not a Lipizzaner. He's a mustang."

Banner keeps hassling Goliath with her spurs. Goliath's tail is ringing in time.

I say, "He's going to blow up."

Justin says to me, "Maybe you should go do something else for a while, Cass. I think you're upsetting him."

"I'm upsetting him? Banner might as well light his tail on fire."

Justin nods. "I'll get to work on that."

I walk away. It's fine. I lost. Not my business. They both know a lot more than I do about horses. But behind my back I hear Justin yelling, "Banner, lay off the damn spurs."

Justin and I avoid each other at dinner. But I avoid everyone. I try to eat my four hundredth serving of baked beans for the summer, but I can't do it. I'm starting to dream about baked beans. I offer my food to Charlie.

"No thanks," he says. Tonight he's looking especially dapper in a jean shirt and a belt buckle that looks like it comes from under my grandpa's bed. "Surprisingly, I have lost my appetite for baked beans as well," he says. "But you should try food. You've been out running around with those mustangs so much you're starting to look slightly malnourished."

"Yeah," I say.

He looks at me seriously. "I heard about your mom and dad. That's hard."

I might wince a little when he says this. For a horse thief I have a pretty poor poker face.

After washing the dinner dishes, I walk down to the corrals.

The sky has gone pink and orange. The cooler air is settling in for the night. Goliath is chomping down his hay, bullying the yearlings like usual. I lean against the fence. "Do you have a minute?"

Goliath leaves his dinner and walks to meet me at the gate. He noses around but doesn't seem too upset when I'm empty-handed. "Hey," I say. "Thanks for letting me ride you. Sorry I blew it."

He hangs his nose in my face and lets it rest there.

"The thing is, no matter what I do, in just a few days

Coulter is going to take you off this mountain, and you probably won't come back here. I won't see you again, or even know what happens to you."

I don't cry. That'd be stupid. I mean, he's a horse.

I look at big, granite-colored Goliath and the mountain. He belongs here. At least one of us should get our happy ending. I look at the gate. It's just one stupid piece of metal that stops Goliath from being where he was before. Free. I reach up and scratch Goliath's neck. Then my hand runs across the Arabic-looking code burned under his mane.

"I'm sorry," I say. And I really am. Because as I touch these symbols I know that Goliath is not a wild horse anymore. He's stamped with a return address. He eats apples out of my hands. He'd be recaptured in a week. And he'd get sent to Rock Springs instead of the auction. They'll never take all the mustang out of him, but the fix is in.

I think about what's going to happen at the auction. The real purpose of why we're going. Even more than the yearlings, Goliath has to show well. Adopting a four-year-old is a risk most people aren't willing to take. And he needs an owner who will value what he is.

"No matter who shows you, Goliath, you have to perform like a champion."

I see Coulter coming up the trail. He walks right up to me and slaps me on the back. "Did you see her ride today? He looks like a maniac with her on his back."

"Is that my fault?"

"Hell, Cassidy. Any idiot can see you've got him eating

out of your hand. You're going to have to teach Banner whatever you did to get that jughead to like you."

"I was just thinking that."

"That's what I like about you, Cassidy. You're a genius. Now fix it."

I walk back to camp and find Mr. Sanchez. I hate what I'm about to do, but I'm going to need more apples.

That night I come back with Banner to the corral. Goliath likes the apples from her hand as much as mine. It about kills me.

"This is what you've been doing in your pj's?" she asks. "Seriously?"

"Otherwise he whinnies. All night long sometimes."

"You walk all the way out here, and you and Justin stand around and watch him eat? That's it? That's so sad," she says.

I try to think beyond Banner. It's not about her either. "We ride him, too. He's sweet on the trail. If you're easy on the rein and give him some space, he has it in him to show well."

"You've been riding him on the trail in the dark? You're crazy and sad, Cassidy," says Banner. "I like that. It's like an old country song. With a dog that dies at the end."

I stroke Goliath. What makes some people think it's okay to look for your weak spot and then drive a nail through it? What makes those same people so arrogant that it never occurs to them that other people have feelings at all? I have to do this for Goliath, but I don't have to be a pansy about it.

"Banner, you're a pain in the ass. But you're a better rider than I am. So while you're out there making yourself look good, make Goliath look good, too. Listen to him. Don't bully him. Sweet-talk him. Whatever it takes, okay?"

Banner laughs. "Bless your heart. Look who grew a pair?"

"That means no spurs tomorrow."

She raises her eyebrows seductively and shrugs her shoulders. Even when she's kidding it looks good. "I'll try anything once."

I walk away and let Banner and Goliath get acquainted.

The next day Banner and Goliath are better. She tells Justin she's "getting the hang of things." And she is. Once she stops bossing him around with her metal heels, Goliath stops fighting her, her riding skills kick in, and she makes him look good. Her body is graceful, measured, and refined when she rides. All the things I'm not. I learn from watching her, but it still kills me inside.

Coulter watches for ten minutes and then slaps me on the back again. So much backslapping. "That's my girl, Cass. Walk over obstacles. Adapt to change."

Sometimes even being good at change supremely sucks.

Chapter Forty-Four

THE VERY NEXT day Goliath has the best ride I've ever seen, even better than with Justin. Not only does he walk, trot, and canter for Banner, but he sidesteps four steps and then walks around the barrels. Alice and I applaud. For Goliath, not for Banner. Alice smiles at me approvingly since I told her about the apples. Banner bows from her saddle. Because, of course, this is all her. Then she does something even more Bannerish. She hops off Goliath and walks over to us so she can stand right next to Justin, like, *right* next to him.

Justin gets a funny look on his face, like there's a fly nearby, but he doesn't move.

I stand still, trying to act natural. Except I'm naturally not okay with Banner even when she isn't right next to Justin. And Justin still hasn't spoken a word to me about that scene in his cabin. In fact, he's barely spoken a word to me about anything since then.

"Wasn't that a great ride?" asks Banner. "We were completely in sync."

"He looked more natural in the bridle today. That was a good idea to get rid of the spurs," says Justin. He still doesn't move. They could press paper flowers they're standing so close.

Alice asks me, "Are you okay, Cassidy? You look like you need some water."

I need water. A few buckets full of it.

"Can you believe it?" Banner asks loudly, putting her arm on Justin's like a stacking chair. "After just a few days he's riding like a perfect gentleman." She twangs the last word so hard I see debutantes in ball gowns. She beams at Justin. "It's like we read each other's minds."

Justin nods to her and then looks over at me, like this is funny. Which it could be. But he doesn't move. I count to one and then let go of the fence and walk away. I've had enough of listening to Banner's southern gloat. And Justin is so entertained. Like he's practically *in sync* with her. Because he's such a *perfect gentleman*.

Alice walks after me. "You know how Banner is."

"Uh-huh. She's a conniving, competitive . . ."

"Okay, but they were just standing together," says Alice quietly.

"This is Banner we're talking about, right? She makes a

T-shirt look like porn. Even Goliath has a thing for her. She could seduce scorpions. And I don't see Justin putting up much of a fight."

Alice asks, "Would you like company? We could throw rocks at something red."

"Sorry," I say. "I'd better overreact on my own."

She's sweet and stops walking. "Hey, Cassidy. Just so you know. I think she did put the salt in the soup."

I don't deserve a friend like Alice. I really don't.

I walk up a bluff overlooking the ranch, and then I walk down. All I get is a headache. I finally go visit Smokey. He's chewing in the pasture. I stand next to him and lean on his shoulder. I don't really think. I just lean. I need to calm down, but I don't. If Coulter wanted us to learn how to fail this summer, I am his poster girl. I should open my own camp. A half hour later I'm still leaning on Smokey when Justin strolls into the pasture to talk to me.

"You okay?"

"I'm fine. Yourself?" I ask. Because I'm still leaning, and I'm leaning toward being pissed.

"I'm tired. That girl's high maintenance."

I stroke Smokey's mane. It's filthy, but he likes it, so I do it anyway. "She looks like she's getting over losing her boy-friend."

Justin digs a hole with his boot and spits in it. "She's cheering up, I guess."

"Absolutely. You lose one, you pick up another one, right?"

"Some people do it like that."

"My dad did."

"Your dad did what?"

"Picked up another. When he and my mom started to fight, he got a girlfriend. Or maybe he got a girlfriend and then they started to fight. I don't know. One of those."

"That's why they're getting divorced? He had an affair?"

"He told me the other day on the phone. I guess I suspected, because that's what usually happens, right? But not my dad, you know. That's what I used to think. Not *my* dad."

"I'm sorry."

Smokey shifts his weight and moves to another part of the pasture. I wouldn't want to stand here either. I walk toward the fence and lean against it, but it's not as soft as Smokey so I stand on my own two angry feet. I try to separate what we're talking about, but I fail at that, too. "People just lie, right? We all have secrets. So we lie. And then we cheat because we can't admit what liars we are."

"Cass." He steps toward me, but I step away. "Not everyone is like that."

"Really? That demo I just saw in the arena with Banner is supposed to make me feel confident? I'm pretty sure everyone *is* like that."

"Come on, Cass. Don't make this what it isn't. Shit happens."

I kick the fence. "I just told you my dad had an affair and your response is 'shit happens'?"

Justin moves backward, keeping his distance. His shoulders are up and his hands start moving even before his lips do. He looks pissed now, too. "Shit *does* happen. People lie and cheat. Nice people get sick, and little kids starve to death. Cass. You know this. I'm sorry about your dad. But don't make this something it isn't."

We both breathe hard and stare at each other.

"Exactly. Something it isn't. I'm leaving at the end of the summer anyway."

"Yes, you are," he says. He shakes his head at me, and then he looks off in the direction he came, like he has other things to do. But then he starts tapping his boot like he can't stop, and it gets faster and faster.

I want to say something. No, I want him to say something. I want him to say that I'm not some shitty summer hobby he uses to pass the time in between horses. But why can't I say that? I just can't. Because I'm a mess for sure, but more than that, I need Justin to honestly talk to me.

When he finally does talk, his voice is loud and uneven. He reaches out his hand to the fence, which is maybe nothing, but it makes me feel trapped. Crazy trapped. "Why don't you just trust me for a minute?"

I move his hand out of my way, and then I kind of lose it and say exactly what I'm thinking. "You want to talk to me about trusting you? You have scars all over your body you won't tell me about."

Justin's eyes flare and then his face goes dark. Like I've hit him, and I guess I have. I'm sorry, but I'm not. He looks at me like I'm dirt. Like I'm nothing. Just some worthless girl who got too close. He says, "I told you I got those riding."

I hate that our fighting about Banner is getting dragged into whatever happened to Justin growing up, but it boils down to the same thing. We don't trust each other, and we aren't going to start.

I say, "I'm going to leave now, okay?"

"You're just using this as a way to hide that you're too scared to go after the horses with me. That's fine. You go back to your tent. Climb in your bag and hide. That's what you do, hide."

I'm stunned by how intentionally cruel that is. That's what he'll do to cover those marks on his back. "I'm not the one hiding, Justin."

He kicks his boot in the dust. "I was tired of babysitting you, anyway. You're just a sheltered little kid. Playing cowboy. Plenty of girls to do that with around here."

I don't need to say anything now. We're done talking. All done. Turns out my mother was right about one thing: you just can't love some people. They won't let you.

Chapter Forty-Five

THE LAST FEW days before the auction float away like dandelions gone to seed. The warm wind blows through the draw in the morning, and the day disappears. We all hustle around putting the finishing touches on our horses' show routines. Sweating. Swatting flies. Cracking lame jokes. Coulter asks me to help the kids like Danny and Granger who aren't quite ready. Devri and Charlie help everyone with their costumes, and Alice and I run around trying to find what all the horses need for tack. I'm glad for the distraction. I stay as far away from Banner and Justin as humanly possible.

Banner never goes to see Goliath at night, so I do. What surprises me is that Banner sleeps like a baby at night now. I haven't seen her with a cigarette since she won the competition. As if she's suddenly exhausted after a summer of scowling at me in the dark. Or maybe she finally has what she wanted.

I have no such luck. I hear Goliath whinny, and I walk the trail.

I don't figure it will hurt Goliath to be ridden outside the arena a few more times before the auction. I tell myself it's good for him because it's bareback trail riding, but the truth is I need to ride him a few more times before he's gone. We don't go far. We stick around the bluff where the other mustangs are in the pasture. Most of the time we just walk. We hear crickets and faraway coyotes, but it's really just me and Goliath under that big Wyoming moon. Maybe I should feel wild or reckless riding alone in the moonlight, but it isn't like that at all. It's more like being part of something. Like I belong here. Like I'm free.

I wonder as I ride if that's what freedom is for Goliath, too. When a horse runs with his herd, he's doing what he was born to do, and that makes him belong. When he rides with a partner, he belongs, too. I hope the person who buys Goliath gets that.

The last day before the auction each horse is polished and trimmed and brushed. They all look beautiful, cared for, and adoptable. Roanie shines up so pretty I wish for the first time in weeks that I had a phone so I could take her picture. When she nuzzles me she smells like fresh-cut hay.

Besides primping horses, my main job is to avoid Justin. I also try to avoid thinking about the gather and Justin going after the horses tonight, but it turns out I stink at that. My mind is on a worst-case-scenario loop. The only way to stop Justin is to tell Coulter, and I can't do that. Both Coulter and Justin have trusted me. So basically there doesn't seem to be a right answer. I finally opt for the wrong answer that I can live with.

I find Justin in the barn around sunset, organizing feed. He's wearing a long-sleeve shirt to keep the hay off and sweating clear through it. Even with the sun going down it's like four hundred degrees in here. Okay, maybe three hundred seventy-five.

I walk up behind him. He turns and stares at me, puffing hard.

"I'll help you," I say.

"I'm almost done. Don't worry about it."

"No. I'll help you."

He takes his gloves off and rubs his red face. He looks out the entryway after me, then looks me over again.

I say, "Let's keep this short. It's hot in here. I said I'll help."

"I thought you said I was reckless."

"You are. I'm not doing this for you."

"I figured that. You know how to whistle yet?"

"I thought maybe we could stay together this time."

"Together?" Justin pauses, like he wants to say something but doesn't. We both stand there sweating and not talking.

Finally, he says, "Yeah. All right. Tonight. Up at the pasture at eleven."

At 10:52 I arrive at the mustang pasture. I walked faster than I meant to. I look around. My heart is racing. And not because of the walk up the hill. The horses are all there but one. I look all around the bluff, keeping as quiet as possible to hear footfalls. All I hear are the mustangs in their pasture. The moon is where it's supposed to be. I am where I'm supposed to be. I look at my watch again. Roanie walks over to me and nickers. Why am I surprised?

Justin and Goliath are gone.

When I come back Banner is lighting a cigarette right inside the tent. So much for not smoking. I don't look at her. I can't stand to. She gets up and walks over to my cot and sits next to me, dangling the cigarette in her graceful fingers. "Why do you try so hard, Cassidy?"

"Try what?"

"To make people happy. To make everything work out. You know it won't."

I don't know what Banner is talking about, or what she knows about what Justin is doing. It makes me sick to think he may have told her about tonight, too. It makes me sick to think they're together. "Why shouldn't I try to make people happy?"

"Because trying to make people happy makes people miserable."

"It doesn't have to be like that. People make it that way."

"Gawd." She pulls the cigarette out in front of her and looks at it. "And to think you nearly made me quit smoking."

"I did what?"

"Well, not just you. It's all this bullshit fresh-air, clean-living rah-rah. But it's not like I don't know what's waiting for me at home. Same old, same old. Daddy on his high horse and Momma waving the Confederate flag of 'What Will the Neighbors Say.' And me being the moody dropout."

"You dropped out?"

"I sure did. Stopped going last semester."

"Me too," I say. "Well, sort of. I stayed in bed for the last couple of weeks and flunked." This tender confession doesn't mean I like Banner. Just because we have this in common. But it's surprising—to have anything in common with the person who's making my life hell.

"Wait . . ." says Banner. "I thought you were on scholarship."

"Scholarship recipient sounds better than charity case."

Her voice lifts, like she thinks I'm lying. "Wait. You? You flunked out? You're, like, relentlessly good and hardworking."

I know she doesn't mean this as a compliment, but it still surprises me. "You think I'm relentlessly good?"

"Please. That shit with the apples? And the way you bust your hump around here? God, you even do stuff for me, and you hate me. It's excruciating. But don't worry. I've seen how much good it does. I'm back to smoking."

"Why do you say that?"

"Good girls finish last. Haven't you noticed?"

I'm not sure exactly what she means. Maybe that she has Goliath and Justin under her red spell. Yeah. She probably means that. But in a way I can't explain, her thinking that just proves to me that she's wrong. I'm not a good girl. At all. I've lied to every person I care about this summer. And I've screwed up more than I've fixed. But hearing her say I've finished last makes me realize something. If my objective is to get Goliath sold, I'm doing that. As long as he and Justin get back okay, that is.

I say, "I guess it depends on the finish line, doesn't it?"

Banner blows smoke into the air. "You're incurable, you know that?"

Sometimes it's nice to be insulted by Banner.

"Good night, Banner."

"Good night, Cassidy."

I move to the stump outside the tent. It's flat but not comfortable. At least I can lean against the tree behind it. I wrap up in a blanket so it's not too cold. Maybe when Justin comes in I can help him. I know he'll be back. Mostly I just want to be outside where I can breathe and see the stars and know when he gets here.

After an hour or so, I hear something.

It's a deer.

I curl up on the stump and close my eyes, and then it's morning.

Chapter Forty-Six

EVERYBODY GETS UP in the dark to load for the auction. Darius and Kaya have borrowed trailers from the BLM to load the horses. We're all supposed to help. Including the youth wrangler.

Ethan storms up to me. "Where's your boyfriend? We got work to do."

"He's not my boyfriend," I say.

"Well, whoever he is, go get his lazy ass up." Ethan is in no mood for slackers this morning. I wonder how he's going to feel if I open that cabin door and Justin isn't there.

I walk up to his cabin slowly. I just don't know if I'm ready for what happens if he isn't there. Justin saunters out before my hand hits the door.

"Hey," he says. Like everything is peachy.

"Hey," I say.

He walks past me to the trailer.

"Thanks for ditching me."

"You're welcome," he says, still walking.

I'm spitting mad and euphoric at the same time. Maybe the mustangs are good, too. I worried for nothing. Everything is fine. But as he walks away I see his left arm is slack and dragging. I notice he has work gloves on before he needs to. Everything is not fine.

"What happened?" I ask.

"I'm fine," he says sharply. "Let's get to work."

Getting nineteen mustangs into trailers is no easy thing. Coulter makes it more chaotic by yelling directions with lots of loud profanity and personal insults. I try to keep my eyes off Justin's arm. I distract myself by watching the ranch entrance for headlights and sirens.

Right before we all get into the truck, Justin corners me in front of the chicken coop. "Look. I'm sorry I lied about taking you. I didn't want you to get involved."

"Practically everyone here is involved if you get caught."

"They tied the white mare up inside the holding pen like bait. She could have hung herself if I hadn't shown up. After I let the horses go I did a little construction work. It will be a while before that pen holds horses again." He sounds proud of himself. Like this is a joke.

So he took the time to wreck the place. Because letting the horses go wasn't enough heat. I look at his arm and shake my head. They are going to find him now. If they find him, they'll blame Coulter. After all our hard work. After every-thing.

I look at the chickens running at my feet. They're scared by all the yelling and rushing around on the property this morning. It's not quiet like it should be this time of day. But there's nothing they can do about it. I walk away from their clatter, and from Justin, toward the trailers. I have work to do.

Chapter Forty-Seven

THE SUBLETTE COUNTY fairgrounds are in Big Piney off highway 189. And they are a trailer traffic jam, even in the parking lot. The population of Big Piney must triple with all the contestants and their families and the people who come from all over to see if they can find a horse they want to take home. To make matters ridiculous, there's also a carnival being set up on the edge of the grounds. It's not exactly the kind of thing you want going on next to an arena where twelve-year-olds are showing mustangs.

We park and get all our horses out and tied up. Everywhere you can hear people hollering to one another and horses whinnying. The air smells like diesel, fly spray, and horse manure. Also cotton candy. The cotton candy smells okay.

Inside the fairgrounds building there are stalls, a large

and small arena, offices, and concessions. All the outside noises get compounded by the echo inside the giant barn. The announcers are already blaring out instructions for the day. I can't imagine a better place to make kids and horses nervous wrecks than this one.

They start vet checking our horses as soon as we arrive. Every horse has to be certified healthy for sale and moved to a stall so the public can come browse between classes. There are four divisions, and all the contestants have to be registered. Props have to be set up. Horses and people have to be polished and buffed one last time. We move as fast as we can while still trying to keep the horses calm.

Justin stays far away from me. I keep telling myself to concentrate on the horses and the auction. I can't get distracted.

Because we're such a huge group, they stick us at the end of the building. Kaya, Alice, and Charlie have painted plaques for each stall telling a little about each horse. Ethan and Scotty and that crew have done all the wood- and metalwork. Devri and her girls have tricked out every mane with braids. The mares all have ribbons, and the geldings all have leather ties. No one else we see even has their horses' hooves blacked yet. It feels good to know that when people come into this barn to see horses, our horses own it.

As I'm putting all the horses in their stalls I notice we have two extra stalls on the roster that haven't been assigned to anyone. Kaya is nearby. "What are these stalls for?"

"The girl that didn't come, the one who would have been your roommate, and Dalton's horse. They already booked out the stalls for us, so we had to keep them."

I look at the two empty stalls. For some reason all the emotions I've been carrying around this summer seem to collide inside me as I look at those empty spaces. I think of all the horses we have just unloaded and prepped for the classes. It makes me feel like I've done something with my summer that matters. I hope Coulter gets to keep doing it.

"Hey. Just out of curiosity, did you talk to Justin last night?" asks Kaya.

"What?" This isn't how Kaya asks a question. Nothing is just out of curiosity with her. "Is something wrong?"

"No," she says. "Are you two still together?"

I shake my head. "We were never together. I was just talking to him that night you came over."

"It wasn't night, Cassidy. It was three in the morning."

I shrug my shoulders. "I don't sleep very well some nights."

"I've noticed," she says. "I bought you something for today."

"You bought me something?"

Kaya pulls a tube of lipstick out of her back pocket. The silver tube reflects the light of the breezeway lamp. She turns it over and shows me the tiny words printed on the bottom of the tube. "Outlaw Red. I thought it would look great with your dark hair and those outrageous green eyes of yours. There's a bathroom down the hall."

I look at the tube. "I've never really worn red lipstick before."

"Since when has that stopped you this summer?" She looks at her watch. "Come on."

"Cassidy!" says Alice, when I walk back to meet her for our yearlings. "What did you do to yourself?"

"Kaya said I needed to spruce up like the yearlings. Is it too much?" Kaya went a lot further than the lipstick once we got in the bathroom. She pulled out her entire show bag and went to town on me.

"You look . . . gorgeous. Kaya did that?"

My face goes hot. "Maybe she'll do it for everyone. She said I looked peaked."

"Are you and Justin fighting?"

"Why does everyone keep asking me about Justin?" I ask, looking around.

"He was trying to find you. He seemed upset."

Worry tightens in my chest. "Where did he go?"

Alice glances over at Banner. "He said he wanted to talk to you after the yearling classes."

I look over at Banner, too. She has her hair tied up neatly in a bun. She and her mustang look amazing together. The perfect couple. She is smiling so big it's startling. She hasn't done a lot of smiling this summer. It looks good on her, like everything else.

"Hey, Banner. How are things?"

"They have never been better. You're so fancy, Cassidy. Did you get a *makeover*?"

I don't take the bait for a change. "Yeah. Have you seen Justin?"

"Justin? I must have misplaced him." Her voice is easily two octaves higher than normal.

I tell myself not to jump to conclusions about Justin. She could sound this happy for a million reasons. Like dead puppies. Or the crushed dreams of little children. "Kaya wants to talk to him," I say.

"Oh, he'll turn up," she says. "It's showtime!"

The classes for conditioning and handling require contestants to take their yearlings into the round pen with a judge and release them, then come back and catch their horses with halters and show the judge how they walk, trot, stop, and back. The judge asks a few questions and checks out how healthy the horse looks.

Roanie shows like a dream. She does everything I ask her to do. After I release her, she comes right back to me. The crowd literally swoons when she comes up and drops her head in my armpit. The announcer says, "Now, there's a horse to break a girl's heart."

I want to yell at him. Roanie would never break anybody's heart. Humans are the only creatures stupid enough to do those kinds of things.

The judge only asks me one question. "What's the best thing about this little mare?"

"She's not a teenage boy." Honestly. I say that. To the judge.

The judge laughs, and he writes something down on his clipboard.

When the class is over Roanie gets third place. That ought to get her some attention at the auction. And I get a white ribbon with the word THIRD stamped on it. It's freaking beautiful.

The classes for the trail events don't go quite as well for Roanie. She's bothered by all the clapping from the audience, and she skitters away from the plastic tarp that is part of the obstacle course. But Alice's and Ethan's horses light it up. Both teams stay sweet and settled the whole time. Ethan takes first, and Alice takes second. Which is not bad for a girl who used to keep her head in her coat and a guy whose horse started out as stubborn as a ketchup stain.

The funny part about it is that Scotty takes sixth. All that groundwork he didn't want to do paid off for him as well. His nanny will be so proud.

What's weird is that Banner's horse doesn't win anything. Banner seems like she couldn't care less about the whole day. She forgets the patterns in both classes. I mean, she looks amazing. But it's like someone turned on a happy light and her eyes still haven't adjusted. Every time I talk to her she just says something that doesn't make a bit of sense and smiles.

The final class of the day for the yearlings is the freestyle. In this event we all have the option to dress our horses in costumes. Kids can bring their own props as long as they don't explode. Some contestants do a Wild West theme, or water theme, or whatever works around the trick their horse is going to do. We didn't have a ton of material to work with at the ranch, but I did manage to make a tinfoil crown for Roanie that she lets me put on her head. And she puts her front feet on a wood block and bows her head. It's cute. But not cute enough to win anything.

And then there's Charlie. He waltzes his horse out with a lion's mane made out of potato sacks and has him chase a cardboard zebra on the end of a wooden stick around in a circle. The crowd goes bonkers. As well they should. There ought to be a grand prize for Charlie and his horse. And a talent scout. A blue ribbon and twenty-five dollars will have to be enough.

The in-hand classes are exhausting and long. I promise myself all morning that as soon as I have a break I will find Justin and talk to him without getting mad. But when I finally get time to breathe, Justin is nowhere to be found. And neither is Banner.

All the other campers get together and eat greasy cheeseburgers for lunch, except Kaya, who looks like she's already got indigestion. Okay, I don't eat one either.

Kaya says, "Coulter will be in the office if you need anything. I have to run an errand."

I follow her out. "What's going on, Kaya?"

"Nothing," she says. "You did great today. I was so proud of you. You make the best of a horse because the horse matters to you."

"Thanks," I say, as she hurries away from me to her truck.

Chapter Forty-Eight

I WALK ALL over the barn and go back to the trailer. Still no sign of Banner or Justin. Coulter stops me when I'm about to go look over by the carnival.

"Have you seen Banner?" he asks.

"No, sir."

"Goliath needs to be warmed up. He's bouncing all over in his stall. This place is making him crazy."

"I know the feeling," I say.

"Yeah. Well. If Banner doesn't show up soon, we are going to have a problem. You go back there, and I'll go this way," he says.

I head to the farthest end of the barn. I don't see anybody down the corridor, but I walk to the last stall before I hear laughing. Banner. I stop walking. I stand in the middle of the breezeway. The sound is coming from the last empty stall. It's a good thing I didn't eat that cheeseburger.

"You are in so much trouble now." Then she laughs again.

There's a wrestling sound. It's muffled a little by being inside the stall, and there are horses whinnying down the row. And by the fact that I'm having a hard time thinking straight. I step forward two steps. I hear a guy moan. I can't be standing here. But I can't move either.

You lose one, you pick another one up. That's all it is. Except I can't pick anything up because everything is detonated inside me. Why is this happening? I'm a crybaby. He didn't care about me anyway. It's just a summer thing. I'm just another girl. And a hundred other reasons.

But I don't believe it. I walk forward until I can peer over the paneling through the bars of the stall grille. I see Banner's big red blanket on the sawdust, Banner's hair, and lots of Banner. Entirely too much Banner.

I step backward. I feel like I just got punched in the stomach. I turn around. I have to walk. I have to find Coulter.

"You find her?"

I can't find anything to make words with.

"You drinking enough water? You got to drink a lot at these things."

"No," I finally croak. "I don't know where she is."

"I can't find Justin either. Idiots. Probably out on those freak show rides. I told everyone not to leave the building if they had a class."

I mumble for a second and then make real words. "How long before she has to go in, sir?"

"You feeling all right, Cassidy? You look pale, even for you."

"I'm fine," I say.

"We've got to warm that horse up. He's sky-high with all these damn carnival rides. Who thought that was a good idea for a horse show?"

"Sir? Should I keep looking, sir?"

"Why do you keep calling me 'sir'? You enlist in the marines or something?"

"I get polite when I'm nervous or injured."

"I guess it's better than when you're mad. You hit people then." Coulter spits in the dirt. "Dammit. That horse needs to be warmed up to get him calmed down. He's worth a bundle if he shows right." Coulter looks at me. "You know her routine?"

My stomach flip-flops. "Yes. But Banner won fair and square."

"If life were fair, horses would ride half the time. Do you want to ride Goliath or not?"

My stomach does a double backflip with a half pike and lands in the splits. "Yes, sir. I want to ride Goliath."

Coulter smiles at me. It's a rich, fatherly smile. Like I can't remember ever having from my own father, although I'm sure I have. It makes me feel like I can ride through steel.

Then he says, "Cassidy, you were born to do this. You've got a god-given gift, but you've sure as hell earned it, too.

You ride with that in your stirrups, and people will be falling down to buy that horse. Now I have to go get you set up with the office. You go get Goliath. And if Banner shows up, I'll tell her she missed her chance. You can do this, right?"

My heart is pumping too hard. I don't think Banner missed her chance. I think she took it. And now I'm going to take mine. "Yes."

He squints at me. "They disqualify you if you fall off."

"I'd better stay on then."

Coulter puts his arm out to me and rests it on my shoulder. His big beard touches my cheek. And I think I am for sure going to cry because it's like when I was little and my parents would find me wiped out on my bike. I was completely fine until they felt sorry for me, and then I melted into sobs. But I don't cry this time. I want him to know I can do this. Because I probably can.

Chapter Forty-Nine

FOR THE FIRST few minutes I'm warming Goliath up, all I can think about is Banner showing up to claim her ride. The thought of seeing her face messes me up so completely I think Goliath wonders if I'm someone else. But when Banner doesn't appear, it occurs to me that Goliath and I are really going to do this. And we have to do it like it was the plan all along. The judges don't care that I'm a substitute. Goliath is tail-swishing and head-swinging all over the place, and guess whose fault it is? I bring Goliath in from his warm-up. He walks up next to me and blows his muzzle right in my face.

I gag and wipe my face with my sleeve. "Yeah, okay," I say. I get it.

I tie him back in his stall. I go into the bathroom, clean my shirt off, and recite our routine in the mirror. I put on a fresh coat of Outlaw Red lipstick. I may not be Banner, but I'm going to give Goliath the ride he deserves.

The class procedure is simple. First, you walk in and saddle your horse from a saddle rack set out in the middle of the arena. Then, you walk, trot, canter, and back. Then, you have three minutes to impress the judge with something unique. Unlike the in-hand classes, the winner gets a trophy and a big chunk of change because all of these horses have gone from being wild to talented performers in less than ninety days. Doing that with a horse is not a bad trick for anyone, but especially for someone who's under eighteen.

I draw a late ride, so I have to sit through all the other performances, thinking about what I'm going to do. I have this terrible feeling the whole time that I need to hurry up and get inside the arena—as if I'll be safer in there. I don't know if it's because I'm afraid that Banner will come and demand her spot back or because something else bad is going to happen, but I know I need to get going.

I don't talk to the other riders. I'm afraid of getting distracted. Even watching them messes me up. Of the seventeen horses competing, two bolt, three buck, and one crashes her rider's leg into the fence so hard the girl doesn't finish.

I pat Goliath on the neck as he prances and paws next to me. He doesn't want to be here. I look up in the stands. From where I'm standing I can look up over the arena fencing and see my friends wander in from the carnival, sitting up front in the stands with bags of roasted almonds and painted faces. I don't think they can see me. They're here to cheer on Banner, and when I walk in with Goliath I'm not sure what they'll think.

When they call my number, I practically jump into the arena. I wipe everything out of my mind but the ride. All I have to do is stay on. Goliath knows what to do, and he's magnificent. "Here we go, boy. Let's make it good."

The judge is waiting with his clipboard. The steward has already put my tack on the rack for me. I make Goliath stand with all four feet square in front of the judge.

He says, "This one's a little bigger than the last filly you showed."

I nod politely and stand at attention.

When he's walked around Goliath five times he says, "They let a little thing like you ride this great big horse?"

"Well, if the horse doesn't mind, then I don't see why people would, sir."

The judge tilts his head to me. "You've got a spark, young lady. I'll give you that much."

When the judge turns his back to me I peek up in the stands and see Coulter, Kaya, and Darius. I see Ethan, Charlie, and Alice. I have a spark. I wish I could yell that to them. At least no one is booing me. In fact, they're smiling, and Alice is giving me a thumbs-up.

I saddle my friend and mount. *Walk, trot, canter*, I think. *Piece of cake.* And it basically is. Goliath does everything seamlessly. His head stays dropped down and collected, just the way Banner taught him. He picks up the right lead on the first ask. As we canter the announcer says, "Look at this little lady. Talk about grace under pressure. Look at her go."

I bring him to a stop, back him up, and let us both take a breath. The crowd is restless. Or maybe that's me. I look out in the stands. All the campers are sitting together, except Banner or Justin. I can't think about that. Right now there is only the ride.

"And now the freestyle portion of the competition."

We walk out into the middle of the arena where the judge is standing next to the saddle rack. I dismount and take off my saddle. The crowd goes quiet.

I grab Goliath's mane and look up. I can do this. I imagine my pink boots flying up in the air when I was seven. I see the first night I climbed on Goliath in the dark. There are no big rocks to give me a boost tonight. I take a big hop and throw myself up. I'm not graceful like Justin, or Banner, but I get a leg over and scramble on. I cluck and we walk and in two steps we're trotting. The bounce goes through me like a wave. Then I pick up speed in a few steps and we're cantering. The crowd applauds. Which I could live without, honestly.

I ride forward, gaining speed. I clutch the reins with one hand and Goliath's mane with the other. We gallop like we were on the ridge, but without Justin. I look ahead, lean forward, and ride. We make a figure eight. We do it one more time, but now we go so fast my hat flies off and hangs on my neck by its string. We're covering ground. The crowd goes crazy. I can feel how happy Goliath is. We both know we can do this.

I need to go the other direction. I turn right in front of my cheer squad. My eyes catch Coulter, standing there watching me. His face is tight. Scared. So is Kaya's. Something must be wrong. What's wrong? I can't get distracted. "Here we go, boy. One more time," I say.

We canter in a circle to get back our rhythm. Goliath is going too fast. I forgot to let out my breath. My reins slip in my hand. I lean back. I feel my seat going out from underneath me. And then out of nowhere I see my mom crying. I see Justin with his arm hanging down. I see red hair and a blanket. I can't get my balance. I can't grip Goliath or it will speed him up. He stumbles with his front foot. I see a blur, and I go flying off.

I lie on the ground. The air is knocked out of me. The announcer is saying something I don't understand. I see Goliath's head hanging down, sniffing me. I put my hand up and pet his muzzle. I shove down my arm to sit up. Nothing's broken. I've gone off a horse before. I stand up.

I don't know what's going on around me. I can't look. I grab the reins and clutch Goliath's mane. I hop but I don't make it on. It hurts. I hop again. And again. And I'm on his back.

I cluck. First we walk and then we trot and then we canter. My sweet Goliath. We canter. We fly. We do our pattern the other direction. Goliath gives me this incredibly rare gift that I know I'll never feel again. And when we come to a stop I can hear the announcer. His voice sounds funny. He is saying something like, "Not what we usually see, folks." I am so pathetic, I made the announcer cry.

I pat Goliath once on the neck. "That's okay, buddy."

And then the audience erupts in applause. Loud applause from all the stands. I'm so shocked I look around to see what everyone is clapping about.

I dismount slowly. A lot of things really hurt when I hit the ground. I pat Goliath and then scan the crowd. People are standing, cheering, smiling. But what I see is not what I want. It isn't even what I understand. I see Coulter. His eyes are all twinkles and moonbeams. But standing next to him is Officer Hanks. And I may have hit my head, but it looks like Coulter is wearing handcuffs.

Chapter Fifty

I EXIT THE arena, dragging Goliath behind me, pushing through the other entrants in the holding pen into the alley. Coulter, Kaya, and Officer Hanks are waiting for me.

"Have you seen Justin?" barks Officer Hanks.

I just stare at Coulter's hands. "Why are you in handcuffs, Mr. Coulter?"

"Do you know where he is?" asks Coulter. Even through his beard I can see him grimacing. "I need you to tell the truth, Cassidy."

Sometimes it's hard to know which truth to tell.

"I haven't seen him since this morning. What's going on?"

"Officer Hanks seems to think Justin has been releasing his horses," says Coulter.

"I don't think it. I have video proof."

Kaya's beautiful olive skin is bright red. "Miles Hanks.

You are acting like a fool. No one in this town will ever speak to you again. Starting with me."

Officer Hanks says, "These little punks think they are a law unto themselves. And Coulter knowingly lets them do it. For all I know it's his idea."

Kaya steps forward into Mile's face. "Why don't you arrest all of us, Miles?"

Coulter bows his hat down. "You don't want to do that, Miles. Trust me."

Officer Hanks looks at Goliath and then me. "That kid's going to jail. He's a brazen thief. And if you know where he is, you'd better get him to come in, or Coulter's going to rot waiting for him."

Coulter says, "Miles, I'm starting to think your mother must not have paid attention to you when you were young. But as usual your timing is impeccable. Kaya and Darius, you two are in charge of the auction." He turns to me. "You did good out there, Cassidy. Real good."

"Thank you," I say.

He smiles through his beard. "They'll be falling down to buy him."

Chapter Fifty-One

I STAND WITH Kaya and Darius while Officer Hanks takes Coulter to his truck.

"I have to go to the bathroom," I say.

Kaya says, "You did so good out there. Are you hurt?"

"Hell of a thing," says Darius. "Must have thrown you five feet."

"I have to go to the bathroom," I say.

I walk down the hallway as fast as I can. I see Alice and the guys coming toward me down the alley, so I walk fast. I go into the bathroom and stand in a stall. *Breathe*, I tell myself. *Breathe.*

I hear the bathroom door open. I hear feet coming toward me. Lots of feet.

"Are you in there?" asks Alice.

"Yeah, I'm going to be a minute," I say.

"Why did they arrest Coulter?" asks Charlie.

Ethan says, "Do you know where Justin is?"

"The last time I saw him was this morning. And he wasn't too happy." It's Banner's voice.

I push open the stall. Three's a crowd for this horrible little bathroom. Banner is standing in front of me. I want to put my fist in her face, but I'm too distracted by the person standing next to her. A Hispanic-looking kid about six feet tall, with a weak mustache and a whole lot of tats. He's holding Banner's hand.

"Where have you been?" I ask.

"Spider, I'd like you to meet Cassidy. Cassidy is my roomie."

"This is Spider? Your boyfriend who dumped you?"

"He changed his mind. He drove his motorcycle all the way across the country to tell me."

Spider turns to Banner and laughs in a slow, private way. "She doesn't look like an eighth grader, Banner. She's kind of *linda*, if you ask me."

"Didn't ask," says Banner.

My head swirls for a minute. The stall. The noises. The assumptions. When I get through the maze of what this means I ask, "What about Justin? What was he doing when you saw him last?"

Banner frowns. "Talking to his dad."

My mouth falls open. I have to shut it by swallowing. "His dad? Wait. His dad?"

"Yeah. I didn't even know that BLM dick was his dad. Did you? No wonder he's so messed up."

"Officer Hanks?"

Banner taps me on the shoulder like she's waking me up. "Um. No, honey. The bigger, older, meaner BLM dick."

"Officer Riker? That's Justin's dad? How do you know that?"

"Justin introduced me to him. And his first name is Riker. Riker Sweet. Didn't seem like they were getting along much. Big surprise."

"Did Justin leave with him? Why didn't you tell anybody?"

"I just saw them talking. And I'm not in a hurry to see Coulter right now, if you know what I mean," she says, looking at Spider.

"You blew off Goliath."

"I heard you two did fine without me," she says. "I knew you would."

I close my eyes.

Alice says, "Everybody outside. Cassidy needs some air."

I wait until they are gone before I open my eyes. Alice is still standing next to me.

"Is Justin in trouble?" she asks.

"Yes. A lot of trouble."

"Do you think he really stole horses from the BLM? Wait, did you do it with him? Is that what you were doing at night?"

"Do you really want to know?"

"Why do you think I wanted to go with you?"

"Okay. Well, I didn't think of that. But yes . . . no . . . We didn't steal horses, we released them. Justin, mostly. And if they really have him on video, he could go to jail. So if Riker really is Justin's dad, and he came in before Hanks but didn't turn Justin in, Justin is probably with him. And his dad's . . ." I don't know how much to say. "He has a temper."

"What are we going to do?"

There is a lot to process right now, and my head is still zinging from my rendezvous with the arena floor. Banner is not with Justin, she's with a six-foot ink mural. Justin's dad is the officer who shot at him in the dark, and Justin never told me. Kaya and Coulter never told me. Coulter is in custody, and there is video of Justin letting the white mare go. But none of this seems as essential as the information that Justin is almost certainly with a man who is capable of hurting him. Again.

"How would you like to help me borrow Coulter's truck, Alice?" I ask. "We need to find Justin."

Alice looks at me, but she doesn't shrink into her jean jacket. Instead, she straightens her neck a little taller and nods. "I thought you'd never ask."

Chapter Fifty-Two

BEFORE WE LEAVE, I go back to the empty stalls with Banner and Spider to talk. It's a little more awkward for me than anyone else since the last time I was here I saw the Red-Spider reunion show.

I ask, "Are you two going to run away together, or is this just a visit?"

"Why? Are you going to rat us out?" says Banner. "You and Justin being horse thieves has created the perfect opportunity for us to leave."

"Yes. Well, you're welcome. But maybe you could cut Coulter a break and not run off while he's in jail? It's hitting a guy when he's down. Plus, if you think your dad hates Spider now, he's going to hate him a lot more if he feels like he kidnapped you."

"She has a point," says Spider, putting his colorful arm

around her. His words rush rhythmically together. "We need to think this through if we're going to do this."

"That's very responsible of you," I say to Spider. I'm not being sarcastic.

"GAWD," says Banner, glaring at me. "Do not encourage him."

I turn to Banner. And it startles me. Suddenly, after months of looking at her and envying her and hating her, I see something I have never seen before. Myself with a better costume. Okay, not better, just different. "Banner. Don't go, okay? Your parents, and the law, will take it out on Coulter and Spider. Not you."

Banner steps back from me and throws her hands in the air. "Like you have room to talk? You're the one sneaking around at night with Justin. You're the biggest hypocrite I ever met besides my dad. And he's a preacher. You're not going to stop me with your do-good bullshit. You screw up everyone you think you're helping because you're so afraid."

It takes a second to absorb all that, but I do. "I'm not afraid, Banner. Not right now, anyway. That's the trick. Doing something for someone else is hard, but it's easier than doing it for yourself."

It gets quiet in the stall. Banner looks at Spider. He looks at her. Then she looks at me.

"I'll see you around, Cassidy," says Banner.

"I hope so, Banner. I really hope so. Nice meeting you, Spider."

By the time I find Ethan and Charlie in the breezeway my brain is going a hundred miles an hour in two different directions. They look at me like I'm crazy or maimed or both.

"You okay?" Ethan asks, not smiling.

I try to act natural. I need him to trust me. "Yeah. I'm fine. But do you remember that day you told me you wanted to be a ranger?"

Ethan looks at me and then Charlie. "I was kidding, girl," he says sharply. "Kid-ding."

"She took a pretty big hit to the head," says Charlie. "But I can see you saying that, Ethan."

I look into Ethan's dark eyes. He sure has beautiful eyes for a guy who wants to follow the rules all the time. And far be it from me to mess that up. I take a deep breath, wait for a few seconds, and start to squeeze little drops of water out of my eyes. "Hey." I rub my face with the back of my hand. "Do you think you guys can handle the auction without me?"

Ethan puts his arm around me. Which feels so good I want to stay there. It makes me feel deeply rotten for fake crying. So bad I'm almost real crying.

"We got it covered, Colorado. You take Alice with you and get some rest."

It sure feels awful to lie to Ethan. I cry a little more. "Charlie, in private? It's kind of personal."

Charlie looks concerned but also confused. "Of course."

We walk around the corner. I stop crying.

"Alice and I are going after Justin. But you can't tell Ethan. Or anyone else, for a few hours. But especially Ethan.

I think they frown on officer candidates who associate with horse thieves."

"You're a horse thief, too? That's a real thing?" Charlie looks at me wide-eyed.

". . . Horse releaser. Say I'm having a meltdown in the bathroom with Alice. If you don't hear from us by the time it gets dark, you can tell Kaya we're at Riker's trailer. The BLM holding pen out by the ranch. She'll know where it is. She'll also probably kill you on the spot, but the horses will be sold, right?"

Charlie's back to being concerned. "You are surprising, Cassidy. Will you two be all right? Based on his behavior at the rodeo, Justin's father seems capable of violence."

"We'll be incredibly careful," I say. "I'm not going to go barging in there. I don't even know if that's where Justin is."

Charlie takes off his bolo tie. He was wearing it when he won his class. He puts it over my head like I'm being knighted by Sir Charlie. I kind of am. "For luck and courage."

I touch the clasp. "Thank you, Charlie. You're a great friend."

Charlie nods gracefully. He looks so different from when I met him the first day. It's not that he's that much thinner; he probably isn't. He just looks happier. Even right now, when he's worrying about me.

"Do you know what's wrong with you, Charlie?"

"I overcompensate with theatrical dressing?"

"Nothing is wrong with you. Your parents are idiots."

Charlie tips his head side to side. "Yes. They are. Thanks."

Chapter Fifty-Three

THE KEYS ARE right where Coulter left them in the wheel guard this morning. The part that worries me is driving out of the fairgrounds without being noticed. We don't exactly look inconspicuous as we fumble around pulling the gooseneck horse trailer off the hitch.

"Can I drive?" asks Alice. "You don't look like you feel very good."

"Can you handle this big truck?"

"I drive the vans for my parents' business sometimes. In San Francisco."

"Clearly I have not asked enough questions this summer. You drive."

When we inch out of the fairgrounds we're both so short we look like ten-year-olds stealing our dad's truck. Luckily, everyone seems to be preoccupied with getting into the auction, and the one guy who really looks at us just smiles and waves. I guess kids driving giant trucks in Wyoming isn't that unusual.

The truck has a gigantic tank, so we have enough gas to get back out to the holding pen. Or I think we do anyway, if we don't get lost trying to find the right road in. That's a lot of time to worry either way. So we talk a little, and then we worry a little.

"You think his dad hits him?" Alice asks.

"Somebody has. I've tried to get him to talk to me about it and he won't. But it's clear that Justin doesn't live with Riker or even acknowledge him in public. All Justin's ever said about his dad to me is that he's an alcoholic. So I'm making some assumptions that his dad is the one who broke his nose, for sure. The thing is, this summer I've learned I'm wrong all the time about people. I mean, all the time. Like, I thought you couldn't handle, you know, things that are dangerous."

"Everyone thinks that." She pauses thoughtfully.

I was right about one thing at least. Alice does think a lot. She says, "Anxiety is different from fear. It's being afraid of things that haven't happened, things that are unknown."

I look out over the two-lane highway and consider this. "Everything ahead of you is unknown."

"Exactly," she says.

"I'm sorry, Alice. I haven't been a very good friend."

"Don't feel bad about this, Cassidy, but you can be a little unfocused sometimes. You don't always notice what's going on around you."

"Yeah. Wow. I'm sorry." Alice's shiny hair bounces along with the motion of the truck. Her knuckles are white from gripping the steering wheel. She has a scar on her arm I've never seen before. "I'm a terrible friend. What else haven't I noticed?"

She looks over and laughs gently. "You aren't a terrible friend. You're the very best kind of friend. You made me want to try things, do things, and be brave. And look what I'm doing right now."

"I don't know if this is being brave or stupid. But we can't just call the police and say that Justin is with his dad so they should go get him. We don't even know if he's with his dad. The list of things I don't know is pretty long, really."

"That's what I mean."

"What?"

"You just run at stuff and figure it out. Even if you have no idea how. But then you usually do figure it out."

"I hope we can figure this one out with nobody getting hurt."

"What are we going to do when we get there?"

"It depends on what's happening."

"Right," says Alice. She shakes her head. "Right."

I recognize the view the second we pull onto the plateau. "Damn."

"Are we lost?" says Alice.

"I know where I am. It's just not where I wanted to go.

We should have taken that other turnoff we passed. I think that's the other road in. But don't turn around just yet. From here we can see the outside of the trailer and maybe get an idea of what's going on."

In the dark those few weeks forever ago, I didn't see the dirt road we're now parked on. When the engine turns off we're suddenly alone with how nuts this is. We both sit silently in Coulter's truck. Birds chirp. I close my eyes.

Alice says, "Cassidy? Are you praying?"

I'm actually panicking. I whisper, "Just clearing my head. Now we have to be super quiet; every sound carries. And watch out for the poison ivy."

"What does that look like exactly?" she whispers.

"Leaves of three. Let it be."

Alice tips her eyes down to my hands. "I guess you learned that the hard way."

"That's how I learn everything."

She nods sadly.

We walk to the edge of the cliff, and in the evening light we see the grubby trailer and the holding pen with the BLM flag waving from the fencing. The holding pen is empty, but the trailer isn't. Within a minute of us getting to the ridge, the trailer door flies open. We both drop to a crouch. Riker Sweet walks out.

"I want this whole thing packed up when I get back from town," he yells back into the trailer. "The whole thing. You got it?"

There is a pause but no sound.

"You got it?" he yells.

If there is a response, it isn't loud enough to carry up the ridge.

Alice grabs my arm hard. I nod and try to look calm.

Below, Riker shuts the trailer door and climbs into his old truck. He's wearing his BLM jacket, even though it's still warm outside. He turns on the engine and lets it rattle to life. He adjusts his two-way radio, and we can hear him getting dispatches through his open window. Much to my relief, he speeds away, leaving a cloud of dust and the other occupant of the trailer behind him.

When he's gone Alice grabs my arm again. "How do we get down there with the truck?"

I smile as optimistically as I can. "*We* don't. I need you to watch and make sure that Mr. Sweet doesn't come back while I talk to Justin. And it's going to take a while to get around and back down there with the truck. If you stand on this rock here you can see all the way up the road. Then Justin and I can just scoot up the trail. We won't even leave a tire track."

"What do I do if Justin's dad comes back?"

"Can you whistle?"

Alice nods. Of course Alice can whistle.

It's slower but a lot easier to get down the cliff trail to Riker's trailer on foot in the light than on a horse in the dark. Something about being able to see just makes all kinds of things easier. I scurry as fast as I can and am down and crossing the open ground in no time.

I don't know what else to do but knock. No one answers.

"Justin, it's Cassidy."

Nothing. I hope my instincts are right. I can see Alice's silhouette on the ridge. I wave, and she waves back. She's so short she looks like a little kid up there on the ridge, but she's the little kid that just drove Coulter's truck like a boss. At least if I'm going to have a problem she can notify my next of kin.

I squeeze open the door to the trailer. No sound but the squeaking hinges. The trailer smells like sour milk. There is no light but the sun coming through the small, dingy windows. "Justin? It's Cassidy. Are you in here?"

I step into the room and wait for my eyes to adjust.

They can't adjust to what I see. Justin is lying lengthwise on a narrow couch with his head back. Beer cans and other garbage litter the floor. One leg is on the couch and the other is sprawled next to it, like he was thrown there by a sudden blast. An arm is draped over his face like he's trying to keep the sun away, but he isn't moving, and there is a foul gray light in the room. "Justin?"

Justin's arm moves, and he turns to me. His eyes are sunken and outlined in dark red and gray. His mouth looks swollen. Same beautiful, terrible nose. No blood. No bruises. Justin. But when he sees me he lets out this gasp. I don't even know. It's like it's the last bit of strength escaping from his mouth.

I cross the cluttered floor and kneel beside the couch. When I touch his arm it bumps his side, and he flinches so hard his whole body lifts into the air, like something popping on a burning-hot skillet. "Aaa," he cries.

I jump back. "Justin? What happened?"

He stays down, like he's flattened with pain. His hands have a slight tremor. One of them is clinched in a fist and bright red. His other hand lifts to me. "You shouldn't have come out here, Cass. Hanks has me on video." Talking seems to hurt him. "You could get in trouble just being with me."

I stand still, staring at the way he's holding himself. "What happened?" I ask again. "Are you hurt?" The last phrase echoes in my head, resonating with stupidity.

He takes in a breath that doesn't sound right. Shallow. Forced. "At least I get to say good-bye this way. Looks like we're moving to Canada. My dad knows somebody with a cattle ranch."

"You can't even move across the room. Is this from last night . . . or today?"

He laughs, but it comes out high and sad, like broken bits of something flying loose. He looks down at his body like it belongs to someone else. He covers his ribs with his hand but doesn't actually touch them. "No. I'll be fine. Just a little stiff."

"Why are you lying?"

"Who says I'm lying?"

I lean forward like I'm going to touch his rib cage, and he flinches again before I'm even close.

I run outside and stand on the step into the trailer. "Alice!"

She whistles back.

"Bring. The. Truck."

She waves her arm. "Okay!"

Justin lifts his head. "Alice? Damn, Cassidy. You brought Alice out here, too?" Then he looks out toward the door. "Wait, Alice can drive a truck?" He laughs again and then winces. "I'm sorry I missed that."

"You can see it for yourself when you come with us."

Justin shakes his head. "Look. I'm not coming with you. Hanks will throw me in juvy, or even jail, maybe. And I can't do that again. I can't do jail. The jail fence kills me."

"Because you're looking so awesome right now. This was your dad, right? Why didn't you tell me Riker was your dad? What is wrong with you? What is wrong with everyone? Don't cowboys know how to talk?" I look around the room. There is nothing to use as a crutch. I can be a crutch, but he's going to have to walk on his own. "No one is going to jail but your dad, Justin. He broke your ribs." I let that float out there for a second, the naked version of what we're not talking about. "We can fix the rest of it."

I'm not totally sure how we fix it, but I know I can't let Justin go off with Riker. People care about him around here. They seem to care about his dad, too. They haven't cared enough to stop this, but they care. Justin needs help. Real help. Even if it means he has to go somewhere else to get it. Everybody, but especially him, has to stop pretending this isn't happening.

There's a strange pause. Like just for a moment Justin

thinks about what I've said. Then he says, "You don't get it." He pushes himself up to sitting, then he arcs with pain and has to shove his hands behind his back to keep from keeling over. His voice cracks all to pieces. "I can't stay here. I blew it. Like I always do. I had a shot with Coulter, and I blew it."

I don't understand why Justin would go with his dad, but I know how hurt can feel like failure. I know I have to get him away from here. This isn't a philosophical decision. Cracked ribs trump any discussion, except how best to get him to the truck. "You go in. You make a deal with Hanks. Whatever. But you don't go with someone who hurts you."

"Stop it, Cassidy." He can't breathe, his ribs hurt so bad, but he can yell. "Stop trying to fix this. You can't fix *everything*."

I slide back next to him. More gently than last time. Not touching him.

He jerks away. "Get out of here. Leave me alone. It's not safe."

"Like I care about safe. You're coming with us." I reach my hand behind him to help him stand up.

He pushes me away. "I mean it. Get out of here!"

I stumble to get my balance.

"Sounds like a good idea to me."

I hear the twinge of hinges behind me. I whirl around.

Riker Sweet is standing in the doorway.

Chapter Fifty-Four

"WHO'S THIS?" HE asks coldly. I can smell whatever he's been drinking from across the room, like he's been rotting in it.

Justin speaks so softly I can barely hear him. "Just a girl from the ranch. She's leaving. Her truck's down the road."

Riker walks in and leans against the inside of his crumbling trailer. When he hunches over his paunch makes him look pregnant. He's Justin's height but a lot heavier. He pulls a toothpick from somewhere in his mouth. With a sick shock, I recognize the eyes, the mouth, even the broad shoulders. Riker is how Justin could look in twenty years, minus the broken nose.

"Why's she here?" says Riker. His words are slurred lightly so they rattle. But softer than I remember. He and Justin kind of sound the same, too.

I say, "I came to get Justin. Coulter needs him."

"Coulter, huh? Coulter's in jail."

Justin doesn't say anything. He just leans forward on the couch.

"You trying to get my son arrested?"

I say, "Not at all, Mr. Sweet."

"—Mr. Sweet? Listen to those manners. You're coming up in the world, Justin. Well, look, young lady, you need to understand something." His watery eyes stare through me. "This is not your house or your business. Justin is all done working for Timothy Coulter. And you need to leave."

He takes a few steps toward me. He may be drunk, but he moves just fine.

Justin puts both feet on the floor and braces himself with his arms. "She's going."

I turn to Justin. "Come on, Justin."

Justin nods. "I'll walk you to your truck."

"Like hell you will," says his dad. All the gentle is out of his voice. He's the guy at the rodeo. Then he turns to me. "I bet you think you've got yourself a real cowboy. He's a cowboy, all right. Justin gets a kick out of stealing and wrecking things. Loves those damn horses more than his own father. He's disgraced me in my own town. I've given up everything for him. And now I have to give up my job to keep him out of jail." He rubs the gray stubble on his chin. "Unfortunately, my son is also a piece of ungrateful gutter trash."

"Stop it, Mr. Sweet," I say.

"Trust me. I'm doing you a favor. Let's go, boy. We'll stock up when we cross the border."

Justin pulls himself to standing. He won't look at me.

Riker's voice goes icy. "I told you to start packing. That asshole Hanks could be here any minute."

I know Justin doesn't want me to see this. This trailer is his private hell. Justin keeps his head down. "I'm going to walk her out."

Riker grabs an empty cardboard box and holds it out to Justin. "Don't go showing off. She found her way out here, she can find her way home. We need to get gone. You done enough damage."

Because that's not ironic.

Justin takes the box and puts it down next to him. It's crazy. Even though he's a lot taller than I am, it seems like he's shrinking right in front of me. "I'll be right back."

"I'm not messin' with you, boy," says Riker. "You got to think about our family now. You owe me that."

"Walk me out, Justin," I say.

Mr. Sweet looks at me and steps closer. The smell alone could kill me. "People are always sticking their nose in where it doesn't belong." His voice goes hard. "They just want to judge you and tell you what a bad father you are. No one seems to care when you got no help and a kid who can't stay out of trouble to save his own life."

Justin steps toward the door.

His father is across the trailer in two steps, standing in front of Justin, clenching a fleshy hand. I can't help it. My feet won't stay still. I bolt. But I'm not running away this time. I'm right between Justin and Riker. It all happens so fast there are no thoughts or words. But I know that Justin can't take one more blow. I won't let him.

Then I feel the full weight of Riker's hand swing across my face, and I'm lifting sideways. I'm airborne in a blur that ends with me smacking into the corner of something with my face. Pain cannonballs into my cheek and jaw. Everything spins. I close my eyes, and when I open them I see the outline of Justin's face over mine.

My guts are in my ears. It feels like someone just ice-picked my cheek. "I'm okay," I blurt. Then I suck back something like a groan.

Justin takes both my hands and pulls me up. He looks at his dad, who is shoving things into a plastic shopping bag.

"She's fine," his dad growls. "Let's get going."

"No, Dad." Justin's voice is so quiet I can barely be sure what he said. Or maybe that's because I'm distracted by trying to stay conscious. "I'm not going."

Riker Sweet doesn't even look up. "Yes, you are."

Justin's voice is louder this time, but still shaky. "I'm taking Cassidy to her truck."

My head is spinning. I'm not entirely sure what I'm seeing is actually happening. Riker squares off in front of Justin. "They'll put you in jail. Coulter will get it, too. Your precious pony ranch will be gone for good. Is that what you want? For what? If you come with me, we get a fresh start. Just you and me. Like it used to be."

"Like it used to be?" says Justin, his voice dipping down.

His father nods. "You and me."

"Can you walk, Cass?" Justin asks me.

My eyes are splitting with pain in the back of my head. "Sure."

Then, unbelievably, Justin says, "Okay. I'll see you later then, Cassidy."

I say, "What? You can't go with him."

Riker smiles. "Blood is thicker than water, sweetie." I watch with horror as he reaches for Justin.

Then Justin reaches, too. With his fist. That rock-solid arm I have been looking at all summer swings through the air and lands in the middle of Mr. Sweet's face. And then the other fist follows. The big man howls in pain and stumbles backward. I sway back against the counter trying to get out of the way.

Riker slams into the wall of the trailer. I wait for him to lunge out and beat Justin to death in front of me. But he doesn't. He doesn't cry out at all. He just stands back up and holds his face. His nose is bleeding.

"You see this?" He holds out his hands and shakes them at me. "You want him? You can have the worthless piece of shit. I should have left him long ago. I gave up my life for him. Quit the rodeo so I could take care of him when my wife died. Took a dead-end job. And this is what I get in return."

This isn't what I expected. Any of it. I hate Riker, but I feel sorry for him, too. Riker lost his wife and his rodeo career. Justin lost his mom. But Riker takes his sickness out on Justin.

Justin says, "Go to Canada, Dad. I'm going to tell the social workers everything, so you shouldn't come back. I'm done running from you. Or anyone. You do what you want. But I'm done."

"You tell those judgmental little pukes all you want. Your record speaks for itself. Can't blame everything on me, boy. Gotta take your own licks once in a while."

Justin looks at his father, bleeding from his own hand. "Good-bye, Riker."

I feel Justin take my elbow and lead me out of the trailer. We walk a little, and then I hear the gravel of a truck approaching. Everything is black and fuzzy except for the headlights. I keep hearing the expression *deer in the headlights* replaying in my head. That's what I am. Except I want the truck to give me a ride.

The truck door opens. "Cassidy? Justin?"

Alice jumps out and puts her tiny arms around us both.

"Don't," we both shout at the same time.

Once I'm in the truck I'm sure I'm going to throw up. One too many hits to the head today. Maybe two too many. Justin takes my hand. I hear Coulter's truck turn and drive out of the yard. Everything hurts. I wish I could see straight. It's really dark.

Justin says, "I can't believe you faced off with my old man, Cassidy."

"You did that?" asks Alice. "He hit you?"

"Then Justin punched him. Twice." It's not like I think that's so great. It's awful really. But it's what happened. And

Justin is here. Not with his dad. Not going to Canada.

I listen to the gravel under the tires. Everything is still spinning. But it's okay. It's just that I have to tell Justin something else. Before anything else happens. It's something important. Something he has to know. About me and all the things I can do now that I couldn't do before I came here. About him and all the things he can do if he'll just give it a chance. About us. Because there is an us, and it doesn't end when I drive off across the Wyoming state line. I'm not sure where it ends.

I just need to sleep a little first.

I'M SITTING UNDER a tree. I sit there for a long time. I can't get up. My head hurts. And then I look up and see my grandfather on his old buckskin. He's exactly like I remember him.

Seeing him feels more real than being awake.

I stand up and start running. As I get closer I can see every crease in his weathered face. I can hear him humming with an old, wobbly voice, and I can see his long, intelligent fingers. One hand is holding the reins to his horse and the other is waving to me. He's riding away.

"Stop!" I have serious questions about him, and about me.

He doesn't slow down. I can smell him from where I chase after him, even though I'm not close enough for that. He smells like coffee and leather and horse.

"Stop!" I yell. I have questions.

He goes through a gate. He waves to me, not hello or good-bye, just a wave. Then he's gone.

I look around. There are mountains far off. Around me there are miles of alfalfa and clover. Miles and miles and miles. And the only thing I have of my grandfather is that I'm standing on the road where he left me. Alone, but standing. And I'm not afraid, at least not like I used to be.

I guess where I go from here is up to me.

Chapter Fifty-Five

WHEN I WAKE up the next morning, I'm tucked under the covers in the ranch house sickbed. I vaguely remember coming in here last night. Alice called Kaya and told her what happened. Officer Miles got on the phone, and he told her to stay put and he'd come to us. And I remember Justin putting his arm around me when we walked into the house.

When my eyes finally focus I see Coulter staring out the window by the bed. With his back to me, I think it's my grandfather. When he turns around I'm mostly sure this is real.

"That's quite a dream you were having," Coulter says. His sad Santa eyes look red and blurry.

"I thought . . ." I don't finish. My dream still feels real.

"You thought what? You'd died and gone to heaven when you saw me? You ain't the first woman to say that about me."

I'm startled that he calls me a woman. But I guess I am. A woman with a sore face.

"Where is Justin? And Alice? Are they okay?"

"You think just because you get knocked around a little everyone wants to talk to you?" His hands curl up as he talks to me. He puts them down and does his best impression of a smile.

"You're out of jail?"

"Miles got sick of holding me as soon as I hired a lawyer. For now Miles can't prove I helped Justin. Without that, he doesn't have much of a case. He can still run me into a poor house trying to prove it if he likes."

"Is Justin okay?" I ask.

"He's got two cracked ribs for sure, but they'll heal. Kaya and Miles took him to the clinic to make sure he didn't puncture a lung. Miles agreed not to arrest him until he's spent some quality time with a doctor and that social worker who keeps track of him in town."

I breathe out. Okay. Justin's alive, not in jail, and not with his dad. People are taking care of him.

"Alice is back at her tent." He chuckles. "That girl grew a tough streak."

"What about Banner?"

"She's here." He sighs. "At least for now. Let's just say we've had some words. Loud ones. And then she had some words with her parents. And then they had some words with me. But damned if I don't have the tattooed boyfriend in my cabin until further notice. I swear, what good does it do to help a kid get her mind right if she has to go back to crazy parents? No wonder that girl acts like a wildcat. I tell you what, Cassidy. This is the damndest way to make a living there is."

"Banner didn't take off?" I can't believe it.

Coulter looks at me. "Did you know she was planning to run off when I asked you where she was at the auction?"

I shake my head. "I saw . . . something in the back stall. I thought she was with Justin."

"Oh," says Coulter, frowning down into his beard. "You thought she was rolling in the hay with Justin? And you didn't turn them in? You're a strange kid, Cassidy."

This makes me feel tired for some reason. Just the whole thing. Tired everywhere. But I'm not done asking qustions. "Did someone buy Goliath?"

"Indeed. A big man out of Missoula bought him. Needs a sturdy horse that can pack him all over God's country. Paid big money, too. Some of which belongs to you. He couldn't get over your ride. But he said what got him into the buyer's box was the way Goliath stopped the second you fell and came back to you. Said he'd take good care of him."

"Did they take him already?"

"He's gone. Sorry, sis."

I'm happy for Goliath. I know it's what's best. But it's hard. "What about Roanie?"

"Went to a greenie couple from Colorado. They'll probably move her into their house and buy her a flat-screen TV. All but two of the yearlings sold, too. So thank you for that."

I sit up and straighten my shirt. My head has too much thinking in it. And my dream is still bothering me so I just keep going. "Was my grandfather really a thief?"

Coulter leans back and nearly falls over laughing. He laughs so hard he starts to wheeze and cough. I think he's going to die before he can tell me. "Are you really still worrying about that?"

"I just had a dream about him."

Coulter stops laughing. "You too, huh? Bastard haunts me all the time."

"I need to know," I say. "The truth this time."

Coulter rolls his sleeves up. The man is theatrical. "The truth is that the day I met your grandfather I was stealing a horse out of his barn. It wasn't my first time stealing either. He offered to not turn me in if I stayed and worked for him."

Coulter was the real horse thief? I can believe that. But I still don't get it. "Why would Grandpa want you to work for him after you tried to steal from him?" I ask.

"Your grandfather had the hide of a shyster, but he was a good judge of horse flesh, and people flesh, too. I was so surprised and grateful to him for being good to me, and your grandma made me so fat with apple pie it turned me responsible. And now look at me, nursemaid to a bunch of city kids and a staff of people who are one check away from the poor house."

"So that's why you didn't stop Justin? You knew he was doing it, didn't you?"

Coulter pulls a chair over and sits down next to me. "Unlike most folks around here I don't buy that a few wild horses are the main threat to the land. The horses are just living and dying like they always have. But I don't have a solution either. So I train them, get them homes, and hope it works out."

Adults are a mystery to me. They seem every bit as confused as kids but with more power to make mistakes. "So you let Justin break the law because you couldn't?"

"Oh, I broke the law. I housed a criminal who I think of as my own son." He pauses. "Best not to broadcast that information."

It dawns on me that he really is Justin's dad. A dad is someone who takes care of you, who teaches you stuff, and who loves you enough to give up their own desires for your happiness. I start to miss my own dad.

Mrs. Sanchez comes in. Her mouth is pulled tight in a small hard circle and her heavy eyes avoid me. "Timothy, there is a phone call for you. And I think it is time that this one goes back to sleep."

"Yes, ma'am," says Coulter. "I was just leaving."

"I'm sorry," I say to Mrs. Sanchez. "I've made a mess of things again."

She gazes at me severely. "You saved that boy's life. You be proud of that, my little chef."

And now I miss my mom, too.

When I wake up the next time I feel a lot better and a lot worse. My head doesn't hurt so much, but I'm alone in room and it's way too creepy quiet. I can't hear anything but the ancient grandfather clock clicking off time in the hallway. I don't even hear horses whinnying outside. I used to crave silence in my bedroom at home, but I seem to have lost my taste for solitary confinement. Even Banner is better than the lonely ticking in the hallway.

I get my clothes on, which have been washed and folded. Mrs. Sanchez is a saint. I'm so freakishly stiff it takes me like five minutes to slide things on. It feels like Riker sideswiped my entire body, not just my face. Or maybe it was the tumble off Goliath. Or maybe it's just the last two months in general.

I look in the old-fashioned oval mirror hanging behind the dresser. The antique glass makes me look like even more of a stranger to myself. Half my face is splotchy and swollen, with a cut where I hit the counter. I look kind of tough actually. I step back from the mirror and then step closer again. It's strange to see myself after so many weeks. My eyes are puffy with dark circles. But my body looks amazing. I make sure no one is silently watching me through the door, and then I flex my arm in the mirror like a body builder. I have a muscle in my arm. It's not big, but it exists. And I swear I'm taller. Like at least a full centimeter.

I walk out into the sunlight, which is viciously bright. I walk up to my tent without seeing anyone. I wonder if I've missed a few days and everyone has gone home. Then I hear Ethan's laugh. I walk faster. Inside our little tent a party is commencing. Everyone, all seventeen campers, are crowded all over our four cots and on the ground. Talking, drinking from cans of soda, and eating large amounts of contraband snacks that came from who knows where. In the tent. So against the rules. Spider and Banner are cozied up together, but everyone else is scattered all over the place. Danny, Granger, Devri and company, all hanging out together like they like one another. Alice propped up so high on her mattress and pillows in between Ethan and Charlie she looks like the queen of campers.

Everyone looks up. "Cassidy!" They all say together.

Alice jumps off her purple throne. "Are you feeling better?"

Ethan stands up to get a closer look at my face. "That is sexy, girl."

"Not really," I say. I touch my bruised and cut face. I mean, Riker slapping me is not sexy. Getting hit is hideous. Still, I feel a little bit of that thing Mrs. Sanchez was talking about. Not pride. Because the whole thing is just sad and awful about Riker and Justin. But I'm okay with the fact that I'm standing here right now with my friends and that Justin's safe from his dad. "What's going on with Justin? Is he back yet?"

"Justin, Justin Justin," says Charlie. He has a chocolate chip cookie in his hand, which he tries unsuccessfully to hand to me. "We are your fun friends. You have to sit down and eat unhealthy food with us before we get all serious again." Charlie might be high on sugar.

Alice says, "Justin's still in town. He has to finish with the social worker before he can came back here. But Officer Hanks is going to press charges."

Charlie says, "Alice. You're a buzzkill. But not nearly as big a buzzkill as Officer Hanks."

Ethan says, "Officer Hanks has a video of Justin vandalizing federal property and letting mustangs out of the holding pen. Kid's got a problem."

I say, "He has a lot of problems, Ethan. But I've been thinking about it. I mean, I thought you guys could help me figure out a way to help him."

"You really are relentless," says Banner, walking across the tent toward us. She's in a red tank top and ripped-up Daisy Dukes. The girl has way too much attitude, but there is nobody like her.

It's such a relief to see Banner I accidently hug her. She's so surprised she almost falls backward over Scotty's legs, which are right in the way. "Whoa, girl. You don't want to spend all that in one place."

"Sorry," I say. Luckily my cheeks are already bright red. "Coulter told me you decided to stick around. It's awesome he let Spider stay here."

"Yeah, the old man can be okay. Did he tell you my dad is threatening to fly out here and get me one day before we all go home? I told him if he so much as steps on a plane, I'm gone. But if he lets me come back on my own, with Spider, I'll come back and go to school in the fall. I even promised to stop smoking." She rolls her eyes at me when she says this and looks over at Spider. He's watching her from across the room. His eyes are smiling. *Gaah.* The way he looks at her kind of melts me.

"Is your dad going for that?" In my head I'm thinking about what my parents would do if I wanted to drive cross-country on a motorcyle with Spider. They would fly out here, too.

"My mother is being sort of sane. For her, anyway. She says that she's tired of fighting. And the smoking thing broke her will. She started praising Jesus when I told her."

"You're relentless," I say.

"GAWD yes," says Banner leaning away from me. She gives me the once-over like she did the first day I was here. "Look at you. All hardcore and badass with that cut." And at least part of her meaness is gone. I'll miss her when I'm back in Colorado. It's like living next to a fire station. I never know what she's going to do next. Maybe my baby sisters can torment me if I get too lonely.

Banner turns and steps over Scotty, who is staring up at her teeny tiny shorts. She flicks his boot with her painted toes and laughs. "Don't chase something you can't handle, Scotty. And you can't handle this."

Scotty dies and looks away.

No. Nobody like Banner.

Chapter Fifty-Six

OFFICER HANKS DRIVES too fast through the ranch gate right as we are all about to eat dinner. He drives up to the house and parks on Kaya's favorite wildflowers.

Coulter turns to Darius. "This guy doesn't quit, does he?"

"Want me to rope him, boss? Just say the word."

"Then we'd have to keep him."

When Miles gets to the fire he singles me out in a hurry, which surprises me. Maybe the plan I've cooked up with the gang isn't going to work after all. He's sweating through his hat. Nobody makes a joke or says anything at all to him. Ethan raises his eyebrows. I hope I know what I'm doing.

Miles looks at Coulter uncomfortably. "I need to talk to Cassidy, in private. Can we talk in the house?"

I look over at Coulter and Mrs. Sanchez, who are giving team shade to Miles.

Darius says, "Evening, Miles, you here to arrest Cassidy, too? Your quota low today?"

Mr. Sanchez takes a few slow steps toward Miles. "Can't you take one of the lazy ones? I like this girl." He smiles at me. He must think that Officer Hanks is kidding around.

Coulter looks less amused. "I'll walk down with Cassidy. No reason for her to talk to you alone. Seems like that might be against some kind of law or another."

When we get to the dining room Officer Hanks asks me to sit down at the table. Coulter sits down next to me. Officer Hanks says, "It really isn't necessary for you to stay, Tim. I'm just going to ask a few questions."

"It's necessary to me, Miles. I like to do things by the book, too."

"Look. It's some questions, okay? I've heard that Cassidy and Justin spent a lot of time together. I hear they're a thing."

I would not have predicted that Kaya would be gossiping about me and Justin to Miles.

"A thing?" bursts out Coulter. "And why in the name of hell are you interested in my campers' love lives, Miles?"

I am either about to be interrogated or break up a fist-fight.

"I can save you both some time." I look carefully at Officer Hanks. I need to see his face, but horses have taught me to watch the back hooves, too. I say, "I released your horses."

Officer Hanks looks at me with disgust. "No, you didn't. Justin released my horses."

"Aww hell," says Coulter. "You did not release horses, Cassidy."

"Yes. I did. I'll testify to it in court. Because I'll also testify that Officer Hanks"—I don't look at them—"allowed a whole bunch of federal laws to be broken, too. He chased horses, including pregnant mares, in the heat. He let horses get hurt and then didn't do anything but let them bleed. He gathered them without court permission, just because a rancher bullied or bribed him into it. He even tied up a mare with enough slack to hang herself. That video he took probably shows that he broke more laws than Justin."

Coulter chuckles. "Welcome to my world, Miles."

"Miss Carrigan?" Miles's voice is testy. "I'm here to ask you questions about Justin."

I say, "Officer Hanks, I'm not trying to be disrespectful, but do you even have room for all these horses you're gathering up?"

"That's not what we're talking about. Justin broke the law."

"So did you."

"Careful, Miles. She might put you on YouTube. You could get famous."

I say, "Viral is more like it." I'm totally bluffing about making my own video, but I like how it makes Officer Hanks look when I say it.

"The laws I broke aren't workable." Officer Hanks's voice rises. "Do you think I like chasing mustangs? They kick and bite and throw up dust. The gathering facilities are full.

Why do you think I've been keeping the horses in those awful makeshift pens out in the desert? It's a giant waste of time and money. I'm just trying to keep the peace."

"I know, Officer Hanks. But it's not working." My brain is on an adrenaline high. Charlie said my idea didn't totally lack merit. Ethan told me I was a dangerous woman. Alice told me not to forget to talk about money. I know there isn't an answer for everything. But there has to be a better answer than Justin going to jail.

"What if you moved the herds someplace else?"

Officer Hanks sighs. "That's just moving the dirt around on the floor, Cassidy. It doesn't change anything."

"Well, what is putting them in a holding pen? My mom is an accountant. She says that when you have a big problem you have to start with the bottom line and work up. You're spending millions to house and feed these horses, right? Like millions and millions. The more you gather, the more you have to feed and take care of. What if you stopped putting horses in holding facilities so much and moved them places that ranchers don't want? I mean, even if you have to build water holes and tell the oil and gas people to share the road, aren't you still money ahead? The Red Desert is ten thousand acres, right? Then every mare you catch you inject with birth control while you ask the federal government to get longer-lasting stuff, instead of just talk about it. I mean, I know the ranchers and oilers need to be protected, too. But treating the horses badly doesn't help. You can't even kill mustangs to save money.

You start euthanizing thousands of horses, and you'll get sued so much it will cost you bazillions."

Coulter is rolling his eyes at me.

In a deeply patronizing voice Officer Hanks says, "I love that you know all those things, Cassidy. But it isn't that simple. The mustangs destroy the range area. They mess up water holes. They cause big problems. Gathering is the best solution we have right now."

"Officer Hanks, I know this is a complicated problem. But I think some problems are like stampeding horses. You have to make yourself big and run at them. You have to use what you have in a bigger way. And you need people who care enough to find a solution. Because they're from here. And they want to make things work."

Miles grimaces. "Justin's going to detention, Cassidy."

"What good does that do? Then you have to feed him, too. Come on, Officer Hanks. You're not a bad guy. Kaya wouldn't have secretly gone out with you if you were." Officer Hanks's face yanks to one side when I say this. I'm not the only one who doesn't like being gossiped about. "You and Justin can help each other. You've seen him. He can bring horses in with a whistle. He can help you do things more safely, and you save money. He doesn't end up in jail. Everyone is better off. And maybe Kaya won't be as angry at you as she probably is right now."

Officer Hanks goes popsicle red. "He damaged my holding facilities."

"What if Coulter offers to pay for the damages as a good-will gesture?"

"What?" asks Coulter. "I can barely afford to buy the drink I'm going to need after this conversation. I've got a preacher threatening to sue me for not killing his daughter, or at least her boyfriend." Coulter looks like the week is catching up with him.

Officer Hanks isn't looking at Coulter. He's looking at me. He's thinking, too.

Time to act bigger than I am. "If you drop the charges against Justin, I'll give you all the money I got from selling Goliath to fix things, and if that's not enough, Coulter will pay you, too. Right? It's not a bribe. It's compensation."

"No way," says Officer Hanks. "Justin broke the law."

I say, "You said you want peace. Maybe peace looks different than you think."

Officer Hanks scratches his head. He folds his arms. "I don't know what the answer is, Cassidy. Nobody does. Or they would have done it. But you can't just start doing whatever comes to mind, making up your own rules. I'm doing the best I can, and it's still a train wreck on fire."

I sit up a little taller in my chair. "So try something different. Sometimes you have to fail to figure stuff out."

Officer Hanks shakes his head. But he doesn't say no.

Coulter gets up from his chiar. He looks at me and then looks at Officer Hanks. "I know, Miles. I hate children, too."

Chapter Fifty-Seven

IT'S TWO IN the morning. I'm awake, but Goliath's gone. The upper pasture is as empty as Justin's cabin. Not even the mice are moving around in our tent. I grab my boots from under my bed, tip them upside down, and slip them on. The moon is still out there.

I walk past the ranch house. Kaya's truck is parked out front. My stomach flip-flops. The lights are all out. I could sneak in, just to see if he's there. I stand and look at the dark windows, breathing heavier. I turn around and keep on walking. Since when do I just break into people's houses at night? This summer, I guess.

I'm nearly to the turnoff up the hill when I hear rustling behind me. It's not cold, but he has a coat on. And a small duffel bag hanging on his good shoulder. He walks unevenly, heavy on one side. My heart is pounding too hard for blood to get to the thinking part of my brain. I run. But when I get closer I see by the way he's glaring that he isn't glad to see me. I stop and stand stupidly in front of him, not sure what's happening.

"Hanks let you come back?" I ask breathlessly.

"Yep." His voice is cowboy flat. He puts his duffel down in the dirt.

"And he's going to drop the charges?"

"You fixed the whole thing. Tied it up in a little bow. Hanks wants me to work with him and help him kidnap horses. Then I really will be my old man."

My words come out in a flood. "Not if you don't want to be. I thought you could help him find a better way. Maybe a much better way. Everybody has to give a little, Justin. I didn't fix anything. I have no idea how to fix anything. Some stuff just stays broken. But I just . . . want you to be okay."

He looks away.

We wait a few seconds like that. Finally I say, "Where are you going to go?"

"I don't know. I'll find something."

"Come on, Justin. You've already found something. Coulter cares about you. You belong here, at least for now. Stick it out."

Justin throws his head back. "Coulter doesn't care. At least, he doesn't want me around. He told that social worker I need to see a full-on psychiatrist. What good am I to him if he thinks I'm crazy?"

"Saying you need help doesn't mean you're crazy, Justin. And it sure doesn't mean he doesn't care about you or you aren't any good to anyone. Stay. Figure it out."

"So I can be happy? Is that what's going to happen to me?"

"I don't know what's going to happen to you."

Justin speaks like a punch. "Don't you get it? Look at you. Your face is all torn up because of me. I screw things up. I screw people up."

I hold my hand up to his face. He flinches, but he doesn't stop me. I go slow. My finger traces the curve where his nose is bent out wrong. I feel a shiver go through the both of us. Then I trace down to his swollen lips and brush across his chin. He breathes out hard and pushes my hand away.

I stand still.

Justin picks up his duffel and walks down the trail. He goes through the gate and drops over the hill. I stand alone in the middle of the road. Just me, the moon, the mountains, and the end of the line. Like in the dream with my grandfather. I stand there waiting. And just like in my dream, Justin doesn't come back.

I find a big rock and sit down. The jagged edges of the stone dig into my skin. Everything hurts. Inside and out. The cracks around my mouth. The dirty cuts in my fingers. A coyote's howl one valley over. The creak of the trees. The empty space where Justin was standing. The whole summer cuts through me, slicing away what I thought would keep me safe. My parents being together. Justin. Goliath. Who I used to be. All gone.

The dry grass rustles in the breeze coming through the

gulch. The cicadas whine. I've read where people say how great it is to be connected to life. Well, it turns out if you're connected, you can feel the awful stuff, too, the pain woven into the fabric of every living thing. And the more it matters, the more it hurts.

Eventually I will get back up off this rock and walk back to the tent. That's what Justin and this whole gut-punching summer have given to me. I'm resilient.

But not right now.

Chapter Fifty-Eight

I'M STILL SITTING on the rock when I see a dull shape moving on the road. The sky has lightened, so I make out that it is a person walking awkwardly. The closer he gets, the faster he goes, and the more my heart speeds up. When he is close enough I hear his boots scrape the gravel in the road. I don't move. When he gets right up to me I slide off the rock, but I don't reach out or say anything. This has to be his idea.

He throws his bag on the ground and breathes heavily. The skin around his hairline is damp with sweat. He holds his arms out. I wonder if he's going to tackle me to the ground or pass out.

"Since the minute I met you you've been driving me crazy. Messing me all up. Making me do stuff. The minute I met you. You ran right at me. You scared the hell out of my horse."

His face is full of anger and pain. I stay quiet. He's not mad at me. Well, mostly not mad at me.

"You bust into my life, and then you try to make me think I can have something else and be something else, and so now what I had before isn't good enough, and I can't go back to being like I was, living like that. I can't do it."

I nod. "So don't."

He picks up his bag again. "Shit. You wrecked me, Cassidy." He glares and turns. He's going to leave now, for good. He's going to walk out of my life and disappear.

"You aren't wrecked, Justin. By me or your dad or anybody else. That's a lie and you know it, or you wouldn't be here right now. You made me fight. Now you goddamn fight, Justin Sweet."

Justin keeps his back to me but doesn't move. The sun is coming up, and it makes him stand out like a figure in a painting. Then he makes a noise, a piercing sound, like he's gasping for air. I force myself to hold still. He shakes his head. He folds his arms across his chest and stamps the earth with his boot. It shouldn't be this hard to let a small portion of misery out after a lifetime of it. But Justin has also had a lifetime of holding it in.

He covers his face with his hands and sways slightly to the side. It's like watching that cloud explode with lightning over our heads. His shoulders heave. I can't see his face, but I know he's weeping. The sadness rumbles through him in waves. He finally drops to one knee in the gravel road.

I wait.

When he stands up he rubs his red, swollen face with his hands and looks at me like he's amazed he's still alive. He pushes his hair back and coughs awkwardly. "Well, that was shit."

I smile a little, and he does, too. Then I wait again.

He puts his hand out for mine then pulls me in. I move slowly so I don't hurt his broken ribs, but I don't let go either. I can't. Wherever we are, we're burned into each other.

We're incandescent.

Chapter Fifty-Nine

DAD COMES TO get me in a new used Subaru, like his last one but with no bike racks. It's a nicer blue color, and it looks like it's seen fewer miles. We hug awkwardly and say hello like strangers.

"What happened to your check?" His eyes are wide.

"I fell."

His nostrils flare slightly. His chest is puffed up. Maybe I should have warned him. "Why didn't anyone call us? Are you okay? Did you see a doctor?"

"Mrs. Sanchez fixed me up. I'm really fine."

He swallows hard enough I can see it. "Well, we'll get it checked out at home. You ready to go?"

"I have to get my stuff."

"You want some help?"

"No, I got it. It might take just a few minutes."

Alice is still packing in our tent. She and most of the rest of the kids are heading to the airport in Jackson Hole in an hour with Darius and Kaya. Banner and Spider are down by his bike arguing about the route they're going to take home. Banner wants to see Crazy Horse Memorial. Through the open flap I see Andrew and Izzy walk past. They've been up in the woods for a long time, but I don't think things are going well. I hear Izzy say, "You are exhausting."

Andrew says, "You know what is exhausting? How fake you are. I can't believe you had a boyfriend this whole time."

When they get far enough past our tent Alice giggles. Not meanly. Just probably because they're yelling so loud about such personal stuff. And then it hits me how cool it is that their yelling is funny to Alice.

I put my grandfather's hat on. It looks dirtier than when I got it. I turn to Alice. "Can you come visit me in Denver? Would your parents let you?"

Alice says, "I'll talk them into it. I'd like to meet your sisters and your little brother."

I nod. "Good luck at your new school. If you go there."

"We'll see. If I like it, I'll stay. If I don't, I'll go someplace else."

We give each other a long, real hug.

"Let's go find the boys," I say. "I think Granger wants your email."

Alice makes the face of pain. "Um. No. But Ethan does."

"Called it," I say.

Then there is too much saying good-bye. Charlie and

Ethan both try to give me money so I can get a cell phone. I give them my email address. And my real address. Snail mail has grown on me.

Ethan's still prickly he was left out of the truck-stealing and fistfighting, especially now that no one is being arrested for it. He towers over me on purpose. "You're a big liar for such a short thing, Colorado."

"I didn't want to mess up your career in law enforcement, if you do that sort of thing."

Ethan shrugs. "Sometimes you gotta break a few rules, right?" Then he gives me his real smile, not his cool one.

"Banner said that same thing before we went after Justin."

"Banner? Stop trying to make me feel bad." He hugs me so my feet come off the ground, and then he puts me down. "Don't let anybody pick on you at home, okay?"

"No way," I say.

Kaya jogs up to our group. "Your dad is looking for you, Cassidy. He asked me to come get you. He seems like he's in a hurry." She says this like my dad may have freaked out.

We walk down the trail together. I say, "I still can't believe you didn't tell me about dating Miles, or Riker being Justin's dad."

"Not everything is your business, Cassidy. Some things are nobody's business."

"Like how you told Miles about me and Justin?"

"That was a mistake. I make those."

"Are you going to date Miles now?"

She cocks her head to the side. "Keep asking questions about Miles and I'm taking the lipstick back. The truth is I don't know what I'm doing. This summer has been tough. I may go back to school and become a BLM officer myself."

"What, really? You'd be great. That is so great."

"We'll see. Maybe I'll fail the hell out it." She smiles wistfully. "Who knows? But I'm sick of trying to get people to do the right thing. If I want things to change I might have to change them myself."

I didn't think Kaya could be any cooler. But yeah. She is. "Kaya, can I be you when I grow up?"

She laughs. "No. Thank goodness."

Coulter shakes Dad's hand very formally and then hugs me like a grizzly bear. "I'll see you next summer, okay, kiddo?"

"Okay." I like the sound of that.

Dad makes a sputtering noise.

"Mr. Coulter offered me a job as a junior counselor. I mean, of course I need to talk to you and Mom about it."

"Let's discuss it." Dad looks like Mr. Coulter has just offered me crack cocaine, but I have a whole year to wear him and Mom down.

Justin comes out of the house and walks up next to me. I turn to Dad. "This is Justin Sweet. He's sort of my . . . friend."

Justin puts his rope-burned hand out to my father. "Hello, Mr. Carrigan."

My father shakes his hand but doesn't look happy about it. "Oh. Hello, Justin. You work here?"

"Yes. I actually live here. It's nice to meet you."

Dad takes in the snaps on Justin's shirt, his split lip, his prizefighter nose. The way he's standing right next to me. I don't know if Dad has finished writing a book this summer, but he's currently an open one. I say, "It's okay, Dad. He reads and everything."

Dad can't get me in the car fast enough.

"Oh my god, Cass. It looks like I got here just in time. I can't believe your mother left you here," he says as we drive too fast on the gravel road out of the ranch.

"It's good to see you, too."

And then we don't talk until we hit the main road.

We drive in and out of The Big Empty, past the rodeo grounds and the convenience store without slowing down. We don't even stop for gas. I think Dad is trying to hold his breath until we cross the Colorado state line. Before long we're out on the open highway, heading for home, and he relaxes his grip on the steering wheel and stops hunching his shoulders.

After a while I ask him to pull over. I jump out and gather a few rocks for Wyatt. A red one for the desert. A white one for the mare. And a gray one for Goliath.

Dad starts up the engine again. "Are you getting those rocks for Wyatt?"

"The gray one is for me."

I look over the desert I saw coming the other direction just a few months ago. I hear the wind on Dad's doors. This time I roll down my window so I can swallow it. I don't know what waits for me at home. I can't really imagine sleeping in my old bed, with sheets and pillows and carpet and air-conditioning. Wearing my old clothes. It hardly seems like they will fit anymore.

But I'm excited to see Mom and the sibs. The closer we get to home, the more I can hardly wait to see them. And showers. I'm going to take a hundred showers. But thinking of home also makes the old sadness creep over me. My family isn't going to be together. School's going to be hard. Nobody knows or cares what happened to me this summer. There will be no horses or campfires or Coulter at home. I feel my throat tighten. What if I go back to being how I was? The sad girl who stays in her bedroom all day.

I look out the window. So much space. So much room.

I won't. I refuse to ride that horse anymore. This summer was for something. And in that way, it is about me. No matter how awful the girls are at school. Or how lonely I feel. Or how weird things are at home. Or whatever happens to me. I rode a half-broke mustang across the top of a mountain in the dark, and then I jumped off a ledge on the other side. I made out with a broken-nosed horse thief that I'm crazy about. I helped Goliath and Roanie get homes, and I stood up to Justin's dad. I told Officer Hanks what I think about what he's doing to the mustangs. I'm not going back to being a miserable, trapped little suburban ghost. I have *coraje*. I am re-friggin'-silient.

"You okay?" asks Dad. "You look a little intense over there."

I might also be a little more intense than I used to be. That's okay, too. "I'm fine, Dad. Really."

"Good," he says, looking at me, obviously worried. He looks back out the window. "Do they get mustangs out this direction?" Dad asks. I think he's trying to apologize, and I honestly want to let him. But he doesn't need to.

"I don't think so," I say. "Not anymore. You have to go farther out to see them."

"That's too bad. I'd like to see a wild horse."

"They have them up by the ranch. At least for now. They might round them all up."

"Oh, that's a shame."

"Yeah," I say. "I hope they leave a few."

That word. *Hope*. It sits on my tongue. I'm not sure what it means, but something different than it used to. Something harder and more interesting.

He turns on the radio but only finds different stations of static. The wind blows fast-food wrappers in the back-seat. They make a dry, nervous noise. He asks, "It's lonely out here, isn't it?"

"Not to me," I say.

"Oh yeah?" He keeps driving. "I'd like to hear about that."

After a while I say, "Thanks for coming to get me."

"I'm happy to do it," he says. He doesn't say anything about how awful I was to him.

"Did you finish your book?"

"Yes. Thanks for asking."

"Can I read it?"

"Absolutely. I'd be honored."

That's enough. For now. It's going to take some time for both of us, but it's a start.

This summer did not go at all like I'd hoped. I did a terrible job of being drama-free, staying away from cowboys, and avoiding mean girls. I got thrown off a horse and was injured—pretty regularly. But the space between what I thought happiness looks like and all the things I didn't want to happen is the space where I found a new happiness, and a new me. I can't make my parents stay married, or let all mustangs go free, but I can make something brilliant with the way things are. That's not lowered expectations, it's braver ones.

I hope Banner and Spider make it back to South Carolina okay and her dad doesn't change his mind and call the police on them halfway home. There's a lot of wind between The Big Empty and Charleston. A lot of sharp turns in the road. You just never know what's coming your way until it comes.

I put my hand out the open window and let it dive up and down. The cool wind skims along my skin, resisting my fingers pointed in the shape of an arrowhead. From here it looks like the sage goes on forever. But the desert isn't empty. The mountains aren't far away. They're beautiful. Like the song humming inside me. Like the clouds that move gracefully over the highway. Like the things I haven't told Justin yet.

But I will. Soon. And after that, we'll just have to figure it out.

KRISTEN CHANDLER lives at the base of the Wasatch mountains with her husband and their herd of eight children, two dogs, and an old cat. In addition to writing, she is a professor at Brigham Young University and an equine instructor for at-risk youth. She has trained mustangs and followed wild herds on horseback in the Red Desert of Wyoming. As a teen, she went from small town to small town showing Quarter horses, getting into more trouble than she meant to, and eventually qualifying for the American Quarter Horse Association Youth Finals.